SPLENDOR *of the* LAND

Books by Connilyn Cossette

OUT FROM EGYPT

Counted with the Stars

Shadow of the Storm

Wings of the Wind

CITIES OF REFUGE

A Light on the Hill

Shelter of the Most High

Until the Mountains Fall

Like Flames in the Night

THE COVENANT HOUSE

To Dwell among Cedars

Between the Wild Branches

THE KING'S MEN

Voice of the Ancient

Shield of the Mighty

Splendor of the Land

THE KING'S MEN

3

SPLENDOR *of the* LAND

CONNILYN COSSETTE

BETHANY HOUSE
a division of Baker Publishing Group
Minneapolis, Minnesota

Published by Bethany House Publishers
Minneapolis, Minnesota
BethanyHouse.com

Bethany House Publishers is a division of
Baker Publishing Group, Grand Rapids, Michigan

Printed in the United States of America

Library of Congress Cataloging-in-Publication Data
Names: Cossette, Connilyn, author.
Title: Splendor of the Land / Connilyn Cossette.
Description: Minneapolis, Minnesota: Bethany House, a division of Baker Publishing Group, 2025. | Series: The King's Men ; 3
Identifiers: LCCN 2024054825 | ISBN 9780764238932 (paperback) | ISBN 9780764244971 (casebound) | ISBN 9781493450749 (ebook)
Subjects: LCGFT: Christian fiction. | Bible fiction. | Novels.
Classification: LCC PS3603.O8655 S64 2025 | DDC 813/.6—dc23/eng/20241213
LC record available at https://lccn.loc.gov/2024054825

Cover design by Jennifer Parker

Author is represented by the Steve Laube Agency.

Baker Publishing Group publications use paper produced from sustainable forestry practices and postconsumer waste whenever possible.

25 26 27 28 29 30 31 7 6 5 4 3 2 1

For those who feel unseen:
The One who lit the stars aflame is calling you by name.

"Do not fear, for I have redeemed you; I have called you by your name; you are Mine."
Isaiah 43:1b HCSB

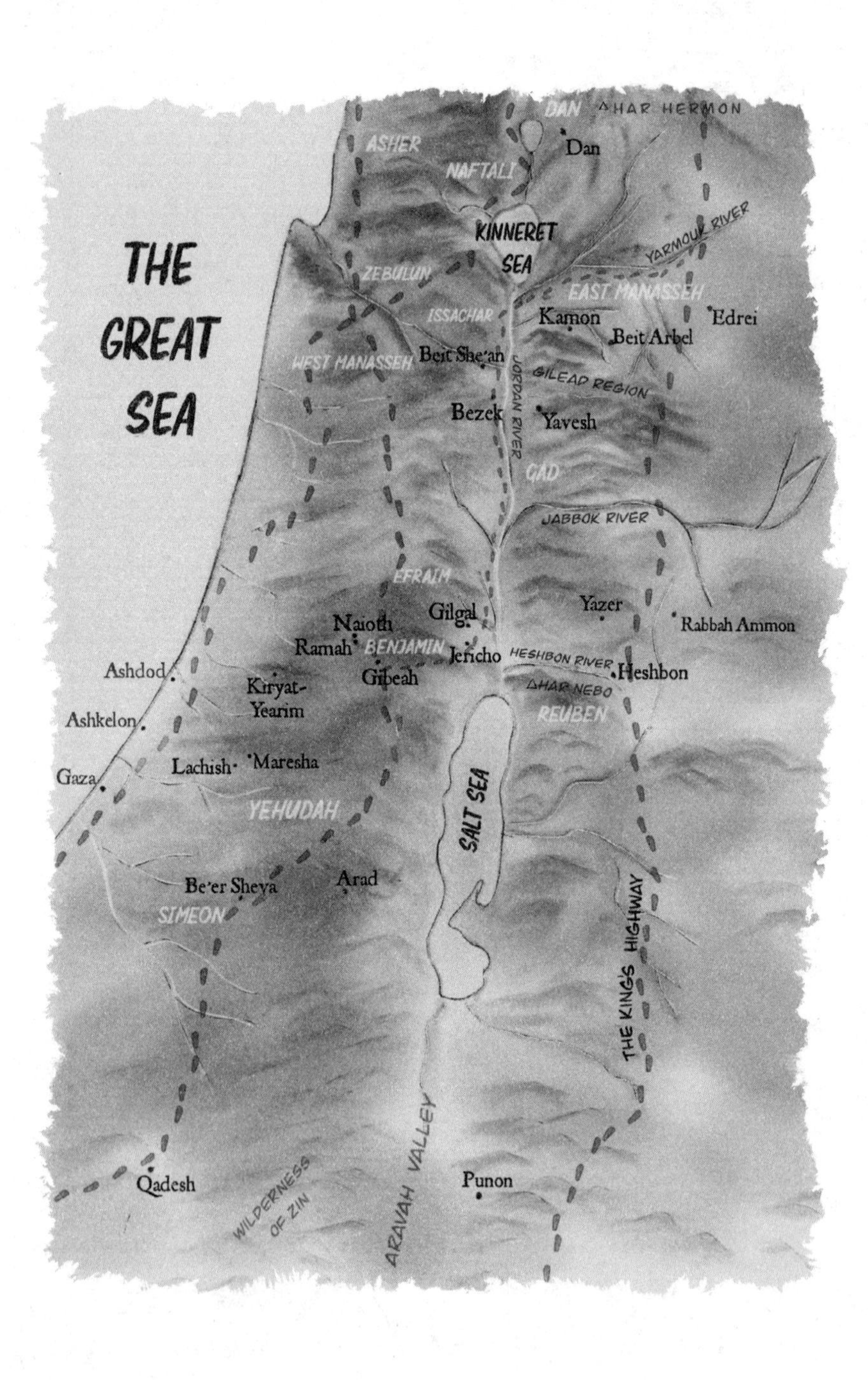
THE GREAT SEA
DAN
HAR HERMON
Dan
ASHER
NAFTALI
KINNERET SEA
YARMOUK RIVER
ZEBULUN
EAST MANASSEH
ISSACHAR
Kamon
Edrei
Beit Arbel
WEST MANASSEH
Beit She'an
JORDAN RIVER
GILEAD REGION
Bezek
Yavesh
GAD
JABBOK RIVER
EFRAIM
Yazer
Gilgal
Naioth
Rabbah Ammon
Ramah
BENJAMIN
Jericho
HESHBON RIVER
Heshbon
Ashdod
Kiryat-Yearim
Gibeah
HAR NEBO
REUBEN
Ashkelon
Lachish
Maresha
Gaza
SALT SEA
YEHUDAH
Be'er Sheva
Arad
SIMEON
THE KING'S HIGHWAY
ARAVAH VALLEY
Qadesh
Punon
WILDERNESS OF ZIN

Then Saul said to the Kenites, "Go, depart; go down from among the Amalekites, lest I destroy you with them. For you showed kindness to all the people of Israel when they came up out of Egypt." So the Kenites departed from among the Amalekites.

1 Samuel 15:6 ESV

A psalm of Ronen ben Avidan

The anointed one shall abide by the counsel of the
Most High,
The voice of the Ancient One to light his every step.

A shield to both the humble and the valiant,
His mighty fortress offers refuge to all who call on the
Name.

From ashes and dust shall his glory arise,
a diadem of splendor to grace the head of the lowly.

His scepter lifted high shines justice across the Land.
Heavenly righteousness, like a river of gladness, flows
from his throne.

Selah.

PROLOGUE

Gavriel

1043 BC
Mitzpah, Israel

"You may be older than me, Zevi. But I haven't been a boy in a long time. I can take care of myself."

I let the words fall hard between me and my eldest cousin, thrilling a little at the flare of indignation in his eyes. Zevi rarely reacted to my jabs, so it gave me a jolt of satisfaction to see him flinch. He was almost as arrogant as Hanan sometimes, and I knew no one as self-satisfied as my uncle.

Ever since my cousins and I had crept up onto the ridge to watch the selection of the new King of Israel early this morning, I'd been aching to get closer to the gathering. Now that I'd seen a fellow Benjamite named Saul ben Kish anointed as sovereign, no one was going to stop me from finding out what was going on in the valley below.

I turned my back on Zevi's judgmental glare but caught sight of the frustration on Shalem's face as I did. The youngest of the four of us, Shay hated being left behind more than anything. I couldn't blame him. I'd lose my mind if Zevi and Avidan coddled me the way they did him, terrified that his parents would flay them alive if he was hurt. The boy needed to toughen up. Iyov and Hodiya couldn't wrap their precious youngest in thick wool for the rest of his days.

Perhaps I should have invited Shay, since he was the only one curious about which warriors had already offered their swords to the new king. But getting close enough to hear what the men were saying was going to be hard enough without a sniveling pup underfoot, pelting me with a thousand questions.

There was no easy path down from the granite ridge where we'd been spying on the proceedings and the underbrush was thick after the long rainy season, but I knew these hills like I knew my favorite blade, and it was easy enough to ghost barefooted through the trees and pluck my way among the boulders until I was within earshot of the group gathered around Saul. From the snatches of conversation that floated toward me, I guessed most of them to be Benjamite, but there were a few others whose subtle accents indicated they hailed from the north, perhaps Efraim or Western Manasseh.

I'd never cared much about who might sit on the throne of Israel before now. I only wanted a leader to crush our enemies. But when it had been a man of my *own* tribe selected, pride for my lineage swept through me like never before. From the very beginning, when the youngest of Yaakov's sons were born, the other tribes had looked down on Benjamin. But not anymore.

Not only was Saul ben Kish the chosen ruler of our nation, he was nearly a head taller than anyone around him. With a thick beard and warrior-wide shoulders, he was a man to be feared, both on and off the battlefield. Our enemies would quiver in their sandals. No more laughing at our "headless" nation, mocking us as a horde of ignorant shepherds and farmers, or stealing our land and oppressing our people. With Saul and his warriors in the lead, our enemies would water the ground beneath their feet when they saw us coming. And I'd be right there alongside my tribesman, my own weapons in hand.

I pressed my palm to the sheathed knife in my belt out of habit. It was the best one I'd made so far. Strong. Sleek. Perfectly balanced. I'd spent days carving the pommel to fit my left hand, the grooves shaped for my grip alone.

Two men stood on the periphery, one tall and dark-haired, his broad-chested form undoubtedly that of a warrior, and the other shorter with fiery red hair but no less built for battle.

"We should take back Efraim first," said the red-haired one. "Or the Philistines will push farther into our territories. We should have sent them back to the coastlands long before now."

The Philistines had captured nearly all Efraimite territory when they sacked Shiloh decades ago. Those who did not escape after the Mishkan was destroyed remained under ruthless domination by those who hated us most.

"He's been king for less than an hour, Emmet," said the taller one. "A campaign like that will take time, resources, and well-trained men—all of which we are sorely lacking right now. Besides, it will require united effort between the tribes."

Emmet scoffed. "It's been hundreds of years since Yaakov sired our tribal fathers. When have we ever been of one accord?"

"We've also never had a king to lead us before. It'll be his first order of business to call for unity, I assure you."

Emmet moved in closer, dropping his voice. "Is he up to it? Do you think?"

The young man was quiet for so long I wondered whether I'd missed his response. I held my breath. "My father will rise to the challenge. I'm certain of it."

Shock buzzed in my veins. This was Saul's *son*? He did have the extreme height and warrior aspect of his father, along with the dark hair and beard.

"He'll have no problem recruiting Benjamites," said Emmet. "But Yehudah and Simeon . . ." He shook his head. "You saw how they reacted to the outcome of the lots."

Saul's son hummed in reluctant agreement. "Perhaps you can be of help in that regard. Your mother hails from the south, doesn't she?"

"She does. Near Arad," said Emmet. "But the Amalekites drove her family north when she was a child. I'll have no sway over any man of Yehudah, regardless of my maternal heritage."

"But it does give you a unique voice," said Saul's son.

"Perhaps," Emmet mused. "Will he put you in charge of a unit?"

"I hope so. I plan to show him I'm worthy."

"You know what else all of this means, don't you, Yonatan? Someday, *you'll* be king."

It was at this moment that my body betrayed me. I'd been crouched in such an awkward position behind the boulder for so long that a muscle in my leg cramped. My foot skidded across the stony ground with a grating rasp and I went down, landing hard on one knee. Eyes pressed closed, I held my breath and prayed no one had heard my blunder.

Too late. A large hand came down on my shoulder, at once grabbing me by the tunic and jerking me to my feet. *Zevi will never let me forget that he was right.*

With my heartbeat thrumming at the back of my throat and dread prickling my skin, I looked up into the eyes of the heir to the throne.

"Catch a spy there, did you?" said Emmet, thick amusement in his voice.

"Indeed," said Yonatan, his piercing gaze taking me in head to foot before he snatched the knife from its sheath. "And an armed one at that."

Instinct battled reason. I was no slender reed, but Yonatan easily outweighed me by a third, was probably equal in height to his giant of a father, and was the son of the new King of Israel. Not to mention there were at least fifteen warriors within a few paces of what had been my hiding spot. So I held still as he examined my weapon. "Where'd you get this, boy? You steal it?"

I bristled. "I *made* it."

Emmet barked out a laugh. "You expect us to believe that?"

My blood went hot, but I swallowed against the glut of rage in my throat. Something about the man reminded me of Hanan, and it made me want to smash my fist into his arrogant mouth. But I refused to waste this, my first impression with the heir to the throne of Israel.

I lifted my chin. "It took me three tries to get the blend of copper and tin just right. The heat had to be perfect, and I found once I added ash to the mold, it worked far better than the first try. Not only can it slice through bone with little effort, but it flies true, I assure you."

I kept my eyes on Yonatan, hoping to prove my words sincere, but Emmet's disbelieving stare singed the side of my face.

"How old are you?" asked Yonatan.

I knew what he saw—a young man who'd not quite grown into his feet and hands, a beard still coming into its fullness over a face that was a shade too youthful to pass for military age. But my shoulders had widened in the past few months, and I'd gained nearly a handspan of height, along with a substantial amount of bulk from laboring with my uncle's men as they loaded and unloaded wagons—a task I relished because it bothered Hanan so much to see me sweating alongside those so far beneath his pristine sandals. But my youth had nothing to do with my skills.

"Old enough to make superior weapons to the vast majority in Hebrew hands."

Their brows flew high at my audacity, but this was no time for false modesty. I'd been taught by a master metalsmith. Since I'd been a boy, I'd studied every weapon I could get my hands on, taking them apart to understand the craftsmanship whenever I could. I'd even figured out how to make leather armor because I refused to give up when I wanted to learn something. The ability to hone in on a task until I'd mastered it had served me well and would continue to do so when I was a soldier. This was my opportunity to lay the groundwork for a future with Saul's army as a master of weapons-making.

After a few tense moments, Yonatan chuckled. "No lack of confidence, I see."

With a blank expression, the red-haired warrior kept his eyes on me. "Fine line between confidence and foolhardiness, if you ask me."

I set my jaw, determined not to snatch up the bait Emmet had laid down. If it wasn't for the red hair, I would lay that fine knife on a bet the arrogant cur was actually related to my uncle.

"This is well-made," said Yonatan, running the pad of one long finger along the edge of my blade. There were no nicks to be found there; I'd sharpened it last night as Avi blathered on with some rambling story about an altercation between two young Levites in Naioth over a woman. Why anyone would fight over one woman was beyond me. There were plenty enough to go around.

Yonatan held the weapon up to one eye and squinted the other, peering down the flat of the blade with a hum of satisfaction for its clean lines. That quiet approval echoed in my chest like a clap of thunder.

I'd spent hour after hour smoothing the metal, ignoring everything else until it was perfect. It had been time well spent, even if my mother had fussed I was ignoring my responsibilities around the house. As if it mattered. As the richest man in Ramah, Hanan employed a bevy of servants to wait hand and foot on my mother and sisters. His efforts to force me into following his footsteps had always been destined to fail. I would never be like him—no more than I meant to be like my father, his worthless brother, who'd left my mother a widow. I would be my own man. And this moment was the first step toward that goal.

Yonatan suddenly flicked his wrist, tossing my knife into the air. With a glimmer of sunlight, the blade flipped twice before landing in the prince's left palm. He grinned. "Well balanced too."

It took every drop of effort to keep an answering grin off my face, when in truth, a shout of pure triumph was demanding to burst from my mouth. But I would not act the boy I'd been twice accused of being today. I locked my muscles tight, willed my breath to remain slow and steady, and allowed only one dip of my chin to acknowledge the praise.

"A left-handed weapon," said Emmet. "You're Benjamite, then."

I nodded. It was a trait our tribe was famous for. Those of us who were not naturally inclined to use our left hands in weaponry were trained to do so from the earliest years. And even though Hanan eschewed any such training himself and did his best to discourage me from doing so, I'd taught myself the skill of using both hands with not only a blade but with a bow and a sling.

The one thing I would not do was learn to write with either hand because it was the only skill my uncle desired me to develop. I could read the symbols of our language, which my mother had taught me before my father died, but I had refused to play the scribe and endlessly etch lines of script and numbers into ledgers like Hanan, a task he adored almost as much as he did my mother and sisters—his one and only redeeming quality in my eyes.

"And you can use this?" asked Yonatan, almost reluctantly handing me the knife by its blade.

I looked the king's son in the eye, banishing the nerves that fluttered in my stomach. "I can hit the center of a target at thirty paces," I said. "Perhaps more on a still day."

One dark eyebrow arched. "Can you?"

"And that knife is only one of my creations. I make spearheads, arrow tips, even metal slingstones that will travel twice the speed of stone, as well as sturdy leather scale armor."

"A man of many talents," said Emmet, his tone entirely disbelieving.

Heat flared at the base of my neck. "I've been smithing since I was eleven. And studying weaponry since I could hold a blade."

"Your father taught you these things?" asked Yonatan.

"No." Bile sluiced over my tongue. "He's dead."

His brow pinched. "I'm sorry—"

"I'm not," I interrupted before I thought better of trampling a prince's words. "What I mean is, I learned most of it on my own and the rest from a . . . friend."

At my vague explanation, a look passed between the two men that I could not interpret. But I was not about to explain that my drunken father had died when I was not even six, and since then I'd spent more time with servants than the man who'd stepped in and married my mother.

"It's a good story. But he stole it, Yonatan." Emmet let out a caustic laugh, and my body went stiff, my face burning. "He's far too young for such skill."

Overcome with equal parts fury and pride, I sputtered, "That's a lie."

Emmet shook his head, unconvinced. "Let's get back, Yonatan. I'm sure your father will address us soon."

My vision blurred for a moment, and if the king's son had not been watching me, I would have plowed headlong into the redheaded fool, no matter how many years he had on me. I wanted to pummel the smugness from his face. I clenched both fists at my sides and breathed through my nose.

Someone called Yonatan's name, and Emmet walked off in answer, not giving me another glance. But to my surprise, the king's son remained, his keen gaze on my face as I held on to what remained of my composure. "What is your name?"

I flinched at the gentle tone. I'd fully expected Yonatan to follow his rude friend without another thought for me. "Gavriel ben Elan of Ramah."

"Well, Gavriel ben Elan of Ramah, when you are old enough to fight for Israel, I'd be honored to have you in my unit. We'll need every weapon we can find. And those who can craft such things will be of great value. Especially if they are of such excellent quality."

I swallowed, too shocked to speak.

"Have you made a sword?"

"No, my lord," I said. "I have only scavenged materials or broken tools to work with."

He folded his arms over his broad chest, frowning. "Our enemies certainly have a stranglehold on the metal trade, don't they?"

With the Amalekites to the south blocking access to the copper mines, the Philistines and Phoenicians controlling the sea trade, and the Arameans, Moabites, and Ammonites dominating the trade roads east and north, there was little opportunity for us to obtain enough ore to make even one sword of quality, let alone the thousands we would need to overcome our enemies.

"Time will come when you'll have plenty of material," Yonatan said. "You'll see. And then, I expect you to make me a sword that will put those Philistine ones to shame." His dark eyes glimmered with amusement. I sensed it was not at my expense but that of his disbelieving friend.

I swallowed hard against the emotion that swelled in my throat as I bowed my head. "I will, my lord. I vow it."

He clapped a hand on my shoulder and squeezed. "Good. Then we have a deal. Until then, keep honing those skills and seeking out new ones. We can always learn more, can't we?"

I nodded, too overcome to respond as the king's son turned to walk away. He was right, I still had much to learn and would not rest until I mastered everything about my chosen craft. But if there was one thing I knew for certain, it was that Yonatan ben Saul was a man I would gladly follow into battle, and I would do whatever it took to ensure that his belief in me was justified.

Gavriel

1033 BC
City of Dan, Northern Israel

Yonatan was going to kill me.

But even if my commander would strip the hide from my bones later, the only thing that mattered right now was how quickly I could slam the grin off the foul mouth of the man standing opposite me. Besides, it wouldn't be the first time King Saul's son called me in for discipline, and I was certain it wouldn't be the last.

Although I was far from drunk, I'd just begun to enjoy a pleasant hum of warmth in my veins. I'd been paid my wages and had plans to spend most of it here in this inn, where I'd been told the drink was good and the cost minimal. But the sight of a woman struggling to get away from a brutish Danite in the corner of the room invoked a flash of infuriating memory that clouded my vision. And when he'd grabbed her by the waist with his meaty paw and laid a sloppy kiss on her unwilling lips, it had been too much. Rage burned through the buzz of drink in my body, and I'd pressed through the oblivious crowd to demand he let her go.

"She's a juicy piece," said the Danite with a curl of his lip toward the serving girl cowering at his side. "But not worth such a fuss."

"Then walk away," I said.

"I'll do as I please." He grabbed the terrified young woman by the jaw and pulled her to him, pressing his face into her hair as she trembled, but keeping his eyes pinned on me in defiance.

I widened my stance. "Only a coward forces a woman's interest."

The Danite's eyes flared at the insult. But instead of releasing the serving girl, he pulled her into his chest. She trembled, begging me with watery eyes to rescue her. Why the innkeeper would even have such a timid little thing in a room full of wolves was beyond my comprehension. Most of the women I'd come across in taverns or inns over the past few years, especially those who worked around soldiers, were nearly as thick-skinned as some of the men I fought beside. This one far too closely resembled my younger sisters, who might as well be made of feathers for all the three of them together weighed. The thought of any one of them caught in such a situation hardened my resolve.

"Release her," I said in a bored tone. "Now."

"Or what?" snapped the Danite. "You'll make me?"

I shrugged lazily. "Can't be all that hard when you have to hide behind a girl."

As I predicted, he puffed up like an adder and pushed the woman to the side. Surprised, she stumbled into the bench along the wall but wisely did not hesitate to dart off and disappear into the crowd. I had no time to be relieved she was safe as the snarling Danite came at me with a curse. My first instinct was to go for the knife at my belt, but this was a fellow Hebrew, not one of my enemies. I could not defend myself by fatal force or I'd end up on trial for murder.

Thankfully, my uncle Natan had taught my cousins and me a

few things from his time as a bare-knuckle fighter, so I pivoted, easily dodging the furious Danite. He slammed into a group of men behind me, their drinks spilling in a cascade of foul words and crashing pottery.

The Danite swiftly righted himself and swung around to plow into me. My jaw hit his huge shoulder, and I bit my tongue, the tang of metallic blood filling my mouth, but I grabbed the back of his tunic with both hands and yanked hard to the right, setting him off-balance. He buckled sideways like an ax-notched sapling.

I let out a mocking laugh. "Perhaps you ought to stick to manhandling girls after all, my friend."

He barreled toward me like a bull, spewing some of the filthiest curses I'd ever heard—and I spent the entirety of my time with soldiers. It took only one breath to realize that not only had I pushed too far but I was still a little drink-addled. I tripped back, trying to firm my stance, and he slammed a fist into my eye. Pain spiked through my head, and my vision split into three foggy scenes, all of which contained a murderous Danite. I swung back, but my aim was off, and I merely clipped him on the cheekbone at the same time he punched me hard in the side. Before I could retaliate, a set of arms looped around my neck, pulling tight until I choked.

Disoriented, I staggered back as two large men came between me and the Danite, one I recognized as the innkeeper himself. "Get out of my inn," he said, then jerked his chin toward the tall man at his side. "Toss him out."

With my breath cut off by whichever of his brutes had me by the throat, I could say nothing as I was dragged toward the door, accompanied by the sound of curses and shouts from the other patrons. Someone even threw their drink on me, which stung my eyes as it sluiced down my face.

I tried to bring the world back into focus, but my head was still faintly ringing from the hit the Danite had gotten in. Perhaps I shouldn't have had more than a couple of drinks tonight, after all.

The men stopped at the threshold, and with all their strength, tossed me into the street, which was surprisingly busy for such a gray afternoon. Tumbling forward into the center of a small herd of pigs being driven by the inn, my knees hit the stones. Pain jolted up my thighs as the swine squealed and scattered. This earned me more curses from their herder, who kicked me in the side with a leather boot inset with what felt like a sharp bone in the toe, the point of which was likely to prod his unruly animals along.

Two of the pigs trampled over me as I lay on the ground, my vision spinning and head muddled, adding a few more bruises to match those already throbbing on my face and torso.

"Don't come back!" bawled the innkeeper from the doorway. "None of you worthless Benjamites are welcome here."

It was doubtful the rest of the soldiers in the small unit I'd traveled here with would bother entering such an inn in the first place, especially since Yonatan had told us to keep to the other side of Dan, where there were a few businesses more friendly to outsiders. But I'd made my choice of establishment for the cheap drinks, not for the welcome.

The door slammed behind me, and I slumped to the ground with a groan. At least the young woman was safe. For now. I doubted the innkeeper cared that she was so vulnerable, only that his purse was full.

"And here he is," said a voice above me. I did not have to raise my head to know that the words came from the mouth of a soldier named Petak. Nor was I surprised when the answer came from his brother, Abenar. They were inseparable, like two halves of a whole.

"Right where Yonatan said we'd find you," said Abenar, "wallowing in filth with the other swine."

With the eye that wasn't already swollen shut, I peered up at the two men I'd fought beside for nearly nine years. Men whose wounds I'd tended after battle. Who'd served with me under Yonatan since before I'd even technically been of military age.

The disgust on both of their faces made it clear they had seen the tail end of my altercation with the innkeeper and his guards, and that they were not pleased to have been sent to haul me back to camp.

Yes, Yonatan was indeed going to murder me, and these men, whom I'd once called friends, would more than likely hand him the first stones.

"I have no time for this," Yonatan bit out. "I have another meeting in the morning with the Danite elders." He paced in front of me, arms folded across his chest. Disappointment hung in the air of the tent like a dark cloud, suffocating whatever remained of my welcome inebriation earlier in the afternoon. The moment I'd stood before my commander and felt the weight of his stare, I'd gone dreadfully sober.

This was not the first time Saul's son had chastised me, but before it had been with the hint of amusement in his eye, as if my slipups with discipline had been tolerable, given my record as a soldier in his command. I'd been with him from nearly the beginning, having petitioned to be in his regiment shortly after the battle of Yavesh, and I could not imagine serving under anyone else. But in all the years I'd been subject to his leadership, I'd never seen him so agitated. At least, not since he'd very nearly been executed by his own father at Michmash.

"We have a mission here, Gavriel. An important one. And I have to go into the meeting with the elders tomorrow with some sort of explanation about why one of my men—one of my handpicked elite—can't keep himself out of drunken brawls."

My stomach wrenched at the bitterness in his tone, but I kept my mouth closed and my chin down. This was no time to talk back. And what could I say anyhow? I'd done just as he said. The fact that it had been in defense of a woman was beside the point. Yonatan was a fair commander, one whose leadership was without rival among Saul's army. But that also meant he took his position seriously and suffered little foolishness. Excuses were not welcome, only unquestionable loyalty and decisive action on behalf of Israel—things Yonatan himself took to heart.

If only the same could be said of his father.

Not that I would dare speak aloud such a treasonous thing. But the entire reason we were here, at the far northern reaches of Hebrew territory on a fairly futile mission to foster goodwill with the men of Dan, was because Saul could not bear to give Yonatan the credit he was due for his part in the victory at Michmash. It was because of Yonatan's boldness that we'd pushed the Philistines back to their coastal cities after decades of oppression and encroachment on Hebrew land.

And yet instead of honoring his son for such courage, Saul had taken most of the credit for the Philistine retreat and even for the presence of the Ark of the Covenant at the battle, which led to the shaking of the ground and the terror among the enemy that handed us the ultimate victory that day.

In the guise of bestowing him the honor of representing the throne, Saul had sent Yonatan as an emissary to the northern tribes for the purposes of garnering support, recruiting skilled soldiers, and keeping a close eye on tribes that had been under their own autonomy for so long they sometimes forgot that Saul was king over *all* Israel.

It was a mission that should have taken only a few months but instead had stretched over the past two years, while in the south other units, under the leadership of lesser men, had the privilege of dealing with our enemies. This northern area was under no immediate threat. The Hittites had left us alone for many years, the Arameans hadn't bothered to face us head-on for decades, and the Phoenicians were far more interested in expanding their seafaring horizons to turn their ambitions southward. I knew this mission for what it was, a punishment for not only showing Saul up on the battlefield but for the events of the following day, when the king nearly slaughtered his heir for a foolish vow.

Yonatan was far more patient than I would have been. I respected Saul as sovereign over Israel, acknowledged he had been chosen by Yahweh himself, and was honored to fight under his banner. But privately, I anticipated the day Yonatan would inhabit the throne. There was no doubt in my mind he would reign with integrity and fairness, the same way he led his men.

Therefore, I would remain silent and take my well-deserved discipline now like a man.

"We are here as representatives for the king. It will be hard enough convincing Dan to send men south to fight with us should another major conflict arise." Yonatan shook his head. "Israel must remain united, throw off the last vestiges of our insular ways and tribal prejudices. I cannot afford to raise their hackles over one fool."

Dread rose as I began to suspect this was no simple disciplinary meeting.

"You are a good soldier, Gavriel. You fight with ferocity like I've rarely seen and are one of my best spies. And of course, your skill in weapon-making is extraordinary. But you are also reckless. Arrogant. And you lack a consistency and focus that would take you from good to great."

All the blood seemed to drain from my head into my mud-covered boots.

"You've been caught twice sleeping during your watch. Both times you were saved because there was no danger in the area but regardless you put this unit at risk."

The back of my neck prickled with shame. He was right. The first time I'd accidentally dozed off was a couple of years ago, when we'd marched almost nonstop for two days from Gibeah to Galilee.

But the second time, I was drunk. We'd been welcomed into one of the towns in Naftali with great fanfare and a generous flow of exceptional wine—not to mention a few lovely girls who served that wine with enticing smiles for the brave soldiers of Israel. I'd forgotten all about my turn at watch while occupied with one of the more accommodating young women and hadn't given myself time to sober up before I was called to stand guard over our camp. That was the first time I'd been the recipient of a dressing-down by Yonatan. In truth, I'd been so sick the next morning I barely remembered what punishment he'd given me.

"I've had more than a few accounts of your hard drinking, Gavriel. Far be it from me to deny a soldier a bit of pleasure when not on duty, a necessary escape from reminders of things we've seen and done, but you've become increasingly irresponsible and less diligent in your work. That last batch of bronze arrowheads you made were so brittle they crumbled the moment they were nocked on bowstrings."

My insides roiled. I could argue that the ingots we'd procured from a load of tribute from the southern tribes was of an inferior grade. There'd been so much impurity mixed into the copper it was nearly impossible to burn it all out. But I suspected nothing I said right now would assuage Yonatan's ire. Besides, he was right that there was little excuse for producing inferior weapons.

"It will never happen again, I v—"

Yonatan threw up a palm to stop my vow, and I was too well-trained to speak over him. "I've put up with far too much as it is. This unit must be cohesive, and the rest of the men have lost trust in you."

My knees nearly buckled. If Yonatan had thrust his sword all the way through my body, it would have hurt less. These men, whom I'd fought alongside for years, whom I considered brothers in many ways, no longer trusted me?

"Therefore, you are released from duty."

Fiery nausea swam up my throat. "But I—"

"Go home, Gavriel. Your sword will undoubtedly be needed in further conflicts. Straighten yourself out so you'll be ready when the time comes."

My mind spun, thoughts crashing around in my skull like rocks in a barrel. He was cutting me from this unit? No. That could not be. I was made to be a warrior. Made to one day stand at Yonatan's side as one of his honored armor-bearers. It was what I'd been working toward since I was sixteen years of age. How could I have so completely ruined everything?

For the first time since I was a boy, I felt my eyes burning with tears. I blinked hard, desperate for my fear not to come flooding out. *"Quit sniveling like a little girl"* spat a ghostly memory. I flinched but quickly got a hold on my composure, determined to cling to the position I'd earned among his elite unit of warriors.

"Please, Commander. Do not send me away. I vow with everything in me that I will do better. This is . . . this is who I am, my lord. I am . . ." I paused to clear my throat of the stupid emotion that had its claws wrapped around my neck. "I am nothing if I am not a soldier."

"I'm sorry, Gavriel. I truly am. I saw your potential from the very first day I met you, but unfortunately, you've squandered it."

Shame crawled up my neck, burning my face like a furnace. Surely this was only a horrible nightmare, I'd only drunk too much and would wake to find myself still in good graces with a man I'd practically worshiped for the past few years. Dizzy, I scrubbed at my face, pressing my fingers into my eye sockets as I tried to drag myself back from whatever hellish dream I'd fallen into.

But Yonatan's tall form still stood before me as the blur began to clear from my sight, the frown on his face hard and unyielding. "Go home."

Dazedly, I muttered, "I don't have one."

The statement was as much a truth as it was a lie. I had been born in Ramah. My mother lived there with my three younger sisters and, of course, the uncle who'd snatched up his brother's wife the moment the fool who'd sired me had landed himself under the wheels of an ox-drawn wagon. I'd grown up with every luxury in a villa near the center of the city that had only grown larger as Hanan's business had flourished. But it wasn't my home anymore. Hadn't been since I'd walked out the door to go fight for Saul at the Battle of Yavesh when I was nearly three years from military age.

Even if my mother and sisters would be thrilled to welcome me back, I had no desire to return to a house whose master considered me the disgraceful spawn of his worthless brother. Besides, even if I wanted to, I was fairly certain I'd destroyed whatever had remained of my welcome the last time I stepped foot in Hanan's house a few years ago.

The look of pity on Yonatan's face gouged into my chest like a rusty knife. I did not want his pity. I wanted to prove he was wrong about me. That I wasn't the sum total of a few foolhardy decisions. I'd worked too hard to watch every plan I'd made crumble into dust. I refused to give up so easily.

I stood straighter, looking him in the eye to display the fullness of my sincerity. "Please, my lord. I know I have let you down. Let everyone down. But give me a chance to redeem myself. If you will not have me with this unit, place me with another. I will give my all. Prove my worth to Israel and to my king."

Yonatan did not respond to my plea, only dropped his eyes to the floor and shook his head. My heart sank into the pit of my stomach. Surely this could not be over. Where would I even go?

Now that he'd chosen to make a life as a timberman instead of a soldier, Zevi and his wife, Yochana, lived in Kiryat-Yearim, among the clan of relatives who inhabited our grandfather's household compound. He still served Saul from time to time training men, but he'd chosen to follow his father's footsteps and stay out of conflict whenever he could, for the sake of his family. He and Yochana would welcome me, I was sure, but as much as I respected Zevi, I had no interest in cutting down trees with my cousin and his father for the rest of my life.

Neither could I find a place with Avidan, since he and his wife had moved their family across the river a couple of years ago to go live with Keziah's people. Avi held some notion of spreading Torah knowledge among the Hebrews who'd been separated from the rest of the tribes for hundreds of years, as well as the idol worshipers who lived among them.

And of course Shalem . . . the youngest of the four of us had been missing for nearly nine years now. Both Avi and Zevi had found clues that he was, against all odds, still alive—or at least had been a few years ago when Zevi insisted he'd crossed Shay's trail on the borders of Philistine territory. But the boy had been traveling with traders, Phoenicians by all accounts, and he could be anywhere at all. Or perhaps he was truly dead by now. We would never know.

For some inexplicable reason, I still carried his little stone knife with me, though it was nothing more than another reminder of the destruction I left in my wake. In truth, I didn't really blame Yonatan for losing faith in me. Even so, I found myself silently pleading with the God I'd not bothered to address directly in over twenty years to soften his resolve.

"All right," Yonatan said.

I sucked in a startled breath, wondering if I'd misheard. But I did not speak for fear of crushing the small crust of hope he'd suddenly dangled in front of me.

"You'll go south," he said. "I've received word that my father means to take on the Amalekites within the next month. He's amassing troops in preparation. We've been summoned to return and prepare the ranks."

We were finally going to war with the Amalekites? They'd been chewing away at our southern borders for decades now, emboldened by the Philistine sacking of Shiloh and the chaos among a loose federation of fractious tribes before Saul had taken the throne. Regardless that we were distant cousins, the bloodthirsty descendants of Esau had been our enemies since Mosheh's day, when they set out to destroy those who'd fled Egypt through the Red Sea, attacking the sick and lame at the outskirts of the procession through the wilderness. From the very start, they'd tried to destroy us when we were at our weakest, but we'd prevailed again and again. Perhaps Saul had finally decided to finish what Yehoshua had begun centuries ago and remove them from the Land of Promise for good.

My hands itched for my weapons at the thought of standing shoulder to shoulder with my brethren on a battlefield once again. Thankfully, Yonatan understood that no matter my faults, I was first and foremost a warrior.

My chest swelled with a potent mix of relief and anticipation. "Of course I will go. It will be an honor to fight for my people against such an ancient enemy."

"You'll not be going to war."

I blinked at my commander. "But you said . . ."

"There is a large tribe of Kenites living among the Amalekites at the eastern edge of the Aravah Valley near the copper mines of Punon. They've been intermingled for some time now—decades, most likely. My father is offering them mercy to repay an ancient debt. You'll go with one of the groups in charge of moving the Kenites to where they will be safe from the forthcoming assault."

I gaped at Yonatan. He wanted me to shepherd a horde of nomads through the wilderness? "I would be of far more use in battle, my lord—"

Yonatan trampled over my words with a half-snarled, "*I* will decide where you are of use, Gavriel. You've wasted your favor with me and are fortunate to have even this chance to redeem yourself."

My breaths came short and shallow as my formidable commander glared down at me, his usually affable expression like stone. I'd truly set fire to the regard he'd once had for me. I had no choice but to submit or be expelled from the army of Israel, perhaps for good. Yonatan may be at odds with King Saul right now, but he was still the man's firstborn son and heir, as well as one of his highest commanders. If Yonatan banned me from fighting in his own ranks, I would not be welcome in others, that was certain.

Swallowing what remained of my pride, I dropped my chin. "Forgive me, my lord. I will go wherever you send me. It is my honor to serve Israel in whatever capacity I am needed."

"I thought as much. Pack your things. You'll be departing in the morning for Gibeah. Move quickly because your new unit is departing in four days' time."

"If I may ask, to whom will I be reporting?"

"Emmet ben Nahvesh."

Shocked, my eyes flew to his. Yonatan's former head armor-bearer, and best friend, hated me nearly as much as the Amalekites hated Israel.

My commander stared back, a hint of challenge in his steady gaze. He was well aware of the sour blood between Emmet and me, but if I wanted to prove myself loyal and trustworthy again, I must submit to his every command.

So I dropped to one knee and bowed low before the man who would one day rule over the kingdom of Israel. "I am grateful for your mercy, my lord. I will not fail you again."

"I know you won't, Gavriel, because you have only this one final chance. Make it count."

Zahava

Punon Valley

The acrid tang of ore in a blazing clay furnace was among my favorite smells in the world. I stared into the dancing green-tinted flames, spellbound as the crushed malachite pulsed a defiant red, fighting to retain form until the fire melted into the cracks between glowing coals.

"Are they still green?" my abba asked, sweat dripping from his beard as he continued the steady cadence of the bellows strapped to his feet.

"They are." Already anticipating his next command, I reached for the iron coal shovel.

"More fuel," he said as I scooped a hefty portion from the nearby pile and tilted it over the knee-high clay furnace. Sparks flared high, the flames following suit, and heat seared my skin through the thick wool wrap over my face. I tripped back a step, leaning on the end of the long-handled shovel to let the fire settle. I'd learned my lesson two years before, nearly singeing my eyebrows off when I didn't retreat fast enough the first time my father had allowed me to feed the furnace.

Once the flare quieted a little, I returned to my stool to take up diligent watch over the flames, waiting for the moment they would signify the copper was purified enough to continue the process.

My father stepped up his pace on the bellows, his thick-muscled legs keeping up a familiar cadence that echoed off the walls of the limestone cave around us. As he pushed air into the blazing red belly of the clay furnace, a dull roar began as the flames eagerly consumed the additional fuel. But still, their tips were painted faintly green, the malachite refusing to completely give up the ghost.

Just as I reached for yet another shovelful of charcoal, my father choked out a series of hacking coughs, his rhythm faltering as his body jolted with the effort.

"Abba!" I cried out. The shovel clattered to the stone floor as I dropped it to go to his side. But he waved me off, shaking his head and slapping his work-scarred palm to his chest a few times until the coughing fit began to wane.

"Tend the fire, Zahava," he ordered, pumping the bellows with renewed vigor. "It can't cool!"

Ignoring the jab of pain in my right hip as I twisted too quickly in my rush to obey, I snatched up the shovel and poured another handful of charcoal into the furnace. He was right, I could not let the fire diminish or the copper would not temper correctly and we'd have to start all over again. And both my back and my hips would not allow me to do so tonight. I would already barely be able to walk tomorrow morning as it was.

I wiped sweat from my eyes with the back of my coal-dust-coated hand. My face was undoubtedly a sooty mess anyhow. I was used to my father's coughing attacks; they were as familiar as my mother's lullabies and went back as far as I could remember, but they seemed to be coming more often now. At times, blood tinged the rag he used to wipe his mouth. It was a common thing among the men who mined the copper ore in this valley and those who worked in the metal shops along the river. But my father had been a master of smithing for my entire life, a craft he'd learned from his own father, which had been passed down through the generations for as long as there had been a Kenite people. No one knew the true origins of our knowledge, only that it was without rival and guarded by utmost secrecy.

Many were the legends surrounding our skills in transforming rock into dazzling pieces of jewelry and inexplicably durable blades. Some said the knowledge had been given to the Kenites by the gods long ago, or that a covenant had been cut with dark spirits for whatever magic occurred within our furnaces, but I knew the truth.

Heat. Time. And above all, patience. All things my father had begun to teach me years ago, in secret.

I wasn't certain when he even began the lessons. I'd been my abba's shadow from the time I was a tiny thing, carried about everywhere on his strong shoulders, because with one leg shorter than the other, I could not keep up, no matter how hard I tried. Since I was unable to carry heavy loads like my mother and sisters, who made two to three trips to the river with heavy jugs on their heads each day and whose never-ending tasks were at times far too painful for me to manage, I grew up in my father's foundry, fascinated by the sights, smells, and energy of those who wrestled rock from the ground, then transformed its purified essence into beauty and strength.

Over the past couple of years, my father had even taken the risk of teaching me the most valuable secret passed down through our family, because he had no living son to divulge such things to. He'd told me he struggled over the decision for months but ultimately concluded that unless he shared the inherited knowledge with someone—even though the recipient was a woman—it would die with him. And so I'd been sworn to strict secrecy, vowing never to reveal the techniques I was taught under the cover of night, ones my ancestors had guarded carefully for hundreds of years.

Over the past few months, I'd finally come to master crafting the pure red-gold jewelry that my father was famous for. And none too soon, because his sight was dwindling away day by day.

"I can try to pump the bellows by hand for a while, abba. Give you a rest." Attempting to do so with my feet like he did was useless. With my right leg a full four fingers shorter than the left due to a childhood illness, I could never hope to get the sort of rhythm and power needed to push air into the furnace. But my arms were strong, nonetheless.

Abba shook his head and let out one more hacking cough. "No. Add more charcoal. I'm fine. Keep your eyes on those flames, tell me the moment they shift."

I knew it pained him far worse than the ache in his lungs that he could no longer detect the subtle color changes that prompted the next step in the process. A handful of years ago, a weak-walled furnace had failed an arms-length away from his face in a terrifying explosion of charcoal, flame, and malachite shards. He'd surprised the healers by retaining his vision once the bandages were removed a few weeks later, but whatever damage had been done that day had been the beginning of a slow erosion of his sight—another of the secrets that my father demanded I keep from the rest of his tribesmen.

Only my family knew Abba's eyes could now only detect rough outlines of shadow and shape, and even then mostly in the daytime or bright lamplight. Somehow, the stubborn man had managed to adjust and mask the worst of his limitations by keeping a strict daily routine, walking only with his staff in hand, leaning into his other senses, and relying on his wife and his daughters to cover any fumbles along the way. But I feared any day the last of his sight would disappear for good.

The flames shifted from green to bright blue, the impurities having finally burned away. And yet I waited, keeping my breaths steady and counting each one until the number my abba had drilled into my head was complete. The time we allowed the copper to remain in the furnace was just as important as the level of heat. Not enough and the metal would be too soft; too long and it would be brittle. And once the copper was mixed with the lump of gold my father had bartered from Egyptian traders, in the exact proportions his own father had shown him, heat and time were again of utmost importance. Mistakes in this craft were costly, a lesson I'd learned during my secret apprenticeship, and as a result, took very seriously.

Once the careful measure of my own breaths was complete, I set down the shovel on what remained of the charcoal pile. "It's done, Abba."

Immediately, he ceased the bellows and bent at the waist, breathing heavily. For a man stricken by the dual-edged sword of near-blindness and dust-filled lungs, he was still extraordinarily strong. Working the bellows was a task for someone with great endurance. And yet I could not help but wonder how much longer he'd be able to man the contraption that was so integral to this work. I had no idea who would aid me at the bellows once he was no longer able.

Yasmin, my eldest sister, and Farah, the second of us girls, wanted nothing at all to do with metal. Both were more than content to spend their days cooking with our mother, weaving cloth, tending goats, or juggling the countless daily tasks that kept our household afloat. Breena, two years my junior, was far too distractable for such a tedious task. And although I adored her, I would find it difficult to concentrate on my work with her vibrant and never-ending chatter. And Anaya, the youngest of us, was only nine.

Once the furnace cooled enough to harvest and quench the solidified copper that formed a hard mass at the bottom, I spent the next hour tapping away the charcoal from the lump of mottled metal, then sifting through the soot and dust in the furnace to ensure I'd collected every precious bead of purified copper.

By the time the small bowl beside me was full, my eyes were bleary, my entire body throbbed with pain, and I was stifling yawn after yawn. The high moon peered through the narrow skylight above our heads, indicating it was long past time for sleep. Dawn would sneak over the horizon far too soon.

"Go to bed, Zahava," said my father. "I'll set things to rights."

He'd been using this former mineshaft as his personal workshop for decades, so familiar with every nook of its enlarged interior that he did not even need to use his staff to find his way around, but I hated to leave the cleanup on his shoulders, even if we were careful to replace tools to their appointed places each time we worked in here.

"I'll stay and help," I said, stretching to work out the ache in my shoulders.

"Go. Your mother will have my head if you do not get some sleep tonight. She said a couple days ago you fell asleep at the quern."

That I had. Somehow the back-and-forth motion of milling barley on the stone had lulled me into a bleary-eyed state after a particularly long night working on new wax molds. Besides, there was no use arguing with my father. Once he had something in his mind, there was no shifting his opinion. I'd received more than one tongue-lashing for voicing my concerns over his safety during our late-night work sessions, so I knew better than to coddle him.

I removed the soot-stained leather apron from over my head, hung it on its designated peg, and pressed a farewell kiss to my abba's cheek, trusting he would find his way back to our tent with his staff on the short path he'd walked every day of his life, each step counted precisely.

I climbed the fifteen limestone steps carved by my grandfather's own hand, steadied by the ledge he'd engraved into the wall, and emerged from the narrow entrance to the cave, which was hidden by a thick hedge of flowering shrubs and towering rosemary. I inhaled deeply of their scent, glad for the crisp air after breathing mostly smoke and soot for the past few hours. The ancient, abandoned mineshaft had been carved into the hillside just above our family tent, so I did not have far to walk, but I took a few moments to look over the valley.

A few fires still burned low among the endless gathering of tents, flickering against the dark landscape like yellow-petaled flowers in the night. Glints of moonlight danced in the river that flowed down from the plateaus of Edom above us, crashing into the valley from great heights. This early in the year, the flow was well-fed by the distant snow-capped mountains but gradually lessened with each turn of the moon until it would be only a narrow stream during the hottest season. At times, our people had been forced to climb the treacherous hills behind us to seek out precious spring water for food and drink and to quench the metals in our furnaces. But we'd lately enjoyed abundant rains, so much so that our people had constructed irrigation ditches and planted crops that filled the valley with unexpected fertility in the vast wilderness of the Aravah.

My father said it was a gift from El Shaddai, even if my friends Niv and Kila insisted it was because the gods of Amalek were well-pleased with the many sacrifices offered by their priests and priestesses at the last solstice. All I knew was that the patch of earth we shared with the Amalekites was far greener lately than it had been since I was a girl—perhaps even since before I'd gotten sick.

I turned my eyes to the sky, brilliant with numberless stars against the deep expanse stretched above me. I'd never heard El Shaddai speak, even if my father said my ancestors heard the Voice address a horde of Hebrew slaves from a fiery cloud atop a sacred mountain near our ancestral lands. I wasn't certain whether that was anything more than a myth. But sometimes, when I stared at the vastness of the starry host above and listened carefully, it was as if there was a *knowing* deep in my bones I could not explain. As if the reverberation of an ancient whisper still trembled there at the core of my being—a tune hummed so low only the most astute of ears could detect its melody.

Yet tonight, that flicker of whatever it was that sometimes called to me remained silent as I sought out my favorite star among the countless jewels twinkling in the heavens. Its distinctly golden hue glittered near the horizon among the multitude of white lights.

"Your father named you not for the gold that men pull from the ground by the sweat of their brows, Zahava," my mother had said when I was a little girl, *"but for that golden star shining like a beacon—like a blessing from on high—throughout the long hours he waited outside the tent, listening for your first cry."*

From my earliest memories, my mother had sung a song about how the Creator had fashioned me with elements far stronger and more precious than pure gold, just as he'd made that beautiful star with no more than a word from his mouth. And after my illness, whenever other children mocked my stilted gait, or pain held me captive, she would wrap me in her arms and sing that song until my tears abated.

But a song could not heal my father's lungs or undo the damage that furnace had done to his eyes. The cough was getting worse, and his eyesight was nearly gone. So recently I'd come to a decision.

I needed a husband.

Someone who would not think me unsuited to work with metal

or demand that I cease my work, and who did not treat me as something broken. And there was only one man who fit that description, one man I'd ever dreamed about: my father's long-time, trusted apprentice, Rahm.

I slipped my hand into the little pouch at my hip and pulled out the two copper cylinders I'd made when my father had been away at the foundry. Because even if he could not see the seals, or what I'd carved on their sides, I did not want to have to lie to my abba. They weren't for me, anyhow. They were simply a means to an end, and time was running out. I had to make Rahm see me as more than Barzel's crippled middle daughter.

A shiver gathered between my shoulder blades, the hair on the back of my neck lifting as the chill breeze curled around me and I tucked the seals back in my pouch. The sooner I delivered them, the better. My father could never know I'd disobeyed his order by what I'd crafted with my hands.

Eyes suddenly heavy and the pain in my hip flaring, I followed the well-packed path and slipped through the tent flap, limping past the slumbering goats penned in the main room and the softly glowing embers in the firepit, and through the partition to where I slept with my four sisters. I slithered under the covers next to Breena, hoping she'd remain deep in slumber, but my head had barely settled atop the goose-feathered pillow when her voice hissed in my ear.

"Your toes are freezing, Zaza."

"Sorry." I shifted my feet away from her and tangled them into the woolen blanket. Apparently I'd gotten more chilled than I realized out there under the stars.

"And you smell like charcoal."

Something else I'd not noticed, but it was not surprising. More often than not, I had charcoal, ash, or ore dust beneath my fingernails. It was a constant complaint from my two older sisters especially.

“That can’t be helped until tomorrow,” I replied. “I’ll wash my hair.”

“What did you make tonight? Another ring?”

Breena was, besides my father and mother, the only one who knew the full extent of my secret training. But only because the little sneak had followed me to the cave one day and spied on me. I’d sworn her to secrecy, made her vow to not even reveal to Abba and Ima that she knew how involved I was in making the red-gold jewelry my father was famous for. And because I was the sister she favored most, she’d been thrilled to be in my confidence. It was only times like this, when Yasmin, Farah, and Anaya were breathing deep and steady, that she would ask about my work.

“I’m too tired to talk, Breena. Can I tell you tomorrow?” My words came out slurred as my body relaxed into the soft pallet and the throb of my right hip began to melt away.

“All right,” she said, snuggling into my side. Faintly, I heard Breena say something more, but I’d already passed the threshold of sleep, where I ran free and easily in a rolling field full of tall grass and lush wildflowers, and Rahm’s dark eyes held promises for the future.

The rickety footbridge spanning the narrow river wobbled as I made my way across. I held out both arms, terrified of pitching sideways. The water rushed along below, and I cursed myself for not removing my sandals before crossing. My father had commissioned the special footwear from a traveling Edomite last year. With the right sole much thicker than the left, they gave my shorter leg a lift but also chafed my soles and made my hips scream after wearing them too long. I’d never told him how much I hated them, and I never would. It would hurt him too much.

Besides, going to the other side of the river was enough of a risk, even if it was only to the Kenite encampment there. Since I did not want to draw attention to myself, I'd worn the elevated sandals, veiled the lower half of my face with my headscarf, and filled my basket with food to take to my abba at the foundry as soon as I was finished with my mission.

Once across the bridge, I checked over my shoulder to make certain no one from home had followed me. With Abba at the foundry and my mother and sisters off weaving tent walls with some of the other women, I'd been left behind to tend my beehives, as I often did. But today, instead of taking the time to separate the honey from the wax, I simply harvested a large chunk of comb from the hive baskets and left it to drip into a pot on its own. I'd deal with the mess later. I had very little time to speak with my friends before I delivered the midday meal to my father.

Keeping my eyes averted the few times I passed someone on the path, I hoped no one would notice the odd cadence of my walk as I sought out the large tent Niv and Kila lived in on the outskirts of Punon. Here, families like theirs, with a Kenite father and an Amalekite mother, had formed their own community, not fully accepted by either tribe. Even though my father and others still regularly did business with them, and with the Amalekites, he trusted neither.

I, however, would be forever grateful to Niv and Kila, who'd rescued me from a small gang of Amalekite boys who came across me a few months ago on the way home from delivering a meal to my abba at the foundry. They had mercilessly harassed me, calling me a litany of hurtful things before knocking me to the ground. The two red-haired young women had come from nowhere, sending the bullies scurrying with their vivid threats. Then they'd taken me back to their tent and tended my scrapes before escorting me back over the river. I'd seen them a number of times now since their father's business was located not far from the foundry. And each time they greeted me so kindly, seemed genuinely interested in me, and never commented on my crippled leg.

I'd only been to their home that one time, so I'd had to backtrack when I found myself lost among the maze of tents. But with the help of some children playing knucklebones in the dirt, I finally found my way, stomach fluttering as I approached the sprawling tent that housed my friends' large family.

Two little boys around Anaya's age, faces and hands smudged with what looked to be date honey, stood just outside the tent. They stared at me, round-eyed and silent.

"Are your sisters here?" I asked, guessing they were brothers by the red hair and copious freckles. "Niv and Kila?"

They nodded, and the oldest one led me inside the enormous tent, which looked to be entirely empty, then pointed to where a heavy partition hung at one end. I remembered this as being the place Niv and Kila had taken me to clean my wounds the first time I'd met them.

"They're inside?"

"Feeling bad," he whispered, then darted out of the tent.

"Shalom? Niv? Kila?" I called out, feeling foolish for standing all alone in someone else's home.

"Mali, is that you?" Niv's voice sounded strange from the other side of the curtain.

"No," I replied, pulling the fabric aside, "it's me, Zahava."

Niv was lying sprawled on the bed they shared, but Kila was sitting on a stool, her head tipped over a pot on the ground, groaning.

"Zahava?" Niv pushed up on her elbows. "What are you doing here?"

Her face was alarmingly pale, her eyes red-rimmed. I set down my basket and knelt beside her, placing a hand on her clammy forehead. "Are you ill?"

Kila chuckled, her long red hair still hiding her face. "You could say that." Then she retched into the pot between her knees.

Niv sat up, gently pushing my hand away. "It's nothing. A little too much celebration last night is all."

I'd forgotten yesterday was a new moon. The sounds of revelry had floated over the river, along with acrid smoke from Amalekite offerings. No wonder this camp had been fairly quiet; everyone was sleeping off the effects of drink and feasting.

Kila spat in the pot, then used the edge of a blanket to wipe her mouth. "Worth it."

Niv cackled. "I wasn't certain you'd even find your way home last night."

Kila shrugged a shoulder as she grinned. "Egan walked me back after you left with your friends."

Niv smirked at her sister. "Did he now? I thought you'd moved on from Egan."

Kila's blue eyes twinkled. "The way he kisses? I think not."

A wash of embarrassment slid up my neck. I wasn't ignorant of the ways between men and women, but the brash and unapologetic way Niv and Kila spoke of such intimacy never failed to shock and unsettle me—as did the rumors of what sorts of things happened during the moon festivals they'd taken part in. But who was I to judge? They'd both been nothing but generous from the very moment we'd met.

"Besides, you looked like you were having *plenty* of fun," Kila countered.

"That I was." Niv winked at me as she braided her fiery hair over one shoulder. "Now, tell us, Zahava. Why are you here? Did you come all by yourself?"

"I did. And I can't stay long. But I had to bring you something."

"Oh! A gift?" Kila clapped her hands, sickness seemingly forgotten as she came over to sit next to Niv on the bed.

I removed the copper seals from the bottom of the basket I'd brought from home and handed one to each sister. They squealed in tandem.

"You made them after all!" said Niv. "I thought you were forbidden."

I swallowed the bile that pooled on the back of my tongue. I *absolutely* was forbidden from making engravings like these. But when I'd confided to Niv and Kila that I sometimes etched copper items with designs—a skill that plenty of Kenite women could boast—they'd begged me to design personalized cylinder seals they could wear around their necks. Of course, I'd kept the extent of my knowledge in metalwork quiet, as I'd vowed to do. They did not need to know that I'd also smelted the copper and pounded it into sheets before carving those designs.

Kila peered at the tiny markings as she rolled it in her fingers. "Is my name on it?"

From my basket, I produced a lump of smooth clay I'd wrapped in a fig leaf, then flattened it between my palms. Taking back the cylinder from Kila, I rolled it across the soft clay to reveal the scene I'd pressed into the copper sheet from memory of the statue sitting on a shelf in this very room: a horned goddess with exaggerated hips and breasts holding a lion-headed scepter, a crescent moon and star, and the symbols that marked Kila's name.

She gasped, studying the depiction as Niv demanded her own seal be pressed into clay. The two were nearly identical, except for their name symbols.

For as glad as I was that they liked the gifts I'd brought them, handing them over gave me little relief. In fact, my own stomach now roiled as the sisters praised my creativity. My father may never know that I disobeyed his explicit order not to carve depictions of such things, but I certainly would.

"*Yahweh forbids the carving of any sort of idolatrous image, daughter,*" he'd told me, "*so even if you have no intention of worshiping the work of your hands, take care not to copy the evil depictions of the enemies of El Shaddai.*"

This is a means to an end. I shrugged off the echo of his voice. *This is the one and only time I'll ever break that law.*

"These are truly extraordinary, Zahava," said Niv after she'd strung the amulet on a thin copper chain around her neck. "I know a dozen people who would pay you a week's wage for one."

I shook my head, guilt pressing a sharp finger into the center of my chest. "These are the only ones I'll make. My abba would have my head if he knew. You cannot tell anyone I made them."

Kila winked. "Our secret, then."

"I have the perfect thing to pay you back with," said Niv, jumping to her feet. "Abba brought home the most delicious balm from Heshbon."

"No." I splayed my palms. "Please, I don't need you to give me anything."

"Of course we do," Kila said, brow furrowing. "You took a risk for us."

Even though I'd come here with this plan in mind, opening my mouth to reveal what I wanted was terrifying. My face went hot. "I need help with something."

Niv leaned closer, intrigued. "Oh, this sounds interesting. What do you need?"

My eyes stung with embarrassment as I took a deep breath and then let my words tumble out in a rush. "I need a husband, and I have no idea how to get the attention of the one I want."

The sisters looked at each other, wide-eyed and mouths gaping for a brief and utterly humiliating moment before they turned twin delighted smiles on me.

"Who is this potential bridegroom?" asked Kila.

My face went blazing hot as I admitted the truth. "A man named Rahm. He is one of my father's metalsmiths."

"Oh! I know Rahm," she said. "He's done plenty of trade with our father."

"A fine choice." Kila winked. "He's certainly handsome enough."

He was that. But what was far more important was that I trusted him not to steal away the thing that was most precious to me—my metalworking.

"Little friend," said Niv, reaching for my hand and squeezing it, "you've come to the right place. If there's anything we know, it's how to get a man's attention."

An hour later, my fingernails were scrubbed clean, my hair oiled and shining, lips and cheeks tinted with henna, and my eyes finely lined with malachite kohl. Kila insisted the green would make the amber in my hazel eyes glow.

I'd never felt more foolish.

"You have a great deal of beauty, Zahava," Niv had told me. *"It's just hidden beneath a coating of charcoal dust and copper filings. Let's show him you are more than worthy to be his bride."*

So I ignored the locusts swirling in my belly, hefted the basket of food higher on my hip, and followed the trail that wound through the army of copper foundries and towering piles of black slag along the river. My right sandal was already chafing, and I would pay for this trek in my hips and back later. But the advice Niv and Kila had offered for piquing Rahm's interest was invaluable—that was, if I could pull it off.

Unfamiliar voices met me as I stepped through the open doorway of the largest stone-walled workshop of the lot, constructed by my grandfather nearly fifty years ago. I'd spent many happy days here when I was younger, perched on a high-legged stool to watch my abba work from a safe distance. Once I'd grown into womanhood, he'd stopped bringing me here, saying it was best if he taught me in the cave, away from both prying eyes and the rough sort of men who worked around this area.

"You must understand, Barzel," said one of the three strangers with their backs to me. "I need some sort of margin for profit."

"You'll reap plenty of profit, Garuzah. Has anything from this shop *ever* not fetched a handsome price from your customers?" My father stood, arms crossed and expression impassive. He knew the worth of every piece his shop produced, whether it be weapon, jewelry, or tool, and was a rod of iron when it came to haggling.

Stretching to see what they were negotiating over, I caught sight of a set of red-gold armbands on the table between them. A thrill went through me. I'd never been present while my father traded any of my own pieces, ones he passed off as his own.

I wasn't certain how he convinced the men he worked with every day that his sight was not as bad as it was. Chances were Rahm, who worked so closely with him, had guessed the damage was worsening after the incident. He and the other smiths handled the smelting and molding now. The work of shaping and polishing blades or tools was one that could be done by feel, easy for a master like my father who'd made hundreds—probably thousands—of such items over the years. However, the intricate wax pattern carvings, specialized filigree, and granulated pieces I crafted were far beyond my father's capabilities anymore.

"Zahava? Why are you hovering by the doorway?"

I startled at my father's booming voice, my face blazing as the eyes of not only the traders but that of Rahm and the five other metalworkers in the shop all landed on me. Curse my father's far-too-excellent hearing.

"I brought food," I mumbled, disoriented by everyone's staring. I glanced at Rahm, who grinned at me from across the room. He knew how much I loathed being the center of attention.

"Excellent!" said Abba. "My navel is touching my backbone. You must have heard our stomachs roaring across the camp."

I squelched a smile. My father was built in every way like a metalsmith—powerful arms and legs, and a wide torso—but in the past few years, he'd developed a bit of a paunch. There was plenty of room between his navel and his spine.

Straightening my own backbone, I willed myself to walk smoothly to my father's side, thankful my walk with the overladen basket was nearly at an end. My left shoulder screamed from the effort of carrying so much weight on that side, and my right hip throbbed.

Rahm came forward to relieve me of the basket and frowned as I shifted the weight to his arms. "This is heavy. Where are your sisters today?"

"Weaving," I said with a little shrug. "I offered to come."

His brow furrowed. "Still. They should not have left this to you."

My belly warmed at the concern on his face. I'd known him most of my life, since my father had taken him under his wing after Rahm's father, one of his distant cousins and a childhood friend, had been crushed at the bottom of a mine shaft when the supports failed. Determined to keep Rahm from the mines for the sake of his mother's heart, he'd taught him the trade of smithing but, for some reason, not the delicate art of jewelry craft the way he'd taught me.

"It's fine . . ." I had been the one to offer to bring the food, after all, with the goal of seeing him.

Garuzah spoke over me. "It's true your work is valued for its uniqueness by many of my customers, Barzel, both in Egypt and in Midian. But they also demand the highest quality, and these are flawed." He gestured to the armbands gleaming in the sunlight.

I stiffened at the accusation. I'd spent days perfecting those pieces. It took every bit of restraint I had not to snatch up the armlets and tell the trader he knew nothing about quality, nor the complicated techniques I'd used to craft them.

My father must have sensed my indignation buzzing from across the room. "Rahm, walk Zahava home."

Although my hackles rose at the silent command to stay out of the negotiation, it would do no good to voice my opinions here. To these men, I was nothing. An ignorant woman. All my defense would do was shame my father for not controlling his daughter and cause suspicion about my knowledge. About whether my father's eyes could even detect flaws in the first place.

When Rahm gently tugged on my sleeve, I turned toward the door, resigned to my helplessness. But just as I approached the threshold, my father spoke with the kind of searing authority I'd rarely heard outside of his gatherings with the other Kenite leaders. "There are plenty of others who will pay what I ask and more. Any fool can see the craftsmanship of these pieces is unparalleled. Not to mention, no one else knows how to make red-gold of this caliber. So if we are done here, I have work to do."

I wasn't the only one who'd been dismissed.

Garuzah's voice followed us out the door, in a much humbler tone than before. "Now there's no need for haste, Barzel. I'm sure we can come to an understanding."

With one statement, my abba had not only lauded my work but beaten the traders at their own game.

"You didn't really think he would let them best him, did you?" asked Rahm, having caught the smile I could not keep from curving on my lips.

"I suppose not."

"If I could be half as shrewd as your father, I would be a rich man indeed." He grinned, dark eyes full of mischief.

I laughed, the sting of being sent away forgotten. My father was wealthy, to be certain. As the eldest son, he'd inherited not only his skills with metalworking and the foundry but plenty of livestock, tended by well-paid shepherds, and a large household whose tents had only continued to expand in number and size since my grandfather's death twelve years ago. My abba may not have a full head of silver hair yet, but he was well-respected among the Kenite leaders, even if he had no sons of his own to inherit such riches.

Rahm pointed out a dip in the path. "So your sisters refused to come today?"

"Not at all. Ima asked them to help the other women with the construction of tent walls for a cousin marrying his bride in a few weeks. She wants them finished in plenty of time to expand his family's tent before he brings his bride home."

Since her husband was the leader of the entire household, my mother's role was one of leadership as well. My many aunts and cousins looked to her to head up such large-scale projects, and Safaa was never one to shy away from delegating tasks to those whose hands were unoccupied. The only reason I'd escaped today was because I could not stand at the looms for hours like the other women, nor maneuver my body back and forth over a ground loom for hours on end.

"Ah, I see," he replied, then put out a hand for me to grasp as we navigated a particularly uneven portion of the path between two black slag piles towering five cubits above the nearest building. The warmth of his skin on mine caused a ripple of awareness to zip through me, conjuring the image of him holding my hand all the way back to the tent. But to my disappointment, the moment I was back on firm ground, he released me again.

Remembering Niv and Kila's instructions to focus on Rahm's interests, I swallowed the deep uneasiness that always came with pushing my nose into other people's affairs and asked a question I'd rehearsed with them. "What project have you been working on lately?"

Unaware how much effort it had taken to ask him, he told me about a sword he was making for one of the high chieftains of the Amalekite tribe, one I knew was rumored to be ruthless with enemies and a collector of both stolen livestock and stolen women.

The rest of the Amalekite men were little better, which was why my father had expressly warned all of us from going into the city without escort. So even though he traded with them in ore and weapons, I was a little surprised to hear that my father had allowed Rahm to work on such a commission. He spoke of the Amalekite leaders the same way he did HaSatan, the great Enemy. In fact, although intermarriages like that of Niv and Kila's father to an Amalekite woman were not uncommon among Kenites, as the head of our clan, my father had strictly forbidden them.

"I won't bore you with the process," Rahm was saying, "or the minerals we add to the bronze to make it more durable, but there are few blades outside of Philistine-made iron swords that are of such strength."

I knew *exactly* which metals and minerals would strengthen bronze, what temperature allowed for proper shaping, and how long to let the object quench and cool before working the metal. Although I now worked mostly with my father's special blend of red-gold, I was proficient with silver, bronze, and pure copper as well. I'd never made any sort of weapon, but the process was similar, at least in the smelting stage.

"My friend Talmar, who arranged the commission, assures me that Agag will be so pleased with it that we'll have no lack of business from him and his strongmen in the future. It'll be a boon for the foundry."

"Does my father agree?" I'd never heard him speak of any such partnership before since he usually avoided doing business with the Amalekites whenever possible.

Rahm bit his lip, looking a little chastened. "I haven't yet told him who it's for."

I flinched, surprised that he would keep such a thing quiet.

He leaned closer, his lovely dark eyes pleading. "Can you keep the secret for me? Just until I prove to him how lucrative this could be for the foundry?"

I wasn't certain such a partnership was what my father would want, but his piercing gaze addled my brain. Who was I to interfere in matters of business? Besides, I could practically hear Niv and Kila in my head demanding I keep my opinions to myself.

"Of course."

His answering smile warmed me all the way to my toes, leaving me even a bit dizzy. If only I could be the one he smiled at every day. "Barzel was right not to cheapen his work by accepting anything less than the highest price," Rahm continued. "The Egyptians and Phoenicians will pay through their noses for such pieces—and clamor for more. But we may need to make a few compromises to see that his work is as famous as it should be."

My face heated. Rahm had no idea his compliment was partly for me. The idea that people in far-flung nations might desire to wear the creations I made was hard to wrap my mind around.

"Where have you been?" Yasmin's voice from the door of our tent startled me. I'd been so caught up in Rahm I hadn't realized we were only a few paces away from our camp.

"I took the midday meal to Abba," I called out. "Didn't Farah tell you?"

She frowned, folding her arms. "By *yourself*?"

My mother hadn't blinked an eye when I offered to take the basket to the men, but Yasmin was never one to hide her worry. For as long as I could remember, she'd fussed over me, doing things that I could have done for myself. She meant well, and I knew she loved me, but even if one of my legs didn't work all that well, I wanted to stand on my own two feet. The last thing I needed while trying to convince Rahm that I would be a good choice of wife was my sister questioning my ability to carry a basket a short distance.

"And we are grateful for it," Rahm said to my sister as we came to a halt in front of her, then turned to me with a smile. "Besides, I had the pleasure of walking her home."

I was certain my face was on fire, but I returned the gesture with a smile of my own. Rahm was exceedingly handsome, with deep ebony eyes that glittered like obsidian when he laughed, trimmed black hair, and a short beard. He may be more slender and finely honed than my father, whose build was all rough angles, but as a man who worked with fire and metal, there was nothing weak about him. And I'd rarely, if ever, seen Rahm without a smile on his face. He somehow managed to befriend almost everyone who crossed his path, be they Kenite, Amalekite, or foreigner. I had to admit a small pinch of jealousy for such a talent. I was no more adept at making friends than I was walking a straight path on my crippled leg.

"It's just as well," said Yasmin with a note of exasperation. "We need help moving the largest of the dye pots, and I haven't found anyone else free."

"See, then," said Rahm, who gave a little bow, "it's fortunate I am here with all my brawn. Put me to work, my lady."

Yasmin rolled her eyes at Rahm's teasing tone, picked up the jug of water she must have come for, and walked away.

He lifted a brow. "She's certainly in a prickly mood."

Yasmin had seemed inordinately out of sorts lately. "I think perhaps Abba will be making a decision soon. About who she is to marry."

"Is that so?" Rahm watched her turn the corner around the back of our sprawling tent where, by the female chatter, a large gathering of weavers was busy making the distinctive brown-and-white pattern that distinguished our family's woolen tents from others of the tribe.

I nodded. "There are two men who desire her hand. I think the uncertainty is weighing on her."

Both of the clansmen who'd pursued her over the past few weeks came from families of honor and practically worshiped the ground my sister walked on. I wasn't sure what was taking our father so long to give his blessing to one or the other.

"What do you think is stopping your father from making a choice?"

"I don't know. It's an important decision. Whomever she marries will likely be his heir."

Rahm's head snapped toward me. "I thought Shulah was his heir."

Our eldest cousin had been the obvious choice for an heir, as the firstborn son of my father's second brother. "For now. But Abba told Yasmin that he would prefer to keep the leadership within the family and would adopt her husband as his own son, to preserve the direct line passed down for hundreds of years. If Abba decides neither man is worthy, I'm certain it will take little time for others to gather around the tent," I said with a quiet scoff. "They can't help themselves."

There are certainly no lines at the door seeking out the hand of the girl with the crippled leg.

As if he'd somehow heard my silent words, Rahm frowned at me, his black brows pressing together. "Yasmin may be a bright and colorful flower that many men want to pluck from the field, Zahava. But a woman with strength of mind and will like yours is rarer than rubies. And worth the effort to uncover."

My breath caught. "Thank you," I said through quivering lips. No one outside my own family had said anything half as lovely to me before.

"Besides, with how you look today, there is no flower more lovely in this entire valley. Any man would be blessed to call you his own." He winked at me, grinning. "Now, I'd better go help with that dye pot before your sister pokes someone's eye out with her barbs."

With my cheeks on fire, I stood blinking in the sunlight as he walked away, shocked to my very core that Niv and Kila's ministrations may have actually worked. I could not wait to tell my friends the next time I saw them. Perhaps my own small compromise had been worth it after all.

I adjusted the bronze mirror over my shoulder, directing the reflection from the skylight above so it illuminated my handiwork. The small worktable in front of me had been created by my father from smooth terebinth planks and topped with a thinly hammered square of bronze, giving me a sturdy work area in a position that was best for my body. I'd been working so long that the cave had grown dim and the shadows long. But I still had a good amount of work to do on the wax carvings, so I stretched my back and neck, adjusted the fat cushion under my backside, and delved back into my task.

There was no better place to make my wax patterns than this limestone cave. Even when the heat outside was oppressive in the deepest months of the hot season, this underground space remained cool. I could carve the hardened beeswax to my heart's content with no worry that my efforts would be distorted.

Using my sharpest bone pick, I scraped away tiny bits of wax from the left wing of the thumb-sized hummingbird that would eventually hang from a chain at the center of a delicate *usekh*, one of the collars favored by Egyptian royalty and therefore coveted by everyone else. Of course, I'd never seen anyone with royal blood wearing any such jewelry, only been told by my father of the vast array of designs he'd seen during his travels to Egypt with his own father when he was a young man. But once he'd explained how they were constructed, my mind had spun with ideas for new styles incorporating gemstones, molded designs, and delicately woven metals.

"Zahava!" My name echoed off the cave walls far before Breena came flying into the room. Everything about my younger sister was loud—her laugh, her voice, her insistence on wearing the brightest colors our ima would allow. I was already smiling by the time she skidded to a stop in front of me.

"Ugh. It's so cold in here!" She scrubbed at her arms. "How do you bear it?"

I shrugged. "I don't really notice it when I'm working."

"Don't your fingers freeze?"

I splayed my hand wide, revealing the wool wrappings around my palms. My fingers themselves were naked. "Can't let the wax melt. Even the heat from my skin can distort my work."

She shivered, letting her teeth chatter. "That sounds miserable."

I laughed, keeping my eyes on the curve of the hummingbird's outstretched wing. "Why are you here?"

"Oh! Zaza! You have to come with me. Right now!"

"I have to finish this, Bree. Abba wants this piece ready by the new moon because a group of traders from the east are due to arrive, and I—"

She snatched the bone pick right out of my grasp. "No. Zahava. It's Rahm, he's talking with Abba right now. About *you*."

I jerked my neck up to look into her wide hazel eyes, the same color as my own. "What?"

The corners of her mouth twitched. "Anaya and I were roasting grain in the oven when he arrived. Dressed in the cleanest tunic I've ever seen him wear, I have to say. And he said he needed to speak with Abba about his daughter." She pointed the bone pick at me. "You, Zaza. He's coming to ask for your hand! After what he said to you yesterday, there is no doubt he is in love with you."

Since I'd been unable to tell Niv and Kila of what all had happened after they polished the tarnish off me, I'd resorted to confiding in my younger sister about our walk back from the foundry. I'd die of humiliation if Yasmin or Farah knew of my hopes regarding Rahm, but Breena had always been good at keeping my secrets.

My heart pounded so loud I feared it may echo off the cave walls. "How do you know they are speaking of marriage?"

"There's only one way to find out." She grinned, wiggling her brows.

Head spinning, I pushed away from my worktable and lifted a hand for her to help me to my feet. She waited for me to stretch the stiffness from my joints before patiently leading me up the stone stairs out of the cave, all the way down the slope toward our tent, and past the group of women still working the looms. Then, like we'd done a hundred times before when trying to avoid chores or hiding during games with other children, we slipped under the back wall of the tent. Careful not to let our bare feet scuffle the ground, we moved as close to the woolen dividing wall as we could and held our breath.

"And why now?" my father was saying. "What has made you wait so long?"

"I wanted to make certain I was prepared," Rahm replied, with far less confidence than I'd ever heard from him before. "I do not take your good opinion of me for granted, Barzel. I have wanted to prove myself worthy of asking for her hand over these past couple of years. I vow to be a man of honor, uphold my responsibilities to you and your family, and above all, treat her with the care she deserves."

Breena squeezed my hand so tightly my fingers went numb, but I did not care. I was going to marry Rahm, and that meant I most likely would not have to give up my work. After all, he'd said that my strength of mind and will were admirable, rarer than rubies. Surely he would value my skills as well.

"Well, I cannot say I am too surprised, Rahm. I've seen you watching her lately."

My pulse thundered as shock tore through me and a gasp nearly burst from my mouth. I'd had *no* idea he was watching when I wasn't looking.

Grinning, Breena pressed her mouth close to my ear to whisper, "You are going to make a beautiful bride."

"Nizar and Yamil will be disappointed," said my father. "They are both good men, but there's no one else I'd rather call *son*. We'll work out the arrangements another time, but you have my blessing to go speak to Yasmin."

All the blood in my body went still. Head swimming with confusion, I looked to Breena, thinking my ears were mistaken. But the tears in her eyes and the remorse on her face confirmed the truth. The man I'd loved for years had just asked for permission to marry Yasmin.

"Oh, Zaza," Breena whispered, her voice thick as she slipped her arms around me, holding me tight. "I'm so sorry. I didn't even think . . ."

I heard little else as the two oblivious men discussed wedding arrangements and marriage contracts that did not include me, and the small hope I'd had that someone like Rahm might ever see me as worthy shattered into a thousand ugly pieces.

Gavriel

Emmet really did hate me. Throughout our journey to the Punon Valley, which lay just south of the Salt Sea, he'd relegated me to the back of the thirty-man squad, put me on watch most nights regardless of how long we'd walked during the day, and had barely said more than a few words to me from the moment I'd reported to him at Gibeah.

His men, too, seemed familiar with my recent reputation before I arrived, as the welcome I'd received had been more than frosty. Only two had even spoken to me directly, an older man named Shachar, whose large, off-center nose looked to have been broken more than once in battle, and the youngest of Emmet's men, an aide named Adin. He'd only recently been selected to serve in this squad and was at least two years from military age. He was likely the son of one of Saul's men, sent along to either keep him out of trouble or toughen his skin.

For the most part, it was Adin sent to give me orders, as if the commander himself would not deign to speak to a worm like me.

If I was honest, Emmet had reason to despise me. He'd always been suspicious of me when we served together under Yonatan, never missing a chance to cut me down to size. But when he'd found me talking up a particularly lovely red-haired woman during one of the ingathering festivals at Gilgal—twirling one of her flaming locks around my finger as I worked to lure a kiss out of her—he'd nearly plowed his fist into my face while bellowing that I was not to even look his younger sister's way if I wanted to keep my teeth. I'd thrown my hands into the air and vowed I hadn't known who the girl was. But it was clear he would never forget the misjudgment.

As we stood now on the edge of the Punon Valley, to where the city of the Amalekites sprawled on both sides of a narrow river, with the Kenite encampments perched on the slopes above, he didn't even bother to look my way as he explained our mission.

"Beniyah, Dag, and Efah," he said, gesturing to his left across the rocky valley, "you're our lookouts to the north and east today. Betsalel, Aziz, and Haim, keep an eye on the southwest. Shachar, Ikavod, Nechemi, Gavriel, and Adin, you'll be coming with me."

I startled. What reason would he have to drag me along to a negotiation with the Kenite leaders? I was a soldier, not a diplomat.

"We'll be going in quietly. Lightly armed and dressed inconspicuously. No armor. The rest of you stay here and wait your turn on watch. The Kenites are peaceful, but we don't need the Amalekites knowing a company of Hebrews is in the area. I'd rather not end up enslaved in the mines."

He gestured toward the hills just to the north of the city, where even from this distance the sprawling mining operation was visible. I was surprised just how extensive it was. There were plenty of long-abandoned holes in the ground, along with a multitude of slag piles. It looked as though this valley had been mined for hundreds of years, long before the Amalekites snatched it from the Edomites.

I'd always thought the Kenites were mostly a nomadic people, moving their tents and flocks to seek out the best grazing by the season. But the area was shockingly fertile, sustained by an intricate irrigation system fed by the river, which flowed down from the plains of Edom and the sharp-toothed mountains that rose up in the east. I was glad it was Emmet and not me charged with persuading the Kenites to pluck up their tent stakes and leave a place with such ample resources both above and below ground. I suspected it would be no easy feat.

One of the men, Obayah, spoke up. "With respect, Captain, there are only thirty of us. How are we going to move all these people, along with their households and flocks?"

"If Mosheh can shepherd millions through this same wilderness for forty years, I suspect we can manage a couple of thousand," said Emmet. "Besides, the Kenites were nomads for hundreds of years. They'll be fine."

"What if they refuse?"

Emmet cast a long look over the valley. "Then they'll die alongside the Amalekites."

Silence reigned at the sobering declaration. Saul had sent us here to persuade the Kenites to leave, out of gratitude for their ancient friendship with our people, but there was no guarantee they would listen to the warning about what was coming for them.

At Emmet's dismissal, the squad swiftly broke up. For a moment, I considered heading for the nearest wineskin to steady my nerves before pleading my case, but instead remained behind, determined to speak without an audience.

Emmet frowned as I approached with the closest thing to a humble posture I could muster. "Captain, a word?"

Similar to Zevi, he was a very serious sort of man, his speech succinct, delegations well-thought-out, and reputation impeccable. He was the type of leader I would normally be glad to serve under—if only he didn't despise the very sight of me. I hoped he would allow me to prove myself and return to Yonatan's squad, even if it was only to be rid of me.

"As you know, I have done plenty of reconnaissance with Yonatan," I said. "Some deep in enemy territory. Perhaps I'd be best utilized by scouting in the city? Looking for weaknesses in advance of Saul's arrival?"

"I am well aware of both your skills and your tendency toward folly," Emmet said. "You'll come with me, where I can keep an eye on you."

Annoyance blazed through me. I was no child to be tended. But this was my only chance to resurrect favor with Yonatan. So I swallowed down the flaming bile in my throat and nodded. "As you wish, Captain."

"I don't want you here, Gavriel," he spat out, his brown eyes narrowed and his freckled skin reddening with anger. "Do us both a favor and go back to Ramah."

I stared, stunned by his candor. I had no interest in ever returning to my hometown, with the exception perhaps of my sisters' weddings. And even then, I'd rather sleep in the servants' quarters than under Hanan's roof. Emmet and my uncle were aligned in their hatred for me. I would let neither one have the satisfaction of seeing me go back to Ramah with my tail tucked.

I looked the man in the eye. "I am here to do my duty to King Saul at the request of Yonatan. I will obey your commands."

He shook his head in disdain. "You may be one of the best weapon-makers we have, but as I saw from the beginning, you are both arrogant and foolhardy—a dangerous mix, in my opinion. Not to mention a drunkard. If it were up to me, you'd have been dismissed long ago. Yonatan is far too forgiving."

From the frustration vibrating off the man, it was clear he'd been ordered by Yonatan to not be hasty in dismissing me. It allowed me a sliver of hope I could pass this test and be reinstated to my rightful squad.

"I *will* prove his confidence not misplaced," I replied.

He scoffed, turning his face away. "You're dismissed. We leave to meet with the Kenites in a quarter of an hour. Try not to cause a brawl."

Even as I dipped a portion of flatbread into the fragrant lentil mash, just one of a surprising array of dishes offered on large acacia platters before us, I kept my eyes moving about the circle gathered around the firelight.

Nearly the moment we entered the Kenite camp, we'd been surrounded by curious eyes. All manner of men, women, and children had watched us walk up the hill to where we were told the heads of households met together every first day of the week. Word traveled ahead of us, and by the time we arrived, our presence was well known, and all but one of the elders had been there to greet us—with varying degrees of suspicion.

Emmet had wasted no time explaining that we came with greetings from King Saul and a message for the honored chieftains of their tribe. But before he was able to announce that we'd come to move them from their home, a barrel-chested man with a thick black beard named Barzel had arrived, the wooden staff in his hand lending an air of unmistakable authority. When he suggested there was no reason to discuss anything with empty bellies, the rest of the men agreed we should partake of a meal together. Although it seemed no single person was head of the tribal council, Barzel was certainly one of the most highly respected, that much was clear.

Emmet, a smoother diplomat than I'd expected for a man who was famous for ruthlessly slaughtering a squad of Philistines with Yonatan, readily accepted their hospitality with almost fawning gratitude. My stomach was certainly glad of it. This food was the best I'd tasted for months, perhaps even a couple of years, when

I last visited my mother. Just the thought of her honey-pistachio cream cakes made my mouth water. No one could cook like my *ima*, but this meal was certainly a close second. It almost distracted me from noticing the two chieftains sitting directly opposite, their turbaned heads bent together as they darted glances our way.

Barzel let out a rumbling laugh across the fire. He, at least, seemed comfortable breaking bread with us, which by the traditions of hospitality, guaranteed we were under the protection of his household. Although his face was overly weathered from the sun and deep grooves spread from his dark eyes, he looked to be about the same age as Hanan. And yet his laugh and expansive gestures reminded me much more of my grandfather, Elazar, who carried the heavy mantle of responsibility for our family as if it weighed little more than a woolen cloak. A sudden pang of longing for him, my grandmother, and the rest of my family in Kiryat-Yearim struck me hard, and I had to force down a lump in my throat.

"What is this?" asked Adin, who was sitting on my right. With three fingers, he scooped up a glop of whitish paste flecked with herbs and held it to his nose.

"Doesn't matter," replied Shachar to my left. "Eat it, or our hosts will be offended."

The rasp of his low voice was a command, not a suggestion, and Adin obeyed without pause. Whatever the creamy white mush was, it was not to the boy's liking. His eyes went watery as he forced it down and then quickly tossed back a gulp of wine.

A quiet laugh came from Shachar. "Goat cheese with horseradish and spring onions."

"Tastes like fire," rasped Adin with a strangled cough, doing an admirable job of not retching but sounding as though his tongue might indeed be aflame.

Again the two Kenite leaders across the group from us caught my eye, scowling as they continued their intense conversation. Something about their demeanor made my hackles rise. The six of us were surrounded by Kenites and only lightly armed, since we did not want to display aggression. But perhaps that had been foolish. This tribe may not have been our enemies in the past, but they'd lived alongside the Amalekites—who most certainly held animosity toward us—for decades. It would take little effort for them to swarm us and either bring us to a swift end or turn us over to our enemies, should they choose to do so.

I slid my eyes to the gap between tents a few paces away. If one of them made a move, we'd have very little time to get away, and I'd have to cover Adin first, since the boy was likely not yet trained to fight for himself.

A large hand settled on my shoulder, squeezing lightly. "Relax. You're making them nervous."

I turned to meet Shachar's dark eyes. He gave a slight shake of his head. "The only one brewing for a fight here is you, son." The words rumbled low in his chest, meant for my ears alone.

Although my blood pulsed hot, I had to acknowledge he was right. There was plenty of laughter and storytelling going on around this circle and very little animosity. There was no need for me to be so ill at ease. Especially when all it would do was undermine our mission here.

So with practice born of many secret missions where I'd had to bend my nature to blend into a foreign place, I forced my body to relax and lifted my cup, tipping it to the older man before tossing the entire thing down my throat.

"We thank you for your hospitality, friends," Emmet said a short while later. "This has been a fine meal indeed."

"All thanks go to my wife and daughters," replied Barzel with a grin. The three women who'd served us during the meal were now gone, but the daughters had been lovely, black-haired and dark-eyed. Yet no one need remind me I should not let my gaze remain on them. Even I wasn't foolish enough to trifle with a chieftain's daughter.

"Then please accept our gratitude," said Emmet. "You are a blessed man to have such a talented wife and daughters. They do you great credit."

"Indeed I am. All five of my daughters are a gift from El Shaddai," the man replied, with a press of his wide palm to his heart. "But we are not here to discuss my girls. So please, do share with us what your king has to say."

The man was certainly forthright, and if I had to guess by his rough-edged demeanor, had no use for overblown negotiation tactics or flowery words. Emmet seemed to be of the same mind. I was surprised, however, that Barzel spoke of El Shaddai, God Most High. I'd not been aware that this group of Kenites venerated the God of my forefathers, even if some of their brethren had lived among our tribes since the time of Yehoshua.

"I must be candid, my friends," Emmet continued. "What I have to say is sensitive information that must remain within this circle. It is a matter of life and death that we put before you."

"Whose lives?" asked another Kenite.

"That of your own families."

As if a cold wind had blown through, the energy shifted around the fire.

"Do you bring word of some threat against us?" asked Barzel, thick brows furrowed.

Emmet cleared his throat. "I do. But before I reveal the warning, I must have your solemn word that what we discuss now stays here, at least until you all come to a decision about how you will respond." He held a solemn gaze as the Kenite elders murmured among themselves.

"Our families are in danger?" asked one of the leaders.

"They will be," said Emmet. "Soon."

"These are all men of honor," said Barzel. "And as heads of the Kenite households living in the Punon Valley, our highest duty is to the people who look to us for protection. Not only our wives and children, but the extended family, servants, and others who make up our households. There are none here today who would ever put a life entrusted to himself in danger."

It was both a promise and a warning. Barzel was seemingly a man of both great wisdom and shrewdness. Again, the similarity to my grandfather was more than apparent.

"Are we in agreement, brothers?" Barzel asked. One by one, the Kenite leaders nodded, even those who'd appeared suspicious before.

"Good. Then here is the message I've been asked to relay." Emmet took a deep breath. "Yahweh has commanded Saul to go to war with Amalek. The king and his forces will arrive before the new moon to finish what our ancestors failed to do."

Stunned silence followed the pronouncement. There was no need to explain the long-standing animosity between the Hebrews and the Amalekites. It didn't matter that they were distant cousins. They hated us. They always had. It was well known they'd attacked us in the wilderness, going after the weak and lame like the cowards they were until Mosheh and Yehoshua waged war against them. A war that truly had never ended.

The Amalekites had been relentless for as long as we'd lived in the Land of Promise, digging their teeth into border towns in Reuben's territory and in southern Yehudah whenever they could—stealing, slaughtering, and enslaving. They were especially fond of attacking when we were busy dealing with other enemies.

The Amalekites were adept at using desert landscapes to their advantage. Their nomadic clans roamed the wilderness areas between here and Midian and all the way to the border of Egypt, the ruthless warriors famous for attacking trade caravans without warning. I wasn't certain why these Kenites, who were for the most part a peaceful people, would entangle themselves with such jackals.

Another elder spoke up. "What does that mean for us?"

"It means you have a choice to make. Our king values the friendship with your people, one that harkens back before our flight from Egypt and was solidified by the faithfulness of the legendary warrior Calev and others of your kin. Therefore, Saul offers your people a way of escape."

One of the two suspicious men I'd noticed earlier spoke up. "Escape? To where?"

"Be'er Sheva," replied Emmet.

Many of the leaders reacted at once, voices overlapping.

"Be'er Sheva!"

"Back near the Philistines? We left decades ago because of them!"

"That's too far!"

"We aren't leaving Punon!"

Emmet lifted his hands, speaking over the chaos. "Please. Let me explain."

A tall leader with an iron-colored beard that trailed nearly to his waist gave a piercing whistle that cut the protests like a blade. "That's enough. Hear the boy out."

Emmet's jaw ticked but he made a heroic show of remaining calm. "Thank you. I know this is sudden. But our goal is to protect your people. The fact is, Saul is already on his way here, with thousands of men. And we *will* have complete victory over Amalek."

"We've been here for decades," said one of the leaders. "Hammered our stakes into these red rocks. We've built foundries and businesses and dug mines with our hands that provide the ore we need for our copper. How could we just leave it behind, especially to go back to where many of our people were slaughtered?"

"That is the question you will have to ask yourselves," said Emmet. "We are here to help in any way we can and then lead you back west. But this time, you will have the benefit of Israel's army to protect you there. Saul is building a fortress with a large garrison at Be'er Sheva. There will be a permanent military presence from now on. What happened before will not happen again."

I wasn't certain to which incident he was referring, but his promises did not seem to persuade them.

"There are no mines in Be'er Sheva."

"No, but your ancestors' furnaces remain, carved into bedrock and mostly intact. And the land is fertile there, even more so than when your great-great-grandfathers settled their nomadic lives to plant fields when Yehoshua was alive. It is still largely uninhabited since most Hebrews built their homes on the northern and eastern edges of Be'er Sheva, along the rivers that flow toward Hebron and Arad."

"How would we survive? We are metalworkers. Miners."

"That is the beauty of Saul's plan. All that is needed is a population of knowledgeable metalsmiths to return, set up foundries in the area, and revive the once-thriving copper trade within sight of the well-traveled road between Egypt and Tyre. Your customers would come to you instead of you being forced to take your goods down to Egypt or up to Damascus and Ammon or rely on traders who undercut your profits. Everyone knows Kenite copper and bronze goods are without parallel."

"Let's say we believe these fantastical promises and abandon our entire livelihood to drag all of our families and livestock through the wilderness to resettle back in Be'er Sheva, where a generation ago we were nearly destroyed. What's in it for your king, then?" said one of the two suspicious men across from me. "There has to be some incentive."

"As I said, the king values our long-held friendship—"

"Don't blow smoke in our faces," said another man.

Emmet lifted his palms in surrender. "Saul believes this move will be advantageous for both our peoples. There are no more talented metalsmiths than the Kenites, that fact is undisputed. And as you know, the Philistines have long prevented the trade of ore from trade routes on the Great Sea. But now that we have managed to push them back to their own cities and retake the port of Yaffa, we can bring tin from Tarshish and other foreign lands. Once we rid this region of Amalek, the mines here and at Timna will be controlled by Israel."

A rumble of annoyance went through the group, but only one of the suspicious elders spoke up. "So you steal our mines and send us away to a place where we have no access to ore and expect us to make a living?"

Emmet shook his head. "No. We take over the mining and bring the copper *to* you. Then you, as the official coppersmiths of the king, will not only be given all the raw materials you need to produce weapons for our men, and be paid well for it, but you will also be afforded protection by Saul's army—the same one that only a few years ago brought the might of the Philistines to its knees at Michmash."

"Gaza is only a stone's throw from Be'er Sheva. Why would Israel care to protect us if they came for us again?"

"The Torah itself guarantees that as resident foreigners in our territory who respect our laws, your people will have every protection afforded to Israelites and will enjoy the blessings of the Land just as our own people do. Saul offers lasting covenant protection for all who go with us."

Emmet waved a hand in the direction of the river at the center of the encampment. "No more scraping in this fickle wilderness for subsistence, trekking for hours to fetch water when the river dries up, or endlessly digging ore from the depths of the earth. Since they are located at the confluence of three rivers and benefit from the seven deep wells built by Avraham, the fields around Be'er Sheva are unfailingly fertile and only need your people to return and tend the soil, expand the irrigation ditches, and reap the benefits for themselves."

"This is ridiculous," said the man directly across from me. "They just want our copper. Surely you aren't falling for this manipulation."

"I for one would be glad to be done mining," said another. "And glad to know that my sons and grandsons would inherit fertile fields instead of trying to scratch food from this miserly wilderness."

Soon, voices were rising again, some arguing the benefits of moving and a few adamant that this was nothing but a trick by a foreign king.

"Listen to me," said Emmet, coming to his feet, "we are cousins. Connected by common ancestry through Avraham himself. We have no desire to deceive you. Everything I have told you is the truth, I vow it on the Holy Mishkan itself."

This bold statement brought the murmuring to a halt. Even the Kenites knew the importance of the sanctuary that had once been indwelt by the glory of Yahweh. Their ancestors had witnessed the fiery cloud that traveled with the Hebrews in this same wilderness and hovered over the Mishkan at each encampment during those forty years of wandering. However, mistrust still vibrated in the dusty air.

Barzel's deep voice cut through the tension. "We have much to think about, brothers. And doubtless we'll have many questions for our friends here. None of this must be decided tonight, does it, young man?"

Emmet shook his head. "As I said, Saul will be here before the new moon. So we have a little over three weeks to move your people away from Punon before he attacks."

"Then perhaps it is best we adjourn for the night," said Barzel. "We can reconvene after the celebration of my eldest daughter's betrothal. A couple of days to think on this proposal will be wise, don't you think, Gabaoh?"

"I do, yes," said the elder with the iron beard. "However, I think it important to remind all of you to keep this to yourselves. We've cultivated peace with our Amalekite neighbors over the years, but let us not be naïve about the nature of that alliance.

It has always been predicated on cooperation in the mines and sharing of resources in this valley, not loyalty to us as a people. If they hear we are even considering leaving and taking both our valuable knowledge and the tools of our craft with us, they might strike us first. If we accept Saul's proposal, it will have to be kept secret until the very last minute. The lives of our families are at stake. The Amalekites may be our allies for the moment, but we all know what happens to those who cross them." He slowly moved his gaze over the group. "So, are we in one accord?"

One by one the men nodded, even those who seemed most doubtful of the plan.

"Excellent," said Barzel, then stretched his arms wide and smiled at Emmet. "And as the father of the bride, I would deem it an honor if you and your men would remain to celebrate my great joy."

"Oh, we could not intrude . . ." Emmet began, even if everyone knew it was only a show of humble refusal for the sake of tradition.

"I insist," said Barzel. "There will be plenty of food for all of you. Music. Dancing. Games and recitations. And more than enough of the best wine you've ever tasted."

At least there would be *one* thing to look forward to if Emmet still refused to let me go stand watch instead. The last thing I wanted to do was witness the betrothal ceremony of a couple of strangers. But at least, unlike the last time I'd been dragged to such a celebration in Ramah, my mother would not be here to poke at me about settling down and giving her grandchildren or to throw some poor unwed maiden at my feet.

I loved my ima with every fiber of my being, but the woman was relentless—and completely deaf to my unwavering vow to remain unwed for all of my days. I'd made that decision long ago and there was nothing that would ever change my mind.

Zahava

"You look so beautiful, Yasmin!"

Our eldest sister beamed at Farah, her dark kohl-lined eyes glittering. "Thanks in no small part to you." She pressed one hand to the crown of her head, where Farah had fashioned myriad braids, all interlaced with shining copper beads that twinkled in the lamplight and jingled merrily whenever she moved her head.

Cross-legged on the ground beside Yasmin, I held her opposite hand in my palm and kept my eyes trained on the intricate designs I'd been painting on her skin for the past hour, instead of looking at Breena. I had no desire to see the pity in her eyes.

Yet, even in my jealousy, I had to admit Yasmin did indeed look radiant. Although it still ached to think of the conversation Breena and I had overheard, I was grateful not to have been surprised by the announcement later that day. I'd been able to force a smile and offer well-wishes to Yasmin, who'd been nearly as shocked as I had that Rahm had chosen her.

"Rahm will be so pleased," said Farah, "knowing he will soon bring the most beautiful bride in the entire valley to his tent."

Yasmin's face flushed. "That's quite the exaggeration."

"It's no such thing, is it, Zahava?"

I refused to look up, in case my eyes revealed the many lacerations inflicted on my heart over the past week. But I would not intentionally hurt any one of my sisters for every scrap of copper in Punon, so instead I nodded as I drew yet another swirling flower over the curve of Yasmin's first finger. "Rahm is a blessed man indeed."

"Are you relieved it was his proposal Abba agreed to?" Farah pressed.

"I am," said Yasmin. "Not that Nizar or Yamil wouldn't have made wonderful husbands. Which was why I was so hesitant to choose between them."

"Neither one is nearly as handsome as Rahm either." Farah grinned and winked.

"Farah, you are terrible." Yasmin swatted at our sister with a laugh. "It's certainly no hardship to look at him. But I am most glad that his family lives so close to our own. I won't be going all that far away when I enter his tent."

That was certainly true. Our father had done his best to care for Rahm's family after his father had died, especially since his twin sisters had only just been born. With no other family to care for her, Rahm's widowed mother had been desperate for help. So my father generously stepped in until Rahm was of age to do so. But still, I would miss Yasmin. And I certainly didn't blame her for marrying the man I'd wanted when she'd never known my heart on the matter.

"He truly is the perfect choice of husband," said Yasmin. "Abba must be glad the man he has mentored all these years will inherit his legacy."

Pain shot through me. I'd been so wrapped up in the shock of losing my chance with Rahm that I'd not considered what this could mean. Now that Rahm was marrying Yasmin, Abba might finally teach him the secrets of making red-gold. Perhaps he would even make *me* show Rahm the techniques I'd worked so hard to master, so he could take my place.

The thought was like a chisel to the heart. Making jewelry had been the one thing I could actually call my own.

"It will be you next, Farah," said Yasmin as I finished the final swirl of red henna across her palm. "Perhaps even one of the men who attends tonight."

Farah scowled as she wrapped a leather tie around the end of her own thick braid. "No, thank you. I've already told Abba I have no interest in a husband right now. Besides, with you gone and focused on helping Rahm's mother with the girls, Ima will need more help."

I winced at the unintended slight. I did as much as I could, many times far more than I should, but I was not as much help to our mother as I should be. And although none of my sisters ever acted resentful toward me, I hated being the cause of extra work for them.

The one thing I did excel at, I could not even reveal to anyone outside our family. And it certainly did not make me a desirable wife. Now it seemed even that would be taken from me.

"Zahava," said Farah, snapping me out of the haze of self-pity I'd been lost in, "it's time for you to get ready."

I blinked up at her in confusion. "I am ready."

Her eyes dropped to my tunic. "That is what you plan to wear?"

"What's wrong with what I am wearing?" I looked down, checking there were no smudges of charcoal or crushed ore. "It's plenty clean."

"This is my betrothal celebration," said Yasmin. "*Everyone* will be here. Abba will want us to look our best and represent him well."

My face warmed as I curled my scarred fingers into my palms. “I hadn’t thought of that.”

Yasmin smiled at me. “Not to worry, sister. Breena, get my saffron dress. She can wear that tonight.”

“No, I can’t. That was a gift from Abba.”

“Hush,” said my sister with a teasing lilt to her dark brows. “I will do as I please. This is my special night, and you will wear what I say. Breena, get the dress. Farah, braid her hair. We will show everyone that the daughters of Barzel are without rival.” She lifted her hands, displaying the designs I’d carefully drawn onto her arms and wrists, which matched the ones on her feet. “These are exquisite, Zahava. And once the henna is dry, I’ll be applying your cosmetics.”

Unable to argue with her requests, on this of all days, I sheepishly complied. And just like the other day, with Niv and Kila, I was caught up in a whirlwind. Before I could catch my breath, the three of them had me wrapped into Yasmin’s saffron dress, along with a creamy linen undertunic that was as smooth as fresh butter on my skin. The dress itself was a good handspan too long, but Farah tucked the extra length into a long, colorful striped scarf that wrapped three times around my chest and waist. The sleeves billowed like wings at my sides as Farah braided my stick-straight hair into a mass of plaits and then wound them into one long braid that trailed nearly to my waist.

Our mother came into the tent just as Yasmin swiped a thin coat of reddish-brown henna over my lips, and her eyes went wide. “Oh, girls. You look so lovely. Yasmin, Rahm will not be able to keep his eyes off you.”

A dart of pain speared through me anew. In all the fuss, I’d nearly forgotten why I’d been cajoled into dressing like this in the first place. Breena’s hand landed gently on my shoulder and squeezed, a subtle gesture of sympathy. But I did not look at her for fear I’d go teary.

"Thank you, Ima," said Yasmin. "Are things ready?"

"They are, and guests are beginning to arrive. We have plenty of help from the other families around us but, Breena and Farah, I expect you girls to make certain our guests' needs are met. Cups full. No empty bowls laying about." She turned to me. "Zahava, you're in charge of Anaya. I cannot keep my eyes on her all evening, and I have much to do."

"Of course, Ima. Where is she now?"

"She's with Rahm's sisters."

Rahm's twin sisters were a couple of years younger than Anaya but still common playmates, along with a few of the other girls in our clan. Now our families would be even more entangled, which meant I would never be able to escape the reminder of my thwarted hopes.

"As for those Hebrew soldiers who came into camp yesterday, your father has invited them to join us tonight," Ima said with a pinch of her dark brows.

"He did?" Farah's voice pitched high. "Whatever for?"

"That is our way, daughter. You know this. They must be treated as honored guests or your father would be shamed for lack of hospitality."

"What do they want?" Yasmin asked.

Ima let out a sigh. "I don't know. He said they brought a message from their king. But he has yet to tell me the nature of the message."

My mother and father were of one mind in nearly everything. I'd rarely ever heard them disagree, so it was disconcerting to know that Abba had not even told her what news these Hebrews brought to our door. As well, he'd been abnormally quiet since they'd arrived, so whatever it was must be unsettling.

"Regardless, we will serve them with the same hospitality as everyone else. We will not dishonor your father by acting suspicious. Understand?"

"Yes, Ima," we said in tandem.

"But also," she said, frowning, "do be cautious. They may be our guests, but they are still strangers. With unknown motives for being here. Keep on your guard."

I knew little about the Hebrews other than we were distant cousins and had ancient ties that went back to before their people left Egypt for Canaan, along with our common worship of El Shaddai. But our alliance with the Amalekites over the past few decades had strained relations between us.

Our father's voice came from the other side of the partition. "Is Yasmin ready? Her betrothed has arrived."

"She is!" Ima pressed a kiss to Yasmin's cheek, then draped a filmy linen veil over her head and pulled aside the curtain.

Abba put out a hand to his eldest daughter, the pride of a doting father in his eyes. "Come. Rahm is waiting."

Yasmin's answering smile as she took our father's hand helped soothe the ache that had taken up residence in my heart. But as the rest of us followed our eldest sister out of the family tent and Rahm came forward to greet his future bride, I had to look away.

Breena's hand was suddenly in my own, her fingers tangled with mine as our family paraded through camp toward the place we gathered as a clan. I leaned on my sister as we walked, glad for her steady presence in more ways than one.

The sun was already sinking into the deep red clouds on the horizon, so the firepits were aflame. Guests sat on cushions and rugs all around the area, chattering, but when they caught sight of Rahm and Yasmin, they stood to their feet to shout out blessings and well-wishes.

Once at the center of the gathering, our father voiced aloud his desire to give Yasmin in marriage to Rahm and spoke of how his great respect for Rahm's father and their longstanding friendship made this union one that pleased him greatly.

A cup of wine was produced, and my father spoke his blessing over the couple before both Rahm and Yasmin took a drink, declaring their intentions to bind their lives together as one as soon as the customary period of betrothal was complete.

Seeking a distraction, I let my gaze wander over the crowd and noticed a group of men standing off to the far right. The Hebrews. There were at least six of them watching the proceedings with interest. One of them had hair that matched the deep red rocks on the nearby hills. One was a little bit older with a large, off-center nose—perhaps he was the leader of the group—and one was surprisingly young and couldn't be more than a year or two older than me. Two others had their faces turned away, so I could not see their features.

But the last one stood at the back of the group, set apart from his companions. His dark, unruly curls hung past his shoulders unfettered, as if he could not be bothered to tie back the mess, and his thick beard was no less untamed. There was a deep frown on his face as the ceremony dragged on, as if he too were here under duress.

To occupy my mind, I began to imagine all sorts of scenarios. Perhaps he'd been ripped away from his own wife soon after their wedding, or he'd lost his whole family in a raid, or perhaps he hated Kenites in general. Lost in my gawking at the man, whose intriguing face might have been handsome had he not been scowling, I flinched when he turned his head and nearly caught me staring. Snapping my gaze back to my sister, I gently tugged my headscarf over my mouth and chin, glad the loose fabric would hide my profile from the Hebrew soldier. My father had always teased that my curiosity was as much a curse as a blessing.

By the time the ceremony was over, my lower back was screaming, and I was thrilled when Farah and I made our way to the women's area at the far end of the clearing. I sank down onto the double-thick cushion that served as my seat at every meal, and Anaya came over to sit beside me, prattling on about some story

Rahm's sisters had told her about two ravens they'd befriended and now brought them gifts in the form of snail shells, stones, and from time to time, pieces of metal or swatches of fabric. Her sweet voice was a balm for both the ache in my hip and the one in my heart.

As well, the delicious food and the hum of conversation from the women around me did a great deal to temper the worst of my heartsickness. Thankfully, from where I was seated, I could not see my sister and her newly betrothed. They were as good as married now, and soon Rahm would come to take her into his tent for good.

As the feasting wound down, the dancing began. Our tribe took every opportunity to celebrate with music and dancing but betrothals and weddings, even more so. When I was younger, I'd often tried to join in, wishing I could keep up with my sisters but could never handle more than a few circuits around the fire. Sometimes my father would swoop me up in his arms and twirl me around until my stomach hurt from laughter and the world blurred around me. But as I grew older, I attempted the dances less and less, until even my sisters stopped trying to include me.

Breena had already gone to join the circle but not before fetching me a cup of wine in which she'd mixed a hefty dose of red sumac and willow bark powder and commanding me to drink every last drop. The herbs would not take away the pain, but they would tame it to a manageable ache.

As I watched Farah and Breena whirl about in a circle of twenty or so other maidens, I drank at least half the wine, but when I lifted the cup to take another long draft, Anaya bumped up against my arm, exclaiming that she wanted to dance too. Startled, I lost my hold on the cup, and it tipped directly into my lap, leaving an angry swath of red across the dress and the scarf around my middle, soaking me to the skin. Yasmin's beautiful saffron dress would be ruined if I didn't act quickly.

"Oh! Zaza, I am sorry!" Anaya's face scrunched as if she were about to cry. Hot tears threatened to well in my own eyes, but I did not want her to feel bad, so I blinked hard against them and forced a smile.

"It was an accident. I'll go wash out the wine and it'll be good as new. You'll see."

She sniffed, tears streaming down her round cheeks. "Are you certain?"

I kissed her nose and smiled. "I promise. All will be well."

I asked one of the ladies nearby to keep an eye on my littlest sister, slipped away from the table, and headed outside the circle of firelight. Thankfully, one of the cisterns was not too far from here, and my eyes adjusted quickly to the dark as I hobbled up the path. Fed both by rainwater and frequent refills by the women of our clan, the cistern allowed fresh, cool water close at hand even in the driest season.

Although I was near enough to hear the music and see a hint of the dancing through the gap between tents down below, there was no one here to see me. I unwound the colorful scarf that Farah had so carefully tied around me and then slipped off the saffron dress, leaving me clad only in the linen tunic. Then, I removed the wooden cover from the cistern and pulled up a measure of water with the jar hanging inside the deep chasm my ancestors had dug from the limestone decades ago.

Wishing I had some natron to help the effort, I tipped a small amount onto the fabric and scrubbed at the stain. To my relief, the color seemed to melt out of the fabric with the cool water. I'd have to dash back to our tent and retrieve a fresh garment before returning, but at least Yasmin's dress would not be ruined. I lifted it high to check for any remaining red in the light of the waning moon.

"What are you doing out here?"

The deep voice came out of the night from close by. I whirled around, off-kilter, and nearly toppled into the outstretched arms of the Hebrew soldier I'd almost been caught staring at earlier.

"Well, hello there," he said with a slight slur as he righted me. I skittered back a couple of steps, heart thrumming in my ears.

He was even more fierce-looking up close, with a deep scar on his cheekbone. But instead of the scowl he'd been wearing while he watched my sister pledge herself to Rahm, he looked down at me with amusement, one brow quirked as his dark eyes perused my face.

Then, to my amazement, a slow smile spread across his own. "I didn't expect a lovely little dove to fly into my arms tonight."

Gavriel

Eyes glittering wide in the bright moonlight, the girl took another couple of steps backward, until her legs were pressed against the low rock wall surrounding the opening of the cistern. It took my foggy head a few moments to discern the fear on her face.

"You don't have to be afraid. I don't hurt people." I huffed a laugh, swiping a hand through the air. "Well . . . only the bad ones."

She just stared at me with her mouth agape.

"So?" I peered at her through narrowed eyes. "Are you an enemy out here to cut my throat?"

Her voice warbled. "I . . . I . . . no. Just washing out a stain."

I frowned. "A stain?"

She held up a dress of some sort. "Spilled wine."

Ah. She must be taking care of the washing for her mistress, although I wasn't certain why a servant would do such a thing in the dark. But who was I to ask questions about the best time to launder clothing?

I wasn't even certain what the hour was. The betrothal celebration had been dragging on for hours. I'd stumbled out of the firelight to relieve myself, and since I'd partaken in my fair share of the excellent drink Barzel had bragged about, I had taken a few extra moments to wander around the edge of camp to clear my swimming head when I caught sight of her.

Dressed in a simple white tunic and with a thick black braid trailing over her shoulder, the young woman had appeared like an apparition out of the darkness, then fluttered toward me with a little cry after I'd startled her. The fragile bird had only been in my arms for the span of two breaths, but she smelled like some elusive spice—cinnamon, perhaps, or nutmeg?—and something earthy that teased my senses and made me wish for just one more deep inhale.

But the last thing I should do was sniff her hair like some lecher when she looked ready to dart away at any moment. And I really didn't like that she appeared so afraid of me. I may be half-drunk, or perhaps a little past halfway, but I'd skewer myself on my own blade before I hurt a woman.

"I just needed some air," I said, hoping to quell the worry painted across her delicate features. "Got a little turned around."

"The celebration is down that way." She gestured down the hill with a pinch between her dark brows. The sound of music, laughter, and overlapping voices wafted toward us, the flicker of firelight beckoning.

But the quiet up here above the Kenite camp was far more enticing. Even though my eyes were still a little fuzzy from drink, I could see the entire valley spread out below. Fires dotted the landscape on both sides of the river as if reflecting the spray of brilliant stars overhead.

"I think I'd rather stay out here for a while," I said with a shrug. "Weddings are not my favorite."

"It's a betrothal."

I waved a hand. "All leads to the same end."

She arched a dark brow in silent question, but I steered away from telling her I'd seen the worst of marriage and that such celebrations stirred both unpleasant memories and deep resentments.

"I'd skip my own sisters' weddings if I could. But my mother would hunt me down and skin me alive."

A soft laugh erupted from her lips before she pressed them together. Then she cleared her throat. "You have sisters?"

"Three. All a few years younger than me. And I told my fool uncle if he marries any of them off before they are at least sixteen, I'll gladly rip out his liver."

Her eyes went wide.

I waved a hand in the air. "Don't worry. My ima won't let them get married too young after what she went through, so his liver is safe. For now." I winked.

Her dark lashes fluttered as she peered at me. "Your uncle? Not your father?"

Usually the mention of my father made bile rise in my throat, but the gentle question in her sweet voice soothed the instinct to snap. I sighed and shook my head. "A long story. My uncle is also my stepfather."

She hummed, the sound full of curiosity but surprisingly did not push the point. "What are your sisters' names?"

"Liorah, Ayelet, and Ruti." Warmth rushed through me at the thought of my girls. It had been far too long since I'd seen them, which I hated. But the last time I'd visited had been a disaster. I also hated that they'd grown up so much since I left home. They still were girls back then, and now all three were considered women. Young wolves would soon be circling, and I was not there to protect them.

"Any brothers?" she asked, pulling me from thoughts that sparked the desire for another cup or two of Barzel's wine.

I shook my head. I'd never felt the lack when it came to brothers because I'd had my cousins. "You?"

"No . . ." She paused. "Only sisters. Four of them."

"Five girls?" I clicked my tongue. "They married?"

She shifted her weight and looked away. "Only one."

Guessing that to be a tender spot, I dropped the line of questioning. But I was surprisingly eager to continue talking with her. I searched inside my muggy head for something to say, but she beat me to it with a blunt question of her own.

"Why are you in this valley?"

Emmet had been clear we were to keep the upcoming move to ourselves tonight. But I had to give some sort of explanation for our presence here.

"Our king is very interested in the metal industry here. He's heard good things about the purity of copper and the quality of bronze coming out of Punon Valley."

A shadow of suspicion moved over her features. "He will *not* get our secrets. We've kept them for generations."

I flinched at the edge of threat in her tone, as if a serving girl was somehow offended I'd even consider such a thing. Strangely, I found myself coming to Saul's defense. "You misunderstand. The king wants to strengthen the friendship between our peoples. He has great respect for the generational wisdom of the Kenites. And truly, your talents are extraordinary."

There was something fascinating about the way she looked back at me with her chin tilted up slightly, as if she took such a compliment to heart. And she no longer looked as if she would flit off into the night at my every move.

"And what do you know of our skills?" Her brow arched in challenge. "You're a soldier, aren't you?"

Perhaps not such a fragile little bird after all. I suppressed a smile at her subtle condescension. "I am. But one who makes his own weapons. And those I saw today in Barzel's foundry were beyond impressive."

"Yes, my . . ." She paused and cleared her throat. "Barzel is a master craftsman. Few among our people can compare."

"Have you seen the jewelry he makes from red-gold? I hate to admit it but it's even more impressive than the weapons—" I began, but she spoke over me, her words jumbling together in a rush.

"Won't your friends wonder where you are?" She twisted the yellow dress she held in her hands, eyes darting to the celebration down the hill. "Or at least your commander?"

She seemed nervous again, ready to bolt, and for some reason, that bothered me very much. I'd known my fair share of women—well, perhaps more than my fair share—but this one intrigued me. I didn't want her to run off so soon.

"I doubt they care much where I am," I said with a casual shrug. "As long as I am not causing trouble."

Her gaze snapped to mine. "Do you do that often?"

"Cause trouble?" I let a slow grin spread over my face. "From time to time. But at least I'm not out in the night luring unsuspecting men into the desert with my magic."

An indignant huff came from her mouth. "Are you accusing me of such a thing?"

"What else do you call a beautiful woman casting spells under the light of the moon?"

Her eyes flared but then she shook her head as if unimpressed with my flirtation. It only made me more determined to see her smile.

"What is your name, little dove?"

She opened her mouth. Paused. Closed it. Then tilted that stubborn little chin up again. "Zahava."

"And I am Gavriel." I bowed my head, hand to my heart.

She hummed in the back of her throat but said nothing. Perhaps she wondered why I did not name myself as anyone's son. But I was my *own* man. And once I earned back my place in Yonatan's company, I was determined to be called armor-bearer to the king's heir and someday even weapons-master of Israel's armies. Those were the only labels that mattered.

After a few silent moments lost in my thoughts, I noticed Zahava's long, slender fingers were tapping against her thigh in an unconscious manner as her body swayed almost imperceptibly to the music in the distance. I wondered whether she was thinking of some young man back down there in the circle of firelight and wishing she was with him instead. What reason did I have to be envious over someone I'd just met? Besides, I had no business trifling with an innocent maiden. I huffed a quiet laugh at my own foolishness.

Zahava startled, frowning. "What?"

"Don't you want to go back and dance?"

She glanced back at the firelight, then shook her head. "I don't dance."

"Now, I find that hard to believe. I would bet you know every step of that one."

She paused, then whispered, "I do."

Somehow the confirmation sounded more like a denial, or as if it pained her to say so. Her gaze dropped to her hands, where she was still clutching the yellow dress to her middle as if it was some sort of shield. I did *not* like the defeated slope of her shoulders. Somehow, I heard myself saying, "Then teach me."

She jerked up her head, blinking at me. "Teach you?"

I gestured to the dancers in the background. "My commander said we should do nothing to offend our host tonight. And I am certain the father of the bride might be vexed should I trample about like a three-legged donkey if I am called upon to join."

A bright burst of laughter flew from her mouth before she caught it with a hand over her lips. A frisson of delight sparked deep in my chest at the gleam of amusement in her eyes, and I was instantly greedy for more.

I put a palm to my chest, where my heartbeat had ticked up, and gave her a pleading look. "Have mercy on me, little dove. You'd not want to see me dragged before the elders of this tribe, would you? Perhaps dropped in one of those deep, dark mineshafts and left for the scorpions to gnaw at my bones?"

She shook her head as if I was ridiculous, glittering eyes reflecting the stars. What color were they in the sunlight?

"I promise to not even touch you." I raised my right hand to vow. "Or may my mother track me down and yank every last hair from my head. Just show me the same steps they are doing." I tipped my chin toward the gathering. "Please. Before the song ends."

She sighed. "All right. I'd hate to see you go bald."

A surge of pure elation swept through my bones, and somehow it was even more potent than the large amount of drink I'd consumed tonight.

She laid the yellow dress over the stone wall that surrounded the cistern and moved closer, slowly, as if she were approaching a bear. I remained perfectly still, worried I might spook her. When she was only an arm's length from me, she lifted both of her hands into the air, palms toward me.

"Put your own like this."

My heart thudded against my ribs. I didn't actually think she would play along, and that elusive scent was teasing my nostrils again. Earth and spice and something intoxicating. I swallowed hard and lifted my scarred hands in the air to match hers. Something vibrated in the space between our palms, as if an invisible cord had been plucked.

How much *had* I drunk earlier? My thoughts swirled hazily as she moved her hands in a wide circle. Reading the expectancy on her beautiful face, which I could see better now that my eyes were adjusting to the dim, I followed her motions as the gentle beat from the gathering down below echoed softly off the cliffs nearby. Our eyes held as she continued moving her hands in slow arcs, up and down, back and forth, then forward until our palms nearly kissed in the middle.

My throat ached as she pulled back again. I'd never wanted

to touch a woman so much in my entire life. But even if she was only a serving girl she was far too sweet. Far too good for the likes of me.

Zahava began to move, turning her left hip toward me, so I echoed the motion, feeling ridiculous but far too encouraged by the smile she directed my way to care. I was so caught up in watching her full lips that when she turned in the opposite direction, I misjudged the move and bumped her shoulder with my elbow, setting her off-balance. She wobbled with a soft cry, so I grabbed for her, but her right leg buckled. She clung to my forearms, fingernails digging into my skin as she completely lost her balance, pulling me with her as she crumpled. Terrified she would hurt herself, I wrapped my arms around her waist and twisted my body so that it was me who hit the ground first.

I landed flat on my back, a groan bursting from my lungs, but I clutched her tight, thankful I had cushioned her fall. Winded from the impact, I lowered my head to the ground and stared up at the stars. Zahava's soft, slight weight was partway across my torso, her head against my chest, breaths coming quick as the two of us recovered from whatever calamity had just occurred.

"Are you all right?" Her voice was muffled against my tunic.

"I'm fine. Are you hurt?"

She shook her head, and although I expected her to jump to her feet and skitter away, she instead began to tremble.

Alarm rushed through me. Instinctively, I pulled my arms tighter around her body. "Zahava? Are you injured?"

She turned her face up, chin resting on my collarbone, and met my eyes as she began to laugh. "I told you I could not dance."

She laughed again, tears of amusement reflecting the moonlight, and I was transfixed—both by the feel of her in my arms and the gentle music of her laughter.

She was so close. It would take nothing at all to lift my head and press my lips to hers. I would only take a taste. Just one. And then I'd send her back to her mistress and stay away from her for the rest of my time with the Kenites.

As if she'd heard my greedy thoughts, her laughter died away, and she stared at me. I had the fleeting idea she might be thinking the very same thing. There was invitation written all over her lovely face.

I took a deep breath and began to lift my head, already imagining the feel of her lips on mine.

"*What* are you doing to my sister?"

Disoriented, it took a bleary moment to swing my thoughts and my eyes away from Zahava's mouth in order to turn my head toward the screeching cry off to our left. Five young women stood a short distance away, three with large water jugs on their hips, and all with gaping mouths and wide eyes.

Zahava went stiff with a gasp and then immediately began to struggle against my embrace. I released her instantly, but we'd become such a tangle of limbs as we fell that she could not prop herself up and instead let out a pitiful cry as she slumped down again.

The woman I assumed was the sister pushed her water jug into the hands of one of her companions and darted forward, grabbing Zahava's arm. "Leave her alone, you brute!" Her bellow echoed off a wall of limestone nearby as she tugged her sister up and away from me.

"No, Farah. He didn't do anything—"

Farah ignored Zahava's attempt to defend me and pressed her sister behind herself before striking out with a hard kick to my shoulder. I threw a hand in front of my face, anticipating her next move, but instead she went for my ribs. A strangled groan burst from my mouth as I twisted away from her. I'd faced some fierce opponents in Saul's army—Ammonites, Philistines, even a giant mercenary who'd somehow allied with a band of Canaanites near Arad—but Zahava's sister was ruthless. I could do nothing but try to block each kick as it came.

As Farah continued her assault, releasing a litany of insults I'd never heard pour from a woman's mouth before, Zahava tried to restrain her, pleading for her to stop and telling her sister that she'd only lost her balance and I had not laid a hand on her. Vaguely, I appreciated her defense of me, but I'd also been very close to stealing a kiss, so I was not as innocent as she portrayed me to be.

Farah kicked me again, this time in my right thigh where I was still tender from a knife wound I'd received a few months ago at the hand of a particularly annoyed innkeeper who'd insisted that I'd not paid for all the beer I'd swilled that night.

Pain shot down my leg and up into my groin. I curled into a ball with a moan. Zahava's sister should fight for Saul; the Amalekites wouldn't have a chance.

"What is going on?" thundered a man's voice. I peeled my eyes open and looked up into the furious face of Barzel.

"What did you do to my *daughter*? And *where* are her garments?"

I had faced plenty of treacherous situations in my twenty-seven years, but never anything so terrifying as the fury of a father. Then again, I'd also never been so foolish as to entangle myself with a maiden before. I'd always stuck to amenable women in taverns or those who made it clear they were interested in nothing more than a dalliance.

Never in a thousand years would I have imagined I would be facing down the father of an innocent, for that's certainly what she was. I'd known it an hour ago, nearly from the first moment she'd spoken, but had been too drunk, or perhaps simply too fascinated by her, to consider the consequences.

Thankfully, Barzel had not shamed Zahava in front of the small crowd that had gathered to gape and whisper. But there would be repercussions for a young woman caught in such damning circumstances—another consequence I'd not taken the time to consider. While her champion of a sister whisked her away, her father had his men disarm and bind me at the wrists and ankles. So now here I was, alone and on my knees in a large tent, waiting for judgment to fall.

Emmet would likely not allow me to remain the night. I'd have to find somewhere in the desert to sleep off what little remained of my drink and then make my way north.

Perhaps I could seek out a mercenary position with one of Hanan's competitors to guard caravans along dangerous trade roads. The thought of doing something that would bother my uncle gave me a small bit of satisfaction, but nothing would be the same as serving in Yonatan's elite unit. And I'd wasted the one chance he'd given me on a woman. Not just any woman either, but the daughter of one of the powerful Kenite leaders we'd come here to persuade in the king's name. If Barzel did not stone me to death, perhaps Emmet would.

Either way, I was not getting out of this tent unscathed.

Neither Barzel nor Emmet said a word as they finally entered, and I kept my chin down in a show of submission, only glancing up in surprise when Zahava herself came inside, her gait a bit wobbly as she came forward to stand next to her father. The poor young woman was likely as nervous as I was, only without my years of practice at remaining blank-faced when emotions ran high.

I allowed myself a fleeting glance at her in the bright lamplight before dropping my gaze back to the ground. She was wearing the yellow dress she'd been scrubbing when I came upon her. Her own garment, not that of some mistress, as I'd foolishly assumed. Perhaps I'd been a bit more inebriated than I'd thought not to see that her face and eyes were painted with fine cosmetics, her hair braided and sparkling with copper beads. Even with her eyes cast on the ground, she looked every bit the daughter of a wealthy chieftain.

"As I said, I invited your men here in good faith, Captain," Barzel spoke to Emmet, his deep voice booming into the tense silence. "I had assumed your king desired our friendship, and our compliance. I would never have dreamed I might have to protect my daughter from the advances of one of his soldiers."

"Rest assured," said Emmet, "this man will be punished and summarily relieved of his position within Israel's army."

And there it was, the end of every ambition I'd ever had for myself. Emmet had gotten his wish after all. I'd lost everything.

Barzel made a hum of contemplation in the back of his throat. "You took advantage of my trust, young man."

I flinched, peering up to find the Kenite leader pinning me with a look that curdled my insides. I could not help but remember this morning, when he had taken us to his foundry, an impressive stone building outfitted with a plethora of metalsmithing tools I would kill to get my hands on. Barzel was a master of his craft, and those working beneath him fortunate to glean from his long experience.

When Adin, the little fool, insisted I show Barzel my sharp-toothed dagger, I'd wanted to throttle the boy. My work was nothing compared to the weapons his workshop produced. But at Barzel's insistence I handed over the dagger. He ran his soot-blackened, callused fingers over the flat and along its serrated edges while my belly spasmed with nerves. When he pronounced it well made, I'd told him I was no master, only an eager student from the time I was a young boy. Barzel had only smiled and said, "*These things take time. One day you'll be a master too. I have no doubt. Just keep practicing your craft.*" I'd found myself speechless by the unmerited praise from such a man. And even though I did not know him, his displeasure now somehow pained me.

Desperation tumbled from my lips. "Please, my lord, let me explain."

"*Explain?*" Barzel's face turned red. "Explain that you came upon my daughter and tried to steal her virtue?"

"No. That's not it at all—" I began, just as Zahava said, "Abba, he didn't—"

Although I was surprised by her defense of me, both of us snapped our mouths shut at the livid expression on her father's sun-worn face. "You have betrayed my trust and soiled my daughter's reputation. Tarnished our family's honor."

"My lord, I would not dream of hurting your daughter. I vow I did not know who she was."

"So you took her for a *whore*?" he snarled.

A strangled gasp came from Zahava, but I could not look at her. I would lose my nerve if I saw tears on her face.

"No, my lord. I did not. I thought she was a servant scrubbing a stain from her mistress's dress."

"And yet she was discovered sprawled over you. Perhaps it was she, then, who lured you? How a daughter of mine could be so brazen, I do not know." The accusation, spoken with utter disgust, made my veins burn with fury, searing away whatever lingered of the drink I'd imbibed. I straightened my shoulders and stared daggers at the man I would have done anything to learn from only a few hours ago.

"That is the furthest thing from the truth. I was wandering outside camp after drinking far too much of your fine wine. I approached her by the cistern, with no intention but to satiate my curiosity about why a woman was out there in the dark. She was kind but wary. Not in any way deserving of your accusations. It was *me* who suggested we dance—in fact, I cajoled her into it. Even then she maintained a respectable distance."

"Then how did you end up tangled together on the ground?" Barzel pressed.

"An accident," I said.

"My foot, Abba," said Zahava in a half-whisper I barely caught.

He raised his brows at her. "Is what he said true, then?"

She nodded, her face pale. She shifted her weight, wincing, clearly mortified as the silence stretched long and her father divided a piercing look between the two of us.

When Barzel finally spoke, his words were like hammer to iron. "There is no other solution to this disaster. You will marry my daughter, without delay."

A tortured sound came from Zahava before she slapped a palm over her mouth. Even Emmet looked stricken by the pronouncement. I'd have been far less stunned had the man ordered me stoned.

"Abba, please. Nothing happened," Zahava choked out.

"It doesn't matter if the two of you are as innocent as newborn lambs. Our honor has been sullied. Rumors are already rampant and will only continue to grow."

Surely the man was out of his mind. I was a stranger to his family, not of his tribe, and a soldier with no intention of ever marrying.

"I have nothing against your daughter, my lord, but I cannot marry her."

"You will if you want our people to leave this valley."

I blinked at him in wordless astonishment. Barzel's people would be destroyed if they did not leave before Saul's army arrived.

"Surely we can come together and decide a more fitting punishment for Gavriel, my lord," said Emmet. "These are two separate considerations."

Barzel splayed his large hands in a gesture of helplessness. "It is your choice, Captain. I won't have my family's honor spat upon. I have plenty of sway with the other leaders, and they are already quite divided. So either this man marries my daughter and protects her name, or I cast my lot against your proposal when the leaders meet tomorrow."

He would truly put this entire camp of people, his own family, in danger over a stain on his honor?

"My lord, Saul is coming," said Emmet, pleading now, "whether you leave or not."

The Kenite folded his arms over his barrel chest, immovable as wrought iron. "Then I trust you'll make the right decision."

Emmet's glare, full of accusation, burned me straight through. There was nothing left to say. I had no choice, and neither did Zahava. Shoulders slumped and head bowed, she still refused to look at me as one tear dripped off her face and fell into the dirt at her feet. The sight of that droplet hitting the ground was like a spear to the center of my chest. She did not deserve any of this, did not deserve to be chained to me. But neither could I let my stubborn vow be the reason this entire mission failed and put every Kenite man, woman, and child in jeopardy. I would not make these people suffer for my foolishness.

I gritted my teeth and lifted my gaze to Barzel's. "It would be my great honor to marry your daughter, my lord."

It appeared my ima would have her wish fulfilled after all.

Zahava

Shadows hovered beneath Ima's ebony eyes, but she refused to sit down to eat, too busy flitting around serving everyone else to enjoy the meal she'd prepared. My parents had been up half the night, their voices low but fervent. Ima's silence now as she filled my father's cup with fresh pomegranate juice spoke far louder than her words could ever do—she was no happier than I was about the decisions he'd made, not that she would dishonor him by contradicting him in front of us.

When my father had declared our people were leaving Punon just before he'd given me away to a stranger, I'd been too distracted to actually consider what that might mean. But the longer they'd whispered while I lay staring at the black ceiling, imagining the worst about my future, the more I'd wondered where we would possibly go. Clearly, something terrible was happening. The red-haired captain's warning that his king was on his way had been ominous, but I'd not had the courage to ask once he and Gavriel had left our tent, and my father had sent me to bed without a word of explanation for any of his actions. My father's word was law in his household, anyway. What good would it do me to protest?

Farah, however, had never been one to let things go unchallenged, and when my father explained that I would be married tonight, she immediately pushed back. "You don't truly mean for Zahava to marry that beast of a Hebrew, do you, Abba?"

His response was swift and sharp. "She will marry who I say."

The sight of Gavriel kneeling on the ground before my father came to my mind. Even if my father outweighed him, Gavriel was a young and well-honed warrior. If he'd had a mind to challenge my abba, there would have been no contest. I could not understand why he'd capitulated so easily.

"I do not mind forgoing a betrothal period, Abba, since Rahm is a friend," said Yasmin, her tone appeasing, "but perhaps you could allow Zahava a chance to get to know her bridegroom a little? What do we even know of him?"

"He could be a murderer for all we know—" Farah began.

He cut her off with a barked, "I am your *father*. That's all you need to know."

Every mouth in the tent snapped shut, even Farah's, as he rose to accept his staff from my mother, who ever anticipated his movements. He swept out of the tent without another word, leaving us all in stunned disbelief. My father rarely, if ever, raised his voice in anger.

Perhaps a small piece of me had hoped he would change his mind, that he'd realize he'd been too hasty in such a pronouncement. Or that my mother might quietly sway him, but he quashed every tendril of hope beneath his retreating sandals. And I had no one else to blame but myself.

When Gavriel had come out of the dark and found me scrubbing at Yasmin's dress, it had taken all my courage not to flee. But he'd been so charming, the fearsomeness of his appearance mitigated by a warm smile and the glint of humor in his eyes.

With no trace of the simmering belligerence I'd witnessed during the ceremony earlier, he'd set me at ease with his quick wit and gentle teases. And although I'd known better than to accept his invitation, I'd seized the opportunity without considering the consequences, thinking it might be the only time I'd be asked by a man to dance. My heart had soared in a new way as we'd moved in tandem before I had tripped and pulled him down with me. And there had been that one luminescent moment when I thought he might kiss me and my lips had begun to tingle with anticipation . . .

I shook my head to clear away the memory. What a little fool I'd been. I'd known he was inebriated, could smell the wine on his breath even if he somehow hadn't slurred a word. I could not even explain my own behavior except that it had felt good to be desired, if only for a few moments.

And now the poor man was stuck with me for good.

"Are you all right, Zaza?" Breena leaned into me, and I realized my mother and sisters were staring at me with pity in their eyes. Even little Anaya looked stricken, her bowl of honeyed yogurt forgotten.

"No," I admitted. "But I will be. I have no choice."

"I just don't understand," said Yasmin. "Why is he doing this, Ima? We don't marry outside our tribe. In fact, he's the one who forbade unions with Amalekites."

"Your father's reasons are his own, girls," said our mother. "He will tell me nothing more than it is a matter of life and death."

"He's not going to send Zaza away with that man, is he?" asked Farah.

Dread sluiced through every one of my limbs. This had been among the fears that kept me from sleeping last night, long after my parents' voices had gone quiet. I didn't know where Gavriel was from, or anything of his family, other than he had three sisters. Was I going to be separated from my own forever, made to live with strangers who resented my presence?

Lightheaded, my vision swam as my midnight fears rose up again.

"No." Ima rushed forward to crouch before me and cradled my face in her hands. "The one thing Barzel promised me was that this Hebrew will not whisk you away." She brushed her thumbs over my cheekbones. "But I will not lie. In the future, we may have to let you go, my sweet girl. As is the way of many young women when they are married to men outside their tribe. But your father assured me he would never force you to leave us."

And yet once I was married, he would have no say in such a thing. My husband would be my head from then on, not my father.

I could no longer hold back the tears, but Ima wiped them away as quickly as they slid down my cheeks. "We must, both of us, trust your father. He and I have weathered all manner of storms under the protection of El Shaddai, and the one thing I know for certain is that the Mighty God of the Mountain will not fail us."

My ima had indeed endured far worse than this, grieving four babies that did not survive to take a first breath, and two young sons who perished in the height of the same fever that had afflicted me.

So many children and youths had been lost in those dark days. The sickness lingered in the valley for weeks, every prayer to El Shaddai unanswered and every sacrifice made to the Amalekites' gods worthless. But then as suddenly as it had appeared, it was gone, leaving my father without heirs and our ravaged tribes to pick up the pieces. Although my mother did not know I'd heard her through the tent wall one night, I knew she'd tearfully pleaded with Abba to take another wife like other chieftains did, one who could give him the sons she could not. It was the only time I'd ever heard him truly furious with her.

"*You are flesh of my flesh and bone of my bone, Safaa,*" he'd said. "*We are one. Do you not remember Sarai and Hagar? Rachel and Leah? Nothing good comes of such arrangements. Only pain.*

So we will trust El Shaddai to provide, just as he supplied the ram that spared Avraham's beloved son."

Unlike the grief my mother had carried on her shoulders with impossible grace, these circumstances were my own fault. And I had no choice but to obey my father, no matter how baffling his reasons for handing me off to a Hebrew might be. However, before I vowed to honor and obey my bridegroom, there was something I needed to do.

So I swallowed a fiery sob and arranged as much of a smile on my face as I could muster. "You're right, Ima. I'll go wash myself in preparation for tonight."

Breena surged forward, her own eyes swimming with tears. "I'll go with you."

I shook my head, dividing my gaze between my sisters. "This is something I must do on my own. I'll be back in plenty of time to dress for the ceremony. Will you help me then?"

"Of course," said Yasmin with forced cheerfulness. "Your bridegroom won't be able to tear his eyes from you when we are done."

My bridegroom. My stomach wrenched hard. Tonight, I would be expected to become one with a man I'd met only yesterday.

I shook off the disturbing thought. There was no use dwelling on that for now. I needed to hurry across the river and warn my friends that King Saul's army was on its way.

I'd felt so beautiful during Yasmin's betrothal, dressed in her saffron dress with my hair braided and my face painted. But tonight I only felt ridiculous. I wore the same yellow gown, but this time, my sisters had added a headdress to the ensemble, fashioned of tinkling copper bells and beads of carnelian and jasper. Long, heavy earrings dangled nearly to my shoulders and a heavy gold collar-piece, borrowed from a neighboring chieftain's wife, lay with suffocating weight on my chest. It was similar to the one around Yasmin's neck, which had been worn by my mother and her mother and grandmother during their own weddings.

Thankfully, someone had had the grace to seat the two of us sisters together at this hastily prepared feast. I'd been so grateful to hold my sister's hand as my father stood toasting our bridegrooms with inexplicable enthusiasm—as if it had been his plan all along to cut Yasmin's betrothal short and give his crippled daughter to the terrifying warrior on my right. At first, the crowd around us gaped and whispered. But soon enough beer, wine, and food dulled their shock, and by the time the music and dancing were in full swing, no one seemed to care about the strangeness of the circumstances.

As for my bridegroom, Gavriel had barely looked at me. He was dressed the same as he had been last night, although freshly washed and with his unruly hair tacked into a tail at his neck. But he was once again the dour-faced soldier I'd first glimpsed at Yasmin's betrothal dinner, and from the two empty cups in front of him, and the full one in his hand, he'd found a way to distract himself from the wedding he'd been bullied into.

I, however, had left my own wine untouched, my nerves stretching more and more taut as the evening wore on and the night ahead of me loomed larger. Our mother had explained the design of babies and bodies without shame to each of us girls at our first flow, but once Yasmin and I were dressed tonight, she'd sent the others away, much to Farah's chagrin, to explain some of the more intimate details of what she called the joyful union between husband and wife, hoping to ease the shock of the inevitable pain.

However, that, paired with the things Niv and Kila told me earlier today about the marriage bed, had only made me more anxious. I could not see how I would ever give myself to Gavriel with anything resembling joy, since he was a stranger to me, and I certainly could never be as bold as my friends. But as soon as he took me up to the borrowed marriage tent set high on the hill, I would have no say at all.

I ate no more than a token bite or two of food, barely hearing the music and chatter around me as I held tight to my sister's hand all night. From time to time, she squeezed back, and I wondered whether that was solely for my benefit or if she, too, was nervous about what came next.

Rahm certainly did not seem upset about the loss of the betrothal period. He was getting what he wanted, after all—Yasmin. I'd been a simpleton to think a man like him would ever consider me over my beautiful and capable sister. I had little confidence Gavriel would ever think of me as anything more than an unwanted burden.

Cup after cup had disappeared down his throat until frankly I was astounded at how much one man could imbibe. Yet he remained perfectly stoic, ate heartily from the spread in front of us, and said not one word to me or anyone else all night.

When someone announced the bridegrooms should escort their brides to their marriage tents, everyone rose to their feet, cheering and calling out blessings. The four of us were ushered away from the gathering by a cadre of well-wishers with flickering torches and led up the hill above camp.

I forced myself not to watch as Yasmin and Rahm broke away with half of the group and disappeared into the night, instead focusing on each of my steps as we followed the narrow pathway toward our own small marriage tent within a copse of blooming acacias. Not that it would have mattered if my steps faltered since my bridegroom walked four strides ahead of me the entire way.

When we arrived, Gavriel pulled back the tent flap, muttered something unintelligible to one of the young men who'd accompanied us, and stumbled in ahead of me, letting the fabric fall closed behind himself. Stunned, I blinked at the door for a few foggy moments before remembering I had an audience. Refusing to meet anyone's pitying gaze, I straightened my shoulders and pulled back the tent flap to step inside.

One oil lamp hung from the center pole, illuminating the small space. The tent held little more than a basket with my clothing and necessities, a leather pack I assumed was Gavriel's, and a wide bedroll stacked with an assortment of blankets, pillows, and soft sheepskins. And one Hebrew warrior, flat on his belly and stretched fully across that marriage bed, snoring.

Gavriel

My wife was curled up on the ground, wrapped in nothing more than a light woolen cloak, with her cheek pillowed on her hands like a little girl.

I was a worm. No, worse than a worm. I did not even remember coming to this tent in the first place, and certainly not passing from consciousness, splayed across the bed in a way that kept her from even having a corner on which to sleep.

My mother's voice chastised me from inside my aching head. "*You left this innocent girl to lay on the ground like a goat?*" And she would be right. I was less than half of a day into this marriage and I'd already proved myself an unfit husband.

Husband. A word I'd never in a thousand years thought I'd call myself. *Soldier.* Yes. *Warrior of Israel*, to be certain. But *husband* . . . never.

I'd seen Avidan and Zevi become men who valued their wives and children above their aspirations. Seen their sharper edges filed away and their baser natures tempered by marriage. And I had laughed whenever they told me I would be next. Time and again, I had vowed to never submit to such shackles.

And yet here I was. Shackled by my own folly.

Taking the opportunity to get a better look at the woman I'd married while she was still sleeping, I tracked the high slope of her cheekbone, the sweep of her long black eyelashes, and the braid that would trail past her slender hips. She was lovely. Gentle and sweet. And far too good for the likes of me, as evidenced by the fact that my mouth tasted like death from the countless servings of wine I'd imbibed last night.

I'd started out telling myself I would only have a couple to toast my bride and help me relax, but the more miserable Zahava looked, the more drink I swilled. The young woman who'd grinned at me with such amusement at the cistern did not smile all night long. Her large luminous eyes, once so bright in the moonlight, were dull and flat as she vowed herself to me and then accepted the only bridal gift I had to offer. Instead of jewelry or fine cloth or even livestock as her portion, Zahava had received the knife from my belt. She had drawn a very bad lot indeed.

And so I drank while she barely looked at me. I drank while she picked at her food. I drank when her sister and her sister's new husband got up to participate in the traditional bridal dance to many shouts and claps and whistles of delight from the crowd, while Zahava's cheeks had turned rosy when she quietly declined the invitation to take part. I drank until I couldn't remember being led up here to the marriage tent, where Zahava's family had prepared a soft and inviting marriage bed, scented with fragrant blossoms and alluring spices that now clung to my rumpled clothing. It wasn't the thickest haze I'd ever woken in, and I was only slightly nauseated, but my bladder was full to bursting.

I was tempted to slide my hands under Zahava's slight frame and move her to the bed, but I feared she might wake to find me looming over her and panic. So instead I picked the thickest blanket from the bed and, without touching her, laid it over her body.

Then I stumbled out of the tent and went in search of a place to relieve myself and for something to clear the rot out of my mouth. The first task was easily managed, since the tent had been pitched on a hill high above the rest, tucked into a grove of trees to afford privacy. The second had me stomping past the other marriage tent set on this high ridge—where I was certain Rahm's bride was *not* asleep in the dirt—and heading off to seek out the cistern where this whole mess had begun.

Instead, I found my commander coming from the direction of Barzel's tent.

"What are you doing here?" he barked. "Where is your wife?"

"Sleeping" was all I managed to say. "I just came down for a drink—"

"Of course you did," Emmet interrupted with a sneer. "You've probably not stopped all night. You smell like an overripe vineyard."

Anger swelled, but I swallowed it down. "I *meant* a drink of water." Even if, yes, a cup of wine might take the edge off both the nausea and the headache that seemed to be growing by the moment.

He stepped closer to point an accusing finger at me. "When Yonatan said he was assigning you to me, I was livid. You were the very last man I wanted in my unit. But he insisted. Said you have potential far greater than your failings. But my instincts were right. You've endangered this entire mission because you can't keep your hands off wine or women, but it ends now, do you hear me?"

Before I could form an answer, he poked my chest hard with that damning finger. "I went along with this marriage scheme because Barzel insisted and he has a powerful voice in the council. But I don't know why he would possibly want an arrogant fool like you for a son-in-law."

I'd asked myself the same thing over and over last night and still had no answers.

"But we have no other option," Emmet continued. "These people are vulnerable without our help, and our mission is to remove them from this valley. We can't afford any more of your blunders. So, you are forbidden from drinking anything but water until Yonatan offloads you from my unit, or until you get yourself killed by your father-in-law for going after another woman, whichever comes first. Can you handle that? Or are you too much of a fool to understand what I am saying to you?"

I'd never wanted to punch a man in the teeth more. Emmet had always been disdainful of me, but now he was speaking to me like I was a child.

And yet I had to admit he was right. I'd made a grave error and had no choice but to comply. One woman and water only. I could do that. I could show him that Yonatan's unlikely faith in me wasn't misplaced.

"I understand," I responded. "What can I do to help?"

"Nothing. You'll only be in the way right now. For now, your job is to stay in that tent and make your new wife extraordinarily happy. Because she is the absolute apple of her father's eye, and if you mess it up, I'm fairly certain he'll skin you alive with one of his fancy knives." He smiled, seeming delighted at the thought, then shook his head and left me staring at his back—quite having forgotten what I'd been doing in the first place.

"He's right, you know," said a young female voice, which had me whirling around to find a girl of about fourteen a few paces away, a basket perched on her hip. "My sister is the apple of our father's eye, and if you so much as harm a hair on that beautiful head of hers, he'll make you wish you never laid eyes on her." The girl narrowed her own, which were a few shades darker than Zahava's but had the same exotic tilt. "And I'll make certain that you wish your ima had never given birth to you in the first place."

I restrained a hard flinch. She had no idea I already felt that way most days. But for some reason, that wound was a shade more tender this morning than it had been before.

"I have no plans to harm your sister," I said. "My only goal is to protect her honor and help your people."

She peered up at me, her expression sharp and assessing. "Why did you give her a knife for a bridal present?"

Her odd question threw me so it took a moment to form an answer. "Because it's the most valuable thing I possess."

Her brows arched high. "Where did you get it?"

"I made it." I had other weapons—a sword I'd taken off a Philistine at Michmash, along with a few knives—but Zahava's now-bridal gift was beautiful. I'd never forget the moment I pulled it from the mold and knew immediately it was without flaw, even before I began the laborious work of honing and polishing each tine. It was the first time I had actually been fully satisfied with something I made.

"You're a metalsmith?"

"I've made plenty of weapons and armor, but I don't count myself a master like your father."

Something glittered in her dark eyes. "Ah. It makes sense, then."

"What does?"

She ignored my question and handed me a basket. "This is for the two of you. Zaza hates mornings, so tell her Ima put some of her favorite cakes in there, along with strong mint tea."

I accepted the basket, which was far heavier than I expected a girl of such slight stature to heft about. But if I'd learned anything about Barzel's daughters, it was that they were far stronger than they looked. I still had the bruises on my ribs to prove the force of Farah's fury. I'd probably do well not to underestimate Zahava either.

"She may be crippled in body," the girl said over her shoulder as she walked away, "but her mind is nothing of the sort."

I blinked in confusion, but she'd already disappeared.

Crippled? Zahava appeared whole to me, even if she'd looked like she was at her funeral instead of her wedding last night.

The mystery followed me back up to the ridge, where I found my new bride a short distance away from the tent, the blanket I'd left for her wrapped around her shoulders as she stared toward the sun rising slowly over the sharp-toothed mountains. Sunlight limned her black hair with crimson-gold, setting it aflame, and I was struck by the oddest sensation of wonder.

I'd thought her enticing when I believed her a servant and lovely when dressed as my bride, but I could not speak for the way she dazzled my eyes in this moment. With her waist-length hair in sleepy disarray and her sun-kissed skin glowing like warm honey, she resembled some untouchable goddess on a mountaintop.

"I brought breakfast," I managed to say, once I had mastery of my tongue again.

With a sharp inhale, she jerked her head toward me, wide-eyed and high-cut cheeks flushed. And then, as she took a few steps my way, her younger sister's warning suddenly made perfect sense: Zahava was indeed crippled in body. With every step, she wobbled from side to side in an almost painful way, one that had my instincts flaring to rush over and sweep her into my arms. It took every bit of torture training I'd endured to keep a bland expression locked in place as she approached. What in the name of everything precious under the sun had Barzel been thinking to tie such a fragile creature to a brute like me?

Zahava

The stranger I now called *husband* stared as I walked toward him, barefoot and doing nothing to disguise my limp. What use would it be? He'd known last night what he'd taken on. I expected him to look at me with disdain, perhaps say the affliction was worse than he expected, but instead, he held out a basket. "Your sister brought this."

I scrambled to make sense of his relaxed demeanor. "Which one?"

He scratched the back of his head. His long dark curls were a disaster, his eyes red-rimmed, and his face oddly pale as he peered at me. "I think she is younger? Not the lioness who kicked my ribs in, and not the one who was married yesterday."

I restrained a smile at the way he spoke of Farah. She'd probably enjoy that description a little too much. "Breena, then."

"What are the names of the others? In all of the . . . confusion, I did not hear."

I'd married a man who did not even know the names of my sisters.

"The eldest, the one who married last night, is Yasmin. The one who attacked you is Farah. Then I am next in line. Breena is a year younger, and then little Anaya is nine years old."

"No brothers?"

I winced at the question, but we were married now, and he had every right to know. "There were two boys who lived past infancy. Both died in the same plague that caused this." I pointed at my leg.

He frowned. "You were not born this way?"

"I was struck with fever like so many others in our tribe, mostly children. Both of my legs were paralyzed for weeks. One recovered, but the other one never seemed to catch up as I grew."

"Why did I not see this before today? You seemed to be less . . ." He stumbled around the word.

"Crippled?" I looked him straight in the eye, both to gauge whether he was in earnest and to prove I was not shy in speaking about it. However, he seemed genuinely curious. Perhaps he had simply been too drunk, or too in shock, to notice before.

"My father had a special sandal made with a thickened sole to help even out my gait, but it hurts to wear too long. I will try to wear it as much as I can, so as not to shame you."

He recoiled as though slapped. "Shame me?"

"Having a wife with such an affliction will reflect poorly on you. There is no use denying it. It is why I have never before had any interest from potential bridegrooms."

Gavriel stared at me, a deep pinch between his brows. "You will wear the sandal if you feel like doing so. Not out of consideration for my reputation. Burn the thing for all I care."

My lashes fluttered as I stared back in complete astonishment, words escaping me.

He shook the basket. "I could devour a lion this morning and you ate no more than four bites last night, so you're probably just as hungry. Let's eat."

Bewildered by his easy dismissal of the affliction that had always been such an embarrassment, I followed him back to the tent and brought out my thick cushion while he relaxed against a tree. We shared the food in almost companionable silence as the sun lifted over the plains of Edom, gilding the hills around us with rose-gold. The thought of leaving this beautiful valley, everything I'd ever known, made my belly ache with grief.

"I won't hurt you," he said quietly, his gaze on some far horizon point. "Your sister Breena seems to think I will do so. I know we are strangers, but you have no need to fear me. I am not the sort of man to force myself on a woman."

I very much had feared I would find Gavriel trying to take what was lawfully his. So I'd lain there on the ground far into the night, bracing myself for the inevitable. Instead, he'd snored loud enough to raise the dead, and when I'd awakened, I saw he'd covered me with one of the blankets. It almost felt like an apology.

I did not understand this man. The first time I'd seen him, he was every bit the terrifying warrior and simmering with belligerence. Then, at the cistern, he was flirtatious and witty. He'd been drunk and brooding during our wedding, but this morning was all sober solemnity. So I remained quiet, giving him space to reveal more of himself if he so chose.

However, shouting broke into the expectant silence between us, a ruckus from down near my family's tent.

"What is that?" I asked.

He sighed. "I'm not certain, but I fear word may be out about your people fleeing. If so, there could be trouble."

I felt the blood drain from my face, thinking of my hasty warning to Niv and Kila. "What kind of trouble?"

"Your father vowed the other chieftains to silence because if the Amalekites discover you are leaving, they'll be furious."

Guilt wrapped long fingers around my throat. I'd told my friends to keep the warning to themselves until a decision was made by the council, but what if they'd told their father and he'd told others?

Surely not. They'd brushed away my concerns without a second thought, eager instead to discuss my wedding night.

Gavriel rose. "I'll go find out what is happening."

Awkwardly, I pushed to my feet. "I'm coming with you."

"No. It's best if you stay in the tent—"

Was this the beginning of being expected to remain quiet and keep myself out of sight? The instinct to flare at him rose up, but I took a calming breath before I spoke. "Please. My family is down there. I am worried for them."

He looked to me, then toward the commotion below, a pinch of frustration on his brow. "All right. We'll go. But if the Amalekites already know, we may need to run."

My heart slammed into motion. "Do you think they will attack us?"

"Maybe. If they know what is coming for them, they might see it as preemptory."

"What exactly *is* coming?"

"The entire might of Israel's collective armies. Saul's call went out from Dan to Be'er Sheva, and many answered. When we left Gilgal to come here, there were already tens of thousands preparing to march south, perhaps more."

"Amalek's armies are strong," I said, my head swimming at the thought of war coming to this valley. "They are feared by everyone in this region. Hasn't Israel tried to run them off before and failed?"

"True," said Gavriel. "But this time, Saul has declared a vow of utter destruction on all Amalek's cities."

The breath was nearly knocked from my lungs. "Including this one?"

Gavriel's expression went dark, but his voice was gentle. "Including this one. Which is why your people *must* go."

Or we'd all be destroyed too.

"Coming?" He was already moving toward the trail.

Stricken speechless by his revelations but grateful he was not leaving me behind to fret in ignorance, I followed. To my surprise, Gavriel did not rush me as we trekked down to camp, even though I could feel urgency rolling off him like waves of thunder. If he was annoyed by my slow pace or my stilted gait, he kept it hidden.

We heard overlapping voices before we even reached the edge of the gathering, where at least fifty agitated heads of households were circled around my father and the tribal council, in the very same place where our marriage had been celebrated last night.

"Where are we to go?"

"This is our home!"

"King Saul's men have come to lead us west," called one of the council members.

Cries of "Where to?" and "Away from the valley?" grew with a fever pitch, followed by "The Hebrews want our mines!" and "They've taken everything!"

My father waved his hands, trying to calm the frantic shouts. "We are going to a fertile place with plenty of room to settle our families. Have no fear!"

"Why should we trust them?"

"I have nothing left! They took my herds!"

"They have the foundries surrounded. I can't even get my tools," shouted another.

"Brothers!" My father's booming voice rang out. "I have lost as much as you—possibly more. If we remain, we will lose that which matters far more than earthly belongings. I will not put my family in jeopardy for sentiment. I have to leave the bones of those I love here, just as all of you do. But I will not risk those who still take breath when we have been offered protection and a new home by Saul's men."

A somber hush came over the group.

My father's eyes moved over the crowd, and even though I knew he could only see shapes and blurs, his gaze was as piercing as ever.

"I cannot speak for the rest of the council or any of you, but my household will not remain to be slaughtered alongside Amalek. Because when it comes down to it, there is one nation that worships the God of our forefather Avraham and one that worships the gods of this earth. I'll take my chances with Israel."

It took only a few moments for more arguments to break out, some refuting my father's words but many shouting support. I was jostled against Gavriel by more men pressing into the clearing, some adding their own voices to the cacophony that only continued to grow in fervor.

To my surprise, Gavriel put his arm around my shoulders and pulled me close to his side. "This is dangerous. Let's get you out of here."

Never relinquishing his grip on me, my new husband waded us back through the crowd, ignoring a few rude comments from some of the men we pushed past. But all gave way to Gavriel and the dark looks he aimed at anyone in our path. Once we were free, he released me but remained within arm's length as I led the way to our family tent. My mother, Breena, and Farah were bustling around the campsite, packing our belongings in baskets.

"Ima!" I called. "What is happening?"

She blinked a few times as if she didn't quite recognize me. "Zahava, dear one. What are you doing here?"

Before I could respond, Yasmin came toward us, Rahm in her wake. "What is going on? We heard the commotion."

"The Amalekites took the foundries," said Farah, "even Abba's. They overpowered the night guards and killed most of them. The mines, the shops, everything is under their control. Even most of the herds have been stolen—including ours. Payback for daring to sneak away, they said."

No wonder my father looked as though he'd been knocked in the jaw. Not only did he own a large herd of sheep and goats, but he'd inherited that foundry from his own father. Now it, along with three generations of tools and the smelting furnaces he'd built with his own hands, was gone. There were some tools in the cave, but most of the weapons he'd planned to trade, and those his men had still been working on, had remained in the shop under guard.

"Who?" I asked. "Who was guarding the shop last?"

"Zafir and Ashan," said my mother, her crestfallen expression telling me the two men, both with young families, had been struck down.

Pain gripped my chest as my mother explained how the council had planned to meet secretly this morning to vote on whether to leave with the Hebrew soldiers, but the Amalekites had struck in the middle of the night. By daybreak, panic had spread, and some households had already fled south, not trusting Saul would ensure their safety.

My right leg wobbled but I waved off my mother's suggestion to sit down. "What did Abba say? Where are we going?"

"Be'er Sheva," she said. "And we must leave before sundown."

All I knew of Be'er Sheva was that it was far to the west of here and that my pregnant great-grandmother had fled from that city with what remained of our tribe after the Philistines had killed her husband during a raid. They'd roamed the wilderness for a while but eventually made a pact with the Amalekites here in Punon: our metalworking skills for their protection. But now was not the time to ask why we would return to a place that was no safer than this valley, in my estimation.

"I barely know where to begin." Ima sighed as she surveyed the campsite around us with shimmering eyes. There was no chance we'd be able to take it all. We were among the few Kenite families who owned a wagon, but even so, most of it would have to be left behind.

"We will help, Ima." I reached for her hand and squeezed.

She nodded, blinking away tears. "Of course. And we will be together. That's what is important."

I startled when Gavriel spoke beside me. "What can I do?"

My mother quickly wiped the surprise from her own features at his offer. "If we are to leave before the sun goes down, then the tents must be packed up and the wagon loaded with as much food and water as we can carry."

My new husband nodded. "And I will make certain you all arrive in Be'er Sheva safely. I vow it upon my own life."

The promise sounded strikingly sincere. My father had always been a strong and capable protector of our family, but with his sight so limited and the fragility of his lungs, he would be at a terrible disadvantage if something happened along the way. Perhaps having a frightening warrior for a husband wasn't such a terrible thing after all.

"Thank you, Gavriel," Ima said. "And welcome to our family."

By the time the sun slid halfway down the sky, we were ready to go. All around us the detritus of our lives was scattered about like pieces of a shattered pot. There were stools, baskets, jugs of wine that were too heavy to load in our wagon, even piles of blankets, rugs, and clothing items that could not fit in packs—all of it handmade by my mother and the other women of our family. Years and years' worth of carefully woven items left behind like trash.

We'd taken as much as we could from the small plot of herbs and vegetables my mother dutifully tended each day, along with whatever foodstuffs fit into the wagon bed under the rolled-up tents and stacked poles. Gavriel had helped me gather as much honeycomb as possible from my hives before I tearfully whispered my thanks to the bees for their generosity and left them behind.

Our family was fortunate. Most had only pushcarts to heft what remained of their belongings, and every donkey, mule, and camel was fully laden. And still so much was left for those who remained to scavenge. Among our clan, a few smaller herds of sheep and goats hadn't been taken by the Amalekites, but all our family had left was the little group of goats Farah tended—four does and their kids that were always penned up in our tent at night.

Some of the larger households were broken in two, with whole clans or singular families choosing to stay behind and take their chances, either disbelieving the king's warning or insisting the Amalekites would protect them for remaining loyal. I refused to dwell on what it meant if they were wrong as I tried to push the leather satchel full of my tools into a gap between bags of grain in the wagon bed.

"Let me help," said Gavriel, whose dusty face and hair were slick with sweat from his labors on my family's behalf.

I flinched as he reached for the satchel and then yanked it close to my chest. "I have it."

Brows arched high, Gavriel raised his palms at my waspish response to his offer.

"It's only that these things are . . . important to me." Those tools were far more precious than any other item I'd packed today. My chisels, files, and wax-carving picks could not be replaced. Each one had been specially made by either my father or my grandfather.

He nodded. "Understood."

A young Hebrew jogged up to us, his eyes on my husband. "The captain says they need to move everyone out—now. The Amalekites are gathering on the north side of the river. Our company will take up the rear to make certain they don't follow."

"All right," said Gavriel. "Did Emmet say anything else?"

The young man, who did not look old enough to fight in any army, shrugged. "He didn't send me. But Shachar and I thought you should know."

"Of course he didn't." Gavriel huffed a rueful laugh, then slapped the boy on the shoulder. "Thank you for letting me know, Adin. It's good to know not everyone in the company despises me."

"Everyone knows what your record is with Yonatan's company." The look on the young man's face made it clear he worshiped my husband. "The captain and the others will come around. You'll see."

"I very much doubt that. Emmet has hated me from the first moment I met him." His tone suggested he didn't care all that much, but I remembered the way he'd submitted as he knelt before the red-haired captain. There had to be a reason Gavriel had given in to my father's demand when it had been obvious it was very much against his will to marry me.

But these were questions for a time when we were not fleeing for our lives. I finished squeezing my treasures securely into the gap between grain sacks while Gavriel and Adin concluded their conversation.

Shortly after, my father called together the entirety of his household, made up of at least seventy-five of my aunts, uncles, and cousins, as well as Rahm's family and a variety of others who'd found their way under my father's mantle over the years.

"Let us seek a blessing over our travels," said Abba, lifting his weathered and scarred palms high into the air as he'd done each Shabbat at sundown and before each festival celebration the entirety of my life. My father was not just the head of this household; he was, in all respects, our head priest.

"El Shaddai, Mighty One, we seek your protection over our family. Over this tribe and over all those traveling with us. We trust you to watch over us just as you watched over the Hebrews while Mosheh shepherded them through the wilderness. Guard our steps, God of Avraham. Lead us safely to the place you have chosen in your sovereign will and keep our eyes on your goodness with every step. And have mercy on those who have not heeded your warning."

A few choked sobs and sniffles echoed around the group once my father's words died away. Many were leaving friends and loved ones behind to an uncertain fate. If only Niv and Kila would have listened to my own warning yesterday.

"We'll be fine," Niv had said after I'd told her what I'd overheard, while my hip screamed from my hasty trek over the river. *"Our mother is Amalekite, remember? And our father's second wife is as well."*

"But what if the Israelite king takes Punon?"

Kila laughed. *"Don't be ridiculous. Agag won't let them anywhere near this valley. He's the most ruthless chieftain in the Aravah and has been for decades. He easily crushed the Edomites who held this place for hundreds of years, didn't he? Some little upstart Hebrew playing king won't have a chance."*

Niv grinned. *"Now tell us about this soldier you're supposed to marry. Is he handsome . . . ?"*

As my father remained with his arms held wide, his eyes focused somewhere in the dimming sky, I peered over my shoulder at the valley that had been my entire world. My father had always said El Shaddai brought us to Punon for a purpose and prospered us here because we worshiped him alone. So why was he driving us away, back to a place that held so much sorrow?

As the first blush of sunset began to bloom in the west, my father's hands came down and my mother moved to his side, where she'd been through every storm past and present. With no other words, the two of them climbed up onto the seat of the mule-drawn wagon. My father took the reins and began to lead us toward that distant horizon.

Gavriel

If it were only us soldiers marching through this wilderness, it would take four days at most to reach Be'er Sheva. But the pace of this caravan was achingly slow. Most of the Kenites had little more than pushcarts full of belongings, although there were quite a few heavy-laden camels and donkeys in the caravan as well. Taking into account what remained of their herds, not to mention myriad little ones and elderly on foot, it may take us two to three times that long, perhaps more.

Thankfully, the land had been fairly flat as we'd crossed the wide Aravah Valley under moonlight. Emmet led us directly toward the dark hills in the distance, and by sunrise, we'd made it nearly halfway across the sandy plain where little grew but scrub brush and a few scraggly weeds that dared poke their heads above the arid soil.

Following Barzel's wagon, I pushed an overflowing handcart as the girls—including my wife—trudged along together. I'd tried to persuade Zahava to ride on the wagon, but she stubbornly refused, insisting she was fine with her father's walking stick. With Breena on one side and Anaya on the other, she valiantly kept pace with the wagon while Farah shepherded their little pack of goats just behind.

The moment I saw Zahava falter, she was going on that wagon, whether she wanted to or not. She may put on a brave face, but no matter how hard she tried to compensate, she had to be in pain after walking all night long. It made my teeth grind to think of her hurting like that, which only aggravated the headache that had been growing for the past few hours. The sudden appearance of Adin at my side only added to my frustration.

"Shalom. Shachar sent me to check on you."

"Is Shachar my ima now?"

The boy squinted at me, humming in mock assessment. "Perhaps. I think I can see the resemblance. Something about the jaw, maybe? Not the nose, though. Nothing could match that travesty."

A smile twitched at the corner of my mouth, but I squelched it, not wanting the young pup to know he amused me. "So he tired of your yapping and foisted you off on me?"

He shrugged a shoulder. "He said something about virgin ears."

I held back a chuckle. Despite his rough edges, or perhaps because of them, I liked Shachar. He reminded me a bit of Tabbish, the old servant who'd taught me how to work bronze, both men composed of equal parts wisdom and off-color jests. A pang of melancholy struck me square in the chest. Tabbish had died a few years ago while I was off somewhere with Yonatan's unit. I'd never gotten to tell him good-bye or thank him properly for bothering with an annoying eleven-year-old who harassed the poor man until he'd taught me the basics of metalwork and then let me hone my newfound skills in his foundry. He never complained about me being in his way and patiently answered thousands of my questions. But he also never let me get away with anything. I had to treat his tools with respect and clean up after myself or I wasn't allowed in his shop—no exceptions.

I should have gone to see him at least once after I left home with my cousins.

"*Ungrateful brat.*" The accusation in my head was an old one, something I hadn't heard in a long while. But somehow it was far louder now than it had been in years, nearly competing with whatever was buzzing in my veins and causing bile to rise in my throat.

A bulging wineskin, dangling from the side of Barzel's wagon as it bumped along, caught my eye. I could practically taste the drink on my tongue. Emmet didn't have to know, did he?

"What's wrong with your wife?" asked Adin, snapping my attention away from the call of the wineskin and back to Zahava. But although she looked exhausted and her arm was looped with Breena's, she was still hobbling along, leaning on Barzel's stick. I'd seen hardened soldiers with less determination than my wife.

Wife. Even in my head, the word felt awkward, like a sword in my right hand instead of my left. *What was I going to do with a wife when I was sent back to Yonatan's unit?* I shook off the thought. I'd deal with that when my skull didn't feel like it was being squeezed by a vise. But regardless of the many complications she represented, the instinct to protect her flared surprisingly hot.

"There's *nothing* wrong with her," I said, my brows lifted to make my point. I'd fought beside men who'd lost an eye or a hand, and many who had far more scars on their bodies than I did—and I had more than my fair share. Zahava having one leg shorter than the other was a battle wound as far as I was concerned.

Adin lifted his palms. "I meant nothing by it. My apologies."

I didn't reply but tipped my chin to accept his regrets. We walked in silence for a while, and I wondered if he'd give up and leave me alone.

No such luck.

"I heard you joined the army before you were of age," he said.

"Did you?" I'd been barely seventeen at the time. Thankfully, I had a full beard by then and enough talent that none of the commanders bothered to ask my age.

"Wish I could wait," Adin muttered. "Or avoid it altogether."

"You don't want to be a soldier?" I wasn't certain I'd ever met a man, other than my uncle Natan, who didn't want to fight for Israel. Even my cousin Avi had been desperate to do so. Though once he'd actually had the chance to fight in a battle, it was clear he was not cut out to wield a sword.

"No," Adin said. "I've never wanted to. But I don't have a choice. I'm to serve as an aide to the captain until I am twenty and then be a chariot runner in Gibeah in preparation for becoming one of the king's guard. Just like my *father*."

The way Adin spat the word sounded more like a curse than a term of respect and my intuition flared. I had good reason to regard my brute of a sire with loathing, but what could cause Adin to do so?

"And you don't want to be like him," I stated, hoping my instincts were off.

His expression went hard, like a soldier who had seen far too much. "I'd rather drown in a cesspit."

Intuition spiraled into a ball of something ugly in my gut, so I pressed him, just a little. "Can a man trusted by Saul be so bad?"

"If you ask his fellow guards or our neighbors, then of course not. But if you ask my mother, who died with his hands wrapped around her neck during a fit of unmerited jealous rage, then yes."

The revelation knocked me back two decades. My mother's screams reverberated in my head for a breathless moment as words I'd only half-understood at six flew like knives—*whore, worthless, probably not even* my *bastard*—while my small hands beat with futile fury against the beast who'd pinned her to the wall.

I blinked away the horror, stomach churning. It seemed Adin and I had far more in common than I wanted to believe. But before I could form a coherent response, Beniyah, one of Emmet's fastest runners, came from behind us at full speed.

"That doesn't look good," said Adin with a frown.

"It does not." Curiosity raged, but Emmet had commanded me to remain with Zahava's family unless summoned.

However, when Beniyah appeared ahead of us a few minutes later with Emmet and Shachar in his wake, I made a quick decision and veered left out of the flow with Adin at my heel and we blocked their path with the handcart. I'd catch up to Zahava's family once I knew what we were dealing with.

"What's going on?" I demanded.

Emmet scowled. "Fill him in, Shachar, but keep everyone moving forward, and don't spook them. Adin, you're with me."

"Amalekites," said Shachar as soon as Emmet and Adin took off running. "They're in the far distance—not yet in swift pursuit, but the captain isn't taking any chances. It's likely Agag means to punish the Kenites for daring to leave."

Shachar's dark eyes tracked to Zahava's family, who'd slowed their pace to wait for me. "Better catch up. I'll send Adin back if you're needed."

My skin prickled with annoyance as I steered the cart back toward Barzel's wagon. Even under threat, Emmet was continuing to punish me, though I'd done everything he'd asked.

"What's going on, Gavriel?" asked Barzel, once I'd come alongside his wagon. Emmet was right, there was no use panicking the Kenites unnecessarily, so I kept the truth tucked away for now.

"Emmet plans to give everyone a rest once we reach the hills. There's bound to be some shade along the Tzin River." Once we reached the foothills, we'd be turning north on the road toward Arad, which if I remembered correctly, was the ancestral home of Emmet's mother.

"I'm glad to hear it. We could all use a rest."

Relieved he'd accepted the misdirection easily, I slackened my pace, glad to have my eyes back on Zahava, and for the skiff of clouds that had formed overhead to give us respite from the harsh sun. The whisper of breeze cooled my skin but did little to alleviate the steadily growing throb of dull pain at my temples.

We were still a good half hour from the foothills. Far too vulnerable for my comfort when the clouds turned darker, the wind strengthened. Dust stirred by hundreds of feet swirled in the overheated air.

From behind us, a shofar blasted out a series of urgent signals I knew as well as my own name. *Alarm. Forward. Double time. Take up arms.* I didn't wait for the signals to repeat.

"Move!" I bellowed. "Head for the hills! We're under attack!"

Cries and shouts followed my call as the ram's horn bleated out the warnings again, and the pace of the caravan quickened. There was little we could do if we were overtaken in the open desert, but if we made it to the foothills, the Kenites might be able to hide in wadis or caves so we could defend them.

My next thought was Zahava. She could not run anywhere at all. I dropped the handles of the cart and headed toward her, meaning to throw her over my shoulder, if necessary, and into the wagon bed. Barzel's mules could outrun the rest of the caravan, and I wanted my wife safe before I ran back to face the Amalekites.

But just before I reached Zahava and her sisters, the movement of the group ahead bogged down, coming to a rambling halt. I reluctantly pulled my eyes from my wife and to the sky, where a bank of iron-gray thunderclouds had dropped, obscuring the hills beyond. And at the front of the storm, a towering wall of dust was rising, coming straight for us.

We were trapped between a dangerous *khamsin* and a furious enemy. There was no way to avoid either. But only one of those would roll over us within moments.

"Get down!" I shouted, waving my arms. "Cover your faces! Close your eyes!"

There was nothing else to do. Many of the animals were instinctively huddling together within their herds and either turning their backs to the storm or dropping to the ground. Thankfully, the people followed their example, taking shelter under wagons and behind carts, pressing together in groups, covering their heads with scarves and blankets and rugs while I continued to shout about keeping eyes and mouths closed. Already a fine mist of sand had reached us, pushed ahead of the billowing dirt, rolling across the landscape like a wave.

Throat hoarse and skin stinging from the sand, I took a much-needed breath as I scanned the group to make certain everyone had heeded my warnings and heard my name being called from about ten paces away. Disoriented by the wall of sand nearly upon us, I saw the horrified eyes of my new wife pinned on me as she repeated my name with an edge of desperation.

I ran to where she was huddled near the wagon with Breena and Anaya, shielding them against the onslaught of whirling dust. I threw myself down and pulled her into the cove of my chest, turning my own back to the sandy winds. She came willingly, dragging her two sisters into the shelter of my body as well.

"Cover your face," I demanded. "Close your eyes and do not breathe in the dust if you can."

They obeyed, and I tightened my grip on them, glad they were all small enough that I could take the brunt of the roaring wind against my back. My long hair blew over my face, sand whipped at the exposed skin on my neck, and my vision blurred before I slammed my eyes shut and pressed my face into Zahava's hair. She smelled the same as she had the night I met her, like desert blossoms, honey, and some alluring spice, and I inhaled deeply before holding my breath while the khamsin whirled around us.

Willfully, I blocked out everything but the knowledge that she was safe in my arms. This extraordinary woman had not uttered a word of complaint about marrying a stranger or even packing up her life at the behest of a king she'd never seen before, and had shielded her sisters with the courage of a lion.

I may never have wanted to marry, and I wasn't certain what lay ahead, but by the time the thick brown cloud had passed over, leaving behind a caravan of dust-covered travelers blinking sand out of their eyes and an endless valley shockingly empty of any sign of pursuers, the duty to protect Zahava with my life had settled deep into my bones.

I slid my gaze over the black horizon, alert for movement among the shadows. Half the company was on watch tonight, stationed atop various vantage points above camp, while the other half slept. And although I'd been relieved Emmet had called me back to duty, I'd found myself wishing that I could at least set my eyes on Zahava to assure myself she was safe. Thankfully, we'd seen nothing more of the Amalekites who'd been pursuing us before the sandstorm. It was as if a giant hand had swept over the Aravah to whisk them away without a trace. But that didn't mean they wouldn't return, so for now, my place was here.

Shachar belched. "It's been far too long since I've enjoyed Kenite fare. My ima cooked with the same spices, ones that burn all the way down to my belly."

I huffed a laugh. These people did seem to enjoy fiery flavors, some so potent they made my eyes water. But however enticing the meal, I'd been too nauseated to enjoy it. So I'd offered the rest of my portion to Shachar, who practically inhaled it.

"Your mother is Kenite?" I asked.

Nodding, he wiped the back of his hand over his mouth. "Her tribe has lived in the territory of West Manasseh since Yehoshua's time. Abba saw her one day on the beach collecting seashells and had to have her." He clicked his tongue on his teeth with a wink. "These women are beauties, no?"

My wife was that, for certain. She was slender, even more slight than her younger sister Breena, likely due to the illness that had affected her leg. But what was far more intriguing to me than her sun-kissed skin, her striking hazel eyes, and silken black hair was the smile that rarely wavered as we'd traveled, even though she was clearly in pain. She'd endured so much and yet I sensed no resentment in her, only quiet acceptance of her lot and selfless focus on those around her.

Thankfully, my cousins weren't here to see just how taken I was with the woman I'd been forced to marry less than two days before. I'd ribbed both of them for turning into besotted fools, after all. They would no doubt eagerly repay me in kind.

Shachar opened a skin of beer and took a long drink. The smell of it teased my nose and my mouth flooded with want as he smacked his lips in satisfaction. He stretched his arm to offer it to me, then stopped midair with a wince. "Apologies. I almost forgot."

I tensed. Apparently, Emmet had made it known I was banned from strong drink. The thought grated against my raw nerves. I already had a sullied reputation with this company. Did I need them coddling me too?

Shachar gave an apologetic shrug. "We've all had our failings, my friend, vices we must overcome. We're for you. Not against."

"Emmet is most definitely against me."

He hummed in wordless agreement. "But you'll prove him wrong, won't you?"

That I would, or die trying. I was a warrior. I wouldn't let a roiling stomach or a pounding headache get the best of me.

"You've got a good thing here, Gavriel," Shachar said, "even if it wasn't your choice. Don't take your wife for granted like I did."

"You were married?"

"I was. Chose to find satisfaction elsewhere, and she ran off with someone else." His tone was full of dark regret. "It's been many years since then, and I've yet to forgive myself. Especially when I am fairly certain she was with child when she disappeared."

Although shocked by the candid admission, I kept my mouth shut, knowing from experience that words would do nothing to ease his guilt.

"All I'm saying is that we all have our regrets. You can choose to either wallow in the filth or climb out of it. But you can't do both."

I chewed on Shachar's admonition for the rest of our watch, after I'd hurled up my guts on the way back to camp, and again while I sought out Barzel's wagon among the disorganized and hastily prepared camp along the river. I found Zahava's family asleep near what remained of a fire, Barzel and his wife on one side, and Farah, Breena, and Anaya pressed together for warmth under a heavy wool blanket, with a few of the goats bedded down beside them. But Zahava was nowhere to be seen.

My pulse ticked higher as I searched the shadows around the campsite, panic swirling in my unsettled gut until I was nearly ready to vomit again.

But then I saw her curled up beneath the wagon, and relief sluiced through my limbs, followed swiftly by dismay. Aside from the two goats cuddled against her, she was once again sleeping on the ground, alone. At least this time I could do something about it.

After retrieving one of the wool blankets from the handcart, I crawled under the wagon to carefully stretch the covering over her small form. Then, hoping I'd not frighten her if she woke, I slowly slid in beside her. I'd always radiated heat in sleep, so hopefully she'd glean some of my warmth, even a handspan away. With a sweet sigh, she nestled closer, and I held still, scared to breathe, lest she startle awake.

Shachar was right; this may not have been the life I'd chosen for myself, but I had to make an effort to do right by her. She deserved that much, even if she was far too pure for the likes of me. But the truth was, I didn't know how to keep myself from tumbling back into my own muck. I'd never been good at fending off dark thoughts or ignoring the voice that constantly reminded me how worthless I was and listed all the ways I'd let down everyone around me. My mother. My sisters. My cousins. Shalem. Odds were I'd fail Zahava too. It was only a matter of time.

My thoughts spiraled as nausea burned at the base of my throat. Soon it became a chore to lay still, my legs restless and hands trembling. Eyes open and fixed on the black underside of the wagon as my heart thrummed unsteadily, I couldn't fend off the echoes of the past. *"What are you going to do, boy? Take me on? You're pitiful. Get out of my way."* My body twitched as the memory of an open-handed slap made my ears ring.

"What's wrong?" came a whisper as Zahava shifted beside me. "Can't you sleep?"

I gritted my teeth, annoyed with myself for waking her. "I'm fine."

She turned to fully face me in the dark. "You pushed that cart all day. Aren't you exhausted?"

I was, body and soul. It was my mind that would not relax. And my heartbeat, which refused to abate. It pulsed in my temples like the insistent beat of a war drum.

I knew what I needed. Knew what would calm the roiling in my stomach, the shaking hands, the twitching muscles, the racing pulse and racing thoughts. But I'd eat my own dusty sandals before giving Emmet the satisfaction of dismissing me for giving in to the sweet oblivion at the bottom of a jug.

"I'll be fine," I lied, hoping I could hold down my sick long enough to sleep.

Zahava went quiet for a while, and I wondered if she'd drifted off again, but then her gentle voice came out of the darkness.

"Gavriel, I don't know you well, but I can tell something is very wrong. How can I help you?"

Her compassion made warmth contract in my chest, and the truth poured out unbidden. "I need a drink."

She shifted, beginning to rise. "I'll go get a waterskin."

I set my hand on her shoulder, partly because I didn't want her to bother, but mostly because I didn't want her to leave. "I meant I need wine. Or something stronger."

She was silent, waiting for more.

"I haven't drunk anything in nearly two days now. It's . . . been a long time since I've abstained like that." I was grateful the dark hid the hot shame washing over my face.

I could practically hear curiosity trembling on her lips, but she only repeated, "What can I do to help?"

She deserves so much better than me. I huffed a rueful laugh. "None of this would have happened if I'd not been soused the night we met."

She let out a soft hum. "Perhaps not."

"Emmet thinks I'm too weak to stop. And maybe he's right."

"Who is Emmet?"

"Our captain. The red-haired one."

"Ah. Yes, he certainly seems to have something against you."

The darkness made me bold. "I tried to seduce his sister."

She inhaled sharply.

"In my defense, I didn't know who she was. But truthfully, he never liked me." I told her the story of the day my cousins and I had sneaked down to watch the king be chosen and how I'd come across Yonatan and his friend. "I don't think I ever had a chance with Emmet. He mistrusted me from the start. Yonatan, however, remembered me a year later when Zevi, Avi, and I ran off to fight at Yavesh-Gilead. He ignored the fact that I wasn't even military age and allowed me to be in his company. He encouraged my weapons-making, even though I ultimately let him down."

If Emmet had been my commander from the start, I'd never have made it this far. He would have sent me away in shame at my first mistake. And I would have deserved it. No matter that I'd always sworn I would not be like my father, here I was. A drunkard and a fool. Just like Hanan said I would be.

She let out a little gasp. "Are you . . . did *you* make that knife?"

"What?" My thoughts had been spinning again, and the question brought them to a grinding halt.

"The bronze knife you gave me as a bridal gift. Are you a metalsmith like my father?"

I felt my face heat again. She had to be disappointed with such a paltry offering. If I'd not refused to be a part of Hanan's business dealings, I could have given her fine gowns, jewels, a beautiful home—anything she wanted.

"I've made weapons, yes. But nothing compared to your father's talent." Seeing the exquisite metalwork Barzel and his apprentices produced had made me realize just how much I still had to learn.

"Of course," she muttered. "Now it makes more sense."

"What does?"

She ignored the question. "Who taught you?"

"A man named Tabbish. He ran a foundry for my stepfather."

"He doesn't run it for himself?"

"The foundry is only one of Hanan's many business endeavors." Distaste coated my tongue. "He's the richest man in Ramah. I grew up in a palace."

"Why do you sound as though that was something bad?"

The darkness, or perhaps it was simply her sweet voice, loosened my tongue even more. "He is not just my stepfather. He is my uncle. He married my mother within weeks of my father being run over by a team of oxen."

"Oh, Gavriel," she whispered.

"My father deserved it. Most of the memories I have are of him beating my mother."

Horrified silence followed my pronouncement.

"I was only six when he died," I continued, "and knew little more than my abba was gone. There were times when he was the best father a boy could want, carrying me on his shoulders, wrestling with me while I laughed until I got the hiccups. And then there were times when he would come home at night only to slap my mother around and accuse her of horrible things before disappearing again."

I'd never forget the sound of my mother's muffled cries, nor the smack of his palm against her beautiful face. Most of the time, I'd cowered in the other room, shaking and trying not to let him hear my sobs.

"Only once did I attempt to get in the way, so he hit me too. Beat me half-senseless." Zahava's hand reached for mine. I savored the warmth of her skin as I continued. "My mother is no bigger than you, but she reacted like a lioness with her claws out. She screamed and slapped and scratched at his face and told him to leave. And to both of our surprise, he did. Until then, she'd always taken the abuse, but I think something snapped in her when he went after me. He came back a couple of days later, telling us both he was desperately sorry. Crying, even. But not long after that, he was trampled in the street. We moved into Hanan's house soon after."

I had hated it. Hated the nice clothes. Hated his big house at the center of the city and the way my ima slept in another room so I had to sleep alone. The stone tile was cold, and my footsteps echoed in the large, empty rooms. Our little two-room house had been all I'd ever known until then, and I'd missed the cozy warmth, the earthen floors, and the friends who now lived on the other side of Ramah and refused to play with "a rich boy." My entire world had been ripped away from me, and it was Hanan's fault.

"Your uncle was abusive too?" she asked after I'd been lost in memories for a while.

"No. He's far more prone to lavishing my mother with gifts

and spoiling the girls when she allows him to—his *one* redeeming quality, since they deserve the sun and the moon and all the stars."

"Then why do you speak of him with such disdain?" she asked, perplexed.

I swallowed against the knot in my throat. "Because I was nothing but a burden to him. A reminder of his useless older brother."

She huffed, as if offended on my behalf. "Surely he did not say such a thing."

"Not in my presence. But he made it clear I was a disappointment. I had no interest in learning his business or spending my days bent over ledgers and lists like he did. I couldn't sit still for any amount of time and only wanted to be outside wrestling, shouting, or playing war. When my uncle hired two Levites to teach me reading and writing, I put far more effort into playing tricks on the young men instead." The letters and numbers had refused to stay in their places anyhow, so I'd seen no point in trying.

It was shortly after the Levites had fled the house that I overheard Hanan and my mother arguing—something they never did. *"If he doesn't learn something other than fighting,"* he said, *"he'll end up face down in the muck someday too."*

From then on, I'd spent all of my time outside, away from his disapproving glares and the pleading, concerned ones of my mother. It was much easier to hang about with the servants, learning bronze and leather work, than it was to be trapped in a palace and constantly reminded of how much he loathed me.

"He's just like my brother . . ." he'd said that night. *"Elan couldn't control himself either . . ."*

I'd proved him right, hadn't I? I was a drunkard just like his brother. I was on the cusp of losing my entire military career over my idiocy. And the beautiful, kind young woman beside me was chained to me for life.

The fleeting image of Zahava cowering in a corner and shielding herself from me caused the nausea to flare again. If I hurt her,

I'd never forgive myself. In fact, I'd gladly fall on my own sword before I lifted a hand to strike her—

Blessedly, her voice cut off my spiraling thoughts. "So you learned metalwork instead? To work with your hands?"

"That, and because Hanan hates weapons. Anything that hints at violence. He refuses to even fight for Israel. Hires mercenaries to take his place in Saul's army and to guard his home."

"But he let you work bronze in his foundry?"

"He either didn't know or didn't care."

She hummed in response, then to my relief, she changed the subject. "That knife you made is quite unique. I've never seen a serrated knife of such strength and quality before. The tines are usually far too soft unless the bronze is alloyed with iron or . . ."

As her voice trailed off, I wondered if perhaps I'd been making things up in my head, that the burn marks and scars on her hands were from cooking, but I had a few matching ones, and I'd rarely seen her near the cookfire.

And then there was the enigma of her father. The man was very near to blind, if I had to guess. He hid it well with plenty of bluster and the help of his walking staff, but over the past three days, I'd seen his wife point out dips in the ground as they walked and hand him items that he should be able to find easily. And it was Safaa driving the mules, not Barzel.

"You made that jewelry, didn't you?" I asked, finally voicing the suspicions I'd been mulling over as we marched through the desert. "Those delicate pieces made of red-gold he showed us in his foundry."

She went rigid. "No . . . I . . . my father . . ."

"Your father can barely see, isn't that true?"

She audibly caught her breath. "How do you know?"

I told her what I'd witnessed, and after a tremulous exhale, she told me about the explosion of the furnace and how Barzel's eyes were getting worse and worse.

"*Please* don't say anything to anyone," she said in an urgent whisper. "He has so much pride, and no one knows he's been teaching me. He doesn't have a son to pass on his trade, and I enjoy it so much."

"How long has it been since you took over making the jewelry?"

She paused, then sighed. "Three years."

"Three? I would have thought much longer." The skill involved in such intricate metalwork was extraordinary. I'd never in my lifetime be able to master such delicate techniques.

"Please don't make me stop," she pleaded. "It's the only thing I am truly good at. But I will be a good wife. I will cook and clean and make clothing. Well . . . I will try, even though I am terrible at weaving. But I will do my best."

"Why would I make you stop? You have a rare talent. If anything, I want to learn *from* you. And of course I'll say nothing about your father's blindness. I'd never dishonor him like that."

She muffled a cry. "Thank you."

"So that's why you were so worried about fitting that bag of tools in the wagon."

"Yes, they are my wax-carving tools. It's how I make delicate pieces, by molding them." She yawned. "However, I'm not certain how I'll be able to do so anymore since I had to leave my beehives behind."

"We should sleep," I said, beginning to feel the tug as well. "It won't be long before we must be up and on our way."

"We should," she said, nestling a bit closer. My body thrilled at both her nearness and the small gesture of growing trust—or perhaps she was just cold.

"But this conversation is not over." I allowed my eyes to fall closed. "I want to know more about how the two of you pulled off such a scheme."

Her smile was nearly audible in the darkness. "All right."

I still wanted a drink, could practically taste the tang of red wine on my parched tongue, but my mind was no longer racing, my heartbeat was steadier, and I was grateful for the distraction she'd offered me tonight.

Zahava may not have the blatant beauty of the sister who'd married Rahm, nor the audacious flair of the sister who'd kicked the still-tender bruise into my ribs, but there was a quiet strength in her that called to me and an innate stillness that reminded me a bit of my aunt Eliora. It was probably what had drawn me to Zahava in the first place that night by the cistern—the sense that she was a pool of deep calm to my turbulent waters.

And so, with that calming presence by my side, I finally slept.

13

Zahava

I had awakened at daybreak, before Gavriel, but was loath to move. It had been so cold last night, and his body radiated like a smelting furnace, so in my sleep I'd moved into the cove of his warmth. His heavy arm was now curled over my waist, and his deep, even breaths tickled the back of my neck, sending tingles of awareness over my skin. Not only had he shielded my sisters and me with his own body during the sandstorm, but he'd also made me feel warm and safe all night long. What had at first felt disconcerting, since I'd never been so close to a man, now felt like the safest place imaginable. I mourned the sounds of the camp coming to life, demanding I extricate myself.

I was glad he was still asleep after such a restless night. I'd been so confused why he'd not been able to relax when he was obviously so exhausted, his eyes bloodshot and his expression drawn, until he had admitted the hold drink had over him. I wasn't sure what made him stop imbibing after our wedding night, but I would do whatever I could to help. And right now, what he needed was rest, so I reluctantly slid out from beneath his arm, immediately missing his warmth, and crawled out from under the wagon into the chill air.

My mother and sisters were making bread on a flat rock near the fire, so after I took care of my needs, I awkwardly folded myself down next to Farah, swiped some flour to coat my hands, and picked up a ball of dough.

"Shalom," said my mother. "Sleep well?"

I did not look up, keeping my eyes on the dough as I pressed it between my flour-covered hands, but my face flushed at the gently teasing question.

"She certainly looked comfortable to me, all wrapped up in her husband," said Farah.

Now my face was on fire. They'd seen me tangled in Gavriel's embrace?

"It was cold last night," I muttered and smashed the round of dough harder between my palms.

Farah elbowed me playfully. "You didn't look cold to me."

My mother shushed Farah and Breena as they laughed at whatever horrified expression they saw on my face.

"Girls, leave her alone. I'm glad Zahava is finding comfort in her husband's embrace. It is as it should be."

I swallowed hard. No one knew Gavriel and I had not actually consummated this marriage. I had to admit the idea of sharing a bed with him wasn't quite as intimidating as it had sounded when Niv and Kila had spoken of the intimacies between men and women in embarrassingly vivid detail. And after last night, when he'd confided to me about his difficulties with his stepfather and the adoring way he spoke of his mother and sisters, I'd felt myself drawn to my new husband in a way I'd never felt toward Rahm.

When I'd accidentally revealed my knowledge of metalwork and he'd not forbidden me from using my skills but instead said he wanted to learn *from* me, I nearly kissed the man right there—

which would have shocked us both. Perhaps my abba's decision had not been such a hasty one after all.

Thankfully, Farah started complaining about how her sandals were giving her blisters during the long walk, taking the attention off me, but when I caught my mother's eye again, she gave me a knowing smile, as if she sensed that I'd softened toward Gavriel and approved.

Curses and a loud flurry of activity startled us, and the two small goats that had been sleeping next to me last night scurried out from under the wagon, bleating, followed by a bleary-eyed Gavriel, his hair a tangled mess.

"Are you all right?" I asked.

"I. Hate. Goats." He scowled as he scraped his black curls away from his face and wound them into a lopsided knot at the back of his neck. "Waking to find one of them nibbling on my beard was *not* pleasant." He glared at me, although the expression had little heat, and then strode off in the direction of the nearby stream, all of us staring as he stomped out of the campsite.

Once he'd disappeared into the brush, I looked back at my mother and sisters, all of them wide-eyed and squelching smiles.

Farah lifted a sardonic brow. "I shouldn't ask him to tend my herd, then?"

I lost my composure, laughing until tears trickled down my cheeks as my sisters joined me, the four of us overcome with giggles. It made me miss Yasmin, who was probably busy helping her new mother-in-law and Rahm's young sisters at their own campsite. Hopefully, if Gavriel didn't make me move somewhere else once we reached Be'er Sheva, we'd pitch our tents close together. Because even if she coddled me from time to time and she'd married the man I'd wanted, I still adored my eldest sister.

Shortly after my mother and sisters left to fetch water, Gavriel returned, his hair dripping wet. Beside him was Adin, the young man who seemed to be an aide to Gavriel's captain.

Adin gestured widely as he spoke to Gavriel, who vaguely acknowledged his chatter. There was obvious hero worship in the young man's demeanor, but something was off with my husband. Looking grim, he passed by without a glance to me and headed directly for my father on the other side of the campsite, who was seated in a circle with a few of the other men of our household, including various uncles, cousins, and Rahm. Adin, however, came to sit next to me.

"Shalom. I hope you slept well," he said.

My face heated as I offered him a piece of bread fresh from the hot rock. He devoured the round in three bites, making a loud groan of satisfaction. "Nothing better."

"What's going on?" I asked, tipping my chin toward the men.

"The captain has decided to change course. After what happened with the Amalekites yesterday, he doesn't want to take any chances."

"What do you mean?"

Adin frowned. "Didn't your husband tell you we were followed from Punon?"

My stomach hollowed and I shook my head. "He didn't say a thing."

"Don't worry. The storm chased them off," he said with a shrug. "The lookouts haven't seen any sign of them since. But the captain thinks it's best we turn south here and go through Qadesh instead of going up toward the Salt Sea to Arad."

That storm had been so odd, billowing out of nowhere and disappearing just as quickly. Had the hand of El Shaddai spun up that storm to protect us? I was certain my father would say so. I could practically hear his voice in my ear.

"If He commands the sea to split in two to save the Hebrews, daughter, will he not stir up a little dust for us? It is his Land, after all, every rock and grain of sand."

Ignorant of my silent musings, Adin continued, "From what

I hear, the new way will be steeper, and at least an extra week of travel to Be'er Sheva."

A week *longer*? I didn't know how I would ever make it so far when every joint in my body ached after yesterday's long trek through the Aravah. I knew Gavriel had wanted me to ride in the bed of the wagon, but it set my teeth on edge to be treated like one of the elderly or a child barely able to walk.

"He is famous, you know," said Adin, pulling me out of my self-pitying thoughts.

"Who?"

He gave me an astonished look. "Gavriel ben Elan of Ramah. Your *husband*?"

I opened my mouth and shut it again, battling a haze of confusion. "Famous for what?"

"He's absolutely fearless on the battlefield. It's like he has no concern for his own life. I'd heard about Gavriel long before I'd ever met him. They say there's no enemy he fears and that he's a master of weaponry. Swords, axes, knives, even a sling—he's proficient in all of them. Shachar told me he was barely seventeen when he joined the army and was in an elite unit assembled by King Saul's son by the time he was twenty. Of course that was before . . ." He waved his hand in the air with a knowing expression.

"Before what?"

He raised his brows, then took a quick look around before lowering his voice. "Before Yonatan booted him out for being drunk and causing a bar brawl over a woman."

When I was seven, one of the mules had rammed into me by accident, knocking the wind from my lungs—this felt nearly the same. I had no reason to feel such bitter jealousy since he'd been my husband for less than three days. But what sort of a woman would he have felt strongly enough to fight over? Some long-legged, worldly beauty, no doubt. Not a crippled girl whose whole life had been lived in a tent with a herd of smelly goats.

My mouth tasted wrong.

"He had a bit of a reputation with women," Adin said, not noticing that I'd gone perfectly still. "They throw themselves at him." He laughed. "But don't worry, the captain forbade him from drinking anything stronger than water or touching any woman—except for you, of course. And Shachar said that once Gavriel proves himself again, he'll be restored to his place with Yonatan's unit. . . . Who is that?"

Although I was reeling from the dose of reality I'd been hit with, I followed his gaze to Farah, who'd returned from the river and was now playing a hand-slapping game with Anaya.

"That is my sister Farah."

He said nothing as he watched the two of them chant a silly rhyme in rhythm with their claps, but I had a feeling Adin might be hanging about our campfire a lot more in the coming days.

"Where are you from?" I asked to distract him from staring at my sister with his mouth gaping. Farah had made it very clear she had no interest in marrying any time soon, if ever, so he was wasting his time.

"The territory of Benjamin," he said, sitting taller. "Just like Gavriel."

I'd never even thought to ask Gavriel's tribal affiliation, and he had not offered. It was another reminder of how little I knew about the man I'd married.

"I live in a town not far from Gibeah, where Saul's fortress was built." He told me of the stone palace, with watchtowers on each of the four corners, that sat atop a high hill and could be seen from far in the distance. "My father is among Saul's personal guard." He scraped at something in the dirt with his foot. "He wants me to be a guard as well someday. It's why he sent me to be an aide to the captain." A hint of discomfort bled through the statement.

"And that's not what you want?"

He pursed his lips, gaze flitting over to Farah briefly before he shook his head. "I don't want to be stuck in a palace. I want to travel the world. See new things and places and people in faraway foreign lands." A hint of pink tinted his cheeks.

"That sounds like an adventure."

He sighed, sounding resigned. "I have no choice but to do my duty. My father would kill me if I went against his plans for me." With that ominous statement, Adin popped to his feet. "I should get back to the captain."

Farah walked over with Anaya holding a bouquet of purple wildflowers they must have picked near the river, but the young man was already striding away as if his sandals were on fire.

With a confused frown, Farah watched him flee. "Who is that, and what was his problem?"

"Adin." I lifted a brow as I realized I finally had some ammunition of my own after the way she'd teased me earlier. "And *you* are the problem. The poor boy couldn't take his eyes off of you."

For the first time I could ever remember, Farah's face went red as the tail end of a sunset. "*Zaza!*"

I grinned at her. "See? Not so fun being poked at, is it?"

She hurled the wildflowers at me and whirled off, dragging a very confused Anaya behind her. But I knew she'd forgive me for giving her a hard time over Adin. There wasn't one of my sisters I wouldn't give my life for, and I knew for certain they felt exactly the same way.

By the time all the wagons were reloaded and the caravan organized, I'd determined to not let what Adin had said about Gavriel bother me. I had no choice but to do all I could to be a good wife, no matter what sort of man I'd been forced to marry, or if he chose to leave me behind when this was over. And he did seem to be trying hard to stay away from drink, as evidenced by the continued shaking of his hands, the pinched look on his face that made me think he had another headache, and the twitchy way he loaded and reloaded the wagon and handcart.

Once he was satisfied with whatever rearrangements he'd made, he came to stand directly in front of me.

"Let's go. You're riding on the wagon today."

I frowned at the spot he'd cleared in the bed and held up my father's walking stick. "I'm fine, I'll—"

"You are not fine. You were groaning in your sleep last night."

I was?

He lowered his voice, his gaze pinning me. "It's all right to ride. No one will think less of you."

My belly swirled. *I will.* I was tired of always having special accommodations made for me. I could push through the pain, I'd done it plenty of times before. So I shook my head, determined not to appear weak in front of a man whose entire being screamed strength and vitality.

"I thought that's what you would say." He leaned over, slung one arm around my waist, and pulled me up over his shoulder. I'd barely taken three shocked breaths before I was dumped onto the back of the wagon, directly onto my thick cushion, which he'd placed in that very spot.

"You cannot just manhandle me." I narrowed my eyes at him.

He smirked. "I think I just did."

I huffed, challenge flaring to life. "I am fine to walk, Gavriel. This caravan is slow, and you have plenty to carry in that cart." The thing had already been overflowing before adding the weight of the grain sacks he'd moved over to make a place for me in the wagon bed.

To my surprise, instead of releasing my waist, he pressed in closer. His large body was nearly between my knees and his face only a breath away as he said, "I am your *husband*. You will do as I say."

My hackles went up for a moment, until I saw the wicked spark in his gray eyes. "Is that so?"

He nodded, gaze pinned to mine. "I have no doubt you can push through this wilderness. You are nearly as stubborn as my mother, and she is as stiff-necked as they come. But have mercy on me, Zahava. It's difficult to push the cart, watch for danger, *and* worry whether you are hurting all day."

I held my breath, staring into his stormy eyes and the striking ring of deep blue that encircled the gray. They dipped to my lips briefly and then back to my eyes.

I lost my path of thought completely and scrambled about for words. "I . . . you . . . you were worried about me?"

"You are mine to worry over now, aren't you, little dove?"

Delicious tingles traveled up and down my spine, and heat surged where his hands were still curved around my waist. I could do nothing but nod.

Then he gave me a wink that proved exactly why women threw themselves at him. "Call me Gavi, *wife*."

A series of bleating blasts from the ram's horns startled both of us, and within moments the caravan jolted into motion. Removing his grip on me, he turned back to his handcart and we began the long detour south through unfamiliar territory.

As much as I enjoyed being called *wife* by the famous Gavriel ben Elan of Ramah, I had to remind myself that the designation was, in all likelihood, temporary. As Adin had said, he'd soon be reinstated with Yonatan's unit and I'd be left behind.

Gavriel

Zahava had been watching me most of the day. Her pretty hazel eyes flitted to me every so often as I trudged along with the overfull handcart. Her covert attention had been a pleasant distraction from the splitting headache that persisted on this third day since Emmet had banned me from wine. Step after endless step, I'd pushed this heavy handcart. For her. Because the screaming of my neck and shoulder muscles was worth it to see her riding along comfortably in that wagon bed. And if I was honest, I'd been purposely walking behind the wagon because I quite liked her curious gaze on me.

If there was anything I'd learned about her over the past few days, it was that there was nothing weak about Zahava. In fact, she may be one of the strongest people I'd ever met. Therefore, she must have been in considerable pain to give in so easily. Because although she'd flared at me a little for picking her up without permission, she settled quickly onto the cushion I'd arranged for her, looking almost relieved I'd ignored her protests.

Thankfully, the nausea had lessened overnight and pushing my body to exhaustion with the heavier burden in my handcart had helped as well. That, coupled with the relentless heat beating down on us, had caused thirst for water alone. My hands had finally stopping shaking so violently, and my heartbeat thrummed a steady rhythm, no more zipping about like a squirrel in a barley sack.

In the distance lay a strip of green at the base of the foothills, an oasis out here in the seemingly endless wilderness. It was at least an hour's walk still, but Emmet's scouts had said we'd reach it well before sundown. They said a river flowed down from the hill country, so we would have plenty of water to replenish our stores.

I refocused to find Zahava watching me once again and opened my mouth, meaning to tease her a little, perhaps see if I could get a laugh or at least the promise of a smile, but the wagon jerked hard to the left. Wide-eyed, Zahava cried out, grabbing for something to brace herself so she did not tumble off the wagon bed, but the jolt caused a stack of baskets to slide sideways on top of her. She pressed against them as the wagon veered hard to the right while Barzel bellowed at the mules to stop.

I dropped the cart, little caring that it tipped over, and ran for Zahava. I snatched her off the wagon bed and into my arms, allowing the baskets to tumble down and break open, spilling their contents in the dirt.

"Are you hurt?" I said, still holding her tight to my chest. My heartbeat raced, but this time it had nothing to do with drink. Only the horrifying thought of her being crushed under a wheel like my abba.

"I'm fine," she said. "You can put me down now."

"Did anything hit your head?" I searched her face for blood or scrapes, my pulse galloping even faster as I imagined a fracture in her skull, of that beautiful light leaving her eyes.

"Gavi." She put a hand on my cheek. "I'm not hurt. Really. Not a scratch."

Disoriented, I blinked at her for another couple of moments before realizing that the wagon had stopped. The entire congregation of Kenites continued to stream around us, dead set on reaching that oasis. They must all think I was mad holding my wife like this in public. I set her on the ground and reluctantly released her. "Are you certain you're all right?"

Her cheek twitched, the gold in her hazel eyes sparkling at me. "I am fine. Let's go see what happened."

I followed her around the front of the wagon, where Barzel was bent over, fidgeting with the left mule's bridle. Zahava placed a hand on her father's back. "Abba. What happened?"

He startled. "Oh! Zahava. I didn't see you." He held up a metal piece still dangling from one rein. "The bit snapped," he said. "The broken piece must have dropped somewhere along the way. As soon as Ebenezer realized he was free of it, he tried to turn around, and then when Safaa pulled on Ida's reins to slow the wagon down, she spooked and jerked the other way."

No wonder the vehicle had been swerving.

"Do you have another bit?" I asked.

"I loaned my spare bridle to Rahm for their mule cart."

Rahm and Yasmin likely had no idea we'd stopped. They'd been ahead of us in the caravan today.

"Can you fix it?" I asked. "Or rig something up?"

"I can't. It needs to be completely remade." He frowned, staring at the broken bit, then looked at his daughter. "But Zahava can do it."

"Abba," she said in a harsh whisper, unnecessary with the noise of feet and hooves and wheels streaming around us. "I'd need to build a furnace, carve a wax model in this heat, and then prepare and pour the mold, not to mention smoothing and polishing. I can't do all of that without someone noticing."

"Perhaps not," he said as a grin spread over his face. "But your husband certainly can. Why do you think I made him marry you?"

We set up camp on the far edge of the oasis, since Emmet said we would spend a couple of days here to rest the livestock and give them a chance to graze on the greenery that filled the wadis around the area. The river was not wide at this point, but it was cool and clear. Someone had also discovered a spring nearby, so there was plenty of fresh water for everyone to replenish their waterskins and jugs, something sorely needed after three days trekking through the desert.

Zahava and I set up our own smaller tent a little farther from the rest, but unlike the rest of the group who headed directly to their bedrolls, I spent the next hour digging a small pit in the hard ground nearby, which we would use as a makeshift furnace. As I worked on the pit, Zahava processed wax from the large jar of honeycomb she'd brought from Punon.

"I miss my cave," she mumbled as she doused the lump of wax she'd separated from the honey in a bowl of icy water from the spring. "I'll have to keep it close to the water and quench it constantly to keep it firm. It's far too hot here."

"You worked in a cave?"

She told me of the enlarged limestone mineshaft she'd worked in, which afforded her both privacy and a cold environment to carve her wax patterns. I'd never heard of such a technique and was anxious to watch her work.

"Is this a skill known only to the Kenites?"

"I don't think so. My father said there are masters of the craft who use it in Egypt and Damascus, perhaps other places. But that technique paired together with the alloy of red-gold, this is the secret passed down for generations, father to son."

I grinned. "Until you."

She nodded. "Until me."

Pure gold was soft, unusable for anything but delicate jewelry.

Adding copper or other stronger metals would give it strength but would also heighten brittleness. The knowledge of how to produce red-gold that was the perfect balance between strength and beauty would be valuable indeed. I could see why Barzel was so careful not to reveal that he'd taught his daughter such a skill. It might actually put her at risk. Which further explained why he'd been so insistent I marry her—again proving Barzel to be a man of foresight.

"I was impressed when I thought it was your father making those pieces he showed me at the foundry, but now that I know my wife crafted them, I'm in awe."

Her cheeks flushed at my compliment. "In truth, no one in our family, even my father, has made anything from red-gold that could touch the *Atarah Hod*."

"The Crown of Splendor? What is that?"

"If the stories are to be believed, it was the most beautiful thing ever designed by my ancestors."

"What does it look like?"

"I only know that it was intricate and lovely. I've never seen it. And I never will."

"Why not?"

"Because it was stolen when the Philistines ran us out of Be'er Sheva and killed my great-grandfather. His pregnant wife was forced to flee with little more than the clothes on her back. No one knows what became of the crown, but it was most likely melted down and repurposed."

"Perhaps one day you'll make another one."

She pressed the lump of wax between her palms, rolling it into a ball. "Nothing could ever equal the Atarah Hod."

"Why not?"

"Because legend says there was a special blessing on it, and it was meant to sit only on the head of a righteous king."

"You believe that to be true?"

"I don't have an answer to that. And it doesn't matter anyhow." She shrugged, her attention on her work. "It's gone."

By the time both of us were nearly asleep on our feet, we decided to rest and finish in the morning. Working with fire and wax was not something to be done with bleary eyes.

We unrolled the stack of blankets that we'd hastily packed the day after we'd been married. I expected her to argue, perhaps attempt to make her own bed across the tent from me, but instead she simply washed her hands and face by lamplight, rebraided her hair, and then after blowing out the light, lay herself down beside me. Granted, there was at least a cubit of space between us, but the thrill of victory inside me was intoxicating.

"Gavi?"

Another surge of something warm swam through my blood at the sound of my childhood nickname on her lips—one used almost exclusively by my family.

I hummed in response, not trusting my voice.

"How did my father know to trust you with our secret?"

I'd been asking myself the very same question. "The only thing I can think of is a brief conversation we had that day in the foundry."

A rustle told me she'd turned on her side, as if to watch me in the pitch-blackness. "Tell me."

"He mostly showed us weapons that day, things his men were working on. But then he brought out some jewelry." I'd interpreted the look on Barzel's face as pride for his craftsmanship as he laid out a necklace, a nose ring, and two cloak pins on a piece of soft brown wool. But instead, it had been fatherly boasting, pride for the talent of his daughter. "He said they were the very best pieces he had. That he expected a hefty price when he took them to Egypt in a couple of months. When I asked how they were made, he told me it was a family secret, which was not surprising. So I told him a secret like that should be protected at all costs."

"Only one born of our line can know," she said. "I took a vow."

The scar at the base of my thumb seemed to throb, reminding me that I'd not always held to my own vows in the past. With my head already clearer than it had been in months, perhaps years, I was determined to at least not fail in the one I'd made when I married this woman.

"I may still be a stranger to you, Zahava, and I've made some horrible mistakes in the past. But I meant what I said. I *will* protect you, your family, and your secrets with my life."

A startled inhale was her only response. Quiet reigned in our little tent for a long while, until I thought she'd gone to sleep.

"What mistakes have you made?" she whispered.

Perhaps it was that Shalem was already in my mind, or that it was easier in the dark, but I found myself confessing, "I chose my own ambitions over my cousin's life."

Her only response was to shift closer in silent encouragement, so I told her of how Shalem had followed Avi, Zevi, and me to battle across the river. How I'd refused to take him back to Naioth because I was desperate to prove myself and how when we'd returned to the cave we'd hidden him in and discovered he'd likely been killed by hyenas, I'd ignored Avi's plea to remain and search for him. Because I was frustrated he'd gotten in the way in the first place, and all I could think about was getting back to the army and impressing Yonatan.

"I practically willed him to disappear," I admitted. "And then I just accepted he was dead because it was easier for me to walk away and pursue my ambitions than it was to set them aside. When Avi returned from his search to tell us that Shay wasn't dead but still missing, well . . . let's just say I didn't handle it well."

In truth, that was the first time I took solace in a jug of wine, and even now, thinking about young Shalem, terrified and alone out there somewhere, made me ache for something to quell the choking guilt that rose up. There were jars of wine in the wagon, it would be so easy—

"He hasn't been found?" Zahava's sweet voice broke into my thinning resolve, and I was grateful for the distraction.

"A few years ago, Zevi happened across evidence Shalem was enslaved to some Phoenicians, but he lost the trail at the edge of Philistine territory." Letting out a sigh, I ran a hand over my face and the beard I'd not realized had grown so unruly. "The boy could be anywhere. Or maybe he truly is dead by now. I don't know. Either way, I failed him."

"You were all so young," she said. "It's not your fault, Gavi."

"But it is, though. He was just a *boy*. All he wanted was to be like us, to be included, and I was too mad at him for being in the way to care when he was gone." My voice broke on the admission I'd never spoken aloud before, not even to Avi and Zevi, who were once my closest friends in the world.

"I wish I could wipe away your pain." Her gentle voice was full of compassion. "But my father would say only El Shaddai is capable of that."

I'd been shocked to learn that Barzel worshiped the God my people revered, but perhaps I should not have been, seeing as how our people were distant cousins through Avraham. However, even if I'd seen evidence of his existence with my own eyes, I doubted the all-powerful deity who'd shaken the earth at Michmash cared anything much for me. I'd known that since I was a little boy and he had remained traitorously silent while I begged him to stop my mother from being beaten.

The next day, Zahava carved the wax pattern for the bit by lamplight inside our tent. The original one had been little more than a fat piece of copper wire twisted into a post the length of my middle finger. But she told me the new one would allow for much more control over the mule. Since I knew next to nothing about animals, I had to trust her knowledge. Besides, I was much more interested in watching her work. Her wax-carving tools showed evidence of long use after being passed down from father to son for generations, and she wielded them as though they were extensions of her own hands, in much the same way I did my weapons.

To keep the wax itself firm but pliable, she dipped it in tepid water every so often. The tip of her tongue poked out between her teeth as her nimble fingers smoothed the edges with a bone file. It was fascinating to watch and something I could never hope to do with my large hands and lack of patience. Casting a knife, honing its edge, and polishing it to perfection was one thing, but her attention to the most minute of details was impressive.

Once the pattern was nearly ready, she sent me to ask her mother for a small cooking pot, which Safaa handed over with reluctance, and asked me to fill it with the cleanest sand I could find, straining it with some loosely woven linen to eliminate any debris. This was a step I was very familiar with. I'd carved plenty of wooden patterns for daggers and knives and then pressed them into tight sand molds before pouring the molten metal inside. However, her delicate wax pattern required a soft touch and gentle packing of the dampened sand around her wax creation.

Once the mold was prepared to her satisfaction, it was my turn to take part in the process. We left the tent, and I built a fire in the pit. Once it was hot enough to satisfy her, Zahava placed a few copper ingots and carefully measured salts in a crucible. With her hands wrapped in protective leather, she held the crucible over the fire with long iron tongs while I manned the bellows.

Before the copper had completely melted, Zahava's sister Yasmin and her new husband appeared in our campsite. A flare of annoyance went through me at the intrusion, but I kept up my steady movement with the bellows.

"What are you two making over here?" asked Yasmin.

Zahava smiled at her sister as if nothing was amiss. "Ebenezer's bit broke. Abba asked Gavriel to make a new one, so I am assisting him. What are the two of you up to?"

I had to admit she was an excellent prevaricator. Probably from the last three years of hiding her brilliant skills in a cave. I wondered how much her sister knew about that secret because it was clear Rahm knew nothing at all. Strange, since he was not only her brother-in-law, but from what I'd seen at the foundry, one of Barzel's best bronzesmiths.

"I've missed you," Yasmin said. "I haven't seen much of you since our wedding." From the smitten gaze she set on her new husband, I doubted she'd given much thought to her sister over the past few days.

"I've missed you too. We'll come find you when he is done with the bit," Zahava said, maintaining her sunny expression. Then, without missing a beat, she added, "Gavriel, didn't you say something about needing to put more ingredients in the bowl soon?"

I halted the billows and searched the suddenly blank space in my head for a couple of panicked moments before grabbing hold of her meaning. "Tin. Yes. In that bowl by your knee."

I could practically feel the weight of Rahm's curious attention and cursed myself silently for being thrown off by Zahava's question. I knew very well how to alloy copper and tin to make bronze.

"I'll put them in for you," said Rahm, already snatching up the bowl of tin and swiftly tipping the shards into the blazing-hot crucible, as if to prove his expertise.

"Many thanks," I said, taking up the cadence of the bellows.

"Perhaps I should hold the tongs," he said to Zahava with a playful frown. "Your poor arms must be getting tired."

To my shock, Zahava's cheeks flushed. "I'm fine, Rahm. I'm glad to be of help."

"Don't get too close to the fire," he warned, tugging her long, black braid. "It would be awful if your hands were burned."

What in the—? Was this man flirting with my *wife*? And in

front of his own? Jealousy shot through me as hot as the pit near my feet. Rahm's easy touch and teasing manner with her seemed far too familiar.

"Are you certain I shouldn't take over?" he said to me, a pinch of what I sensed was false concern between his brows. "I know how particular Barzel can be."

"I have it well in hand," I said evenly, when I really wanted to tell the man to step away from my wife or have the fingers that touched her braid removed one by one.

"Yasmin," said Zahava, "can you ask Farah to bring us another jug of water from the spring right away? Gavriel said he needs more to cool off the metal when he's done, and I can't step away while he's working. And also there's a jar of honey right there by the tent door for Ima."

A flicker of confusion rippled over Yasmin's face. She must be just as surprised that Zahava was hiding her skill from Rahm as I was. But she schooled her expression swiftly.

"Of course!" She wove her fingers through Rahm's, dragging him along with her to fetch the jar. "Ima made a fresh batch of yogurt, and I love it with a drizzle of honey."

I watched them go, my hackles rising again when Rahm took one last look over his shoulder at us, belatedly giving me a tight smile and a nod. I stared back, blank-faced, practically daring him to come back and push me further.

I didn't know what exactly his issue was with me, but one thing was certain: He would be staying away from *my* wife in the future, or he and I would have far greater matters to discuss than a broken mule bit.

Zahava

Thankfully, Ebenezer's new bit held up well, since the next few days of travel were among the most grueling. Consistently uphill, the terrain wound through narrow valleys, some of which only allowed one wagon or handcart to pass through at a time. Our progress was slow, so I could have walked, but I was silently grateful Gavi still insisted I ride. There was no way my hips would be able to withstand such an arduous hike. There had been no more whispered conversations under the wagon at night because Gavi was asleep nearly the moment he laid his head down, after countless hours of pushing that cart. But at least he finally was sleeping deeply and undisturbed after those first few restless nights.

The shouting began not long after sunrise on the tenth day after we'd left Punon, while we were breaking camp. Screams reverberated off the hills around us, causing Gavi and me to pause with the tent wall we'd been folding suspended in the air between us. Our eyes met over the woolen fabric as more voices added to the chaos.

"An attack?" I asked.

He shook his head, coming forward to press the corners of the fabric into my hands. "Sounds more like an argument. I'll go see."

My curiosity sparked. I dropped the tent wall on the ground beside me. We could finish folding it later. "Take me with you."

My husband frowned. "Zahava . . ."

"Please, Gavi. I hate being left behind."

He flinched, as if what I'd said had struck a nerve. I held my breath, expecting him to ignore my plea and command me to wait for him to return. But then, to my surprise, a gleam of amusement came into his gray eyes. "All right. But stay close, my curious little wife."

We followed the shouts, Gavi kindly shortening his long stride for me as we wove through camp to where a group of onlookers was gathered around a couple of tents with unfamiliar patterns woven into their walls—certainly not anyone within my father's household.

In front of one of the tents, belongings were strewn all over the ground. Two veiled women huddled in the dirt with a few children clinging to them, and all of them in tears. Three men were brawling nearby, two against one.

"Stay here," Gavi said to me before heading straight into the fight without pause. He grabbed the first man he reached, snagging him by the tunic, and jerked him away from the one being beaten.

"What are you doing?" my husband demanded.

"I've been robbed. I want my silver." He twisted out of Gavi's hold just as the other attacker landed a vicious hit to the victim's jaw—although I wasn't certain how much of a victim he was if he'd robbed someone.

Gavriel tussled with the two men, shouting at them to stop fighting, but it wasn't until he knocked the first man on his backside and caught the other in a chokehold that either attacker listened.

From his place on the ground, the first man cursed Gavi. "Why are you taking the side of a thief?"

"I'm not," Gavi said, his grip on the second man remaining firm. "I'm merely trying to get the two of you to calm down so we can discuss this."

I'd known my husband was strong—that much was obvious by looking at him—but watching him take on two men alone, I was more impressed than I should be at such a show of brute strength. No wonder Adin said he was famous; if he was as skilled with a sword and spear as he was with his hands, he'd be formidable indeed.

"What is there to discuss? He robbed me, and I want it back."

"I did nothing of the sort," said the victim. "You had no right to ransack my belongings and frighten my wives."

"You had no right to steal from my wagon," snarled the first man.

"Let me go," rasped the second attacker, neck still clenched in the crook of Gavi's thick-muscled arm.

"My brother was only trying to help me," said the first man.

"I'll let him go if you'll stop fighting so I can figure out the truth here. If need be, we'll take it to my captain."

The second man lifted his hands in surrender, and Gavi released him. All three men were bloodied from the scuffle, but the victim had the brunt of the injuries, his nose gushing like a river.

"Now," said Gavi, looking amazingly unruffled, even though his tunic was soaked with the man's blood, "tell me what happened."

"We returned from the spring with water and found my handcart had been dug through, my purse missing."

"And why do you think it was this man?" Gavi pointed to the victim.

"Because when I asked around if anyone had seen anything, he refused to look me in the eye."

Not an admission of guilt, but certainly suspicious.

"I told you. It was not me," said the victim, pinching his nose with his fingers in an effort to stanch the blood. "I have no reason to steal from anyone."

As the crowd around us grew, the twitch of the door flap on the tent behind them caught my eye. Someone covertly peered out to witness the argument, and I blinked hard a few times to make certain I was not seeing things.

Wide-eyed and face pale, Niv stared back at me for a moment before disappearing inside the tent again. Stricken, my gaze was drawn back to the two veiled women and the boys clinging to them, all with distinctive red hair, just like their older sisters. Even after my warning, I'd never once considered that their family would try to join this caravan. Not only had Gavriel's captain made it clear that no Amalekites were to be among us on this journey—regardless of intermarriage—by order of King Saul, but Niv had told me her father would never leave Punon and that they would be well protected by the Amalekites because of their heritage. And yet here they were.

"Then it was one of your women," the first man was saying, turning to Gavi. "Search them."

"You already ripped our tent apart and terrified my children," snapped the man who must be Niv and Kila's father. "What more do you want?"

"I want my silver! It's all I have!" shouted the man, then without warning dashed toward the women. He grabbed the headscarf of the first one, yanking it off her head and away from her face. "One of you has it!"

A gasp traveled through the crowd around me. It took a couple of moments to realize why. The moon and star of Astarte was tattooed on her chin.

"She's Amalekite!" called someone.

"Look, an idol!" a woman shouted, pointing at something on the ground. "It's true!"

And sure enough, there on the ground, half hidden by a pile of bright-colored scarves, was a clay statue about the length of my forearm of a bare-breasted goddess, her beckoning arms outstretched to the sky.

Suddenly, no one cared much for the man's stolen silver. Calls went up around us for the council to be summoned.

The scene devolved again into chaos as someone else snatched the veil off the other woman to reveal her matching tattoo, the children wailed in terror, and Niv and Kila's bloodied father ran to defend his wives. When my two friends were dragged out of the tent, screaming, my knees nearly buckled. Was I to watch the young women who'd once come to my defense be stoned to death in front of my eyes?

Gavriel's eyes swung to me across the crowd, and as if I could see the conflicting thoughts written on his face, I knew the moment he decided it was a lost cause to try to keep order and to come for me instead.

He plowed through the baying crowd, eyes never leaving mine until he was directly in front of me, then without a word, he swept me into his arms and ran.

Gavi took me straight to my parents and had barely put me down before he began explaining to my father what was happening. Abba sent Farah to alert the other council members and then asked my husband to lead the way back to Niv and Kila's tent.

Dread filled my stomach to overflowing as they strode away. I was concerned for my friends, to be sure, but now I knew for certain that the Amalekite attacks that sent us fleeing was my fault. I was the one who'd divulged our imminent escape from Punon to Niv and Kila, and their father must have spread the news to his contacts in the city. I was the reason Zafir and Ashan had been killed, leaving behind their young families, and the reason my father and so many other Kenites had their flocks stolen and foundries ransacked.

Paralyzed with guilt, I sank down before the ashes of the cookfire as my mother directed Breena and Anaya to go to Yasmin's camp until she came for them. I barely noticed when she folded herself onto the ground beside me. It took only one stroke of her warm palm down the length of my back before the truth poured out: my friendship with Niv and Kila after they'd protected me, how they'd made me feel accepted, and how I'd set off such a horrible chain of events.

"And now they may be killed too. Everyone was so angry, Ima. . . ." I shook my head, too horrified and in shock to even cry. "I'll have not only Zafir and Ashan's deaths on my soul but Niv's and Kila's and their whole family as well."

"Are you so powerful, then?" she asked, with another comforting stroke down my hair.

I blinked at her. "What do you mean?"

"I mean that although you should have obeyed your father, it was their father who snuck in among us and hid the identities of his wives, against the express wishes of King Saul. I'm not certain how he even did so; he must have had some help. But regardless, you are not El Shaddai, and as I have told you girls, you are not responsible for any footsteps but your own."

I swallowed down the lump of tears forming in my throat. "But my actions caused so much loss. The flocks. The metalworks."

"On this score, at least, I can ease your burden greatly, daughter." She nudged my chin upward so I was looking at her. "It was not you who spilled the secret to the Amalekites, Zahava. It was two of the Kenite chieftains. In exchange for a cut of the spoils taken from our own people and the guarantee of protection, they went to Agag himself. You were in no way responsible for Zafir and Ashan's deaths, nor the loss of our flocks and herds."

Relief poured through my bones, and I slumped forward into my hands, tears finally spilling over as she slipped her arm around me and pulled me into her side. "As for the rest, my *kohav zahav*, haven't I told you all your life what you are made of and who made you?"

I nodded. The words of her song had been imprinted on me for as long as I could remember.

"Then you know that the Creator fashioned you from elements far stronger than iron and infinitely more precious than diamonds, my love. You have no need to turn to anyone but him for protection or to define your worth."

She pressed a kiss to the top of my head, and I stared into the ashes, waiting for Gavi and my father to return with news of Niv and Kila, and pleading silently with the Creator my abba and ima trusted so implicitly to show me how to do the same and make himself so apparent to me that I could not help but understand exactly who I was in his eyes.

However, by the time my husband and father did return with matching solemn expressions, followed by Rahm, no pillar of fire and smoke had manifested to show me the way, no voice trumpeted from the heavens to shake the ground.

"Barzel," said my mother, "what happened?"

My father hesitated, his nearly sightless eyes lifted to the northern hills. I chanced a glance at my own husband, but his attention was locked on the ground at his feet, his arms crossed tightly over his broad chest. Only Rahm met my eyes, frowning, with a look so piercing that I caught my breath and held it until his gaze slid away. What had happened to make all three of these men so unsettled? Had they indeed been witness to a stoning? A shiver raced up my spine at the thought of Niv and Kila suffering such a fate. Surely not their brothers too . . .

My father's deep voice broke into my morbid thoughts. "The man and his Amalekite wives have been sent away. They'll have to fend for themselves."

"They'll never survive," said my mother, "not in this harsh landscape."

"That is for El Shaddai to determine," said my father. "It is his decree that was flouted, after all. We were to disentangle ourselves completely from the Amalekites, without exception, in order to be protected. Such disobedience put this entire caravan at risk."

"Talmar is a good man," said Rahm, his voice sharper than I'd ever heard before. "He doesn't deserve to be cast out like this."

At the mention of the man's name, two things reordered themselves in my mind. The first was that I'd heard it before, when Rahm had spoken of the friend who'd arranged the commission of the sword for Agag, and the second was that Niv and Kila had told me of the connection between their father and Yasmin's husband.

"You knew him?" asked Gavi, his voice flat.

"Since I was a boy," Rahm said. "Our fathers were friends. He was only trying to protect his family. To provide for them. And the council has practically sentenced all of them to death with such an edict."

The hair on the back of my neck prickled at the vitriol behind his words. My mother had said Talmar must have had help to join our caravan. Surely it hadn't been Rahm, had it?

With an expression of banked fury, my father faced his son-in-law. "The council of this tribe made their decision based on the law given to Mosheh by El Shaddai himself. As resident foreigners among the Hebrews, in his mercy, we are to obey that law if we are to live in peace and safety in the Land. *Complete* separation from Amalek, and indeed from all idolatry, is not only necessary but essential to the survival of our people. There is no room for compromise."

"Is there no room for compassion, then?" Rahm said. "For the women and children?"

"Compassion cannot come at the expense of obedience. Yahweh is God above all others, able to discern the heart of each man and woman. He can see what we cannot—past, present, and future. So we must trust the Creator, even when it makes no earthly sense, or suffer the same consequences as those destined for destruction."

My father and Rahm stared at each other for a few long,

breathless moments, both unbending. For as long as I'd known him, Rahm had treated my father with the utmost respect, so to see him on the edge of defiance was truly shocking. But then, to my relief, Rahm's shoulders slumped, and he dropped his chin. "Of course you are right, Barzel. Forgive me for questioning your wisdom."

My father put his hand on Rahm's shoulder, giving it an affectionate squeeze. "It is not my wisdom you must honor in this, son, but that of El Shaddai. Now go find Yasmin and prepare your family to depart within the hour. We must get as close to Qadesh as possible by sundown."

Once Rahm had walked away, I came to my feet, breathing easier. My stomach ached knowing that Niv and Kila were out there in the wilderness now, in a place that Gavi told me was full of hostile desert tribes, but I was grateful the leaders had given their family mercy.

"Was the stolen silver found?" I asked my husband.

He cleared his throat and nodded without actually looking at me. "One of the man's daughters had it hidden on her person. It was returned to the rightful owner."

I caught my breath at the revelation.

"Also found on the girls were these," said my father, stretching out his hand. Two copper chains dangled from his fist, and on them, the two cylindrical seals I'd made for Niv and Kila.

I flinched as my father stared into my eyes, the disappointment in his own slashing into me like a sword. He knew I'd made them. Knew I'd defied his express command never to carve idolatrous images.

"Abba . . ." I began, although I wasn't certain what I could possibly say to mitigate what I'd done.

"Talmar's daughters were quite forthcoming about where they'd gotten these blasphemous objects, along with your reason for making them."

The air punched from my lungs and humiliation burned a path from the top of my head to the soles of my feet.

"They'd hoped their association with you would earn them a measure of mercy, but the decision of the council was final."

More shame rained down. Had all the Kenite chieftains been witness to the revelations of my foolishness and blatant disobedience? Worse, had Rahm? Had *Gavriel*? I could not even bear to look behind me, knowing I'd shamed him, too, with my deceit. Perhaps this fragile, unconsummated union between us was over before we'd even made it to Be'er Sheva.

That thought was the final blow. I sank to my knees before my father, tears dripping into the dirt as I bowed to prostrate myself at his feet.

"Forgive me, Abba. Please forgive me. I have no defense of my actions other than fear. I thought I would be forced to give up metalsmithing, that it would be forbidden if I married someone else."

"Had I ever given you the indication that would happen? That I would marry you off to someone who would strip you of my gift?"

"No—"

"I would not, Zahava. I would never give you to a man I did not believe would honor your talent or protect you from those who might take advantage of your knowledge. But Rahm was never for you. I'd always expected him to ask for Yasmin, which was why I did not choose from among the others. I was only waiting for him to gather the courage. He has worked hard in my foundry and will take over once I am no longer able to lead. But the ancestral secrets I passed to you are yours alone. No one will take them from you. You should have trusted me and your mother enough to know that we would choose the right man for you, one who would willingly lay down his life for you if necessary. You and Gavriel may have forced my hand with your exhibition that night, but when he looked ready to take my head off when I pretended to accuse you of harlotry, I knew he was the perfect choice."

I lifted my head, shocked. "You . . . that was an act?"

His brows pinched. "Of course, Zahava. You are the farthest thing from a wanton I can imagine. After the way Gavriel praised your work, before he knew it was yours, I was satisfied he would value your knowledge, but I had to make certain the man would vehemently defend you, even from me."

My eyes dropped to the seals in his hand. "Please forgive me for making those, Abba. I vow to you, I will never again carve anything that is an offense to El Shaddai."

"I'm glad to hear it." He handed them to me. "And since you made them, I expect *you* to destroy them."

I nodded, glad for the opportunity to wipe away at least one of my foolish decisions. "But will you forgive me for making them in the first place? For not trusting you?"

My father squatted down to look me straight in the eyes. "You are my precious daughter, given to me not just once but *twice* by the Creator and Protector of life—once when you were born and once when you were spared from the plague in his great mercy—mercy I did not deserve after I shook my fist at the heavens and cursed the Most High when my sons were taken from me."

My heart twisted at the revelation. I'd never known that my father had been so angry with Yahweh for the death of my brothers.

Abba lifted his leathery, burn-scarred palm to my cheek. "So why would I not forgive you, Zahava? When I myself have been forgiven so much?"

Gavriel

I was a coward. Running away while Zahava wept at her father's feet. But I could not bear to hear another word. It was too much. Instead, I went to help a few other Kenite families repack their carts and wagons and organize them back into a line, my head too muddled to do anything else but mindless labor.

And when the shofar blew to move out, I avoided looking in Zahava's direction as I retrieved the handcart, then let myself fall back into the endless sea of travelers as the caravan lurched into motion. I may be known as fearless in battle, but right now I had no idea how to face my wife.

With a jolt that shook my bones, the handcart shuddered and tipped sideways. Scrambling to right the top-heavy load, I gripped the handles, but whatever rut I'd hit was deep. The cart toppled to the left, spilling Barzel's belongings in a billowing puff of dust.

Staring at the mess, I bit my tongue against the explosive curses that welled up, kicking the side of the fallen cart, sorely tempted to just walk away and leave the fool thing there. From the way the

Kenites veered around me, there was probably a fair bit of violence on my face, enough that no one dared try to help.

This was ridiculous—all of it.

I was a soldier, not a pack mule. What was I even doing here in this godforsaken wilderness with a company that didn't trust me, a captain who despised me, and married to a woman who wanted someone else?

You'll never be enough.

My eye snagged on a wineskin peering out from beneath a jumble of blankets. I hadn't noticed it hidden in the handcart before but now I couldn't look away.

It was right there. All I had to do was reach down and grab it. Untie the spout and dump the contents directly into my throat. My hands twitched, and my mouth watered.

Just one drink. . . . It won't hurt anything. . . .

No! My fists balled against the driving urge. I would *not* give in. I was a warrior, and this was merely another battle I would win. I just had to fight harder. Dig in. And not give up. I wouldn't let Emmet have the satisfaction of stripping me of everything I'd worked for.

A low whistle came from my side. "Having some trouble there, Gav?"

I flinched but pointedly ignored Shachar. The last thing I needed right now was his jibes.

"Need some help?" Adin appeared at my other side.

Eyes dropping closed, I groaned. It was just my luck that the only two soldiers in this company who didn't avoid me would be here to witness my unraveling.

Of course, Shachar, being the blundering boar he was, disregarded all evidence that I was on the edge of losing my mind. "Where's your wife and her family? They banish you?"

I gritted my teeth. "No."

"So, what? You lost?"

More than he could ever guess, but I wasn't about to spill my guts alongside the contents of the handcart.

"Is Zahava all right?" asked Adin. "After what happened earlier?"

I leveled a glare on him. "Why, what did you hear?"

Brows high, he lifted his palms. "All I know is the captain said there was some sort of scuffle with the Kenites, and that you and she were there."

What had happened earlier had been far more than a mere scuffle. By the time I'd returned with Barzel, it had devolved even further. But thankfully, his booming command for quiet carried over the crowd, and even before the council had gathered, those who'd picked up stones to throw at the family had dropped them.

Honestly, I couldn't blame them for their anger. Talmar had endangered every man, woman, and child in this caravan with such deception. And I highly suspected Rahm had been involved in the scheme as well. He'd shrewdly submitted to Barzel before revealing his entanglement, but I'd be keeping a close eye on him in the future—for more reasons than one.

"Everything is fine." The lie tasted acrid. Although Zahava's father had been incredibly gracious to forgive her own deceit—and indeed, I'd actually been stunned by the man's benevolence with his daughter—I had no idea how to untangle my own thoughts about any of it.

"Why don't you go check on Barzel's family?" Shachar told Adin. "I'll help our friend here with his cart."

Adin frowned but gave me a friendly pat on the shoulder before walking away. I wasn't certain why he reminded me so much of Shalem. They looked nothing alike, so perhaps it was just that he always seemed to be underfoot when I was at my worst.

"Out with it," said Shachar once the young man had disappeared into the crowd.

"Excuse me?"

"Whatever has you a handsbreadth away from knocking back that bag of wine you were staring down . . . Tell me."

His demand was like a rusty blade over a raw wound.

"There's nothing to say."

He scoffed. "I'm not a fool, Gavriel. I haven't seen you more than a few feet away from that woman unless you were on watch since we left Punon."

My teeth ground hard against each other. Everything was a jumble in my head, and my tongue felt like it was tied in knots, so I said the first thing that spilled out.

"She doesn't want me."

"Well, that's a load of manure if I've ever smelled one."

I shrugged "It's true. She wants her sister's husband."

He wrinkled his features. "She told you that?"

"Unfortunately, I had to hear it from the daughters of the man who was expelled from the caravan. Apparently, my wife paid them to help her lure him into marriage."

Shachar scratched his cheek, looking perplexed. "And these women are trustworthy?"

I cleared my throat, thrown by the question. "Well . . . no. They were trying to barter for mercy with Barzel."

He folded his arms. "You think she'll be unfaithful, then?"

I winced. In truth, I couldn't even reconcile how she could ever entangle herself with those women. Not only because they were quick to give up her name at the first opportunity, but also because, to my shame, I'd known plenty of women like them over the past few years—the sort who did anything for attention and reveled in the power they had over men by flaunting their bodies. Zahava was nothing of the sort.

"Of course not, but I'd rather she not be pining after anyone else."

I was the worst of hypocrites for being jealous, especially when I'd known her for barely more than a week and had chased after plenty of women before I met her. But I could not help myself. No matter how it had happened, she was *my* wife now, and just the idea of her wanting that fool Rahm made my blood boil.

"Well then, make her pine after *you*, fool."

"I don't . . ." I blinked at him in bewilderment, then let out a hiss of frustration. "I don't have any idea how to do that. I've never tried to win a woman for more than a night."

He laid a heavy hand on my shoulder. "We've got a long walk ahead of us, my friend. We'll think of something. But first, let's lighten your load a bit."

With a grunt, Shachar squatted down, yanked the skin of wine from beneath the mess, then untied it and dumped it in the dirt. "There. Now let's get this thing upright."

Armed with the plan Shachar and I had devised, I pushed the handcart through the mass of Kenites already lifting tents and building cookfires just to the east of Qadesh, searching for Barzel's campsite. It wasn't long until sunset, and there was little time to waste in preparing for nightfall.

The moment I saw the wagon in the distance, my eyes searched for Zahava. But although Barzel and Safaa were working together to prepare a makeshift tent on one side of the wagon while Breena and Anaya were retrieving supplies from the baskets, Zahava and Farah were nowhere to be seen.

"There you are, Gavriel!" said Safaa, approaching with a smile that made no sense. "I need my best copper pot for the stew, and you have it in the cart."

I searched for the pot in the handcart and gave it to Zahava's mother. "It may have a dent or two," I admitted. "You must forgive me, I hit a rut and the load toppled."

She smoothed a palm over its sides. "Not to worry, this old

pot has been through plenty. A dent or two won't keep her from her purpose."

"How can I help?" I asked.

"Your friend Adin escorted Farah and Zahava over there with the goats a while ago." She gestured toward the hill just to the south of us. "There's some lovely grasses on the slope up in those trees. Perhaps you can help herd them all back before the sun sets?"

"Of course."

"You've taken good care of my girl so far, young man." She reached up to pat my cheek. "All will be well. Trust Yahweh."

It was almost as if my own ima were standing in her place, with her round face and wild black-and-silver curls and unconditional love in her brown eyes. I cleared my throat twice before I was able to speak. "I'll make sure she . . . they all get back safely."

"Don't take too long. My sabra stew is not to be missed. The girls found some along the road. With some garlic, onion, and dried meat, along with my own blend of spices, you'll go to sleep with a full and satisfied belly."

For five years, I'd stayed away from Ramah. I'd only seen my mother and sisters when I managed to attend a handful of festival gatherings in Naioth—which I knew Hanan rarely attended. Maybe it was because of Zahava and her sisters, or that my head wasn't so hazy now, but for some reason over the past couple of weeks, my family had been on my mind a great deal. Safaa's kindness, in spite of everything, not only made my heart ache for them but also caused guilt to coat the back of my tongue. No matter what had happened between me and Hanan, I should not have stayed away so long.

"Gavriel, can I have a word?" Barzel called out, waving me over.

My stomach twisted, but I sucked in a deep breath, preparing myself for whatever Barzel had to say about my disappearance today. The man had every right to excoriate me after I'd selfishly abandoned his family on the road today.

"I have a favor to ask of you," he said before I could form a coherent apology.

"Anything."

"Tomorrow, a group of Kenites are going into Qadesh to trade for supplies. I believe your captain is sending in a few of your fellow soldiers as well. I need to sell some of Zahava's jewelry, but I'd rather not bumble around in a city I don't know." He frowned. "It was hard enough when I knew every trail, every tent by heart in Punon. Perhaps you'll go in my stead? It's important we get the best price. We don't have much of value left after the Amalekites ransacked my foundry. Until we can set up a workshop for her in Be'er Sheva and get our hands on some ore, things will be lean."

I was astonished he would put his trust in me, especially with so much at stake. I gave a small bow. "I would be honored to do so. And please, forgive my disappearance today—"

He cut me off with a wave of his hand. "You had much to consider, son. Think nothing of it. I knew you'd be back for her."

"I made a vow to her."

He peered at me with such piercing intensity it was hard to believe his eyes were damaged. "I went against generations of tradition to marry my daughter to you, Gavriel. You are not of our clan. Not even a tribesman. But I meant what I said. You *are* the right man for her."

"How can you know that?" The words came out in a choked whisper.

"Because for months—years, really—I'd been asking for divine wisdom in choosing a husband for her. And then as you knelt before me, half-drunk and terrified I would have you killed for shaming Zahava in front of the entire tribe, Yahweh told me clearly, 'This one.'"

I flinched. "What? Why?"

He shrugged. "I don't ask the why of the Almighty One, Gavriel. I simply trust him and obey."

It took little effort to find Farah and Adin, along with her little herd of goats that were enjoying the sweet grasses around a copse of wild olive trees. With their backs to me, the two of them had been talking so intently as they plucked ripe olives that they both jumped when I asked where my wife had gone.

"She's up there," said Farah, pointing to the top of the ridge. "Said she wanted to see the sun go down."

"Your mother says to hurry back for the meal." I turned to Adin. "And I would guess Emmet is wondering where you are."

He blanched, as if he'd entirely forgotten he had a job to do. And it *wasn't* flirting with Zahava's sister.

He cleared his throat and looked to Farah. "I'll help you get the goats back."

A smile quirked her lips. "I've been driving this herd since I could walk. I'm fine. Run on back to your captain."

He winced at the clear dismissal. Farah had not only made her lack of interest clear but implied he was little more than a child.

Adin stiffened, gave her a nod, and silently walked away.

"And I thought it was bad when you kicked my ribs in," I murmured.

She watched him go, a tiny wrinkle between her brows. "He's a boy."

"He's a year older than you."

"Doesn't matter. I don't have time for that nonsense."

"I said the same thing for years." I chuckled under my breath as I looked toward the ridge. "And yet . . . here I am."

Farah glanced over her shoulder. "You'll keep her safe?"

I let out a slow breath. "Always."

She nodded, then summoned the goats, who immediately trotted toward their shepherdess, calling out with their odd, warbly voices as they came. I didn't wait for them to get any closer before striding away. There was just something about those strange rectangular pupils that raised the hair on the back of my neck.

I found my wife on the ground under an olive tree, arms around her knees and eyes pinned on the far horizon, where the sun had just set foot on the hills behind Qadesh, gilding them in red-gold. I settled down beside her, and together we watched as the sky turned to fire. Although I'd planned with Shachar what to say, my mouth had gone dry. I couldn't seem to find the right words to begin.

She beat me to it.

"Those ideas I had . . . about Rahm, I mean. That was all before." She swallowed hard, skin flushing, her gaze still on the brilliant display in the sky. "It was before I'd met you. Before the announcement was made of their betrothal. And it wasn't a true possibility, anyhow. It was simply the foolish imagination of a girl with no prospects, I assure you. There was never any reciprocation."

A foolish rush of relief tunneled through my veins. Whether or not I'd had a right to be jealous of her hopes before I'd barreled into her life, it was good to hear there'd been nothing mutual. My murderous thoughts toward Rahm ebbed slightly, even if I still didn't trust him.

I cleared my throat as I tried to find the right words for my own confession. My tongue felt thick and clumsy. "I have no right to judge you for anything that happened before our marriage and certainly not for wanting a husband to protect you and your talents. I'd never planned to marry and so I lived like . . . like an . . . unattached soldier." I cringed at my own admission, heat crawling up my neck. I'd gone many years without caring what others thought of my woman-chasing ways, but it turned my stomach to think of Zahava being horrified by my dissolute behavior.

"I know," she said. "Adin told me about your . . . *affinity* for women. And theirs for you."

With a groan, I scrubbed a hand over my face. "Of course he did."

"It's all right. You were forced to marry me, after all. You never expected this." The resignation in her voice shamed me.

"I want you to know that I would *never* dishonor you, Zahava."

Finally, she turned to face me, resting her cheek on her knee. "I believe you."

"You do?"

"I may not know you very well, Gavi, but you have been nothing but honorable in a situation you did not choose for yourself." Although her words were generous, her tone was flat. She may believe I would not shame her by chasing after other women, but I suspected she did not fully trust me. And I did not blame her. I barely trusted myself. But I would do my best to be worthy of Zahava, who was everything good and kind. And I would start by following Shachar's advice.

"I have something for you." I reached into the small satchel tied to my belt, past Shalem's little knife, and tugged out my gift. The broken ax head was coated with a thin green patina but was weighty—fully bronze, if I had to guess. I handed it to her.

"Where did you find this?"

"Shachar found it in a wadi, half-buried in the ground. He gave it to me."

"I don't think it's fixable," she said, turning it over in her hand. "Not unless you find the other half, and even then it would require a very hot flame to weld it together."

"It's for you. I mean . . . I was going to pick some flowers." I scratched at the back of my neck, feeling like an utter dolt. "They were yellow, and I remembered Barzel called you his golden star, so I thought maybe you would like them. But then Shachar gave me this and—" I shrugged, my face hot as a crucible. "I figured you'd have some use for it. To make something that would last longer than a handful of dead flowers."

Zahava's hazel eyes met mine and held as she wrapped her hands around the ax head and pulled it close to her abdomen, almost as if she was fearful I would snatch it back. "This is so thoughtful, Gavi. Thank you. I'm certain I can make something of it."

Victory buzzed in my bones. Who knew pleasing Zahava in such a simple way would feel better than felling a giant? It made me blurt out the idea I'd had on the walk up here.

"Your father asked me to barter for supplies in his place when the others go into Qadesh. Would you like to go with me?"

Her long black eyelashes fluttered. "You want *me* to go?"

The delight in her voice sent another ripple of triumph through me. Above all things, I'd learned that Zahava *hated* being left behind. *Just like Shalem*, an accusing voice whispered, but I forced it away.

"Isn't it dangerous?" she asked.

That was true. From what Shachar said, although Qadesh was technically with the territory of Yehudah, the city sat at the crosspoint of trading roads that served plenty of hostile areas. There was no way to know who might be friend or foe. But I'd been in plenty of cities like Qadesh before.

"You'll be with me, Zahava, and I'll always protect you." The vow was easily given, and I meant it with every drop of blood in my body. "If anything, your presence will detract from suspicions. A man traveling with his wife is of no consequence. Besides"—I grinned, knowing the leverage I had—"it's your work I'm trading. Don't you want to see what price we can secure?"

Even in the dimming twilight, I saw her eyes go wide. I'd guessed she'd never gone with her father when he traded her pieces and that her natural curiosity would make my case for me.

"I would love to . . . but I don't want to hold you back. What if—?"

I spoke over her. "You are not a hindrance, Zahava. You are an asset."

She pressed her lips together, her eyes reflecting the last of the golden light edging the hills. "Then I would very much like to go."

Again, that odd sensation of triumph welled up in my chest. "I'm glad to hear it. Now, your mother sent me to fetch you for the meal. Should we head back?"

She let out a sigh, her attention drawn back to the deepening sky. "I'm not quite ready to go back to camp. It's so quiet up here."

Although my empty stomach was eager for some of Safaa's stew, the chance to please Zahava again won out, so I stretched out my legs and settled against the olive tree. "Take as long as you need, little dove."

Zahava

I'd lived in the Punon Valley my entire life and yet had never been inside the city walls, since my father declared it unsafe for Kenite women to venture into the Amalekite stronghold. So riding into Qadesh beside my husband on the wagon was like entering an entirely different world.

Stone buildings two and three stories high ushered us deeper into the city as merchants called out their wares from shop windows beneath multicolored awnings. My eyes could not alight on any one thing as we rambled toward the central market. With hordes of stalls boasting every sort of good imaginable under endlessly vibrant canopies, a stream of camels, mules, and other pack animals, and flocks of tradespeople and customers speaking languages I'd never heard before, my mind could not contain it all. Pulling my headscarf tighter over my face, I pressed a little closer to Gavi and his increasingly reassuring presence at my side.

Even though he was dressed only in a simple tunic and a thick leather belt, having left his armor behind, he'd assured me he was taking no chances today. There were daggers strapped to both his thighs and knives tucked stealthily into his belt.

"Relax your body, little dove," he murmured, giving two gawkers a friendly nod. I wasn't sure how he could be so calm with all this jarring noise and chaos flowing around us. But there was no fear on his face as he met my gaze. "I am glad you came today."

"You are?" I thought for certain he'd regret the invitation.

A little smile ticked on his lips, which were easier to see since he'd trimmed down his crazy bush of a beard. He'd even oiled his curls and pulled them into a knot at his nape. I'd been startled at the change; he looked a great deal younger and vastly more handsome. Even Farah had mentioned the drastic difference, poking at me for staring at my own husband all morning.

"You're going to run someone over," called Shachar from the bed of the wagon. "How about you look at the road instead of your wife?"

Gavi glared over his shoulder. "You want your jaw to match your ugly nose?"

In the wagon bed beside Shachar, Adin was red-faced from holding back laughter. Gavi's toothless threat broke them both, their guffaws drawing far more attention to the four of us than was wise. Still, I could not help joining in the laughter. Although Gavi called them both idiots before turning back to drive the mules, he gave me a covert wink.

Gavi drove as close as possible to the main square before the street became too crowded to continue, and then we left Shachar and Adin to watch over the wagon and began our search for a jewelry merchant.

To my surprise, Gavi reached for my hand as we walked, keeping me close and steady as we passed by stalls of fresh fruits and vegetables, baked goods, grains, spices, fabrics of every hue and pattern, leather goods, and pottery, along with animals of every shape and size. The dust kicked up by myriad feet, hooves, and paws stung my eyes, and the heat of so many bodies pressed into the marketplace made sweat trickle down my spine.

Once we emerged from the worst of the crowd, Gavi spotted a shop at one end of the square, with long tables boasting a variety of copper necklaces, rings, and bracelets. None of which I, or anyone with a true eye for such things, would consider high quality.

"There's nothing of your caliber," Gavi murmured, echoing my thoughts. I glanced pointedly to where two armed guards stood near the open door, which meant the real treasures lay inside.

Thankfully, Gavi understood and approached the merchant manning the table. "Is the owner available? I have a trade to offer."

"And what is it you have?"

"That's between myself and the owner."

The man pressed his tongue into the wide gap between his front teeth. "I'll make that call."

"The shop down the street was much more amenable. Come on," Gavi said to me with a lazy shrug, "we'll take their offer after all."

He tugged me with him as he took a couple of steps away, then halted when a raspy female voice called out, "What do you have?"

An Egyptian woman a little older than my own mother stood at the threshold of the shop, piercing black eyes focused on my husband.

"I'd be happy to show the owner," he said with a challenging arch of his brow.

She narrowed her eyes for a moment, her gaze moving back and forth between the two of us. "It had better be worth my time."

Gavi didn't so much as blink. "It is, I assure you."

She beckoned us inside with a jerk of her chin.

My husband leaned to speak in my ear. "I may not have experience bartering jewelry, but I do know how to charm a woman." He gave a little wink as he stepped over the threshold.

However, a quarter of an hour later, I'd decided perhaps he'd overestimated his persuasiveness, at least with a woman like Thema, who was far more stubborn than Ebenezer and Ida combined.

"That's the price I can offer." Hands splayed in a gesture of helplessness, she remained unmoved on her end of the bargain, nearly half the price the jeweled necklace and twin bangles on the table between us were worth. "I have to make a profit, you understand."

None of Gavi's flatteries had yielded anything but flat looks from Thema, and she brushed aside his every attempt at softening her resolve. I could practically feel the frustration vibrating off my husband as his hopes for a profitable trade evaporated. I, however, had spent the time they'd been dickering back and forth examining the rest of the shop's offerings. The pieces were vastly better than the ones outside on the table but not anywhere near the quality I produced. It was an insult to my hard work that she'd try to undercut their value.

Unbidden, my own frustrations tumbled out of my mouth. "You have nothing in this shop to compare to the pieces we brought here." Gavi turned to gape at me, bewildered by my interjection. But it was too late to reel back my words now. I wouldn't let him go back to my father empty-handed. We needed those supplies.

"Strength and beauty, love refined, in you his perfect craft combined . . ."

With the words from my mother's song echoing in my heart, I gestured to where a few golden rings were displayed cleverly on carved wooden hands, all set with various precious and semiprecious stones. "Most of these are so soft they'd fall off a wearer after a day or two. And the stones will disappear long before that for the weakness of the settings. They may look beautiful, but they are useless."

Although my knees trembled, I set my gaze on Thema. Her expression was still flat, but there was a spark of curiosity in her dark eyes. I took her silence as invitation to continue.

"And these—" I gestured to a row of necklaces sprawled over

a black wool table covering, each bearing Egyptian-style amulets of various gods and goddesses. "The clasps are sloppily crafted, patched together with brittle joints, and won't bear the weight of those amulets."

Pulse thrumming, I continued to make my way around the shop, describing the faults in most of the offerings, except for a set of gold armbands in the shape of serpents, which truly were masterfully crafted, and a set of silver haircombs inlaid with brilliant turquoise, which were exquisite by any measure.

When I was done, I faced the formidable woman again. "On the other hand, the pieces we've brought are without question superior. They were made by Kenite hands, which, by virtue of their origin alone, will fetch you three times or more in Egypt than the paltry sum you've offered my husband. So either you adjust your offer accordingly, or we will indeed find another merchant to give us what they are worth."

Thema's fists had gone to her ample hips as I spoke, her chin high as she stared me down for a few tense moments. Then, to my utter astonishment, a smile played at the corners of her thin lips. "So it's like that, is it?"

I remained still as stone, lifting only one brow in acknowledgment of her challenge.

"You have more?" Expression knowing, Thema directed the question to me, *not* my husband.

I swallowed hard. Admitting the truth that I was responsible for these pieces, and therefore breaking the promise I'd made my father, could either be the most foolish thing I'd ever do, or the wisest. But without a place to sell the things I made, there was no use for them at all. I could only hope my father would once again forgive me for the sake of rebuilding everything he'd lost.

I let out the breath I'd been holding. "I do. However, we plan to settle near Be'er Sheva."

Thema's shoulders fell a little, but then she rapped her fingers on the table. "I have a man who travels up through there every couple of months. You save your best pieces for me, and I'll make certain the women of Avaris will scratch each other's eyes out to get their hennaed claws on them."

"I'll need ore."

"Done. Shipments from the Timna mines come directly through Qadesh on their way north to Gaza and Damascus. And I have a contact for gold shipped directly from Ofir via the Red Sea."

Ofir? Even my father had never found a source from the gold mines famed for unmatched quality. My heart thumped. *Am I truly going to do this?*

I considered the other promise I'd made to my abba, one I had no intention of breaking again, even if it ended this negotiation. I straightened my shoulders. "I do not carve idols or make graven images. Ever."

Her brows pinched, but she waved a dismissive palm. "As long as you make beautiful things, I can sell them."

Relieved, I exhaled a shuddery breath. "And no one knows who made the jewelry. *Especially* not a woman. Do we have a deal?"

Thema pursed her lips, her dark eyes studying me from head to toe and then back again. Then her face softened, wrinkles forming at her eyes as a wide smile stretched over her face.

"We have a deal."

18

Gavriel

Zahava was still shaking when we arrived back at the wagon, the purse around my neck heavy with silver. Not only had Thema given us above the price we asked, but she and Zahava had spent nearly an hour discussing what sorts of items the women of Egypt would salivate over and scheming together about the fledgling partnership they'd formed, including Thema's promise that Zahava would have plenty of metal and an array of gemstones to work with.

"Where have you two been?" asked Shachar, sweat curling what remained of his light brown hair.

"Ask my wife. The businesswoman." Zahava's face went red as a pomegranate. "She drove such a hard bargain with the shopkeeper, the woman was practically on her knees." I'd never reveal the truth about why she'd been so successful, but I would not let her get away without taking some credit today.

Before they could ask more, two of Emmet's men approached, their backs laden with supplies.

"Saw some Kenites at the tavern," said Obadyah. "Bringing a little too much attention to themselves."

Everyone had been given explicit instructions about our conduct here. Emmet would not be pleased.

"Why are you telling me?" I asked.

Tuval folded his arms over his thick chest, battle scars on full display. "Because one of them is your brother-in-law."

Rahm. The man had become a thorn in my sandal. What was he even doing here? He was not the head of a large household like Barzel; only those within his own small family unit.

Hands on my hips and head down, I let out a long sigh. I'd been looking forward to purchasing our supplies and returning to camp well before sundown, but I could not leave Rahm behind. Besides, Barzel would want me to make certain Rahm did not get himself into trouble.

Leaving both my wife and the purse with Shachar and Adin, I followed Tuval and Obadyah to the local tavern, a large establishment near the marketplace, where even the benches outside were overflowing with patrons of every ilk.

I took a deep breath before going inside. The smell of beer hit my nostrils like a team of horses, hanging so thick in the air I could practically taste it. Unbidden, my mouth watered. My eyes landed on a full cup of strong drink in one man's hand as he told a story to his tablemates, and I could feel the liquid sliding down my parched throat, warming my belly, and seeping into my veins.

"He's over there," said Obadyah, breaking into my rebellious thoughts.

I blinked, holding my breath for the count of three before following his gesture to where Rahm and another Kenite I'd never seen before sat with a few men whose origins I could not divine from across the room. Egyptians, perhaps, by the cut of the linen kilts around their hips. Rahm barked a laugh, his eyes bright with drink.

Weaving my way through the packed room, I positioned myself directly in Rahm's sights. He didn't notice, too busy regaling his new friends with the details of a sword he'd been working on for some powerful Amalekite. My neck prickled. *Drawing attention to himself indeed.*

His friend noticed me first and nudged Rahm, giving him a tip of his chin to alert Yasmin's fool of a husband to my presence.

"Ah! If it isn't my *brother-in-law*," Rahm slurred. "Where's our little Zaza?" He peered past me as if I'd bring my innocent wife into a place like this, where at least four scantily clad prostitutes were draped over patrons around the room. My stomach roiled at the idea of Zahava anywhere near this building, along with the realization that not that long ago I would have thought nothing of pulling one of those wantons onto my own lap.

You are worthless. Filthy, the voice whispered.

"Time to go," I said, forcing aside the accusations. "Your own wife is waiting on you."

He laughed and shook his cup at me, and it sloshed onto the table. "I'm not done yet. Sit down! Have a drink. Oh! Wait." He slapped a palm over his mouth. "You're not allowed, are you?" He clucked his tongue. "Water only. Isn't that right? I wonder what you did to be put in the corner?"

He and his friends guffawed as chills broke out on my neck and arms. Who had told him about Emmet's edict? But I shook my head. It made no difference. All that mattered was getting these two out of here without causing more of a scene than they already had.

"Let's go," I said, infusing my voice with authority I did not actually possess.

"Let the man finish his drink," said one of his tablemates with a heavy accent. "We were having a conversation."

I took a closer look at the man, at the ivory plugs in his ears and the black symbols scrolling down his thick arms as well as marking the sides of his shaved head. My blood went cold. These were no Egyptians. These were Philistines.

Alarm pulsed through my limbs. Not only had I met men like these on the battlefield, I'd grown up fascinated by similar tattoos on my uncle Natan, the only part of his heritage he could not scrub away when he'd entered into Covenant with Yahweh and his people.

Visions from Michmash, of men like these with feathered headdresses and blood-spattered faces charging toward me, thundered through my head. But I'd been trained by the best: Yonatan ben Saul. And I'd spent plenty of time in enemy territory, acting the part of a mercenary-for-hire who was disgusted with my own king and eager to betray my own people for silver.

I arranged my features into a lazy grin. "Well, my friends, I'd be happy to do so, but his mother sent me to drag his sorry hide home. She's threatening *her sandal*." I loudly whispered the last two words behind my hand, eyes wide. "And Rahm here hates disappointing his ima."

The look of pure hatred from Yasmin's husband was unsurprising, but after a couple of drawn-out moments, he tipped his cup back and drained it in a gulp, then slammed it on the table.

"Remember what I said," he told his new friends.

The men said nothing but watched Rahm weave through the crowded room, his companion stumbling along at his heels.

"What are you doing with those Kenites, *Hebrew*?" The Philistine spat the word like a curse, his keen gaze tracking over me, as if he could sense the weapons tied to my thighs and hidden in my belt.

"Didn't you hear the man? I'm married to his wife's sister. His people are mine now." It would be nothing to slip my knives from my belt, let them fly across the table, and hit them both in the throat. But for Zahava's sake, I tipped my chin in the semblance of a friendly farewell to men who made my skin crawl and, against every screaming instinct, turned my back on my enemies.

I took no more than five steps across the room when a man twisted to the side and hurled his stinking guts on the floor a handspan from my sandals. Drooling, the drunkard wiped his hand over his mouth and gagged again, spewing bile down the front of his own tunic. Then, eyes rolling, his head crashed to the table, sending his half-empty beer cup rolling into another patron.

Steering around the putrid mess, I headed for the door.

That was you, came the voice. *That disgusting mess. You've woken in your own sick more times than you can count.*

It was true. I'd been just as bad. Just as out of control. Just as pitiful as the men who were probably drinking away most of their day's wages, just as I'd done.

But even if that old voice continued to rail at me, to spit accusations, my mind was sharper and clearer now that it had been in years. Yes, I'd been that man. I'd let down my commander. My fellow soldiers. And my family.

But if Zahava could shoulder pain every day of her life without complaint, suffer the humiliation of being treated as some sort of broken vessel with grace, and hold her head high when others took credit for her extraordinary talent, then surely I could become the sort of man who was worthy of her—or at least attempt to come close.

Rahm was waiting outside for me, his back against the stone wall. "Don't need a nursemaid. I'm plenty capable of handling myself. I was making business contacts—profitable ones."

"Apparently you do. Besides, those aren't the sort of connections that will benefit us."

He sneered. "You *aren't* one of us, Hebrew. You never will be."

It was odd how much the sharp-edged quip smarted.

"I am married to Zahava," I said. "Therefore, her family is my own."

His eyes narrowed as he pushed off the wall. "You won't get it. I won't let you."

"Get what?"

"The inheritance. It's *mine*."

I threw up my hands in surrender. "I know nothing about an inheritance."

His face twitched. "I know he's nearly blind. It's only a matter of time before he turns it over."

"I don't know what—"

He cut me off with a curse. "I'm not a fool. I *know* what's going on. Your little trip to that Egyptian jeweler today confirmed it."

Hair rose on the back of my neck, but I held very still. Any reaction on my part might only serve to confirm his suspicions, whatever they may be.

"If Barzel thinks he can cut me out and replace me with some thick-skulled foreign soldier who hasn't spent the past twelve years slaving away in his foundry, then he's very wrong. The other chieftains won't countenance such an action, anyhow."

I held back a relieved sigh. This was about misplaced jealousy, not about Zahava's talent. "I have no aims to replace you, Rahm. You are married to Barzel's eldest daughter. You'll have to discuss his choice of heir with him. And truth be told, I have no need for any sort of inheritance. Zahava is all the reward I need."

The truth was easy to speak. I'd never given a moment's thought to what sort of woman would complement me, since I'd never planned to marry at all. But I was beginning to think Zahava was the only one I would want to be at my side. Besides, if all the riches in Hanan's treasury didn't tempt me to bend my knee to him, Barzel's wealth—whatever was left of it—certainly was no enticement.

"Perhaps I married the wrong daughter, then. Apparently, your *wife* wanted me first, anyhow."

I refused to let him see the fury searing through my body. He was drunk, spouting off and trying his best to get under my skin. A couple of months ago, I would have already knocked the smug look off his face. But for the first time in my life, I had no problem walking away from a fight.

I'd promised Zahava that I would protect her. And I was not going to let her down. However, I couldn't resist getting at least one good shot in before I walked away and left the two drunkards to stumble back to camp alone.

"Well, she's mine now, my friend. So your choice is on you."

Zahava

Gavi returned from the tavern with a grim expression I could not decipher. But he was far too focused on procuring goods and returning to camp for me to ask what had happened with Rahm. Whatever it was had stolen the smile from his face after our triumph with Thema and replaced it with single-minded determination. I'd have to be patient and ask him later. Perhaps once we were under the wagon in the quiet place we'd found there, tucked away from the world.

In fact, I'd come to yearn for nightfall just so I could lay beside him, even when he was too exhausted to do anything but sleep. But the nights when we whispered together, about anything and everything, long after the moon rose, had become my favorite. I'd even come to begrudge the sight of first light because it meant disentangling myself from Gavi's strong, warm arms.

Adin was left with the empty wagon while Shachar took a few pieces of silver to purchase grain. Gavi and I headed back into the crowded marketplace to look for olive oil and other perishables to sustain us until Be'er Sheva. I was surprised at the vast array of fruits and vegetables available in this town, but we came to discover that Qadesh was situated near four springs, allowing for prolific cultivation one would not expect in the vast desert. No wonder the ancient Hebrews had spent much of their time here during their forty years in the wilderness.

Once the wagon was loaded and Gavi had lifted me to my seat at the end of the bed, we left Qadesh behind, setting a steady pace toward the camp two hours back. Shachar and Adin rode on the wagon bench while Gavi walked a few paces behind, his gaze roving the road ahead and the area around, alert for danger as always. I spent the ride dreaming up new designs for jewelry Thema could sell in Egypt based on some of the beautiful patterns I'd seen on the fabric at the market and painted on pottery from places as far away as Midian and Tyre.

An hour into the journey, two of Emmet's men caught up to us at a swift jog, full packs of provisions on their backs, and asked whether Gavi had heard about Punon. My stomach jolted at the ominous question, along with the concerned glance Gavi flicked my way before saying he'd heard nothing.

"Saul wiped them all out," said the tallest of the two Hebrews, whose thick hair was shaved nearly to the scalp.

Dread trickled through my veins. *All of them?* I'd known there was to be a battle and everyone who remained was in danger, but did that mean the women too? And the children? My throat ached. There were plenty of Kenites who'd stayed behind to take their chances in Punon. Were they slaughtered as well?

The other, a shorter man with half of an ear missing, grinned widely. "Rumor is he even has Agag on the run."

"Saul vowed to pursue whoever is left from Havilah to Shur," said the tall one. "Amalek will never bother us again."

"Yes, and I heard they—"

Gavi raised his palm, halting the crowing of One Ear about

the king's victory. "You'd best hurry on and take the news to the captain, Korach. My wife does not need to hear the details."

The men blinked at him in confusion, then shifted their gazes to me. I saw the instant they remembered my heritage.

"Of course," said Korach, smacking his companion's chest with the back of his hand. "Let's go, Ithiel."

Shame-faced, they mumbled apologies and then jogged on. We traveled in silence until Shachar announced we were in sight of the camp, but I wasn't quite ready to return to hear my family discuss what had happened in the Punon Valley.

Besides, my tailbone was aching from sitting so long.

"Stop the wagon!" I called out.

"What's wrong?" asked Gavi, hurrying to catch up.

"Nothing, but I need to get off. Now."

"Halt!" Gavi cried out over the clatter of hooves and wheels on the dry streambed we'd been following.

Shachar jerked the mules to a stop, peering over his shoulder. "What's wrong?"

I did not wait for Gavi to help me down, slipping off the end of the wagon bed, then grabbing my father's staff. "Nothing. I'm walking the rest of the way."

The men exchanged glances.

"It's all right," said Gavi, "You two go on back. Let Barzel know we'll be there soon."

The wagon clattered on, sloping down into the valley where more than a few cookfires flickered, the peaceful scene promising rest and nourishment. And yet even the thought of food caused my stomach to roil.

"I'm sorry you heard that," said Gavi without looking at me. "I should have stopped him."

I sighed. "I would find out sooner or later. Everyone in camp will know by nightfall. But I don't understand. Did he mean that Saul slayed women and children too?"

He paused, looking off in the eastern distance, as if he could see all the way to Punon. "He did."

Nausea rolled up my throat at the confirmation. "But why? I knew there would be war but *slaughter*?"

Gavi shook his head. "I wish I had the answers, Zahava. The command from Yahweh through Samuel was very clear: *Every* Amalekite was to be killed, without exception."

I'd spent my life hearing my father tell stories of the Mighty God of the Mountain, of how he'd led his people out from Egypt and into the Land of Promise. I knew Yehoshua went to war with the tribes of Canaan that had refused to leave, but to wipe out an entire people? That did not reconcile with what I knew of Yahweh.

"You have to understand," said Gavi, "it's been hundreds of years since Yahweh declared Amalek's destruction at Yehoshua's hands, an edict that was not fully obeyed."

I knew the fraught history between Amalek and Israel, had listened to the stories of Yehoshua's conquest of Canaan, but had no idea that Yahweh had declared the destruction of the people my own had allied with for so long.

"We have been dealing with constant threat of annihilation from Amalek and its allies for as long as we've been a nation. And every generation is brought up to nurture hatred of us. They seethe with it from their early years. You know this; you've lived among them."

I did know it. Even though I'd had little contact with Amalekites over the years, it was common knowledge they had no greater enemy than Israel. Rumors of raids into Hebrew territory were common. In fact, the only Hebrews I'd seen before Gavi and his unit came into the valley were slaves either forced to work in the mines or chained to drudgery in Amalekite households, treated as little more than chattel.

"We've made peace, however tense, with most of the nations around us, or intimidated them enough to leave us alone. Except, of course, the Philistines and Amalek. Both want the Land. They will not stop until every last Hebrew is in the ground. We have to protect our people or there won't be any of us left."

"I understand that," I said. "I just don't understand why that means annihilating everyone. Even the innocent."

"That is a question I don't think any of us can answer, Zahava. I am a soldier. I follow orders. I've had to do things that keep me up at night sometimes. But I follow those orders because I trust that my captains, my commanders, my generals, and even the king know more than I do about the situation. Perhaps Yahweh can see all of it from whatever great height he resides in—beginning, middle, and end—and there is some sort of divine purpose in such a decree." He shook his head. "Maybe I am wrong. I usually am."

We let the conversation go quiet as we continued walking, both of us lost in trying to comprehend the incomprehensible.

"You were magnificent today, by the way," he said after a while. "With Thema."

I'd never forget the look on the shrewd woman's face when I began pointing out the flaws in the jewelry she called her finest. "I couldn't let her cheat us."

"The way you brought her to her knees was a sight to behold." He grinned, his gray eyes dancing in the waning light. "Saul's commanders should take a lesson from you in keeping troops in order."

I laughed at the ridiculous notion. "As if they'd put a woman in charge. A crippled one, at that!"

He scoffed. "Your leg has nothing to do with it. You are the strongest person I've ever met."

"That's ridiculous, Gavi. I've had to ride in the wagon most of the way. I can't carry water jugs or even stand at a loom."

He stopped and turned to stare at me with such ferocity that I came to a halt as well. "That's not the type of strength I mean and you know it. You have been dealt a lot that would cause most people to wallow in self-pity. You don't hide away. You don't complain. Ever."

"Of course I do," I said. "I've hidden myself away many times, especially when I was young and children, sometimes even adults, were so cruel. I rarely played with others aside from my sisters. And I've complained in my heart countless times over the years, even if I don't say it out loud. Perhaps it is only because I have seen my parents suffer far worse and still hold fast to hope in El Shaddai that I keep it inside."

The truth shamed me. Even after my brothers were lost, my parents lost infant after infant until Ima was finally able to carry Anaya to her first breath. And although the two of them grieved each loss deeply, and it sounded as though my father had been more conflicted than I'd known, they ultimately chose to trust Yahweh's will. Whereas I had let my fear and mistrust drag me down a path that led me to disobey the most fundamental of the laws given to Mosheh.

"Why do they?" he asked. "From what I've seen not all Kenites seem to worship Yahweh."

"My father would say because his direct ancestors witnessed the fire atop the Mountain, heard the Voice shake the earth. And because Mosheh himself taught his forefathers the Ten Words sometime during the forty years your own wandered in the wilderness."

"And what do you say?"

I hummed, contemplating his question, one I'd never been asked before. "I'm not certain I have an answer."

I gazed to the west, where the sunset had spread her robes across the horizon in brilliant display against the red-tinged hills and the blooming acacias that surrounded this small basin, an ever-shifting pattern of color that was never the same on any given evening. Soon, myriad stars would shimmer above us, endlessly traveling their mysterious paths in the heavens. And as I turned my eyes upward to seek them out, my mother's song began to flow from my lips.

Look to the stars, my child, and know,
The heavens speak of what you're shown.
More precious than the diamonds bright,
More costly than the purest light.
Your worth is far beyond the earth,
Crowned in splendor before your birth.

Lift your eyes to skies afar,
And remember, child, just who you are.
The Master's hand, with skill untold,
Has shaped your heart of pure red-gold.
Strength and beauty, love refined,
In you His perfect craft combined.

The One who lit the stars aflame,
Is He who softly calls your name.
His mighty hands designed your soul,
A radiant mystery to unfold.
Endowed with worth from Heaven's throne,
You are His child, His very own.

As the words drifted into unbroken silence while Gavi and I stood side by side watching the first of the glittering stars twinkle into view, I felt it. That low hum in the depths of my soul, the pull of something unknowable, something beyond human understanding. And suddenly, I *did* know the answer to Gavi's question.

"The truth is here, isn't it?" I declared, stretching out my arms. "This Land, these heavens, such inexplicable splendor point to a God beyond all gods. And if Yahweh made all of this, then who am I to question his goodness? Or whatever unknowable plans he has for his own Creation? For me?"

Gavi shrugged, his eyes still on the deepening sky. "To be honest, Zahava, I've spent far more time chasing my ambitions than contemplating such mysteries. But I felt the ground tremble beneath my feet when the Ark of the Covenant was brought to the battlefield and saw vicious enemies shaken to their knees. I've seen a raging storm come from pure blue sky when Samuel the Seer called on the name of Yahweh and disappear just as quickly. I can certainly never explain it as anything but acts of a Mighty God. But I've also seen the terror on my mother's face as my father beat her senseless. I've seen men—good, brave, devoted men—cut down before my eyes. And I've seen the anointed King of Israel, supposedly chosen by that same God, nearly murder his own son."

I sucked in a gasp. "Surely not."

He shook his head, scoffing. "Like I said, I don't have any answers. And the ones I usually have are wrong."

For a man with so much brash confidence, so much strength and courage, sometimes Gavi seemed almost uncertain of himself. It made little sense. Especially to someone like me, who'd hidden herself in a cave and let her fears drown out everything she'd been taught her entire life.

"Perhaps we're just not meant to have all the answers," I said. "But to keep listening for the only One who does."

Gavi turned his eyes to mine. "You are extraordinary, Zahava. I've never known anyone like you." There was a note of something like wonder in his low voice.

My face heated at the compliment. "That's kind of you to say."

He leaned closer, his warm breath whispering across my cheek. "I mean it. I am proud to call you my wife. I will do everything in my power to be worthy of you."

Tears pricked my eyes at such a sweet and sincere pronouncement. No matter what Gavi thought of himself or what his doubts may be, no one, outside of my family, had ever made me feel so valued. He'd been so gentle with me, so patient in waiting for this marriage to be made true. He'd said he wasn't one to force himself on a woman, and I fully believed that to be the case. I wasn't certain I was ready for such intimacies, but after today and how

I'd been able to stand up to Thema, surely I could take a small step in his direction. Couldn't I?

I turned my face toward him, my hands trembling as I gazed up at the man to whom I'd pledged my life. "I am glad Yahweh planned for our paths to merge, Gavi. Even if it was not what either of us expected."

"You are certainly unexpected, little dove." His lips quirked, his eyes dipping to my mouth as another sort of song vibrated in the air between us. My body drifted toward him as his strong arm came around my back. But instead of pressing a kiss to my tingling lips, my husband let his own drift gently across my temple and merely held me close for a few breathless moments.

"We should probably get back to camp," he rasped low, then cleared his throat. "Your father will wonder if something happened to us."

Glad the dim light hid the flush on my cheeks for such presumption, I mumbled agreement and let him take me by the hand and lead me along the path to the valley, now lit only by stars.

"Besides," he said softly, "I cannot wait to tell him how his daughter convinced one of the most formidable and frankly terrifying women I've ever met to double her offer."

Gavriel

"Why are we not unloading this wagon first?" asked Haim as six of us took our places around the tilting vehicle. The ox cart had broken down just before the caravan stopped yesterday so the elderly couple had been forced to leave it behind, unable to repair the wheel on their own. They'd taken only their ancient ox and a few necessities with them, leaving the wagon a good half-hour walk from camp.

"Waste of time," said Emmet. "We need to get moving. Prop it up, change the wheel, and move out. I want to be in Be'er Sheva before sundown."

Although we were only a few hours from our final destination, Emmet had decided to give everyone extra time to visit the springs in the nearby wadis to refresh themselves and their animals before we set off on the last leg of this journey.

Emmet shouted, "Lift!" and we complied, each of us straining to heft the overladen wagon. The moment it was aloft, a few large rocks were pushed under the axles while we held it steady. By the time Emmet gave the command to set the wagon back down, my palms smarted and my leg muscles screamed. But truth be told, I was glad for the distraction after a restless night.

I'd been so tempted to close the narrow distance between Zahava and me last night on the road. Every drop of my blood had roared as she'd surprised me by turning up those enticing lips, practically daring me to steal a taste of her mouth. I'd been only a breath from giving in but held back, suddenly and ridiculously terrified.

I'd never put so much consideration into a simple kiss before, never thought it even mattered all that much. But with her, it was not a moment of fleeting pleasure; it was a full embrace of the woman who'd taken up the largest share of my thoughts for days now.

Everything about Zahava called to me. Her kindness and patience since being tied to me, even when I was retching my guts in the sand. Her intriguing skills and sharp mind. Her pure delight at besting Thema. Her courage. Her eyes. Her smile.

What a fool I was to be such a coward about kissing my own wife. Next time I'd be ready to enjoy those lips, ready to breathe in her honey-spice scent and hold her in my arms . . .

"What are you smirking about?" Obadyah nudged me in the ribs, knocking me out of my head while Haim and Ithiel worked together to remove the broken wheel from the axle.

Tuval chuckled. "No mystery there. He's the only one of us with a woman in this camp. And a pretty one, at that."

My face went hot. Had I actually been smiling to myself while thinking about kissing Zahava? I refused to let them know they'd gotten under my skin, so I narrowed my eyes on Tuval. "My *wife* is none of your concern."

"Oh, now. We mean nothing by it. We're just glad you aren't snapping and snarling like a half-starved mongrel anymore," said Obadyah, patting my shoulder.

I elbowed him, but the tease invoked a sense of camaraderie I'd not experienced in a long while. These men, whom I'd not even gone into battle with, were treating me as one of them. There was a time when the men of Yonatan's unit had done the same, had known I could be trusted to have their backs. Yet somewhere along the way, I'd stopped caring, squandered their good opinion. It shamed me that I'd been so reckless.

"Tuval. Obadyah," said Emmet as he approached. "Stop standing around and get the replacement wheel ready."

The two men hurried to obey the captain, and Emmet took their place by my side. We stood, arms crossed, watching as the four men exchanged the broken wheel for another. Unfortunately, the new wheel was a bit larger than the first, so it would be a bumpy ride for the elderly couple who owned the cart, but at least they'd be able to limp into Be'er Sheva with their belongings.

Emmet did not turn to me as he spoke. "Your wife's family ready to go?"

"Not sure. I'll head back when we are done here." I'd hated leaving them to pack up the campsite, but Emmet had sent Adin to fetch me for this repair, and I couldn't ignore an order.

"I must say, you've surprised me, Gavriel."

I held my tongue, but he was the one who'd surprised me with this conversation. The man had said little to me for most of this journey, but I'd seen him watching me with Zahava's family a few times.

"I've spoken with Barzel, and he had nothing but good things to say about the way you've conducted yourself since Punon. And from all accounts, no one has seen a drop touch your lips."

"Water only," I affirmed.

"It seems you've finally begun to take Yonatan's discipline seriously."

In the past, his condescending tone would have scrubbed salt into all the raw places. But now that the haze of drink had finally cleared, and along with it, the bitter taste in my mouth for Yonatan's decision, the more I could see that it had been justified.

In truth, dragging Rahm out of that tavern had shaken something loose in my head. Last night, after Zahava fell asleep beside me, I began to remember times I'd put everyone at risk that Yonatan didn't even know of, times when I wasn't certain who I'd spoken to or where I'd been on a few mornings after I'd overindulged to the point of blackness. I'd not slept most of last night for the hounding guilt of knowing that it was Yahweh's mercy alone that I hadn't gotten anyone killed.

"He was right to cut me," I said, knowing to my bones it was true.

Emmet faced me now. "You admit it, then?"

"My recklessness was a danger to my comrades. He should not have given me any mercy."

He huffed a laugh. "My recommendation exactly."

It was no surprise Emmet had wanted me gone, but one question had risen above the others last night. "Why *did* he give me another chance?"

Emmet shook his head. "It's certainly not because of his upbringing. His father is merciless."

I blinked at him in astonishment. Such blatant disrespect of the king within the ranks of this army was grounds for punishment—or worse, an accusation of treason.

He scoffed but spoke in a hushed tone. "Oh, don't pretend you're more loyal to Saul than Yonatan. We were both at Michmash. If the lot of us hadn't practically threatened mutiny, he would have slaughtered his own heir for an ill-conceived vow. He cycles through armor-bearers and advisers like dirty tunics, dismissing them for foolish reasons or for no reason at all."

I'd not heard such rumblings about Saul's inner circle, but it did not surprise me. I'd been as excited as any other Benjamite when Saul had been anointed king, but soon after the victory of Yavesh, rumors of double-mindedness and impulsive decisions began to filter through the ranks. I'd ignored most of it, glad to be under Yonatan's direct command since he was twice the man his father was. But even I had never been bold enough to speak my reservations about the king aloud to anyone other than Zevi and Avi.

Even now, I offered only silence in concession to his brash words. But it seemed I was not the only one who questioned why Yahweh would select such a man to inhabit the throne.

"Do you still want to return to Yonatan's unit, if you can hold it together until I report this change in your attitude?"

Once again, Emmet had shocked me. Returning to Yonatan's unit had been my every thought since the moment he'd sent me away, but somehow over the past couple of weeks, the urgency had diminished. Did I want to go back to spending endless months spying among enemies? Following Yonatan on countless missions to strengthen ties with other tribes?

My mind flashed immediately to Zahava. I certainly could not drag her with me to far-flung places where she'd be in danger, especially when it meant she'd be all alone and away from her family. The entirety of my time in the army I'd never had to give a second thought to anyone but myself, and now she was the only one I could think about.

"I . . . I have to consider Zahava's safety. . . ."

He tilted his chin, peering at me sideways. "I honestly didn't think you'd take this marriage seriously, regardless of what you said to Barzel."

"She is a good woman. Worth my loyalty."

He raised a brow. "Enough to stay back from battle for a year?"

My blood went still. How had I never considered this until now? Many Hebrews ignored Mosheh's edict for a man to withdraw from war during his first year of marriage, but Zevi had risked everything to request the provision of King Saul himself. And to everyone's astonishment, he'd relished the time so much he'd never returned to full-time soldiering. Yochana, and the young family they'd started during that time, proved far more satisfying to him than the vengeance he'd thirsted after for so long.

I looked down at the dirt in front of my sandals. "All I can say is that if you would have asked me that three weeks ago, I'd have said nothing was more important than being a soldier and returning to Yonatan's unit. Now . . ." I shrugged. "I'm not certain the answer is as clear."

All I'd ever wanted was to be my own man. Pursue my ambitions. Become a master of weaponry. But everything had been turned on its head since I arrived in Punon.

"You know, that day we found you behind the rock, Yonatan told me you had the potential for greatness."

My mouth gaped. I'd not been certain Emmet even remembered that meeting. He'd never mentioned it before now. "He did?"

Emmet nodded. "But he said unless you were brought low, you'd never reach it. Because only a man on his knees can see what he is lacking most."

I tried to come up with a response and found no words.

"That's what makes Yonatan different from Saul," he said. "He *starts* on his knees. I saw it first on the day we climbed up that cliff to the garrison at Michmash, and then a hundred different times over the years."

Even if I'd not been as close to Yonatan as Emmet, who'd served as his armor-bearer for many years before being raised to leadership, I'd witnessed much of the same.

"It truly astounds me," Emmet continued, "how opposite a man can be from the one who sired him."

The comparison struck like a spear to my chest. *"He's just like*

Elan . . ." I swallowed against a knot of bile in my throat. "He will be a great king one day."

Emmet bowed his head, nodding as he went quiet for a long moment. Then he let out a sigh. "He will. And if I were you, I'd never again take his confidence for granted."

I nodded, too entangled in my swirling thoughts to form a response. At that moment, Tuval called for us to take up our places to set the repaired cart back on the ground. But before I joined them, I turned back to Emmet. "I never would have gone near your sister had I known who she was. I swear it."

He chuckled. "Sarai is a flirt, Gavriel. Well, she was before my father married her off to a man who could take her in hand. She was as much to blame as you for that mess."

"Regardless. I want to sincerely apologize for disrespecting her. And you, that day."

He sobered, nodding. "I appreciate that."

I'd taken only three steps toward the wagon when the screaming began in the distance. Every one of us whirled toward the horrific sound of terror from the direction of the caravan ahead, instantly sliding weapons from our belts.

"Go!" shouted Emmet, but we already on the move toward whatever danger had crept up on us while we'd been off-guard, complacent by virtue of proximity to Be'er Sheva and being firmly within Yehudite territory for the past two days.

Foolish. Foolish, I thought before I fixed my mind on reaching Zahava. Ahead of the others, I dodged screaming women and children fleeing toward the rocky hills just to the east of the road, then veered toward the campsite where we'd laughed together last night as Anaya and Breena had entertained us by acting out a story by the flickering light of the cookfire.

A white-faced Adin was suddenly in my path, but I did not slow my pace as I shouted, "What's happening?"

"Bandits. A lot of them."

My stomach heaved. "Emmet and the others are just behind me. Go!" The shouts and cries grew louder as I passed him, pushing harder north. Barzel's family had been traveling near the middle of the Kenite caravan.

I saw Barzel and Safaa among the fleeing Kenites, Zahava's mother stumbling along as she led her husband toward the hills. I skidded to a halt in front of them, and Safaa let out a terrified shriek, jerking back into Barzel and nearly knocking the man to the ground.

"Where is she?" I demanded.

Tears streamed down Safaa's face. "The girls went up to the pool to bathe. You have to find them!"

"Take Safaa with you!" His eyes wide and face pale, Barzel pushed his wife toward me.

"No," she shouted, gripping the sleeves of his tunic. "I'm not leaving you."

"You will go. Now!" he ordered with all the force of his considerable authority. "Our girls need you."

Barzel may be half-blind, but he could clearly see that if I was to find Zahava and her sisters, I could not wait for him. And there was no time to argue with a man who I knew would gladly give his life for any one of them. I pointed to my right, toward the thick carcass of an olive tree about fifteen paces away. "Can you see that tree?"

Barzel nodded, already moving toward what was likely only a shadow. "*Go!*"

Safaa sobbed his name, but I yanked her along with me as we ascended the slope toward the wadi. "I'll come back for him, I promise. We have to find the girls. Run!"

Catching a flash of movement in the corner of my eye, I barely managed to push Safaa aside as I spun to find a heavily tattooed man swinging an iron dagger at my face. I slashed my knife across his forearm, then jammed my elbow into his throat. He fell back a couple of steps, gagging and cursing, but swiftly recovered and came at me again. I swept his left leg, and he went down hard. I pounced before he'd fully landed on the ground and plunged my knife into the side of his neck. I didn't pause to watch the light leave his eyes but glanced toward the caravan to where Emmet's men were now engaged with a large number of attackers, some on horseback. My instinct to join the fight was only superseded by my bone-deep urge to find Zahava.

At the bottom of the slope, Obadyah stood between one of the bandits and Rahm's mother. Ten paces away from them, Rahm himself stood with his hands high in the air, the point of a sword at his chest. And on the other end of that sword was one of the Philistines from the tavern.

Confusion roared inside my head, but I had no time to parse out what it meant or leave Safaa vulnerable here to turn aside and help them. I had to trust Emmet's men. Zahava needed me.

I yanked Safaa up from the ground where she'd collapsed in a sobbing heap. "We have to keep moving!"

Heart galloping, I headed toward the steep path that led to the pool, where I'd bathed early this morning before Emmet had sent Adin to summon me. Zahava and the girls must have headed up there soon after I left to help with the ox cart.

Once Safaa and I got a little farther up the narrow path, I took quick measure of the chaotic situation below. Animals and people were screaming and scattering in every direction. Women and children hid under wagons and handcarts. Although the Kenite men weren't soldiers, they were doing their measured best to fend off the invaders, if not with weapons then with ox-goads and staffs and rocks. But there were already a few bodies littering the ground.

"Yahweh, have mercy!" Safaa's body shook violently as I dragged her along.

"Don't look. Let's find the girls."

It was the only mission that mattered right now. Once Zahava and her sisters were safe, I'd go help deal with the enemy. Emmet was a capable leader. He and his company had been sent by Saul to protect these people for a reason.

Safaa and I pushed past boulders lodged near the mouth of the canyon, probably the aftermath of a flash flood, and through the tall brush that I hoped would camouflage the entrance from the invaders below.

Scrambling along the twisting path, Safaa and I reached the pool, but it was empty, the green water still. I swung my gaze around the wadi, desperation pounding through me. The answer to Emmet's earlier question was now clear as glass—*of course* she was worth giving up war for a year. She was worth a *lifetime*.

"Gavi! Ima!"

The echo of her voice off the canyon walls was the single most beautiful sound I'd ever heard. My knees wobbled with relief as Zahava peered out from behind a boulder, eyes red-rimmed, black hair dripping wet, and her face nearly as pale as the sandstone around us.

With a choking cry, Safaa tripped forward as Breena, Anaya, Yasmin, and Rahm's two little sisters emerged, along with a few other terrified young women and girls. But I only had eyes for my Zahava as she limped toward me.

I ran for her, scooped her into my arms, and locked her trembling body into my embrace. Her feet dangled in the air as she sobbed against my chest.

"What's happening?" Breena clung to her mother. "We heard screaming, so we ran from the water and hid."

"Caravan raiders," I said, unable to soften the blow.

"Where's my father?" Zahava turned her face up to me. I would end the world to wipe the horror from those hazel eyes.

I set her on the ground. "Hiding."

"But he's helpless!"

"Your mother's safety was his priority." I pressed a swift kiss to her forehead and turned away. "I'll go get him."

"Girls! Where's Farah?" Safaa's desperate question jerked me to a halt.

Breena let out a choking sob. "She took the goats to graze. Someone has to go get her! She's all alone."

"What about Rahm?" asked Yasmin, tears trickling down her cheeks as she pulled her husband's sisters close to her body.

From what I'd seen, things did not look good for either her husband or his mother. "Emmet's men will protect them."

I abhorred leaving Zahava, but neither could I just let Farah fend for herself. And if I didn't hurry back down to the olive tree, Barzel would have no chance at all. Torn in a hundred directions, I had to make a snap decision. "Which way did Farah go?"

Yasmin gestured toward the rocky cliff to the north. "She found a shaded stream in the neighboring canyon with a place for them to graze."

With barely a thought for our audience, and with none at all for the excuses I'd given myself last night, I yanked Zahava to me and kissed her soundly. "Hide. I will be back with Farah and your father."

Then, leaving my shocked wife behind, I strode back toward the valley, barely feeling the whip of scrub brush against my legs and arms as I navigated the rocky path and laid out a plan to get Farah and hide her here while I went for Barzel. Then I'd go back and fight alongside Emmet's men.

However, when I reached the mouth of the canyon, I slammed to a halt, bewildered by the scene in front of me.

It was over.

In the distance, almost to the far western ridge, a group of horses was at a full gallop, dust swirling behind. Below me, a few dazed Kenites stood with their eyes on the retreating raiders, while others tended the wounded and the dead. Already the sound of ululating tinged the air with grief.

There was nothing I could do for any of them. I had to find Zahava's sister and ensure she was safe. I followed the sloping curve of the terrain into the next wadi, where after about forty paces I found her little herd of goats grazing blissfully on lush grasses near the trickle of a stream.

But no Farah.

I called her name. When there was no answer, I pressed farther into the wadi, repeating my call over and over. Only the echo of my own voice returned from the crumbling sandstone walls of the canyon.

All I could hope was that Farah had gone to find her family, maybe even joined her father. But when I arrived at the olive tree where I'd sent Zahava's father to hide, neither of them were there. Worry swelled into thick panic as I headed toward Barzel's wagon.

Rahm's mother lay on the ground not far from where I'd seen Obadyah defending her, eyes wide and sightless. And about three paces away, Obadyah too was in the dirt, gore spilling from the gash in his abdomen.

I'd seen plenty of death on the battlefield, so the sight of guts and severed limbs did little to turn my stomach anymore, but nausea flamed at the back of my throat as I remembered how he'd teased me just an hour ago for smiling like a fool over my wife. The young man would never have the chance to do the same in this life.

I scanned the area for Barzel. For Farah. But most everyone I saw was a stranger to me.

And then Adin was stumbling toward me, bleeding from a slash to his forearm where it looked as though he'd defended himself from a knife blow. The boy was fortunate. If it had been a sword, he'd have no hand left.

"What happened to the raiders?" I demanded.

"They just . . . stopped." His face was ashen, eyes dazed. "One of them bellowed for a retreat and they just turned around and left."

I surveyed the caravan. None of the wagons looked to have been pilfered, no carts overturned.

"Did they take anything?"

He let out a muffled noise, and I turned to find him with his hand pressed to his mouth. Dread started at the base of my spine and surged upward.

"Adin. What did they take?"

"Hostages," he said, his voice small. A tear trickled from one eye. "They took Farah."

I flinched, gutted for Zahava and her family.

"I tried to get to her, but they dragged her onto a horse so quickly." He raised his bloody arm. "Swiped at me before I could get a grip on the reins and then took off." He swallowed hard and I could practically hear the guilt sloshing around inside his belly. He would see those moments in his mind for years, again and again, and castigate himself for not reaching her in time. It was the same for me now that I did not have drink to dull the memory of leaving Shalem behind to suffer unknown terrors.

"They took Rahm too," he said. "He was one of the first they captured. Held him at sword point until he showed them where Barzel was behind that dead olive tree."

It took everything I had to remain standing. I shouldn't have left him, should have forced him to come with Safaa and me. I'd taken too long to hunt for Farah . . . or maybe I should have gone for Barzel first—

"I don't understand, though." Adin's trembling voice broke through my guilt-ridden haze. "Rahm went wild when his mother was killed, screamed something about betrayal until they gagged him and dragged him away."

Fury burned a fiery path through my insides. Rahm had been in on it. He must have told those Philistines in the tavern exactly where we'd been heading. If he wasn't dead already, I would kill him. But for now, I needed to get back to my wife, and then we had to get all these people to safety.

"Where's Emmet?"

With a shudder, Adin swiped his sweaty and dirt-stained face, smearing it worse with his bloody palm. "The captain is dead."

Zahava

Eighteen people were missing. Among them, my father, my sister, and Rahm. Seven soldiers had lost their lives defending the caravan, including the captain. And ten Kenites had perished. Four more were seriously wounded, needing a skilled healer, which we did not have among us. The only woman who'd come close to that designation was a midwife, and she had lost her life protecting a young pregnant woman from the raiders.

And so, with no choice other than to take only what was necessary, we'd had to flee.

Without a captain to lead them, the soldiers looked to Shachar and Gavi for direction, which surprised me a little, given what he'd told me about feeling like an outsider among them. But something had happened during the onslaught, as if there'd been a shift inside Gavi I could not explain. The others around him must have noticed it as well.

We left the handcarts behind, unloaded the wagons of all but the barest essentials, and filled them instead with the wounded, the elderly, and small children. Camels and donkeys were relieved of much of their burdens so they could move quicker. One of the wagons carried the hastily wrapped bodies of our dead, since we had no time for burial.

We'd been less than a three hours' walk from Be'er Sheva this morning, but now the Hebrews were determined to get us to the city as swiftly as possible. They were taking no chances in case our attackers returned to finish whatever they'd begun.

None of it made any sense.

They'd taken eighteen people but nothing else. They did not touch the wagons or carts and had no interest in our livestock. And then they simply galloped away. Caravan raiders didn't do that. They did not conduct an ambush to steal nothing of value. And slavers would not take three tribal leaders, two of whom were elderly and one who was nearly blind, leaving a slew of capable young men and women behind.

I could practically see the thoughts cycling through Gavi's mind as he drove the mules as fast as they could go with a full load of people in the wagon bed. I had no doubt he'd been running the attack over and over in his head, wondering what he could have done to prevent it. He'd said little since we'd departed the scene of the attack, our belongings strewn about the valley floor like scattered leaves after a storm.

What remained of the herds had also been left to wander there. A few Kenites had loudly argued against doing so. Gavi told them they were welcome to remain behind to drive them, without escort. No one took him up on the challenge.

I held my little pack of tools against my chest like a shield, the only thing I'd cared to take with me.

What was supposed to have been an exciting return to ancestral land had instead become a dash for refuge by a horde of stricken and confused Kenites. The only noise other than the whisper of hundreds of sandals and the clatter of mule and ox hooves on the stony trade road were a few scattered sniffles from those riding in the back of our wagon.

Gavi had insisted on keeping his eye on what remained of our family, so my hollow-eyed mother, with Anaya and Breena on either side of her, walked ahead of the wagon, with Yasmin and Rahm's orphaned sisters just behind. None of us had been able to speak of what had happened or how our two families had been shredded to pieces.

A few hours ago, I would have thrilled at the sight of the fertile area that would be our new home. I'd have scoured the horizon, wondering where my family would pitch our tents, and gazed in awe at the ancient hilltop city where Avraham himself had once lived, and where generations of Kenites had settled just after Yehoshua conquered Canaan.

But now I didn't care about the abundant green along the two rivers that crossed through the valley or the varied herds that grazed along irrigation canals. Nor did I care that the city was undergoing construction, with new thick walls and a garrison being raised. King Saul was obviously making his presence known, both to the tribe of Simeon that had ruled this territory for generations, and whichever enemies were in the region.

But I was not impressed by such a show of strength and expanding wealth by the King of Israel. I just wanted my father and sister back. What I really wanted was to crawl into Gavi's lap, lay my head on his chest, and cry. But that would have to wait until our people were safe.

For as heartbroken as I was, poor Yasmin was gutted by both the loss of her husband and the death of her mother-in-law in addition to our missing father and sister, but somehow she was holding it together for the sake of Rahm's sisters. The girls had clung to her constantly ever since their mother's death. So, if Yasmin could be a bulwark in the face of so much devastation, then certainly I could hold myself together.

When finally we were within sight of the gates, or what would be the gates once they were finished, a group of guards jogged down the long slope to meet us, and the caravan came to a standstill.

Gavi halted the mules and handed me the reins, then jumped down to go meet them, Shachar and a few other soldiers joining him. After a fair amount of gesturing back the direction we'd come from and what looked to be fervent discussion, my husband returned with his shoulders not quite so tense.

"They're going to lead us into the city," he said. "There is plenty of room in the garrison courtyard for us to sleep tonight."

Relief flooded through me. "What about the wounded?"

"They said there are a few healers in the area. They're sending messengers to alert them to our arrival."

I swallowed back a glut of hot tears. Were my father and sister wounded too? Where would they sleep tonight? In the cold? Neither one had even been wearing a cloak.

The caravan lumbered up the sloping hill and through what would undoubtedly be a grand entrance to the city on completion. Many curious townsfolk had stopped their various tasks or halted in the street to stare at the bedraggled Kenites shuffling into their city.

I expected disdain or suspicion, but instead I saw more than a few expressions of sympathy on the faces of people we passed. A few of them even darted forward to hand off loaves of bread or handfuls of fruit to the children. My throat ached, tears swimming in my eyes at the kindness.

Once we were inside the large garrison courtyard, there was a flurry of activity as families scurried to reunite with those who'd ridden in wagons, then spread out within the walled area to claim places in the shade, while wounded Kenites were carried inside the nearly completed garrison itself. From the size of the building, it looked as though Saul planned to assign a large contingent here.

Gavi brought the wagon to a halt and dropped his head to his chest with a sigh that sounded as though he'd carried the entirety of our tribe here on his own back. Then he turned to me, looking into my eyes for the first time since we'd fled. "I'm sorry."

I flinched, confused. "For what?"

He pinched his eyes shut for a moment, scrubbing at his forehead. "I shouldn't have left him behind. I should have insisted he come with us."

The poor man was feeling guilt over my father?

"Gavi. No one can make my father do anything. He is the most stubborn man alive."

The word nearly choked me. *Was* he alive? Was Farah? I knew what enemies did to female captives and refused to let my mind linger on what could be happening to my beautiful spitfire sister, things more horrifying than death. But none of this was Gavi's fault.

I slid my hand over his, letting my scarred fingers settle in the valleys of his large, capable ones. "You saved my mother, Gavi, like he asked you to do. And you couldn't have known Farah was in the wadi by herself. None of us blames you for what happened today. Especially me."

Our gazes held as the tail end of our caravan entered the courtyard and barely organized chaos swirled around us.

"I don't deserve you," he whispered so quietly I had to read the words on his lips.

Before I could respond, someone called Gavi's name, startling us both. A dark-haired soldier strode up to the wagon, palm lifted in greeting. "Is that really you?"

"Zevi?" Gavi's jaw gaped, then to my surprise, he jumped down from the wagon to embrace the man. "What are you doing here?"

Zevi returned the embrace, slapping Gavi's back affectionately. "Training the guards Saul appointed to this garrison. He wants them well-prepared since it's so close to Philistine territory."

Releasing his hold on the man, Gavi set his hands on his hips, stance wide. "A wise decision on his part."

"And who is this, cousin?" asked Zevi, turning curious brown eyes to me. He was taller than Gavi, with dark wavy hair trimmed short, along with a well-tended beard and golden skin that was only a shade or two lighter than my own. They may be cousins, but the two looked nothing alike. Even so, from their easy camaraderie, I guessed this was indeed the Zevi who featured in many of Gavi's childhood stories.

"This is Zahava," Gavi said. Then he paused for a moment, looking almost . . . shy? "My wife."

Zevi's jaw dropped. He stared at Gavi as if my husband had sprouted horns from his head. "Your *what*? I think perhaps my ears are playing tricks."

A flicker of amusement ticked at Gavi's mouth. "You heard me just fine. This is my wife." He put out his hand, gesturing for me to come down from the wagon. Still clutching my tools to my chest, I accepted his help.

Zevi shook his head, incredulous, as Gavi slid his steady arm around me. "She is the daughter of one of the Kenite elders—one of those taken hostage."

His cousin's face went blank. "Tell me exactly what happened."

I'd thought perhaps Gavi would ask me to go find my mother and sisters while the two talked, but instead he kept me by his side, his hold on me never wavering as he explained the attack in swift terms. Zevi's expression turned dark as Gavi described how the attackers had taken nothing but a small group of people before galloping away.

"Philistines?" he asked.

"A few of them, for certain. I suspect most were mercenaries. A couple of the dead ones looked like Amorites. But what concerns me most is that it was a targeted attack."

"What do you mean?"

"I recognized one of them," said Gavi. "I saw one of the Philistines in Qadesh at the tavern."

I stiffened, peering up at my husband in bewilderment. Why hadn't he said anything before now?

Zevi folded his arms over his wide chest. "How do you know it was the same man?"

"Because Rahm, the husband of Zahava's sister, had been drinking with him and a few of his cohorts. I traded a few words with them when I came to fetch him. And Rahm was one of the first hostages they grabbed."

"Could he be in on it?" asked Zevi.

Gavi's hold on me tightened, as if bracing me for what came next. "From what one of the men said, he may have been. There was talk of betrayal, as if whatever had been planned went awry after Rahm's mother was killed in the melee."

I trembled at the revelation. It *couldn't* be true. Rahm was married to my sister, had been practically part of our family since he was a boy. I couldn't reconcile any of this with what I'd known of the man I'd once hoped to marry.

Although he kept his gaze on his cousin, Gavi's palm smoothed up and down my arm. "Unfortunately, the Kenite I saw with Rahm at the tavern was killed, so there's no way to find out for certain. But the raiders took only people, nothing of value from the wagons. Very strange."

Brow furrowed, Zevi stared at the ground for a few moments before lifting his chin. "You're right, it's all very odd. But right now we need to get these people settled. My men will go back for the belongings and livestock as soon as the wagons are unloaded, with whoever wants to come along. We'll figure out the rest in the morning."

More relief. At least the lot of us would not be completely destitute if they managed to retrieve our worldly goods. Hopefully, nothing had been pilfered by passersby and the herds hadn't completely scattered into the wilderness.

"I ordered everyone out of their rooms in the garrison," said Zevi. "We can shelter a good number inside. And from what I understand, some of the women in town are already organizing food. There is a deep well in the center of town, so there's plenty of fresh water."

A tear slipped from the corner of my eye. I never expected the people of Be'er Sheva to be so kind to a horde of foreigners. Pulling me a little closer, Gavi gently squeezed my arm in a soothing gesture.

Zevi's eyes tracked the movement. "You and your wife will take my quarters."

"Thank you, Zev. But Zahava's family is my responsibility. We need to stay with them."

His cousin blinked at him for a moment before seeming to shake his head clear of confusion. "Of course. There is plenty of space for them in the adjoining chamber."

Gavi nodded his head in silent thanks.

"I'll have someone lead you there. I need to go organize my men." Zevi reached out to clasp Gavi's shoulder. "I am glad to see you, even if the circumstances are unwelcome. It's been far too long. You've been missed."

Gavi swallowed hard, as if he were struggling with his response. "Have you heard any news from . . . Ramah?"

Zevi gave him a soft smile. "I traveled through there when coming back from Gibeah. Your family is well. Your sisters are growing up far too quickly."

Gavi cleared his throat. "And my mother?"

His cousin chuckled, backing away. "Doda Miri will likely fall on the floor in a dead faint the moment she hears you are married."

Once Zevi left us, I turned to peer up at my husband. "Do you really think Rahm was involved in this attack? Why would he put our family and Yasmin in danger? Not to mention his own mother and sisters?"

"I don't know." His brow furrowed and his slate gray eyes filled with determination. "But I promise you, I will find out. And I *will* get them back."

22

Gavriel

Even with Zahava safe beside me, I barely slept all night. The attack ran over and over in my head with startling clarity, in a way I'd never allowed a battle to do before. She may say she didn't blame me, but Barzel and Farah were gone and I absolutely blamed myself.

At dawn, I slipped out of Zevi's private quarters, passed the larger adjoining room where Zahava's mother and sisters slept, along with Yasmin and the two motherless girls in her care, and wound my way through the barracks.

Tents had been raised all over the courtyard, the Kenites relieved to be in possession of their belongings since Zevi's guards-in-training had run to the scene of the attack and brought back most everything before the sun set. For them, it was another of his relentless training exercises. For the Kenites, it was a miracle. A few of the men had remained behind to round up the animals and herd them to Be'er Sheva. For Zahava's sake, I hoped they'd retrieved Farah's goats from the stream. Her family had lost enough.

The most vulnerable refugees had taken shelter in the nearly completed barracks like we had, and a few had even been taken in by kind townsfolk. But the sheer number of bodies, animals, and belongings jammed into the courtyard made it seem far smaller than it was. It took me a while to find my cousin, who was near the entrance to the garrison, giving orders to a group of young men.

"Keep an eye on the horizon. The moment they are back, you let me know," he said before the soldiers peeled away, heading for the gates. Only Zevi and one other man remained in place as I approached.

"Who are they looking for?" I asked by way of greeting.

"Scouts," Zevi replied. "We sent three of them out from the scene of the attack to see if they can find a trail, some clue where the hostages were taken."

I'd been tempted to do so myself yesterday, let the others lead the caravan to Be'er Sheva, but I'd been incapable of leaving Zahava's side until I knew she was safe. And I may be arrogant, like Emmet and Yonatan accused, but I wasn't foolish enough to think I could have done anything on my own against forty raiders on horseback.

"Eliyah," he said to the man at his side, "would you mind taking your unit back toward the attack site to help the others herd the animals this way? My trainees are exhausted after running there and back last night. I plan to keep them on light duty today so they can refresh."

"Certainly, Commander. Mine are ready to go." The younger man gave me a nod and walked off.

"Who was that?" I asked.

"Captain Eliyah ben Resev, from Lachish. He brought his unit down to help build the fortress a few months ago. He joined my company just before the battle at Michmash."

That must be why the man looked familiar. I'd seen Zevi after he'd been promoted to commander of four hundred men but my memories of that time, and really much of the years after, were blurred.

"You sleep?"

I huffed, shaking my head. "But thank you for the use of your quarters. I was glad Zahava's mother and sisters didn't have to sleep in the courtyard."

"How's your wife?" he asked.

"Heartbroken. But still made of stronger stuff than half the men I know." She'd held in most of her grief, keeping a brave face for her mother and sisters, and then when we were alone, she finally let the dam break. Her silent tears had been like razors slicing into my skin as she cried against my chest until she finally passed into exhausted oblivion.

"I still cannot fathom you breaking your vow, Gav. She must be an extraordinary woman."

"She is," I agreed. "But I didn't really have a choice."

His brown eyes flared. "Is she with child?"

I glared at Zevi, and he raised his palms. "Apologies. That was uncalled for."

But I had to admit there was little reason for him to assume anything different. He'd seen my behavior with women for many years—since I first discovered the distracting enticements of a pretty girl, really. So, I told him about my dismissal by Yonatan. Being put under Emmet's command as punishment. How I'd drunkenly gotten Zahava and myself into such a mess. And how Emmet had commanded me to stay away from drink.

"It's thanks to him I'm thinking clearly for the first time in years," I said, wishing I wasn't talking about Emmet in the past.

"He was a good man. Yonatan will be devastated to hear of his loss. They'd been friends for many years," Zevi said. "However, I am truly happy for you, cousin. I look forward to getting to know Zahava. Yochana will be thrilled as well. She's been worried about you."

"How is your bride?"

"She's well," he said, "but tired. Our youngest is a little over a year now and he's already running all over the mountain. It's a good thing there are so many family members around to keep eyes on him. Her official role as perfumer to the king takes up much of her time, but she also has a number of apprentices now. A few traveled from as far north as Sidon and Tyre to learn from her."

"Zevi," I said, still fixed on his first statement. "You have a son!"

His grin was as wide as the sky. "I do. His name is Lukio."

"I'll wager your father was honored you gave him that name."

Although Uncle Natan had publicly shed the name he'd been given at birth when he joined himself to the Covenant, his wife still called him Lukio as a term of affection.

"Between you and me . . ." He leaned in. "He wept."

I chuckled. "That would've been a sight to see. The Champion of Ashdod sobbing over his namesake."

"That it was. Where do you—"

"Commander!" The call from a messenger cut off whatever Zevi had planned to ask. "The spies are almost back. They'll be at the gates within moments."

Zevi and I broke into a run, following the young man to the entrance of the city, where even now, mudbricks were being lifted by workers to form the gates of Be'er Sheva. No longer would the inhabitants of the surrounding valley be vulnerable to invasion by the Philistines; they'd have a strong refuge to run to. One with thick walls and the protection of Israel's ever-expanding army. Saul's growing might and wealth were on full display here, a warning to our enemies and a comfort to the people of this region—including the Kenites who would now call this place their home. The question of whether this would be my home with Zahava was one without an answer, but I'd make those decisions after Barzel and Farah were rescued.

Zevi and I arrived just before the spies did, who looked as though they'd run all the way back from wherever they'd been. However, Zevi gave them little time to catch their breath. "What did you find?"

"We found the trail," panted one spy, palms on his knees. "But it didn't continue south toward Qadesh like we expected."

"Instead, they doubled back and followed the Besor River northwest," said the second spy.

Zevi's expression turned grim. "Into Philistine territory?"

Frowning, the spies nodded in tandem, and my stomach lurched. It was bad enough these people had been taken. But dragged to Philistia? Did they mean to sell them as slaves? I had to swallow back nausea as the attack rolled through my mind again. There was no end to the loop of questions about things I could have done differently that day. No end to the persistent voices reminding me of how I'd failed.

Zevi continued pressing the spies. "Do you know where they took them?"

The first man wiped his mouth, having just taken a long draft from a waterskin. "We thought maybe they'd turned northeast at a brook, but we came across hoofprints in the mud headed west. Then, we were fortunate to cross paths with some Egyptian traders on the Way of the Sea, and they told us they'd seen men on horseback thundering by their camp, headed toward Gaza."

"We couldn't go any farther," said the third spy. "We weren't prepared to go that far into enemy territory in the first place. We were fortunate to make it back unnoticed."

"That's all right," said Zevi, a hollow note in his voice. "You did well. Now we at least know where they've been taken."

Gaza. One of the five chief Philistine cities and an impenetrable fortress guarded by a standing army the extent of which no one truly knew. We may have surprised the Philistines at Michmash, aided by the shaking of the ground caused by the Ark, but not even the entirety of Saul's combined armies could take Gaza right now. The last Hebrew who'd had any measure of success against that wicked city had died beneath the rubble of the enormous temple he pulled down with his own two hands. And I was no Samson.

It's hopeless.

Even if I managed to find my way into Gaza without being revealed as a Hebrew, where would I look? From what I'd heard, it was no small place and boasted ancient fortifications going back to Avraham's day, perhaps further. It had been founded by Canaanites, conquered and expanded by Egypt, and now was held by Philistines who ruled the surrounding city-state from within its walls.

I'd promised Zahava I would get her loved ones back, and now I'd have to tell her she should count her father and sister as dead, because if they weren't already, they would probably be glad for death when it came. If there was anything the Philistines were famous for, it was cruelty.

I wandered away from the group, since Zevi was occupied with pressing the spies for more information. To what end, I had no idea. There was nothing that could be done to save them.

Hopeless.

Useless.

Failure.

I should go back and check on Zahava and her family, but my feet refused to turn toward the barracks. I couldn't face more of her pain. Couldn't watch her suffer. And I didn't want to return to the garrison where a group of soldiers had been looking at me as if I was somehow one of the leaders in the unit I'd been sent to as a punishment.

So instead, I passed through the half-built gates of the city, walked down the long slope into the valley, and then, harnessing the buzz building under my skin, set off at a swift jog heading south on the trade road. Losing myself in the thud of my sandals against the wagon-packed path, I easily caught up to Eliyah's unit and offered my help with the mission to retrieve what was left of the Kenite herds. The young captain must have sensed my desperation to keep myself occupied because he asked no questions, just told me to fall into formation.

We met Zevi's men and the chaotic mass of sheep and goats that they'd formed into one unruly herd about two hours later, not all that far from the site of the attack. Taking up positions around the livestock, we drove them toward Be'er Sheva, none of us skilled in shepherding but doing our best to keep them moving all the same with waving hands, shaking sticks, and loud cries. Thankfully, most of the animals followed their own leaders instinctively, and by early afternoon, we were within sight of Be'er Sheva.

At least I would be able to offer Zahava one small comfort today because halfway through the march back to the city, I recognized one of Farah's goats. She had a distinctive speckled pattern across her back and one horn that had been broken off before we'd left Punon, as well as twins tagging along behind. Around her was the rest of Farah's little herd. I'd leave them with the other goats being driven toward a lush patch of land just south of the river, so the women would claim them once they were ready.

Yet even with this small piece of good news in hand, I couldn't face them just yet. I spent the rest of the day with a group from Eliyah's unit digging a canal, glad for the heavy labor, the easy conversation between soldiers about nothing of any importance, and the rhythmic cadence of my adz breaking the stony ground. For the most part, it kept the hounding voices in my head at bay—the ones saying I would only continue to let Zahava down and I would never be anything but an echo of my worthless father.

Near sundown, we packed up our tools to return to the city. But as I went to part ways with Eliyah's men and finally face my grief-stricken wife, they insisted on buying me a drink in gratitude for my help with the canal.

I let them tug me toward the tavern. Let them slap a cup of strong drink on the table in front of me as they discussed how long it would take to finish the job in Be'er Sheva so they could get back to Lachish and their families. And as the chatter and clamor of the packed room lifted around me like music I'd half-forgotten, I curled my fingers around the cup on the sticky table. The liquid shimmered in the dance of firelight from the oil lamps dangling overhead, and the smell of it wafted toward me like the sweetest perfume.

I closed my eyes, breathing deeply of its aroma, knowing exactly how it would feel sliding down my throat, how it would hit my belly with that first delicious spike of heat, then the floating sensation that would ebb through my veins, tingling through my body all the way to the tips of my fingers and the soles of my feet. Oblivion called to me, whispering its name in my ear as my hand clenched tighter around that cup.

"Just like his father . . . he'll end up face down in the muck . . ."

The longer I hesitated, the louder the voices grew.

Worthless . . . failure . . . you'll only let her down . . .

An image rose up of Zahava's haunted face peering out the window of Zevi's room, searching the countryside for me, and then was overlaid with a hazy memory of my own mother pushing me into the next room, urgently whispering for me to stay quiet and promising that she wouldn't let *him* hurt me.

I flinched but for some reason could not release the iron hold I had on the cup. *Why?* I'd been fighting this beast for weeks now, refusing to let it have victory over me, and just as I had in every battle, I'd succeeded.

Did you?

The question was barely a whisper in some secret place deep inside, but it thundered in my ears just the same. Somehow, I knew the answer was no.

Zahava had said it was Yahweh who caused our paths to merge, and without that chance encounter with a little dove by a cistern, Emmet wouldn't have laid down his edict. And the day I'd tipped the cart and nearly succumbed to my thirst for that wine, it had been Shachar who'd dumped it on the ground.

Could it be, like Zahava said, that the God who'd set the stars aflame cared enough to order my steps and send others to intervene? That he cared enough to rescue me from my own foolishness?

"She's waiting!"

My eyes flew open at the startling exclamation from the young man beside me. Disoriented by the sudden rush of sound into my thoughts, I searched the faces of my companions. Were they talking about Zahava?

"She won't wait long," said another man across the table from me, his gap-toothed grin wide as he waggled his brows. "She's far too pretty for that. You haven't even approached her father, have you?"

It took me another few moments to realize they were discussing someone else's woman, not mine. But the spell of the drink before me was broken. I peeled my fingers from the cup and excused myself from the table, leaving behind my new friends and every last drop of drink in the tavern.

As I wound through Be'er Sheva, I was grateful nightfall had sent most of the people into their lamplit homes or to their beds. The darkness and empty streets allowed me time to consider what I'd realized at the tavern.

I'd been self-destructing for many years. Somehow, I'd become the very thing I hated—a man who squandered everything he'd been given and ended up a scourge to his own family. *Just like his father . . . pitiful . . . worthless . . . You let Zahava down . . . just like you let Shalem down . . .* Even out here, where the air was crisp and clear, the accusations in my head were relentless.

I stumbled over something in the street and tumbled, landing so hard on my knees that a shock of pain blazed up my thighs. Bleary-eyed from the agony of slamming into stone, I fell forward, palms flat on the ground, waiting until I could see straight again before sitting back on my heels.

I turned my face up to the sky and let out a long breath. Exhaustion pulled at my body. I'd been pushing myself without sleep for what seemed like days. If I could curl up on the ground right here, I would. But my wife, and our warm bed, were waiting. And even if her grief pained me, I needed to go back, face my brokenhearted wife, and hope she forgave me for running away and hiding from her like a fool.

The stars were not nearly as bright here as they'd been in the Punon Valley, or even the night Zahava and I walked back to camp after she'd sung me her mother's song, but still, myriad lights looked down on me from above. One in particular caught my eye, pulsing golden in the southeast. It was the same one she'd pointed out to me during that walk as she told me the story of her birth.

As I stared up at that mysterious golden light glittering against the midnight fabric of the skies, her honey-sweet voice rose up in my mind. *"Perhaps we're just not meant to have all the answers. But to keep listening for the only One who does."*

Again, a whisper of something nudged me from inside, this time telling me that the accusing words I'd carried around like stones in a satchel were lies. That I'd collected them and polished them and hoarded them as if they were gems instead of the refuse they truly were.

Emmet had been right. Here, on my knees, I could see far more clearly than I ever had before. And for the first time in years, those accusing voices were gone, far overshadowed by the voice of the

King of All Creation. I bowed my head and listened instead for the truth, basking in the relief of surrender.

When I finally crawled back into bed with Zahava later that night and she curled into me with a relieved sigh, I fell into sleep with the bone-deep reassurance that even if I had no answers about how to find Barzel and Farah, Yahweh would direct my every step. I only had to listen and obey.

Zahava

When Gavi suggested the two of us fetch Farah's goats this morning, along with Breena and Anaya, I leaped at the chance to leave the barracks, where grief still hung in the air like smoke.

Hand in hand, the girls walked ahead of us but as usual Gavi kindly shortened his stride as we descended the sloping road down into the valley. I didn't blame him for engaging in hard labor while we waited for answers and had told him so when he'd poured out apologies for disappearing. I wished I too could lose myself in work to distract my shattered heart. My fingers itched for my tools.

"How is Yasmin?" he asked as we turned onto the path that led to the Kenite encampment on the south side of the valley.

"She's doing her best to keep the twins occupied," I said. "She hasn't spoken much of Rahm at all."

Gavi and I had decided not to reveal the role her husband might have had in the attack. It would only cause her more pain. Besides, we didn't know the actual extent of his culpability.

"Do you think she suspects anything?"

"I don't know. My sister is no fool." What I could not understand was why he would do such a thing. My father had been so generous to him and his family, had taught him so much, and had given him his eldest daughter without reservation. If Rahm had truly been involved, the betrayal was too great to comprehend.

The revelation that my father and Farah were likely being held in Gaza was no secret, however. Within hours of the spies' return, everyone in Be'er Sheva knew just how dire the situation was. Gavi wouldn't tell me much, only that they were working on a plan.

Although our family remained in the barracks, at Zevi's insistence, many of the Kenite families had already set their tents in the area Saul had allotted for our tribe, the heads of households eager to stake their claim on the fertile land. My four uncles had come to tell my mother they had done so for our family as well, in my father's absence. Yaniq, the eldest of them, had unofficially assumed leadership for the family, but no one dared speak of what would happen should my father not return.

I'd never seen my mother so stricken, even when I'd watched her grieve both my brothers and multiple lost infants. But perhaps the double loss of her husband and her daughter had been too much. I was determined to get her out of Zevi's quarters and into the sun later today, along with Yasmin and Rahm's sisters, who'd not been more than a pace away from my eldest sister since news of their mother's death. Yasmin was, for all intents and purposes, their mother now.

At least I'd succeeded in getting Breena and Anaya outside, with the lure of a hunt for the goats. With our mother so uncharacteristically withdrawn, they'd turned to me for comfort. And that morning when Gavi had gone missing, they'd spent the entire day tucked into the bed on either side of me, the three of us comforting one another as best we could.

Even so, I'd missed waking beside him and drifting off with his warmth beside me. No wonder my mother was so bereft. I'd been married to Gavi for a matter of weeks; she'd been married to my father since she was Breena's age, barely a woman. After so long, it would be like having your heart ripped from your chest.

"There she is!" exclaimed Breena, a note of excitement in her voice for the first time in days. "There's Barodi!"

The girls ran toward the spotted doe Farah had nursed by hand when her own dam had died and who'd become one of the most prolific breeders and milk providers in all of my father's flocks. The sight of her, her twin kids, and the other goats my sister tended like her own children sent a wave of searing grief through me. Farah would be so glad her flock was safe. If only I could know that she was safe too. I could not bear to think of her suffering.

A sob burst from my mouth, but before my knees could buckle, I was in Gavi's arms, pressed tightly to his chest. He did not shush me or tell me not to cry but simply stroked my back gently as I wept in his strong embrace.

Once my tears slowed, Gavi pressed a kiss to my forehead, using his thumbs to wipe my cheeks. "We will not give up hope, little dove. I know it may look bleak, but I've seen Yahweh shake the ground under my feet to terrify the Philistines. He kept Zevi alive after traitors shot him full of holes and left him for dead. And I am convinced Yahweh even stirred up that dust storm to keep your people protected from the Amalekites in the Aravah. If he did all that, then he can lead us to your father and sister too."

I stared up at him in disbelief. "You told me before that you weren't certain about the benevolent nature of Yahweh. What changed?"

"You told me to listen for the answers. And I finally got low enough that I had nowhere to look but up." He told me how he'd been so close to throwing away his resolve in the tavern and how clarity had come when he needed it most. He'd also told me how my golden star had been a lodestone for him, drawing his eyes to the heavens as the Voice of the Eternal One had whispered truth to his heart.

"We won't give up," he said. "You know that, don't you? Zevi and I are working on a plan."

"How would you even find them in Gaza?" I mused. "Especially without being revealed as Hebrews?"

"That's the difficult part," he said. "There aren't many of us who could enter the city without raising suspicions."

"Perhaps you'll have to find a legitimate reason to be there, then. Who would be brave enough to go into a city with such a reputation?"

"Traders, perhaps . . . mercenaries . . . or . . ." His words faded away, his slate gray eyes tracking to some point far beyond my shoulder. Then he clapped a hand to his thigh. "That's it. I know *exactly* how we can get in."

"How?"

A laugh from Anaya drew our attention before he could respond, the sound foreign after these past few days of mourning. She was making circles around the trunk of the terebinth, with Barodi's twins tripping along in her wake. The sight was a balm over the raw places on my heart. Breena too looked much less bereft as she knelt down beside Barodi, preparing to milk the doe.

"Thank you," I said to Gavi. "For bringing us out here. We needed space to breathe."

He pulled me into his side, his palm stroking down the length of my arm as we watched the girls with the animals. "They've been carrying too much. You all have. If I can help lift some of that burden, I will."

From my first impression of this fearsome warrior at the betrothal, I'd never have guessed Gavi would be such an affectionate man. But although he'd only kissed me on the mouth that one time, right before he dashed off to go find Farah in the wadi, he'd taken to touching me without hesitation these last couple of days.

A brush of his palm across my shoulders, a squeeze of my hand, or a gentle touch on the small of my back as he passed by me . . . it was almost as if he needed the constant reassurance I was safe. And even though we no longer slept outside in the cold, he still enveloped me in his arms at night, sharing his warmth.

So why, when he was so free with his affection and we had Zevi's little room to ourselves, did he not make me his wife in body? He hadn't even hinted that he desired me in that way, but I had no idea how to even broach the subject without perishing from embarrassment. Even now my face heated from my own thoughts, so I was glad he was staring off at the horizon.

But suddenly his body went rigid beside me, and his arm dropped away. Disoriented and wondering if I'd somehow spoken my ridiculous thoughts aloud, I looked up to find him staring intently at something in the distance.

"What is it?" I asked, blocking the glare of sunlight with my hand. A donkey ambled slowly along through a barley field, but no one seemed to be driving it forward. It looked to be laden with a burden on its back, so perhaps it had run off from its master.

"Stay here with the girls." Something in his tone caused the hair on the back of my neck to prickle as he jogged toward the animal.

The donkey halted as Gavi approached, standing still as my husband reached to lift one side of the burden bowed over its back.

Realization hit me like a blow to my gut. It was not a burden of goods my husband was studying; it was a body. A head and arms dangled over one side, and its feet nearly touched the ground on the other. Panic and horror exploded inside my chest.

"Bree. Stay with Anaya," I commanded. "I'll be back."

Breena looked up from her milking with a frown. "What's wrong?"

"Do not move from this place. Do you hear me?" I was already on the move, ignoring the sharp pain in my hip as I hobbled over the uneven ground toward Gavi. I *had* to know.

"Stay back," he called, one palm in the air. "You don't need to see this."

The donkey had turned to the side. All I could see was a ragged and bloodied tunic and the bound legs of the barefooted man it carried.

I ignored Gavi, continuing forward. "Who is it? My father?"

"No," he said. "Zahava. Stop."

Relief warred with the drive to confirm with my own eyes that it was not my abba slumped over the donkey, which appeared to be half-dead itself, ribs protruding and with a large patch of weeping sores on its withers. I circled around the other side.

"*Rahm.*" His name came out on a choked whisper as I slapped a palm over my mouth to keep from crying aloud. He'd been beaten nearly to the point of nonrecognition, but I'd stared at that handsome face for years, memorizing it as only an infatuated young girl could do. And although it was my husband who held my heart, I'd still know Rahm anywhere. Even bound hand and foot with his broken body tied to a donkey.

"Is he . . . dead?"

"He's breathing," said Gavi. "But he has an iron rod impaling his chest. We need to get him into the city, quickly, or he won't be alive for long."

We sent Breena and Anaya to the city ahead of us to alert Zevi, without letting them see the extent of Rahm's injuries. Then Gavi led the donkey up the sloping road to Be'er Sheva with as much care as possible. Even so, Rahm would often groan in gut-wrenching agony but did not awaken. Gavi had decided not to remove him from the animal's back, lest our efforts cause worse damage.

Zevi met us halfway up the slope, a group of his men trailing behind him. "Who is it?"

"Yasmin's husband," said Gavi. "The one I told you about."

His cousin frowned, surveying Rahm's extensive injuries and the iron rod jammed high into his right side. "He say anything?"

Gavi shook his head. "He's not fully conscious."

"Find anything on the donkey? A note?"

"Didn't look, Zev. I'm just trying to get him to town and save his life."

Zevi gestured to his men, who came forward to carefully lift Rahm from the donkey and lay his bloodied form on a wool blanket. Then, with the blanket stretched between four of them, they headed for the gates.

Before he left us to head for the barracks, Zevi ordered two of the soldiers to search the animal for anything that might give a clue to where Rahm had been, a couple more to go fetch a healer, and one to collect Yasmin.

Before we could follow him, Gavi paused to face me, concern furrowed between his brows. "Perhaps you should head back to Zevi's quarters. None of this will be easy."

I frowned at him. "I'm going with you."

"Doesn't this . . . upset you to see him this way? He was part of your life for many years."

"It's difficult to see him like this." I tipped up my chin and stared into his eyes, grateful for his compassion. "But he also may be at fault for my father and sister being stolen away, and for a number of deaths, including your captain's."

"It's very possible, but—"

I shook my head. "I want to know, Gavi. And besides, my sister will need me."

He let out a sigh. "All right, then. Let's go."

When we entered the small room where Rahm had been taken, I was surprised that Yasmin hadn't arrived yet and neither had the healer. Rahm moaned as we approached the bed, eyes fluttering open and wheeling about hazily. One of them was blood-red, the wide pupil black as it landed on me.

"Za . . . hav?" he mumbled, his mouth so swollen I was surprised he could speak at all. It was bad enough to see him draped over that donkey but laid out here on the bed, which was already soaked with blood, his true state was startling and his face nearly unrecognizable. No matter what he had or hadn't done, no one deserved such torture.

"Someone went to fetch Yasmin. She'll be here shortly."

"No. She . . . can't be . . . here." Each word was labored, spoken in a painful rasp.

"Your wife has been very worried for you," said Gavi at my side. "She'll want to see you."

Rahm squeezed his eyes shut. "I don't . . . deserve . . ."

The last shred of hope I had that Gavi had guessed wrongly fell away, and anger spiked hot in my blood. "Why not?"

He swallowed hard, looking away from me to my husband. "They . . . sent . . . a . . ." He pulled in a painful-sounding inhale. "A message."

"Who?" Gavi pressed.

"Phil . . . stines. Barzel could . . . not . . . make red . . . gold."

My body went numb. "What do you mean?"

"I did . . . not mean to . . ." He paused, taking another gasping breath as blood trickled from the corner of his mouth.

Fury bubbled up. "Why? Why would you endanger my father? And all of us?" Gavi gently squeezed my hand in silent support.

Rahm shook his head, even though the move was clearly agonizing. "He . . . wouldn't . . . listen. Trusted . . . Hebrews . . . instead. I had a . . . plan . . . with Talmar."

So he *had* been involved in the scheme to bring along Niv and Kila's family. What could he and Talmar possibly have had in the works that would cause him to betray everyone?

"So, what? You endangered all of us—your own *family*—by telling them about his skills?"

"I . . . made a . . . deal. Take Barzel . . . Make him . . . show me . . ." He gritted his teeth and inhaled sharply. But he'd said enough for me to slide the pieces together.

". . . the secrets of the red-gold," I finished for him. Perhaps he and Talmar had endeavored to coerce my father somehow once we'd arrived in Be'er Sheva, but when Niv and Kila's family was sent away, Rahm had devised a scheme of his own at the tavern. One that meant making a deal with our enemies so he could reap the rewards. I remembered how he told me not to tell my father about the sword he was making for the Amalekite chieftain. Perhaps he'd been manipulating my father all along.

His battered face twisted. "He . . . refused. Even . . . after the . . . wedding. Said . . . it was . . . a vow."

I huffed a mirthless chuckle. "My father is mostly blind, Rahm. He couldn't teach you anymore even if he wanted to."

Rahm swallowed hard again as a line of bloody saliva dripped from his mouth and his lone working eye fixed on me. "They . . . weren't supposed . . . to take . . . Farah."

My knees wobbled as his implication landed. Gavi's arm went around my waist, holding me up.

"You knew it was me," I whispered. "How long?"

"Eb . . . enezer's . . . bit." He coughed, more blood bubbling at his lips. "Should . . . have known. . . . Didn't . . . guess . . . until it was too late."

Indeed, he should have known it was me. If he'd not been caught up in whatever machinations he'd been planning, he might have realized it years ago. I was the one who spent hours in the foundry and whose hands bore the scars of metalwork. But he'd never actually *seen* me.

So he'd married Yasmin, and when that didn't get him what he wanted, he'd colluded with monsters to kidnap us. Poor Farah had only gotten ensnared in what should have been my fate.

A strangled noise by the door drew my attention away from Rahm. Yasmin stood there, her face pale as she stared at her traitorous husband. "*You* did this?"

Rahm merely nodded.

"Your mother . . ." She paused, shaking her head. "Your sisters are orphans now. How could you?"

"I . . . was . . . wrong," he began, but an ancient man whom I guessed to be the healer, by the large satchel slung over his chest, appeared behind Yasmin in the doorway. He tried to sidle past her to reach Rahm, but my sister threw out an arm to block his path.

"Where are they?" she demanded of Rahm.

"Young woman," huffed the man, who barely reached her eye level, "I need to get that rod out and cauterize that wound or he'll not live much longer."

"Then my *husband* had better tell me where my father and sister are. *Now*."

By the fearsome look on her face, I had no doubt Yasmin would let him die without regret. And it seemed Rahm believed she would as well.

"The king . . . of . . . Gaza said . . . until the goldsmith . . . comes to him . . . one Kenite . . . will die . . . every day."

24

Gavriel

Regardless of Yasmin's bold insistence that Rahm tell us everything before anyone touched him, we learned little more before he was swallowed up in unconsciousness and the healer finally was allowed to step in. We now knew that Farah had been separated from the men, and so far everyone else was alive but locked in a prison somewhere on the grounds of the royal fortress. Rahm said we had less than two days to produce my wife to the Philistine king. And since that was *not* happening, we now had to figure out how to get into the palace in Gaza before Kenites began dying.

It was difficult to feel any sort of compassion for the fool, dying or not. He'd caused the deaths of his mother, Emmet, and so many others. He'd offered up my wife for the sake of his own greed. He was fortunate there were so many witnesses in that room or I may have yanked that rod from his side myself.

Yasmin remained to assist the healer, who'd been unpacking his wound-cauterizing equipment when Zahava and I left the room, and Zevi assured me his men would let him know if Rahm said anything more of importance. I'd seen plenty of battle wounds, and truly, I didn't think the man would last more than a few hours. I guessed it had been the king's goal to have him live only long enough to deliver the message.

In a silent daze, my wife let me lead her up the stairway to the second floor but came to a halt before we reached the door of Zevi's quarters. "I can't let anyone die in my place, Gavi. My father, Farah, *everyone* is in danger because of me."

I turned her toward me and then, caring nothing that anyone in the courtyard below might see us, I held her face in my hands, my thumbs stroking her cheekbones. "We know where they are now, little dove. Zevi and I will find a way to get them out."

She swallowed hard, her eyes shimmering. "But then you'll be in danger too. And I don't know what I would do . . ."

I pulled her close, brushing a kiss to the top of her head and breathing in her sweetness as she pressed her cheek to my chest. "I spent the last few years of my life spying on our enemies for Yonatan, Zahava. This is what I do."

I hated to relinquish my hold on her, but time was not on our side. Zevi and I had plans to make.

"Your mother is probably desperate to hear what happened. Will you be all right to tell her?"

She sniffled as she pulled out of my arms. "I'll have to be careful so the girls don't figure out the truth. Hopefully, Rahm's sisters will never know that their brother caused their mother's death."

I nodded grimly. "I'll be back as soon as I can."

She took a deep breath, seeming to collect herself before turning away. Her bravery never ceased to astound me. I stood by the door for a few moments after she entered the room, listening to the murmur of her quiet words as she explained the situation. Rahm's sisters began to weep, and it made me think of my own. Would they cry for me that way, if something terrible happened to me? They'd always looked up to me, but I'd left home when they were children. The back of my throat burned at the realization that I'd been so mired in my own mess that I'd become little more than a stranger to my own family.

I blew out a breath, pushing off those thoughts for another time, and went to find Zevi. I found him in a shady corner of the courtyard, with a group of men gathered around, hanging on his every word. Young men like Adin practically kissed the dirt he walked on. And truly, he deserved such honor. He was a good man. Loyal to his king, his nation, and his family.

I suddenly regretted the times I'd been less than respectful to him or resented him for having Natan for a father. I'd even been jealous of Avidan, whose father was no Champion of Ashdod but was not shy of boasting about Avi's devotion to teaching Israel's past to Hebrews across the river who'd forgotten the stories. Yet somehow, even though both my cousins knew full well what a disaster I'd been over the past few years, neither one had cut me off the way I deserved. There was still a current of something unresolved between us, because of Shalem, but there was no doubt in my mind that either man would lay down their lives for me. As I would for them.

I joined the group around Zevi, standing between Eliyah on my right and Adin on my left. I hadn't seen much of the young man since we'd arrived in Be'er Sheva, and I was struck by his altered appearance. Gone was the eager light in his eyes and the quick smile. He looked haggard, as if he'd aged a decade over the past few days. I easily recognized the signs of self-torture and sleepless nights, probably over his failure to protect Farah during the raid. Hopefully, Adin wouldn't be foolish enough to drown his guilt in wine like I had. Once this was all over, I'd make a point to take the boy under my wing.

"How do we get in?" asked one of the men, dragging me back to the mission at hand. "They aren't going to throw open the fortress gates to a bunch of Hebrews."

"Ideas?" Zevi asked, his gaze roving the group.

"Perhaps we can come by sea?" said another. "I heard Gaza lies on the coast."

"It's possible," said Zevi. "But that still doesn't answer how we'd get inside the fortress. A small group of us is nothing against the king's guard."

"What happens if we are caught?" said Eliyah. "Could it cause a greater conflict with Israel?"

Zevi blew out a breath. "That's certainly something to consider. We don't want to cause a war. Saul would not be pleased."

It was true. Sending in a group of Hebrew soldiers to a Philistine stronghold could be construed as an act of war. And although they'd been less aggressive since we'd made a mockery out of them at Michmash, I doubted it would take much for our greatest enemies to gather forces in retaliation. Besides, this rescue mission was not sanctioned by Saul.

"We don't send in Hebrew soldiers." Zahava's question earlier had sparked an idea that I'd formed into the semblance of a plan. "Send in civilians."

Everyone turned to stare at me.

"What do you have in mind, Gavriel?" asked Zevi.

"If we go blazing into Gaza, then we have no chance. We'll be cut down. The Philistines have superior weapons, and engaging them in their own territory would be futile. Whenever we've had success in the past against them, it's because we know the terrain. We use the land itself against them, shooting from the hills, from behind rocks, from treetops, choking them in narrow passes, and the like. It's the only way we can succeed when they have fleets of iron-wheeled chariots."

Zevi nodded, tracking my thoughts. "So how do we use their advantages against them?"

"Simple," I said. "Iron."

"I don't follow," said Eliyah.

"Look. The Philistines have the upper hand when it comes to the iron trade. They've developed ways of strengthening iron that we just don't understand. They have furnaces capable of reaching temperatures much higher than ours. Bronze is durable but lacks the strength of iron, which means they have access to weapons that are not only stronger but far cheaper to produce. Iron ore is easy to gather. It sits on the surface of the earth for the most part—unlike copper, which has to be wrestled from the ground in deep and treacherous mines like at Punon."

"What does this have to do with civilians going into Gaza?" pressed Haim, who'd been one of Emmet's trusted inner circle.

"Because the Philistines hold most of the ports on the Great Sea to import ore and guard their production secrets so well, even Hebrews are forced to rely on Philistine blacksmiths to repair tools. Therefore, the way into Gaza is disguised as customers either needing tool repairs or seeking to purchase iron farm implements."

"They hate us. But they won't turn away our silver." Zevi sounded impressed.

"We should enter the city in pairs, not as a large group. Yochaim and I will go in together." Eliyah gestured to the man on his right.

"*You* are not going anywhere near Gaza, Eliyah," said Zevi. "Your wife is near her time. You and your men will be heading back to Lachish as soon as you finish that canal."

"With all respect, Commander—" Eliyah began, but Zevi held up a palm.

"Go home, my friend. Hold your first child. There's nothing better in the world, I assure you."

A sudden longing for a son or daughter of my own hit me with such force that it nearly knocked the wind from my lungs. I was shocked to realize that I was jealous of Eliyah. When this was over, I'd gladly take a year, or more, with Zahava to start a family of our own.

"I'll go," said Adin, dragging me back from the vision of a future I'd never imagined but now desperately wanted.

"No. You won't," said Shachar. "You're not ready."

"I am," said the young man, his nostrils flaring.

"You aren't even of age," said Zevi. "Your father would not allow it."

Adin gritted his teeth. "I could not care less what my father thinks. I'm not afraid to go into Gaza. Besides, who would look twice at me?"

He had a point. The Philistines would not expect a young man, especially one who looked as innocent as Adin, to be a spy. But Shachar was right; he was not ready for such a treacherous mission.

I put my hand on his shoulder. "You'll have plenty of chances to take on the Philistines, Adin. This isn't your time yet."

The boy shrugged me off, his jaw set. No longer did he regard me with anything resembling hero worship. There were daggers in his eyes before he spun around and stalked away, head down. I had a sudden rush of empathy for anyone who'd been on the wrong end of my own disrespect over the years. But I had no time to deal with his behavior right now. We had until sunset the day after tomorrow to rescue seventeen vulnerable Kenites.

"I think Gavriel's plan has merit," said Zevi. "I'd say no more than twelve men, entering the city over the course of a few hours and coming from different directions. We'll ask around here for any broken farm tools that can be carried as props. Maybe even a few of us should be dressed in Kenite garb."

"How will we gain access to the fortress?" asked Shachar.

"Gavriel has spent the last few years in Yonatan's unit," said Zevi. "We'll make some contingency plans, but I trust him to take point on the best way to get inside once he takes stock of the situation in Gaza."

I wasn't certain how we would get into that fortress and find the Kenites once we did so, but I'd find a way. No Philistine king would ever get anywhere near Zahava. I'd lay my life down to make certain of it.

Everyone was asleep by the time our plan was fully fleshed out. As I crept back into Zevi's quarters, I could barely make out the forms of Safaa and Anaya on one bedroll and Breena on the other, with Rahm's sisters on either side of her. Yasmin must still be with Rahm. The last I'd heard, he was still alive but hadn't awakened for some time. The traitor wasn't expected to survive until morning. After what he'd planned for Zahava, I couldn't bring myself to care, even for Yasmin's sake.

I stole into the small chamber Zahava and I had been sharing, opening and closing the door carefully so it did not squeak on its bronze hinges. A beam of moonlight through the high window illuminated my wife on the bed, eyes open and waiting for me.

"Why are you still awake?" I whispered, padding across the wooden floor. Thankfully, there were only stables beneath us, and no one to wake with my footsteps.

"I could not sleep without you."

The statement wrapped around my heart and squeezed. Throat tight, I lifted the edge of the blanket and slipped into the bed beside her. The ropes creaked a little at my added weight, but the straw-stuffed mattress was nearly as comfortable as the wool-and-goose-feather one I'd slept on in Hanan's home.

"You have a plan?" she asked.

"We do. I'll tell you about it in the morning. Let's sleep."

"I won't be able to rest until you do."

I stroked my hand down the length of her braid. "Are you sure you want to know? I don't want you to worry."

"I will worry no matter what, Gavi." She took a tremulous

breath. "Don't leave me in the dark about what is going to happen tomorrow, or it'll be worse."

So as the moon slid across the narrow gap between the two windows high on the wall of Zevi's room, I explained how we planned to get into the city by fooling the Philistines into believing we were there to repair tools. She asked which men would be going, and I gave their names.

"Just the twelve?" she asked.

"Eliyah wanted to go, but his wife is close to having a baby, so Zevi forbade him. And Adin is furious we wouldn't even consider him."

"He's very upset over what happened with Farah, isn't he?"

"I'm certain he thinks it's his fault."

"He was quite infatuated with her," she said.

"Was he?"

"I'm surprised you didn't notice. He stared at her so hard she practically had holes in her."

I chuckled. "I was too busy looking at you."

She nudged closer. "Is that so?"

I pressed a kiss to her forehead. "Once the wine haze wore off, it did not take long to realize I was married to the most beautiful woman I'd ever seen."

She scoffed. "Yasmin is the most beautiful."

I leaned in, speaking close to the shell of her ear. "Yasmin is lovely, but you are the brightest star in my sky, my little dove. There is nothing I would not do for you."

She inhaled at my declaration, then breathed out my name on a sigh.

"Which is why I will not give up until your father and sister are back here with you where they belong."

"But it's not just my father and Farah. There are fifteen other families who are terrified for their loved ones. I just don't see how you can get them all back safely. Or even find them in time."

"Please, Zahava. Trust me."

"I do. I just hate that they are in danger because of me. And now you and the others will be too." The moonlight reappeared through the window, washing her sun-bronzed skin to white and causing her hazel eyes to glimmer with a sheen of tears. "I am one person. I am not worth their lives."

With one finger, I nudged her chin until she was looking into my eyes. "How can you even think that? You are my *wife*. If I could go back and erase the last few years of supreme stupidity, I would never even *glance* at another woman. I just pray you can forgive me. That you believe I will never want anyone or anything more than I want you. You are worth everything to me."

She let out a little sob, then pressed a kiss to my jaw as she slid her leg around my calf, pulling me closer. "And I want you. I want to be your wife, body and soul. I want to be one with you, Gavriel."

Everything went still inside my head for a moment, and then my pulse began to race. "Zahava . . ."

"Please." She nuzzled her nose against my chest, then pressed another kiss to the hollow of my throat. "We don't know what will happen tomorrow. For tonight, can we just pretend it's our wedding night?"

If I'd learned anything about marriage so far, it was not to argue with my wife. So as the moon slipped away from the window, affording us true and uninterrupted privacy, we two finally became one.

A knock on the door woke me from the deepest sleep I'd had in years. A decade, perhaps. Disoriented by the banging, as well as Zevi's voice calling my name, I rolled myself out of the bed and yanked the door open. Had I overslept? We'd planned to leave after sunrise, and the sky outside the window was only just beginning to turn gray.

My cousin's eyes were wide. "Adin's gone."

"What?" I blinked a few times, trying to make sense of his words. "Where did he go?"

"Shachar woke at dawn, found his bedroll empty and his pack missing from the tent."

"Maybe he went to sleep somewhere else? He was pretty angry with all of us after yesterday."

"Shachar thought so at first, so he asked around. No one in the garrison has seen him." Zevi paused. "There's also a mule missing from the stable. One of Barzel's."

My stomach dropped like a boulder. I would throttle that boy when I caught up with him. "No one saw him leave the city?"

"I spoke with the guards on duty early this morning. Since the gates aren't finished yet, there's nothing barring anyone from going in or out at any hour. They said two young men left with a mule a couple of hours ago. Said the animal was in distress and making so much noise braying and kicking up a fuss that it was waking everyone in the garrison. He claimed he'd been told to get it outside the city until it calmed down. My men assumed they were stable boys and didn't think anything of it."

I ran my hands over my face with a groan. Where would he even go with a mule in the middle of the—? A horrific thought cut off my words as my mind spun backward. "Did you say there were *two* boys with the mule?"

"Yes, but I don't know who it could be. No one else has been reported missing."

Zevi may have said something else, but my ears were ringing as dread crashed into me like a wave. I whipped around to stare at the bed on the opposite wall, the one I'd just rolled out of, never noticing the other side was unoccupied.

A curse flew from my mouth as I called her name, my vision blurring for a moment as I stupidly searched the empty room for my precious wife and found that the leather satchel she carried on her lap all the way from Punon was gone as well. There was only one reason she would take her tools with her in the middle of the night.

My wife had gone to Gaza to surrender herself to the Philistine king.

Zahava

Ebenezer was surprisingly fast for a mule, especially when he had only two people on his back, a downward-sloping trail, and no heavy-laden wagon yoked to him. And since we'd kept moving from the moment we left Be'er Sheva long before dawn and all the way down into the coastlands, I was also grateful for his endurance. I could not chance Gavi catching up. I would not allow anyone else to die. Not when I could leverage the knowledge I held for their release.

It was a risk. The Philistines may not believe that I was the goldsmith; they may even imprison me as well. But I could not wait until Gavi and his companions found a way to get inside the royal fortress without getting killed themselves. By that time, my father or Farah might already be sacrificed in my place, and that was a risk I refused to take. And I was certainly not fool enough to think that Gavi would ever agree to taking me to Gaza himself, so I'd set aside the choking guilt and taken matters into my own hands.

I'd hated asking for Adin's help, knowing I was dragging him into danger with me, but after what Gavi had said about his frustration at being dismissed, I'd hoped he'd go with me to Gaza. In the end, it had taken little effort to find him out in the courtyard where he'd been sleeping fitfully with his back against a palm tree, and even less to convince him to come with me after I'd shaken him awake.

Frankly, I was surprised he hadn't even argued with my plan to trade myself for the hostages. But I didn't question why, and neither did he offer up his reasons. Thankfully, the guards at Be'er Sheva thought nothing of a couple of stable boys tending an unruly mule—although I was still apologizing to Ebenezer for surreptitiously poking him with one of my bone picks to prove he was far too noisy to remain penned up in the garrison.

Adin and I passed some of the journey down to the coastlands trading our secrets: me, with my metalworking, and him, his murderous father whom I could not believe was such a trusted member of Saul's guard. It sounded as if Adin and his brothers had endured the worst torture in his household. I only hoped Gavi would be forgiving when I sent him back to explain my actions because I could not bear to think of Adin being punished for my decision, even though it meant Farah's freedom, along with my father and the other Kenites.

Once we'd found our way to the main trade road, thanks to Adin having been in on the early discussions about how the soldiers would get into Gaza, we turned Ebenezer north and followed the well-trodden road along with the other traders and travelers, none of whom paid us any attention since we looked like nothing but a couple of dusty paupers.

We'd snatched garments from clotheslines in the dark courtyard before we stole out of Be'er Sheva so Adin would look as much a Kenite as I did, with the exception of his blue eyes. Head-coverings hid his light brown hair and my own waist-length braid, and I'd smudged ash around our eyes just like our shepherds did to help with the blaze of sunlight in the fields. But even with the disguises, the sight of the walls of Gaza rising in the distance swirled terror through my veins. All it would take was one guard at the gates to take a second look at Adin or to press him on his origins for us to be discovered.

However, even this late in the afternoon, there was a steady stream of wagons, handcarts, and camels plodding along with their burdens, streaming in and out of those impressive gates, which afforded us anonymity in the crowd. And when Adin affected a gruff Kenite accent to tell the harried guard we'd come to purchase food for our journey north to Ashkelon, we were easily given entrance.

With Ebenezer plodding along behind us, Adin and I found ourselves pushed along with the crowds filling streets lined with dazzling white buildings, which were decorated with such an array of beautiful colors and unfamiliar designs that I had to force my mouth closed to hide my awe. I'd never seen anything like the complicated system of ceramic drains lining the sides of the roads, carrying a steady stream of dirty water and sewage toward the sea.

I wasn't certain what I'd expected of Gaza, but the buzz of everyday life surrounded us. Garments fluttered from windowsills. Good-natured chatter and sharp words alike bled from open doorways as we passed. Servants passed us carrying baskets on heads and women with painted faces floated by in many-tiered skirts of every hue. Barefooted children darted through alleyways, wooden swords in hand and feathered headdresses made from strips of linen and seagull feathers to mimic the many well-armed soldiers prowling the streets of Gaza.

However, unlike Be'er Sheva, shrines to the gods were everywhere: in wall niches on shop fronts and beside doorways into homes that stood three and four stories tall. From the yawning gates of the temple complex, the smell of burning flesh nearly choked me as we passed. This was not the sweet smell of a roasted lamb my father offered in sacrifice to Yahweh but something rank and bitter that mixed with the salt-laden humidity.

"What is that?" I asked, hovering a hand over my mouth and nose.

"Burning pig flesh, I would guess," he said, tugging his head-covering over his face. "At least that's what I hope it is."

I did not ask what else it might be, for fear I already knew his answer. My father had never held back his disgust at the horrifying worship practices of the Amalekites, which included the offering of even their own children to Molech at times. I held my breath and kept my eyes fixed on the road ahead of us, shamed to my core that I'd ever turned a blind eye to the fact that Niv and Kila took part in such rituals.

"They must have rebuilt the temple Samson pulled down so many years ago," mused Adin, a welcome distraction from the guilt coating my insides.

"Who is Samson?"

In brief terms, he quietly relayed the story of one of the *shoftim* of Israel, a champion of a man who sounded nearly as reckless as he was mighty. After Samson had given up the secret to his blessing from Yahweh, he'd died beneath the rubble of the temple here in Gaza, taking scores of Philistines with him to the grave.

There was so much I did not know about the history of Israel. Our people only heard scattered rumors at Punon, but now was not the time to ask more, with the streets around us full of the enemies of Adin's people, who undoubtedly remembered how the Hebrew had humiliated them, even with his eyes gouged out and his hair shorn, stripped of everything because of his foolishness.

And not only Philistines filled the streets of Gaza. The marketplace overflowed with people of every shade of skin and a cacophony of languages. Egyptians dressed in fine linens with jewels at their wrists and necks and braided wigs tinkling with tiny gold beads bartered with foreign merchants in stalls, proving the relationship between the land of the Pharaohs and Philistia was more than amicable, even if they'd once been enemies.

"Look, there it is," said Adin, gesturing toward the grand palace looming ahead at the western edge of the city. I'd been awed by the new garrison and barracks in Be'er Sheva, but this was like nothing I'd ever imagined. Stacked layer upon layer with red and blue columns holding aloft high ceilings over open porticos that ran the length of the building, the display of such blatant wealth and power dazzled my eyes. In comparison to this marvel of masonry, Be'er Sheva was a wilderness outpost. It would likely take King Saul decades to even begin to approach this level of splendor.

Swaying palms lined the wide road that led to the ornate gates of the palace, along with manicured gardens overflowing with bright blooms of every color. At least half of the plants we passed I had no name for, having never seen such a profusion of vibrant flora in my life. There were even pools surrounded by limestone that contained enormous blue-white blossoms that floated atop the water among wide leaves, snaking grasses, and trembling reeds.

The closer we came to the entrance, where a cadre of guards stood in shining bronze armor and crimson-feathered headdresses, the smaller I felt. My hip screamed from the walk through the city without the aid of my father's walking stick, and the long ride atop Ebenezer, so I was glad to have the mule to covertly lean on once we stood before the palace gates.

"You two lost?" asked one of the Philistine guards, one hand on the hilt of his iron sword.

Nervous sweat trickled down my back, but I took a deep breath and lifted my chin with as much courage as I could muster. "I was summoned here by the king."

"Were you now?" The Philistine arched one silvering brow.

"It's true," said Adin. "The king sent a message with a hostage he sent to Be'er Sheva tied to the back of a donkey. *She* is the master goldsmith he seeks among the Kenites."

One of the other guards snickered. "A woman?"

My pulse raced. Had I traveled this far only to be sent away?

"Please, my lord," I said, "if you will allow me to see the king, I can prove my skill."

The older man looked me up and down, his penetrating gaze causing gooseflesh to break out on my arms. "Prove it to me first."

I blinked at him. "How?"

"If you're such a skilled metalsmith, you'll think of something."

Mind whirling, I scrambled for an idea. Simply pulling out the tools I'd brought with me might not convince this guard—or even the king, for that matter.

My eyes latched on the plug in the man's left ear. "Is that gold?" I asked.

He touched his earlobe. "This? Yes."

"Are you sure?"

"I received it from the king himself for preventing an assassination attempt. It's *pure* gold."

"Can you remove it?"

He frowned, brow furrowing. "Why?"

"You asked me for proof."

He peered at me with interest, then reached up to push the plug from his lobe. "Now what?"

"Adin," I said, "hand me the smallest iron tongs from my pack, will you?"

The young man practically vibrated with tension but did as I bade. Then I asked one of the guards to retrieve a torch from the niche beside the gate. The head guard allowed it, probably driven more by curiosity than anything.

"I must hold the plug over the fire," I said. "But don't worry, it's not nearly hot enough to harm it."

"You must be awfully confident in that assessment, seeing as how any one of us could gut you in a moment if you are lying."

"And not only that," I replied, "but I am crippled. I can't even run away."

He flinched at my words, surprised by my honesty, I would guess.

"All right. Tenokea, hold that torch still. Let's see what proof she can give us."

His companion lowered the bitumen torch, the wide flame flickering in the humid sea air, and the head guard held out his gold earplug, carved with a symbol of a god whose name I did not care to know. Heart thumping in spite of my confidence in the outcome, I plucked the plug from his palm with the tongs and held it over the torch. Holding it directly in the center of the fire for a slow count of thirty.

"That's enough," said the guard, shifting nervously.

"Not quite," I said. "Just a bit longer."

"If you ruin that . . ."

"I won't. It takes a fire three times as hot as this one, inside a well-tended furnace, to melt gold."

When I'd counted to ninety, I removed the plug from the fire and limped over to the lovely pool a few paces away, quenching it in the water for another count of sixty.

The head guard had followed, watching me warily, lest I let his cherished reward slip to the bottom of the pool. Even if I wasn't adept with every one of my metalworking tools, the water was as clear as a mountain spring, and tiny fish darted about near the shallow floor of the pool.

I held the cooled jewel out to the man, dropping it into his palm. "There. Perfectly intact."

"And what does that prove?"

"If it was alloyed with some other cheaper metal, like nickel or zinc, it would have blackened. But as you can see, it shines even brighter than before. Your king must indeed value your service." I tried for a smile, but it trembled. I may know my metals but I knew nothing of Philistine soldiers. It was possible I'd only offended him by testing the gold and had doomed both Adin and myself with my audacity.

He let out an amused huff. "All right. Just for being bold enough to potentially destroy that earplug, I'll take you inside. But it'll be up to the king to grant you an audience."

My knees wobbled as relief poured through me. "Thank you."

I slipped the iron tongs back into my pack and slung the strap over my shoulder, then turned to Adin. "Tell Gavriel—"

"I'm going with you, *cousin*. Don't bother." His jaw was set as he spoke over me, sounding far older than he was. I could stand here and bicker with him, but I guessed he'd already anticipated my every argument. So I just nodded, swallowing hard against the emotion his loyalty incited.

The head guard told Tenokea to put Ebenezer with the horses for now. I hoped I'd see my father's loyal mule again soon, but if I didn't, at least he would be held in the royal stables.

And then, the head guard, earplug back in place, led us through the gates into a courtyard that nearly rivaled the palace for beauty. The variety of flowers and well-tended trees outside the walls were eclipsed by the sheer number of perfectly manicured gardens spread over the grounds. Even the tiled walkway was a work of art, inlaid with tiny shells and colorful stones. Once we entered the building itself through towering oak doors, the murals on the walls of the main hall were so intricate and vibrant, I wished I could stop and stare.

We were led down two flights of wide stone stairs—thanks to Adin supporting me by hand down each step—and toward the back of the palace. After an abrupt left turn, the head guard unlocked a heavy wooden door and ushered us inside. He'd been astoundingly patient with my slow pace for a man whose people were known to the Hebrews as evil personified.

However, it took me all of three heartbeats before I realized he'd closed the door behind us.

"Wait!" I shouted as the lock clattered shut. "I thought you were taking us to the king."

"The king sees no one without an invitation," he called through the door of the windowless room. "You'll just have to wait until he decides whether you receive one or not."

Adin refused to sleep on the lone bench in our prison cell, not that the floor would have been any more comfortable for me. I slept fitfully and woke with a sharp ache in my lower back that no amount of stretching would relieve and blisters on my soles from my elevated sandals. Only the sliver of light underneath the door told us it was morning.

Thankfully, a guard brought us a tray of food, since neither of us had eaten anything since we'd left Be'er Sheva yesterday. But the longer we waited, the less hope I had that the King of Gaza would bother speaking to me. The head guard likely told him I was nothing more than a delusional, crippled woman.

Adin tried his best to keep my spirits up, asking more about metalworking and telling me how he'd dreamed of boarding a ship for distant lands ever since he'd been a boy and heard about the vastness of the Great Sea.

"And to think"—he gestured toward the western wall of our prison—"it's just right there, not far from where I'm sitting. I could walk to the shore in a quarter of an hour and put my toes in the waves."

We'd seen the expanse of blue in the distance before we'd entered the city, and I had to admit, I was nearly as curious as Adin about what it would be like to stand on the shoreline. I'd never seen a body of water larger than the river that ran through the Punon Valley, and that was easily crossed via any one of the footbridges spanning the waterway.

But as Adin talked about how one could sail for days—weeks—and never see land, my mind expanded to encompass such a mystery. Even here, inside the windowless room, the sticky air was still tinged with the distinct smell of salt. I'd heard stories from Kenites who'd journeyed up to the Salt Sea from Punon and how white crystals lined the shore, sparkling in the sun. Perhaps the shore of Gaza glittered like diamonds too.

The clank of the latch broke into my musings, and I pushed myself to standing. The older guard who had put us in here entered.

"Let's go."

I tensed, clutching my satchel against my belly. "Where?"

"Do you want to go before the king or not?"

Adin and I exchanged a wide-eyed glance. The two of us were dusty, head to toe, and rumpled from a sleepless night. Not to mention my bladder was desperately in need of relief. I'd been holding out against the indignity of using the jar in the far corner.

With Adin supporting me, I hiked back up the two flights of stairs, which was even more painful than it had been last night. To my surprise, the guard led us along an open portico facing the sea. The sparkle of sunlight on the breaking turquoise waves did indeed glitter like jewels, but from up here, it appeared there were no lines of salt lining the beach, only golden sand that spread endlessly along the edge of a vast expanse.

And then we were turning away from the captivating view, ascending yet another set of stairs, and entering a massive hall. Beneath a wide skylight, an enormous round hearth sat at the center, with the remnants of a fire atop its swirling stonework. Along the wall, stone benches lined the hall, with at least thirty people seated in groups of twos and threes—men in finery of every color, and women in gauzy dresses, some with breasts brazenly exposed. They gawked at me as I hobbled with trembling knees toward the man seated on a raised dais and holding a bejeweled scepter to denote his authority.

Authority that could be the end of me, and those I loved, with only a word.

The King of Gaza was a handsome man, with hair the color

of the sand I'd just seen on the beach, and not much older than Gavi, if I had to guess. Tall and slender, his light-colored eyes narrowed on me as we approached. The focused attention from such a powerful man made my stomach lurch toward my throat and everything inside me screamed to flee.

For Abba. For Farah. I repeated the reminder over and over inside my spinning head as the head guard ordered us to bow before the throne. With Adin's help, I dutifully prostrated myself, knowing to refuse meant immediate death.

"I was told you were a woman. But not—" the king's voice was full of disdain—"this."

"Endowed with worth from Heaven's throne, You are his child, his very own . . ."

Unbidden, the echoes of my mother's song arose in my heart. So instead of flinching at the insult, I did as she'd taught me and imagined my bones made of iron, my skin of hardy bronze, and my heart of hammered red-gold.

I kept my eyes lowered in submission as I spoke. "I may be crippled in body, my lord, but my hands are skillful and have mastered every one of my father's secret techniques. As you've discovered, he is no longer able to work metal as he used to, but I can. Please let him go. Let them all go."

He said nothing, and I was too terrified to glance upward during the silence that followed.

When he spoke, it was not to me but his guardsman. "And you say she nearly destroyed the valuable award I gave you, Korrero?"

"If it would have been anything less than pure gold, it would have been ruined, my king," replied the head guard. "But of course your generosity is well known."

The king's hum rumbled in the back of his throat. "You may know how to divine true gold from false, but you are Kenite, a tribe well-known to have extensive knowledge of such things. How do I know you aren't simply lying about your skill?"

I took in a trembling breath. "I would be nothing less than a suicidal fool to walk into your palace on a crippled leg unless I was telling the truth, my lord. But if you require proof, I've brought some of the red-gold my father taught me to craft."

"Korrero, bring it to me."

Heart pounding, I slid the half-completed usekh collar I'd been in the process of making when we left Punon from the satchel at my hip. Korrero took it from me and approached the dais to lay it in the king's outstretched palm.

"It's broken?" snapped the king.

"Unfinished," I replied, chancing another quick peek as he studied my work. "We were forced to flee the valley of Punon."

"Ah yes. I've heard the Hebrew king took on Amalek. Quite a victory, I'm told. And you Kenites were given warning of this attack?"

"We had to flee before the Hebrew army arrived. Therefore, I have not had the opportunity, nor the materials, to complete my work."

He turned the piece over, peering at it from different angles. "This is extraordinary, I have to admit. I've only seen such pure red-gold on the Atarah Hod, but this could rival its craftsmanship."

I gasped, head snapping up. "You've seen the Atarah Hod?"

By the way Korrero stiffened, I'd made a horrible mistake with my interjection.

But instead of ordering my beheading, the King of Gaza chuckled. "It was my great-grandfather who took it. I have it now."

Struck speechless by the revelation that all these years the Crown of Splendor had been in this city and not melted down, I could only stare in shock.

"But you truly expect me to believe *you* made this?" He shook the collar, the pendant rings jingling in the air.

There was no use being modest or shying away from the truth, regardless of the vow I'd taken. Seventeen lives were at stake. "As

I understand you are aware, my father has been slowly going blind for the past five years. I am the only person he revealed these well-guarded secrets to."

"Hm. I see. And who is this with you?"

"Her cousin and eager apprentice, my lord," Adin said with his own eyes still locked on the floor. "I haven't learned much yet, but someone must tend the bellows."

The king paused, likely noting that Adin looked nothing like a relation of mine, but instead of calling out the lie, he let out a huffing breath and jingled the collar again. "All right, then. You'll finish this. Show me what you can do."

Emboldened by the concession, I let my gaze slip upward to meet his eyes. "And you'll let my father and the others go?"

He gave me a patronizing smile that somehow reminded me of a jackal. "That'll depend on how well you complete the task, won't it? Korrero, see she has what she needs."

Before I lost my nerve, I dared speak one more time. "My sister, my lord. I was told she was separated from the others. May I see her?"

Those odd-colored eyes, almost silver in this light, flashed with something sharp and dangerous. "You'd best focus on showing me what you can do, for now. Because if you're lying, she'll be the first to die."

26

To complete the collar, the king had me escorted to a small foundry on the far edge of the palace grounds, complete with a brick smelting furnace, a ready supply of charcoal, enormous foot bellows, and every other tool I might need. The shop was well-lit by a skylight, the smoke directed through a ceramic shaft leading out of the building, but I told the king's men I must have both wax and a cold place to carve molds.

So, I spent the remainder of the day in a wine cellar deep in the earth and lined with limestone, with only enormous jars of wine and oil for company since Adin had been taken back to our cell.

By the light of four large oil lamps in the corners of the dark room, I shaped the purified wax they'd brought me into the three hummingbirds I'd imagined in great detail weeks ago and tried not to dwell on what was at stake. Once those were finished, I worked on the missing collar plate, along with the delicate chains and rings that would hold it all together. By the time I emerged from the cellar into moonlight, I was bleary-eyed but almost ready to pack the molds.

Thankfully, someone had provided us a few cushions, two straw mattresses, and some water for washing by the time I was returned to the cell. I was glad that Korrero had believed Adin to be my cousin, or at least didn't care enough to separate us because I could not imagine being locked in this place alone. But still, I missed Gavi with an ache that refused to abate. As I lay on the thin mattress, hurting body and soul, I prayed he would not try anything foolish. Because especially now that I'd seen this fortified palace with my own eyes and the well-armed soldiers who guarded it day and night, it was clear he and his companions would never have a chance to get inside the walls, let alone free my family and the other Kenites from wherever they were being held.

I was their only chance, a thought that rolled over and over in my head as I packed sand around my wax molds the next morning just after dawn, ensuring the sprues to channel the molten metal inside were secure before heading up to the foundry, flanked by four guardsmen—as if a limping woman who did not reach their bronze-plated shoulders was somehow a threat.

I took a few moments while two of the guards went to fetch Adin from our cell to plead with El Shaddai for favor as I cast the red-gold today. Although I'd done this time and again, I'd never done so on my own, and certainly not in a Philistine workshop. I missed my cave nearly as much as I missed my abba. The image of Rahm's tortured body rose up, and I begged Yahweh to guide my hands to prevent that from happening to anyone else—especially my father or Farah.

The moment Adin set foot in the foundry, we got to work. I directed him how to use the foot bellows, which were larger than those I was used to, and was grateful the young man took to the strenuous task with ease. Then, we brought the fire in the furnace to the exact right temperature, as evidenced by the color, height, and even the sound of the flames, just like my father had drilled into me over the past few years.

However, as the pure gold and copper ingots provided by the king, along with the barest hint of zinc I'd quietly pilfered from a jar on the foundry shelf, melted in the crucible with the salts, I began to fret.

"What if this is taking too long?" I asked Adin. "The king said two days."

"Rahm said you had to present yourself by then," he replied, never slowing the constant pump of the bellows on his feet. "You are providing proof of your expertise, and that cannot be rushed."

"But what if Gavi—"

He shook his head, halting my words. "Your husband is famous for a reason. Trust his experience and that of his cousin, whose exploits at Michmash are the stuff of legends. I understand why you had to do this; the Philistines would not have hesitated to slaughter the others if you hadn't risked everything to come. But I would not have let you step foot in Gaza if I wasn't certain Gavriel will not rest until you are safe."

Guilt curdled in my gut. I'd known full well my husband would be furious when he discovered me missing. What if I'd made everything worse by coming here? Because Adin was right that Gavi would do anything to find me. Panic built in my chest as I watched the liquified metal turn from dull reddish-brown to deep orange in the crucible. I'd not even stopped to ask guidance from the All-Knowing One before I'd embarked on this hasty mission, one that could end in all of our deaths—the man I loved, included.

Forgive me, Yahweh, I pleaded silently as the swirl of metal shifted to a golden hue, what remained of the impurities streaking dark across its surface. I'd made the same foolish mistake with Niv and Kila, choosing my own stubborn path instead of seeking his wisdom, and it had caused only pain. Had I not learned anything?

Sparks popped in the furnace, flaring as bright as the stars that night on the road from Qadesh, when the sky above Gavi and me had inspired me to sing my mother's song. Once again, I let the comforting words unspool in my heart, a reminder that there was nothing about me, even my deepest weaknesses and darkest impurities, that was unknown to the One who set the stars aflame. By the time the last of the dross burned away and the molten gold had turned the brilliant red-orange I'd been watching for, my fears had turned to smoke as well. No matter what missteps I'd made along the way, Yahweh was here, his voice still softly calling my name. *Be still and know I AM* came the deep and inexplicable command at the center of my soul.

As I removed the crucible and carefully poured purified red-gold into each of the molds, trusting the process my father had taught me, I held tight to the silent assurance I'd been given of Yahweh's presence, remembering how Gavi had spoken of the way the Most High had brought him to his knees to give him a similar reminder. I could only hope that the God who'd brought us together once would one day merge our paths again.

The next afternoon, I buffed the completed collar to a brilliant shine with a soft piece of wool. And when I was satisfied with the clarity of my own reflection on every polished surface, I could not help but cry tears of exhaustion and relief, certain that Yahweh himself had not only given me the strength to finish but inspiration to make something even more lovely than I'd imagined.

"No wonder a king is willing to go to such lengths for your skills, Zahava," said Adin, a note of awe in his voice as he examined my work.

"Thank you for your help." I swiped a tear from my cheek. "You made an excellent assistant. Perhaps you'll be a metalsmith too someday."

"I think I'll leave that work to you and Gavriel," he said. "My legs are still wobbling from manning those bellows yesterday."

When I alerted the two guards at the door of the foundry that I was finished, they walked us back into the palace and to Korrero, who was in the middle of delivering what sounded like a scathing rebuke to a couple of chastened young guards for being drunk while on watch. Once the men, who looked similar in age to Adin, scuttled off looking like a couple of kicked puppies, Korrero excused our escorts and then wordlessly put out his hand for the collar. I placed it in his weathered palm, a little fearful he might turn that awful wrath on me.

Instead, his eyes flicked up to meet mine. "This is . . . extraordinary, young woman. King Enesidu will be very pleased."

"He will?"

"Without a doubt." He handed it back to me. Then, hands on his hips, he took a glance around the portico where the three of us stood, as if checking for listening ears before he spoke again in a low tone. "In fact, he will be so thrilled it's likely he will give you whatever you ask. So do not be afraid to ask for the sun, moon, and stars. You have a unique point of leverage with this. Hold steady."

I blinked up at the huge Philistine in astonishment. Why was he giving me this sort of advice?

"I've faced down plenty of adversaries in my day and never had anyone, man or woman, challenge me in such a bold way as you did with this." He gestured to his earplug. "You didn't know if it was pure or not, did you?"

"There are plenty of ways of making gold appear pure. It could easily have turned black."

"And if it had, you would have proved my king a liar. It was a wager you were willing to lose to prove your expertise. I admire that."

"Do you think he will release my people?"

He paused, looking out to sea. "I think no one else can do what you can, and he'll see that. It's why, when a couple of mercenaries came to him with the information that you Kenites were returning to Be'er Sheva, he paid them handsomely to round up a group of riders to bring back someone who made what he calls 'blood-gold.' He's been demanding for years that his own metalsmiths produce it. Many tried. No one succeeded."

That answered the question of why they'd come at us with such numbers. Although Rahm had been a greedy fool to entangle himself with the Philistines, he could not have anticipated the horrific outcome of his scheme.

"Why is the red-gold such an obsession for your king?"

"The Crown. Enesidu became fascinated with it when he was just a child and heard the myths surrounding it."

"Myths?" I knew my own people believed the Atarah Hod was to sit only on the head of a righteous king, but surely the Philistines would not honor our traditions.

"As he said, his great-grandfather was king when it was taken in the raid on Be'er Sheva. And shortly afterward, he survived an assassination attempt while wearing it."

"What happened?"

"He was addressing a crowd and someone shot an arrow from a nearby rooftop. It glanced off the crown and nicked the top of his ear instead. If he'd not been wearing it, the arrow would have pierced his temple and killed him instantly."

"A fortunate happenstance, but how could that give rise to a myth?"

"Because his son was wearing it fifteen years later when he survived a fall from this very portico." Korrero gestured to our left. "Just over there. He'd been drinking during a festival and meant to lean against one of the columns but missed and fell two stories. He broke both arms but did not smash his head open on the ground below. The crown itself landed harmlessly in a bush without so much as a nick."

"So now your king believes it holds some sort of protective magic?"

"Indeed. His father wore it on the battlefield against the Hebrews at Afek and managed to return without a scratch. He raised Enesidu with the belief that he cannot be killed if it's on his head."

"But it's just a crown. Made by human hands."

"Perhaps. But that belief is what may well set your people free."

He arched his silvering brows knowingly. "Use it to your advantage. Now, are you ready?"

My belly was already roiling at the thought of going before the Philistine king again. "As ready as I will ever be."

"You were as brave as a warrior the first time. I've seen grown men wet themselves in front of that throne before." He grinned at my gape-mouthed surprise. "Let's go. He'll have just finished his meal, and Enesidu with a full belly is far more amenable than without."

Korrero led us back to the large hearth room again, but this time, the king was seated on a wide wooden chair not far from the fire, where the half-consumed remains of a pig sat among the ashes. Again, the smell of burning flesh hit me hard, and I held my breath. The swine had been roasted whole, along with whatever foul things were still inside. However, none of the people gathered around the king seemed to care about the stink in the air.

"My king," said Korrero as we approached, "the young Kenite woman has completed the task you gave her."

Enesidu lurched out of his chair and strode toward me, hand outstretched. "Give it here."

Although my knees shook violently as the King of Gaza approached, especially since he was the tallest person I'd ever seen, looming at least a full head and a half above me, I held my ground and placed the collar in his waiting palm.

His gaze flashed to the golden usekh, then to my face, and back to the collar. He held it aloft, examining it from all sides, touching the dangling hummingbirds and making a small noise of appreciation when they swung back and forth, glittering in the bright sunlight beaming through the open ceiling above us.

"If this is what you can accomplish in three days, I can only imagine what you can do in weeks. Or months."

Relief rushed from my head to my feet, making me a little dizzy. Perhaps the risk I'd taken, and the sacrifice I'd made, had been worth it after all. Korrero's suggestion that I not be afraid to ask for the sun, moon, and stars gave me a burst of courage.

"May I see my sister now?"

The king seemed to squelch a smile. "You may."

My pulse galloped at double speed. "And my father?"

His shoulder ticked up carelessly. "Korrero, bring the prisoners."

The guard glanced at me once before striding away, and I wished I could thank him, even if I didn't understand why he'd been so kind. My next request, if my favor continued, would be to release Adin along with the rest of my people.

"Do you want to see it?" asked the king.

I barely heard him, too wrapped up in knowing I would soon have eyes on my father and sister. "My lord?"

"The Atarah Hod."

My eyes flared wide. "Yes, yes . . . of course," I stuttered.

Enesidu told a servant to have it fetched from the treasury, then indicated I should take a seat on a bench not far from his own wooden chair. Wordlessly, Adin moved to stand behind me.

"Hungry? There's plenty." The king gestured toward the disgusting carcass on the hearth, as if I were a royal guest instead of a crippled prisoner.

"No, thank you." In truth, my belly was empty, since we'd been given only a small repast upon waking this morning. But I had no intention of consuming swine flesh, and I was certain Adin was of the same mind, since that was one of the Hebrew edicts we Kenites also lived by.

"What is your name?" asked the king.

"Zahava, my lord."

He raised a light brow. "Your name is literally *gold*?"

"It is. But not for the metal. For a star my father saw the night I was born."

"Interesting."

The servant he'd sent to the treasury returned with a wooden casket, decorated in red, blue, and yellow swirls of paint and symbols that I assumed must be the Philistine language. He unlatched the box and then lifted out the crown, handing it to the king.

The sight of the gleaming red-gold crown stole the breath from my lungs. Not only was it embossed with finely engraved etchings of leaves that curved all around the circumference of the crown—each one a precise work of art in itself—but there were deep red garnets embedded in the gold. Such a feat was difficult, since precious stones had a tendency to crack and shatter with high heat. And with red-gold, such temperature issues were even harder to manage. I'd only accomplished it once before with any measure of success.

"Your ancestors made this, no?"

I nodded. "Generations ago."

"And somehow you, a wisp of a woman with a crippled leg, ended up inheriting this knowledge." He smiled at me, but it was not a gesture of kindness. It was accompanied by a flare of something greedy in his eyes. "And now you are here. I've waited a long time for this day."

My stomach soured. No matter what Adin hoped Gavi might do, I'd known when I made my decision to come to Gaza that it was possible I was giving up my freedom for good. If Enesidu was as obsessed with the red-gold as Korrero said, this may be the last time I saw anyone I loved.

When Korrero entered the room again, he was leading a line of Kenites, wrists bound and feet chained together as they shuffled forward. I knew most of them. Two were shepherds my father employed, one was a third cousin, and two were elders. And there, halfway down the line, was my father.

Elation and horror rose in equal measures as I took in his bruised and swollen face. He looked horribly defeated and thankfully could not see that I was here from so far away but at least he was alive. But then, at the end of the group, another guard came around the corner, leading my sister by the arm.

Her name flew from my lips without thought, and her head jerked up, her eyes going wide. Praise be to Yahweh, she looked unharmed, except for a nasty cut on her swollen bottom lip. "Zahava? Why are you here?"

My father's head snapped up as well, and my name fell from his mouth on a tortured groan. "No! Daughter!"

"Please, my lord . . ." Voice shaking, I turned to Enesidu, desperation outweighing my fear of the powerful king. "You have me in your service now, willingly. Please let them go."

He pursed his lips, considering as he tapped the usekh on his thigh. "I'm not certain that is wise."

Trembling, I lifted my hands in supplication. "I am the *only* one with the ability to make the red-gold. It has been a family secret for generations, and my father has no sons, so he taught me instead and made me vow to guard the knowledge as sacred. I'll make whatever you ask. Our tribe is peaceful. We've never been at odds with Philistia and have no desire to be. These are innocent people who just want to return to their families."

He tilted his chin. "Are they, though?"

I frowned, confused. But on his gesture, another group of prisoners was ushered inside. The king said something else, but my ears rang as my heart began to race and everything around me went hazy, everything except the four shackled men dressed in torn Kenite clothing, who'd obviously been on the losing end of a vicious beating.

Zevi. Shachar. A Hebrew soldier whose name I did not know. And my husband.

Gavi lifted his battered face and peered at me through two blackened eyes. Blood drooled from a hugely swollen lip down his purpling jaw. This beating was a recent one. My heart screamed his name over and over as a thousand futile questions filled my mind. *Why had he not stayed away? Why had I taken so long to finish the collar? Would we* all *die here in this awful palace?*

Although I could feel the intensity of his gaze, along with the shock and horror of seeing me next to the King of Gaza, Gavi's solemn expression did not so much as twitch as he stared back.

Don't react, it said. *Do not give away our connection.*

My entire body trembled, nausea rising in my throat. But I obeyed his silent command and clenched my jaw, determined to remain just as strong as Gavi, for his sake and for that of my father and sister.

"These men were caught trying to break into my palace last night. They got fairly close to where the prisoners were being held, I'll grant them that. But, honestly, did you think you could actually steal inside the most fortified palace of the Five Cities?" Enesidu's laugh was mocking.

I swallowed hard, willing my voice to remain still and my eyes not to track back to Gavi again, or I might lose my nerve for what I had to do. If my husband could restrain the instinct to fight, which I knew for certain every bone in his body was screaming to do, then even in my weakness, I could shake off the terror and fight for him with everything I had.

Give me strength, El Shaddai.

I straightened my shoulders as I met the gaze of the king. "I plead with you, my lord, to release them all and I will remain here, in your service, for the rest of my life."

"Zahava! No!" my father bellowed, the sound of his devastation reverberating around the room. But I held myself still, not allowing my lock on Enesidu's silvery eyes to waver.

He smiled with condescension, as if I were a child. "Oh, my dear, you'll do that anyhow. You had to know you weren't leaving when you approached my gates in the first place."

I inhaled deeply, silently asking the Most High to bless Korrero for telling me of the king's misguided belief that the Atarah Hod was imbued with some sort of magical protection. Without that knowledge, I'd not have the very weapon I needed in this moment.

"That is true," I replied, willing my voice to not break. "But as we've established, I am the *only* person who can craft the red-gold you so desire. But just because you have me in your custody doesn't mean I will do it."

His sharp gaze narrowed on me, all semblance of cordiality gone. "I assume you saw the state of that pathetic fool I sent back to Be'er Sheva, the one whose loose lips revealed your skill in the first place. I hammered that iron stake into his side *myself*. A fatal wound, but not deep enough to pierce his heart so he'd be alive for as long as it took to deliver my message. It's a skill I've perfected over the years after much practice with enemies, both inside my kingdom and out. So, my dear girl, I have plenty of ways of making you do my bidding."

The flippant way he spoke of torturing Rahm was beyond horrifying. It was clear Enesidu reveled in others' pain. But as I'd been reminded, the same Creator who'd breathed the glorious stars into being had also breathed life into this flawed vessel. Therefore, I could trust El Shaddai now, with my final breath, and beyond.

"You can certainly torture me. My body is fairly fragile, as you can see. It would not take much to break my bones or make me bleed. But unless you release these people—all of them—I won't give up the secrets my father gave me, no matter what you do. Instead, everything I know about how to make items like the Atarah Hod will go with me to the grave."

Rage sparked in Enesidu's eyes like silver lightning, and his entire body seemed to vibrate like a plucked bow. "How dare you—"

"However . . ." Speaking over him, I held up one finger, as if that alone could prevent the Philistine king from exploding. And to my surprise, he did indeed hesitate, so I lifted my chin, hoping Enesidu would entertain a bargain the way Thema had. "If you release these people, let them return to their families unharmed, I will gladly make whatever you want. As well, even though it will take time to do so, I promise to take on a few capable apprentices and teach them how to make items from red-gold too. Which means it won't only be me producing valuable pieces for you but a group of us to fill your treasury."

Enesidu leaned toward me, the fury in his eyes replaced with the avaricious gleam I'd glimpsed before. "Can you make armor from red-gold? A breastplate and pauldrons to match the crown, perhaps even ceremonial greaves and bracers too?"

With his belief that the Atarah Hod would protect him from harm, it was not surprising he would desire to cloak himself in red-gold even if bronze scale armor would be far stronger. But I would not argue that point.

"I believe I could, yes, as long as I have something to pattern it from. My wax techniques can form almost any shape."

He made a contemplative noise, as if his mind was whirring with ideas. "*Any* shape at all?"

My lungs seized. These Philistines worshiped a variety of heathen gods. Plenty of votives, along with food and drink offerings were set at the feet of various idols all over the palace. Even the walls were decorated with bright murals depicting gods in various scenes. Some looked to be a record of military victories, some merely pastoral, and others were so blatantly perverse that I had to look away. But I vowed to never again make anything that would dishonor the command of Yahweh to not carve any images for the purpose of worship.

And yet if I refused to make those for Enesidu, there was every likelihood he would slaughter all of us for such audacity. Everything I'd done to set everyone free could be undone with only one word.

As if he'd spoken from across the room, my father's voice suddenly echoed in my mind. "*The Word of Yahweh is life, daughter. Better to die in obedience than live in rebellion.*"

My eyes tracked to his wan and battered face. I knew he could not see me from so far away, but his gaze was heavy on me all the same, a silent reminder to trust the Creator, even when it made no earthly sense.

"Yes, I can pattern most any item from red-gold. However, there are some I will not."

Enesidu's mouth bent into a frown, his annoyance causing my belly to cramp hard. But even though they may be my last words, I had to speak them.

"I worship Yahweh, God of the Hebrews. And he has forbidden us to worship graven images of any sort, nor to make them with our hands. I will not make any object or carve any depiction of things on earth below or in heaven above for such purposes."

The king's expression went flat. "You dare tell *me* what you will and will not make?"

All the hair on the back of my neck stood on end, and I swallowed hard against the instinct to reel back my brazen words. This man was one of the five most fearsome kings of Philistia. Who was I to stand up to such power? I was a woman, crippled, and at his mercy.

"*Your worth is far beyond the earth, Crowned in splendor before your birth . . .*"

My mother's song arose in my heart once again. And like it had always done when children mocked me, it reminded me to look to the heavens for evidence of my value. Value imbued by the Creator of Life itself.

So, I lifted my chin, straightened my shoulders, and replied, "My hands are at your disposal when it comes to metalwork, my lord, but my allegiance will always be to Yahweh first."

After a long stretch of horrifying silence, while the king stared at me intensely and everything inside me trembled, he dropped his eyes to the Atarah Hod in his lap. His fingers traced the vines and leaves that encircled the beautiful crown my ancestor made so long ago as he considered. It would take me years to make something of such matchless perfection.

"I have plenty of artisans to make me votives for my gods." He lifted his gaze, his expression blank. "They can go."

Stunned, I blinked at him while my heart pounded like the feet of an entire battalion. "Everyone?"

He waved a dismissive palm. "Let it never be said I am not merciful. I have what I wanted anyhow."

Victory sang in my bones as any lingering doubts I'd ever had about Yahweh's goodness melted into nothing. "And Adin too?" I gestured behind me. "He only came to make sure I got here safely."

"No, cousin." Adin's response was low but firm. "I'm staying with you."

I turned to glare at the young man over my shoulder. "No, you are not. Go back home."

"You know very well I don't have one," he said with a shrug. "Besides, you need someone to man the bellows."

"There, it's settled," said the king as a menacing smile stretched over his handsome face. "As long as your *cousin* knows any attempt to run off with you will end in his swift and very painful death."

As tempted as I was to plead with Adin to escape such peril, nothing was more important than making certain every one of these people, including the three I loved more than my life, walked out of this horrible city alive. And I could not take the chance Enesidu would change his mind.

I bowed my head, acknowledging the costly bargain I had made—one that meant that I would live out the rest of my days as a slave to a man of little mercy.

"Korrero," said the king, waving his hand eastward, "take them past Ziklag and then let them go. They can find their way back from there."

My throat burned as I allowed myself one last look as the captives were led out of the room by the guards. My abba's head was bowed, his face wet with tears, and his wide shoulders slumped in defeat as he shuffled away, one palm on the back of the man in front of him to ensure he would not fall. Once again, he'd lost another child. I prayed he and my mother would find comfort in the Maker of the Stars, just as they'd always done.

As the guard who'd escorted her here tugged Farah's arm, she sobbed, shaking her head in disbelief as she was dragged from the room. I placed my own hand on my heart, telling her without words that I loved her, knowing she would take care of Breena and Anaya, just as she'd always looked after me.

Then I had only a few breathless moments to meet Gavi's horrified stare before he and the others were led away as well. Gutted, I curled forward with a choked sob. From behind, Adin gripped my shoulder in wordless compassion while burning tears coursed down my cheeks, dripping from my chin to the tiles. If not for the bench beneath me, I'd be in a puddle there as well.

There was nothing I could do but surrender my husband to the One who made him and be grateful he would live, even if I would never be held in his arms again. He was worth the sacrifice. They all were.

Gavriel

Four months later
Gaza, Philistine Territory

The port of Gaza was busier than usual today. Returning fishermen fought the crashing waves to drag their boats onto the beach nearby while a crowd of sponge divers hauled their daily harvest toward the market, and a bevy of merchants, customers, and laborers of all tribes and tongues milled about the docks. But the one person I'd been seeking was still nowhere to be seen among the crowd.

With a long sigh, I twisted my body to crack the tension from my spine, then folded my aching bones down to the sand under the shade of a wind-bowed palm to wait. My back hurt. Even my thighs hurt from a long day of shoveling coal into blazing furnaces and swinging a heavy mallet to knock slag from iron bloom. Four months of heavy labor had taken its toll on my body. But four months without Zahava had taken a much harder toll on my heart. So even if it took four years, or forty, I would not leave this place without my little dove.

I leaned back against the tree as the vision of Zahava's tear-stained face filled my mind, a constant since I'd been led away from her in chains. But as agonizing as it had been to leave her behind, any further attempt at rescue that day would only have gotten everyone killed—including her father and sister. After the sacrifice she'd made to free them, and all of us, I'd had no choice.

So, I'd held silent. Restrained the fury pumping through my body at the sight of her, so small and unnaturally pale, beside the beast who sat on the throne of one of the more vicious city-states among the Philistines. Even though he was a young king, only ruling for the past eight years, Enesidu's brutal reputation stretched all the way to Gibeah and beyond. My wife had been at his mercy for months now and still I was no closer to her than I'd been the day his men had left us shackled together like animals at the edge of Philistine territory. Every step farther from my wife had been excruciating, a painful unraveling of the golden thread stitched into me by Yahweh himself.

A year ago, I might have let my anger rule me. I might have broken away from the group and run back to Gaza, reckless with vengeance and dependent on my weapons alone to mete out justice and rescue the woman I loved. But that was before I'd seen myself clearly, without the haze of drink to blur the truth. When I'd been a disaster and a fool bent on his own destruction. Instead, I'd spent the long hours of the slow journey back to Be'er Sheva formulating a plan.

"You're going back, aren't you?" Zevi had asked when we were finally in sight of the city walls.

"Of course."

He nodded, worrying his bruised lower lip with his teeth for a moment. *"If it was Yochana, I would do the same. We'll get these people back, then regroup—"*

I put up a staying hand. *"No. I'm going back alone. This will take some time. Months. Maybe even years. Go home and be with your family. They need you."*

Truthfully, I'd been shocked Zevi had insisted on going to Gaza in the first place, after the horrors he'd endured at the hands of the Philistines as a boy. But the moment he lifted his palm, displaying the scar at the base of his thumb—the one that matched mine—I knew nothing I would say would dissuade him. Zevi did not renege on vows, even ones made to three boys a lifetime ago. It was not his fault that we'd gotten all the way onto the palace grounds by scaling the wall in the middle of the night when a servant spied us in the gardens and alerted the guard.

"*What do I tell Yonatan?*" my cousin asked. "*He'll want to know why I let you go without his leave.*"

"*Tell him I'll never give up on Zahava,*" I said. "*Not like I gave up on Shay to chase after my selfish ambitions. No matter how much I respect Yonatan, Yahweh entrusted her to me, and his rank is infinitely higher.*"

And if I'd learned anything over these past few months, it was that no matter who sat on the throne of Israel, it was the Most High who ruled over all.

"No matter how many times I see you like that, slick-faced and shorn like a spring ram, I'll never get used to it." Shachar's teasing dragged me out of the memory as he strode across the beach toward me, sand clinging to his legs and woolen kilt dripping wet after emerging from the sea.

"At least I have a little left." I scrubbed my fingers through my filthy finger-length hair. "You're as bald as a pig."

He slapped his palm over his crown with a grin. "I happen to like it. Less fuss. And doesn't get in my way when I dive."

Unlike me, Shachar hadn't fully shaved his beard before he and I returned to Gaza four months ago, so a narrow patch of gray-streaked hair dangled from his chin. That, paired with his deeply sun-bronzed skin from months of diving naked for sponges and mussels, meant that he now easily passed for one of the locals.

Where Zevi had acquiesced when I refused his accompaniment on this mission, Shachar would hear none of my arguments.

"And let you have all the glory after you snatch your pretty little wife from under the nose of the King of Gaza? Not a chance." He'd frowned, arms crossed.

"There's no guarantee we'll make it back at all," I'd said. *"We'll be slithering back into that nest of vipers and staying there for who knows how long."*

"Then we probably should learn how to crawl on our bellies, hadn't we?"

Five days later, freshly shaved and with bruises fading, the two of us had set off for the coast armed with little more than a plan to seek work among the Philistines and a determination to find another way into Enesidu's palace. We'd had success with the former, but the latter still eluded us.

I handed Shachar a packet of oil-fried fish I'd purchased from a street vendor near the wharf before I came to wait for him on the beach, our biweekly habit for as long as we'd been in the city. So far, our regular meetings had gone unnoticed, but we were careful to choose a different place each time and always on days when the port was the most crowded.

He heaved himself onto the sand beside me with a grunt. "How goes the smithing?"

"Dirty. Noisy. Exhausting. Same as it's been since day one."

"You learned all you need to know yet?"

"For the most part. The master smith has been pleased with my progress. It'll take time and practice, but as long as I find access to iron ore and build an adequate furnace, I should be able to reproduce their techniques."

When Shachar and I had made our way into Gaza, separately, so as not to draw attention, I'd stumbled across a couple of blacksmith apprentices while looking for work at the port. One of their fellow apprentices had lost his position for theft, so they brought me back to their master. My tale was simple: my tribe had been run out of southern Kenite territory by Israel's forces and since I "hated" the Hebrews for "stealing" our land, I wanted nothing to do with them.

Thanks to the few words of Kenite dialect I'd picked up and my borrowed Kenite clothing, no one questioned my story, especially once I'd proven my worth at the forge. I had swiftly been promoted from building mud-brick furnaces and basic labor to hammering iron bloom and then to forging the metal tools and weapons. My main goal here was to get my wife back, but if I could return with the secrets of Philistine iron techniques as well, all the better.

Shachar had easily found work among the divers, since he'd grown up on the coast of Western Manasseh's territory to the far north. His family made their living by the sea so he'd learned to swim before he learned to walk. Holding his breath to dive deep for mussels and sea sponges was nothing at all. It also gave him a unique position in the port, where fishermen's nets were as full of gossip as fish and seafaring ships brought news from foreign shores along with their goods.

But in all the weeks we'd been here, neither of us had heard a word about Zahava or Adin. Not even rumors of a talented new goldsmith in the palace. Only terrible, excruciating silence.

It was only by the mercy of the Almighty I'd been able to withstand the lure of drink during the agonizing wait. But whenever my resolve began to stretch thin, I made a point to go lie out under the night sky, search for Zahava's star among the host, and listen for the Voice of the One who breathed the universe into being.

"Anything new?" I asked Shachar.

"Actually . . ." He grinned mischievously. "I *have* heard something of interest. There's a solstice festival coming up in three weeks. There'll be all sorts of debauchery while they sacrifice to their gods. It may be the perfect opportunity to find your woman."

The first good news I'd heard in months. "You think we can get her out of there while they are occupied with their rituals?"

"Possibly. I'm working to find out more. Also . . ." He lifted his palms, brows arched. "It's not for certain, mind you, but it looks like I may have a connection inside the palace."

Wide-eyed, I sucked in a breath. "Who?"

He shook his head. "Not yet. Give me a few more days to finesse things before you get your hopes up too much. Just want you to know I've got something in the works."

"Thank you." I paused to clear the tightness from my throat. "For coming with me. For . . . everything." I wasn't certain why Shachar had chosen to befriend me, especially when I'd been little more than an arrogant drunkard when we met, but his loyalty was further proof of Yahweh's goodness, in spite of the many years I'd turned my back.

He swiped at the sand on his left calf, not meeting my eyes. "Think nothing of it. If I'd fought half as hard as you do, I'd still have a wife. I won't let you lose yours."

Too overcome to speak, I nodded and turned my eyes back toward the sea. For months it had seemed like that entire blue expanse lay between me and Zahava, even though she was only a fifteen-minute walk to the south. Though I would cross any ocean to have her back in my arms, it was good to know she may be a little closer than before.

"All right, then. I'll try to be patient, but tell me about this contact in the palace."

He grinned, a wicked gleam in his eyes. "Her name is Polina. . . ."

Zahava

What did I do wrong?

Hair unbound from the tight braid I always wore while working, I paced from one end of the rooftop garden to the other. The salty breeze was a welcome respite from the searing-hot air of the foundry.

These gardens were my favorite place inside the royal fortress walls, even with an armed guard watching my every move. Thanks to Korrero's petition to the king for an assigned escort, I'd been given leave to explore the grounds. It had become my habit over these past few months to meander among the flowers and trees every evening as the sun blushed pink and orange over the sea. The memory of walking under a similar sky on the road from Qadesh was as close as I'd ever be to my husband again, so I cherished each sunset as a gift.

However, today I could not focus on Yahweh's masterpiece spreading across the sky, or even my precious memories of Gavi. All I could see was the shattered remains of the bracer I'd been working on for the last three days on the floor of the foundry.

I had to have missed something. I hadn't had a piece of metal fail so spectacularly since I'd begun learning from my father three years ago. But I'd retraced every step in my mind, beginning to end, with no clue why the red-gold had been so brittle this time.

I'd spent nearly every day of these past months carving, molding, or polishing each of the many scales that made up the breastplate and pauldrons for the king, along with countless connection rings. Enesidu insisted a pattern of leaves be incorporated in the design to emulate those on the Atarah Hod. If I did not figure out what the problem was with the metal, and quickly, I would have to tell the king the armor I'd promised him by the solstice festival, only six days from now, would not be finished.

I doubted he'd have me killed, since I'd proved my value. But there were still plenty of ways he could punish me, some of them too frightening to dwell on.

So for the tenth time in the past hour, I started at the beginning, imagining each step of the process my father had taught me and trying to determine what had been different from all the times before.

"Zahava!"

Startled, I turned my back on the sunset to find a grinning Adin striding across the rooftop with three young Phoenicians. Their distinctive cone-shaped caps reminded me of mushrooms. White linen swirled around the base of the caps like a half-formed turban, fringed ends flapping in the salty breeze.

The entire city was thrumming with excitement over the upcoming solstice festival and a large influx of newcomers had been pouring into Gaza for a week, eager to participate in the festivities and rituals.

Another sharp pang of worry hit my belly. If I didn't have that armor ready for the opening ceremony at the solstice, Enesidu may punish Adin as well for my failure. I *had* to figure out what had gone wrong.

"I'm glad I found you," said Adin, heedless of my silent struggle to protect both of us. "You must meet my new friends. This is Baalimeq, Oresto, and Mattaniel."

The three Phoenicians bowed low, as if I was someone of note instead of a prisoner of the king.

"It is our pleasure to make your acquaintance," said the one Adin had called Baalimeq. "We've heard you are a woman of unique talent."

Both he and Oresto had a narrow stripe of costly purple on the edge of their garments. Not royalty, I guessed, since the rest of their garb was fairly simple, aside from their strange hats, but perhaps aides to Phoenician nobles who'd come to grovel before Enesidu's throne over the past few days.

I darted a glance at my friend, surprised he'd been so free with information about my work. "Has Adin been exaggerating my skills?"

He lifted his palms. "It wasn't me, I swear it. They'd been told of a female goldsmith before they came to the palace. As you know, the king's servants are horrible gossips."

My stomach churned. My family had kept this secret for generations and now everyone would know. But my knowledge, no matter how valuable, was of far less worth than the lives of my loved ones.

"We look forward to seeing your handiwork during the festival," said Oresto. "We've been told you are making something extraordinary."

It unsettled me that they'd heard anything about my work since only Adin and Korrero were allowed inside the foundry while I worked on the armor. Enesidu insisted the unveiling be a spectacle.

All the more reason to make certain it was finished properly. *Could it be that the gold ingots weren't purified long enough? Or perhaps the salts I used were tainted?*

Adin's voice again broke into my distracted thoughts. "Baalimeq and Oresto came here aboard that ship." He gestured to the northwest, where an enormous vessel perched a short way off the coast, illuminated by the dazzling orange of the sunset so that the ship seemed to be on fire. I could see nothing of its details from this far away, but simply judging by its size, it was truly a marvel.

"Oresto and I are personal aides to the emissary sent by the King of Byblos," said Baalimeq, his tone implying this was a position of high import. "We've been at sea for weeks. So putting into port here was a welcome respite."

"They were in *Egypt*," said Adin, not bothering to hide his jealousy. "They actually saw Pharaoh's summer palace and traveled down the Nile River."

Baalimeq smiled at my friend, entertained by his excitement. "That we did. We sailed downriver so Hannibaal could meet with various governors and establish new trading connections."

"And they saw real crocodiles, Zahava. And animals with necks so long they can eat leaves from the very tops of trees!" Adin's fascination with places far beyond these shores had only grown since we'd been in Gaza.

"Mattaniel has been to places much farther away than we have," said Baalimeq, gesturing to the third young man, who stood nearly a head taller than the others. He wore the same style of mushroom cap but a simpler tunic of coarse brown wool instead of linen.

"Have you?" I asked. "Where?"

"My master went to the far north, seeking tin," said Mattaniel. "It took months to get there and months to return."

"What was it like?"

"Cold. And wet. The rain never seemed to stop. But also incredibly green. It was like a paradise made of emeralds. Especially when the sun came out between rain showers."

There was a hint of an accent in Mattaniel's speech I could not place, and his skin was a few shades darker than that of his companions. He must be from one of the other nations. Egypt, perhaps, or Midian.

"Are you going back?" asked Adin.

Mattaniel nodded. "My master established a good connection at the largest tin mine in the region. Once the festival is over, we'll be back out to sea. It may be many months before we return."

A strong gust of wind suddenly rustled the flowering oleanders around us, whipping Mattaniel's odd mushroom hat off his head. It swirled in the air for a moment before landing ten paces away. The young man gave chase, but just before he could reach it, another blast of wind caused it to skitter off, as if it had a mind of its own.

With a chuckle, Adin dashed off to retrieve the linen strip, which had tangled itself in a nearby citrus tree. Both young men were laughing by the time they returned. I was glad Adin had found others to talk to. I was poor company most days, focused as I was on my work and on the difficult task of not melting into a puddle of sorrow over missing my family and my husband.

"Thank you," Mattaniel said as he rewrapped the linen around his cap. "My master would not be pleased if I was disheveled at tonight's meal with the king."

"As if he would care," said Oresto with a bark of laughter. "I've never seen a master brag so much about a servant before."

Color slashed across Mattaniel's high-cut cheekbones. "My skill with languages is merely a valuable asset when we travel abroad."

"It certainly doesn't hurt with women either." Oresto winked. "You had the daughters of that Egyptian emissary enthralled last night."

Poor Mattaniel's face turned nearly as red as the swiftly setting sun, but I wasn't surprised he garnered attention from young ladies. He was almost painfully handsome, with striking light honey-brown eyes, a tall, lanky build, and sharp features. However, I far preferred warriors with gray eyes and a wild mane of curls. And oh, how I missed strong arms enfolding me in warmth as I nestled into a broad, well-muscled chest.

"You're embarrassing our new friend." Baalimeq elbowed Oresto.

With a laugh, Oresto raised his palms. "No harm meant. If I could wield pretty foreign words to make women fall at my feet like sycamores, I'd take full advantage."

I let out a gasp as the answer to my conundrum hit me square between the eyes. "Sycamores! Of course!"

The four young men stared at me in bewilderment for the outburst I hadn't even meant to speak aloud.

"The charcoal Korrero's men brought us yesterday," I explained to Adin. "They said it was made from sycamore this time, not cedar or oak. It's a much softer wood, so it likely altered the temperature somehow."

"What do you—" Adin began.

"It was lovely to meet you," I interrupted, giving the Phoenicians a small bow. "I'm sorry. I need to get back to the foundry."

Glad for the short walking stick Korrero had brought me soon after I'd come to Gaza, I headed for the staircase on the far side of the rooftop garden, already wondering where I could find some better charcoal.

It took only a few moments for Adin to catch up. "What is wrong?"

I told him about the broken bracer and explained how I suspected the density of the charcoal may have had an effect on the brittleness of the metal. "Which means I have to start over. And now I am three days behind. I'll need to get to the wine cellar and carve another wax pattern tonight so we can pour the mold tomorrow. Then work late into the night to polish it so I have time to make the greaves before the solstice. I don't think I'll be getting much sleep this week."

"How can I help?"

"I'm fine on my own tonight. I'll need your feet on the bellows tomorrow, though."

He frowned, his gaze ticking back to the three Phoenicians. "Are you certain?"

I waved a dismissive hand. "They seem like kind young men. I'm glad you've made some friends."

"They've told me the most fascinating stories. Mattaniel said there are places where men speak strange languages no one can understand. Where trees grow as tall as the sky. And where gold is as plentiful as bread. What I wouldn't do to see it with my own eyes."

The longing in his voice was palpable. I could not help but feel guilty he was stuck here with me instead of off discovering the world for himself.

"If you get the chance to do so," I said cautiously, "you should take it."

His gaze snapped to mine. "I would never leave you behind—"

I stopped him with a palm in the air. "I cannot tell you how much it meant to me that you remained behind. But even here, I trust Yahweh to watch over me. And I am telling you, brother of my heart, if you have the chance to explore those distant horizons . . . *Go*."

29

Gavriel

Making every effort to stride with unhurried purpose, Shachar and I approached the gates of the palace complex. In all my days scouting for Yonatan, my heart had never pounded like this. But we had one chance—and only one—to get Zahava out of this place. Once the breach of the vulnerabilities we'd taken advantage of was discovered, the Philistines would double the guard in the palace. All we could do now was hope that Polina's information was sound.

Shachar may not be the most handsome of men, with his smashed nose and rough mannerisms, but he was tall and muscular and knew how to make a woman feel that his entire focus was on her and her alone. Poor Polina hadn't had a chance.

It hadn't taken him long to cajole the laundress into revealing a detailed layout of the palace. Where the guards were usually stationed. And where Zahava worked on her metals and where she slept at night. When we'd broken into the complex before, we'd come in mostly blind, only having been told by a merchant that he'd heard there were prisoners locked in a wine cellar at the back of the palace.

This time, thanks to Polina's loose tongue, we'd planned our incursion while most everyone, including the entire royal family and their esteemed foreign guests, was down at the water's edge, watching a staged battle between a swarm of pirates and a well-armed Phoenician vessel. We'd have only enough time to execute the rescue before the sacrifice ceremony was completed aboard that same ship, just as the longest day of the year was set to rest on the western horizon. After that, the king and his guests would return for a feast and the palace would once again be swarming with people.

Only two young guards stood at the gates, where torches flickered against the gathering dusk. Either the Philistines were extraordinarily lax tonight since everyone of note was down on the beach or Yahweh had heard my fervent prayers to smooth the way before us. Still, neither Shachar nor I would let our own guard down. Only we, and the two naked men bound and gagged under the thick oleanders on the shadowed side of the fortress walls, knew that beneath our borrowed breastplates beat Hebrew hearts.

Shachar greeted the two young men with an impressive Philistine accent. "Captain Korrero sent us to cover the roof."

"The roof?" asked one of the guards with a frown. "What's up there to protect?"

"Trees? Flowers?" Shachar shrugged, his demeanor light as he chuckled. "I don't question Korrero, do you?"

The two men laughed.

"Not if we like our jobs," said the second man. "He sent a couple guards down to the building crew just last week. The two of us were promoted because of it."

"Oh, really? Why was that?" Shachar set his stance wide, arms folded as if he were settling in for a cup of gossip.

"Drunk on watch," said the other.

"Fools," said Shachar, affecting an aggrieved tone. "If something had happened to the king, it'd be Korrero's head on the wall.

But good for the two of you moving up in the ranks. I'll put in a good word for you with the captain. He and I trained together years ago."

They smiled, devouring Shachar's story like fresh bread.

"That'd be much appreciated," said the first guard.

"We'd best get moving," said Shachar, giving the young man a firm pat on the shoulder. "I'd like to keep my own neck intact. When's your shift done? Perhaps the four of us can go get a drink together. I'll give you some tips to get on Korrero's good side. I heard that Egyptian tavern near the temple has the best wine in the city."

They eagerly agreed to meet up once their watch was complete. Then, Shachar and I strode through the entrance to the palace grounds as if we belonged there. I took a brief moment at the top of the stairs to peer at the golden sky, gauging the position of the sun. We had an hour, at most, to find her.

Be with us, Yahweh. Guide my steps.

For nearly the last decade of my life, I'd relied solely on my weapons, and my skill with those weapons, to protect me and further my ambitions. But I'd spent four helpless months with nothing to rely on for Zahava's safety except the care of El Shaddai, and I was certain that if we succeeded today, it would only be because Yahweh's hand was on us.

The guards at the main doors said nothing as we passed through, accepting our silent salute and disguises as proof we'd been cleared by the guards at the gate, and I breathed another prayer of gratitude to the One who made the stars. Perhaps I'd have my little dove in my arms before the sky overhead even changed from gold to dusky orange.

A bevy of servants scurried about the enormous main hall, preparing for the influx of guests who would soon descend upon the lavish spread of food and drinks, while two whole oxen turned on spits at the center of a huge hearth. My belly snarled. I'd been too tense to eat before I'd walked out of the blacksmith shop for the last time, carrying little more than the invaluable knowledge of Philistine ironmaking techniques I'd earned from four months of grueling labor.

Thankfully, none of the servants questioned our presence, so once we passed through the main hall, we made our way to the stairway at the southwest corner of the palace, just where Polina said it would be.

"So far, my laundress has proven a valuable asset," Shachar murmured as we jogged down one flight of stairs. "Too bad I can't take her with me."

"Ready to be shackled again?"

He chortled. "It'd have to be an extraordinary woman to put up with the likes of me."

We walked the length of the open portico, the sky now completely ablaze, and turned at the next corner, which led to yet another set of stairs to the lowest level of the palace, where Zahava was supposed to be quartered.

This place was a maze we'd never have navigated without Shachar's ability to wrap a woman around his leathery finger and then wheedle information out of her like a master spy. If ever I had the chance to be in favor with Yonatan again, I'd have to recommend my friend for his elite unit.

One of the doors along the narrow corridor swung open, and we found ourselves face-to-face with two servant girls, one holding a broom and a wooden bucket and the other a basket overflowing with dusty rags.

They both gasped and came to a wide-eyed halt. All it would take was one scream and we'd have a cadre of guards descending on us, our entire plan destroyed.

"Well, hello," said Shachar, his tone brimming with flirtation. "Why aren't you two lovelies down at the beach watching the festivities?"

Again, his ability to charm females came in handy. Instead of crying out, one of the young women flushed as rosy as the sunset. "We have to clean the guest chambers while the royals are at the celebration."

The other maid snatched her friend's arm, tugging her close as she veered around us. "Monaca," she muttered, "I *told* you to stay away from the guards. They always get you into trouble."

"Oh, come now, ladies," Shachar cajoled, his bare arms splayed wide to display an impressive set of muscles. "Surely we can be friendly, can't we?"

The older one frowned. "No. We can't. What are you even doing down here? Shouldn't you be guarding a doorway somewhere?"

"Just making certain the palace is secure," he said. "You can never be too careful."

She rolled her eyes at Shachar and tugged her friend along. "With men, that is a given."

"Oh, now don't run off!" he called, then snickered as the two maids scurried away.

Dropping all hint of pretense the moment they disappeared around the corner, Shachar set off at a clip in the opposite direction. "Step it up. Monaca's friend was a shade too suspicious for my liking. Polina said Zahava's room is at the end of this corridor."

When we came within a few paces of the last doorway, lamplight spilled from the open door, and the low hum of voices inside caused a spike of nearly painful hope in my veins.

Please, Yahweh, I breathed, *let it be her.*

However, when I peered into the open door, it was not my little wife lounging on a well-cushioned couch at the back of the small room but Adin, talking with a guard lounging carelessly against the wall.

No longer dressed as a Kenite, he wore a simple Philistine tunic—white linen with a stripe of green embroidery at the hem. His hair was trimmed short, as was his beard, and he was laughing as I stepped into the room. Even the room itself was fairly well-appointed, with a comfortable-looking mattress on the couch, two wooden chairs, and a table with the remnants of what looked to be a healthy meal. This looked far more like the room of a guest to the king and little like the prison cell I expected.

Adin turned his head on my entrance but showed no sign of recognition, due to our changed appearances.

"What are you two doing here?" The guard pushed off the wall to approach.

"We've come to move the prisoner, on Korrero's orders," Shachar said, coming to my side. Our bodies now completely blocked the exit.

At Shachar's voice, Adin's eyes went wide, his gaze moving back and forth between us, but he wisely kept his mouth closed.

"Prisoner?" The guard had gone from curious to suspicious. "I've heard nothing about Adin being moved somewhere else."

Odd. The man spoke as if Adin were a friend, not a prisoner at all.

"Talk to Korrero," Shachar said with a careless shrug. "It was his order."

"Who *are* you?" asked the guard, his shoulders going rigid as he scrutinized our faces. "I've not seen you around the palace before."

"Transfers," said Shachar, "from the city gates. To replace those fools who got caught drinking."

The guard's eyes narrowed. "I met the replacements. And you aren't them."

In the distance outside, shouting arose, and my stomach sank. *Not again*.

Shachar didn't hesitate. He plowed headlong into the man, slamming him against the wall. Thanks to months of daily diving in Gaza's strong ocean currents, Shachar had the dazed guard subdued in moments.

Adin jumped up, rushing forward with palms outstretched. "Don't kill him. He's been kind to me, and to your wife."

As the shouting in the distance increased, Shachar kneed the guard hard in the jaw, knocking him senseless. "We need to get out of here."

"I know a way out," said Adin, grabbing a satchel from underneath a stool in the corner.

"I'm not going anywhere without Zahava."

"She's not in the palace," he said, moving toward the doorway.

"Then where is she?"

"On the ship. With the king. Come on, I'll explain once we are outside."

Adin led us down the corridor, then darted across an empty inner courtyard and past another line of dark doorways. On the far side, we climbed up a set of stairs that led us toward the shouting instead of away.

There was no doubt they were looking for us. And no doubt we'd erased any chance of getting back inside these walls once we escaped. This was twice now I'd failed at rescuing my wife. Had I been fooling myself that Yahweh had heard my plea for help?

Pausing at a corner while a trio of guards ran down the corridor ahead of us, Adin leaned close, voice low. "See that chamber across the way? It's where the priests prepare themselves before they perform rituals for the king. There's a door there to the outside."

Shachar and I had no choice but to trust his knowledge of the palace. Waiting only a couple of moments to ensure the corridor was still clear, the three of us dashed across but skidded to a quick stop when we found the door locked.

Adin cursed as he shook the handle. "We have to get through here. It's the only way other than the front entrance."

"Step back," I said, and Adin complied. I took a few steps backward, and using the full force of the strength I'd gained from working iron for the past four months, I plowed into the wooden door. The latch broke, the door flying open as shards of wood scattered and then slamming back on its bronze hinges with a crash, an iron lock skittering across the floor.

Adin chuckled. "It's a good thing you came. I'd have never gotten through that on my own."

Shachar slapped me on the shoulder as he passed. "But can you hold your breath to the bottom of the sea? I think not."

With a shake of my head, I followed Adin and Shachar through the small chamber, which was lined with gaudy idols of every sort, their sightless eyes staring at us from painted niches. The suffocating stink of incense and old blood permeated the room. The door at the back was locked as well. It took two tries to plow through this one, so my shoulder was screaming by the time we stepped into the twilight. But there was no time to dwell on the pain because we were immediately on the move, following a narrow path between the palace and the enormous fortress walls until we reached the northeast corner of the building.

Shachar raised his fist, a silent demand for us to halt as he stealthily peered around the corner, then leaned back against the wall. "Five men at the gate, that I can see."

Shachar and I were the only two armed with swords. I pulled a knife from the holster tied to my thigh and handed it to Adin.

"How will we get through?" he asked.

"Let me look." I pressed past Shachar to peer around the corner. The gates were about fifty paces from where we stood, and all five men were scanning the area diligently. At least our hiding place was deep in the shadows.

I tugged my sling from my belt. "I'll pick as many off as I can while you two run for the gate. Then I'll catch up."

"It's as good a plan as any," said Shachar, sword already in hand.

"Ready?" I asked as I loaded the first of my iron slingstones into the pouch. Thankfully, I'd planned ahead and pilfered chunks of discard over the past months, which I'd shaped with a broken file

I'd found on the ground in the shop one day. They may not be the high-quality wrought-iron slingstones I'd learned to make at the foundry, but they were hard enough to do damage at high speed.

Taking a deep breath, I pleaded once again for Yahweh's help as I stepped past the corner. *Send them true.* He may not have led me to Zahava, but at least we'd found Adin. Surely that counted as a partial answer, didn't it?

It had been a while since I'd twirled my sling, but after months of swinging a heavy mallet against a granite anvil, my shoulders were stronger than they'd ever been. I locked the closest guard in my sight and with a quick twist and a snap of my wrist, let the stone fly. At the crack of my stone to his head, the man fell with a cry, but I didn't wait to see if he rose before I reloaded the sling and set it spinning toward the next target while Shachar and Adin dashed past me.

I picked off one more before the others came running, full speed. Not wanting to hit my friends, I jammed my sling into my belt and followed them, sword at the ready.

Shachar had one down before I caught up, blood pouring from the young man's side. It was one of the two who'd let us into the palace in the first place.

Adin had another guard engaged, doing his best to fend off a well-trained, well-armed man with nothing more than my knife. The third one came directly for me, so I planted my feet, our swords clanging as he swung. Battle-rage surged through my limbs as I knocked him back with a well-placed kick to his thigh. I surged forward while he was off-balance and caught him in the side of the neck with my sword. Eyes wide, the man fell, blood gushing from the wound.

I stepped past the body to deal with one of the guards I'd hit in the forehead with a slingstone, who'd woken from his stupor and was trying to get to his feet. In moments, his blood too was soaking the ground.

"Let's go," said Shachar, having dispatched the other two guards while I was busy.

Adin looked a little dazed as we ran out of the gates, a spray of red across what had been his pristine white tunic, but he kept pace with us.

Glad for the cover of darkness, we paused at one of the garden pools about fifteen paces from the gates. Shachar and I tossed our headdresses into the water, then stripped the bronze-scaled breastplates and, although it pained me to do so, dropped them into the pool as well.

"Where to?" I asked.

"The center of town," said Shachar. "It's best if we take cover in the crowds for now. Hopefully we can get out of the gates before anyone notices the mess at the palace."

Adin had already taken a cloak from the satchel he carried and thrown it over his bloody tunic. He tugged the hood up over his head. Shachar and I were left with nondescript brown tunics and thick leather belts. The only thing marking us as out of the ordinary were the iron swords dangling from those belts as we merged into the flow of bodies. Gaza overflowed with visitors for the festival, torches and braziers blazing along the streets, so we let our pace match the flow of myriad bodies.

We passed the entrance to the temple complex, where worshipers waited in a seemingly endless line with all manner of votive offerings and full baskets of foodstuffs in hand. Then after slowly maneuvering ourselves to the very center of the herd of revelers, we exited the gates of Gaza, where the guards had obviously not been alerted to the chaos we'd caused at the palace. Not one of them looked twice at the three of us as we left the city.

"I knew you'd come for her eventually," Adin said once we were free of the city walls and following a dark path skirting the extensive encampment of visitors' tents to the north of Gaza.

"Of course I came for her. She's my wife."

"So she's on the ship with the king?" Shachar gestured to the sea, where the red-orange sun was now only a sliver on the horizon.

"He insisted," said Adin. "She's spent the last four months making the most extraordinary ceremonial armor I've ever seen. He could not wait to wear it during the sacrifices tonight to make an impression on the Phoenician emissaries. He's desperate to grow trade between Gaza and Byblos and get his greedy hands on some of their ships. Having a goldsmith whose techniques are unparalleled is valuable leverage in such negotiations."

"So how do we get to her?" asked Shachar.

Adin shook his head. "This is the first time she's been allowed off the grounds. She's always under guard. Korrero has a soft spot for her for some reason and assigns his best men to watch over her. As soon as the sacrifices are finished out there on the water, she'll be ushered back inside the palace. And after what just happened, I'm certain Korrero will double her guard, perhaps even move her to a more secure location."

The frustration in his voice was only a weak echo of my own. We'd never get into that palace again. What good had all my prayers done? Zahava was even more out of reach than she had been a few hours ago.

Shachar clamped his hand on my shoulder. "We'll think of something, my friend. We didn't come this far to give up."

Zahava

The scale breastplate I'd spent weeks crafting glowed like fire, reflecting the last of the sunset over the horizon as King Enesidu received groveling bows from the Egyptian emissaries who'd just boarded the ship. Their late arrival had postponed the ceremony, and the king was not pleased. At the opposite end of the deck, the priests appeared anxious to begin the solstice ritual, and at least ten guards were stationed along both sides of the boat, flickering torches in hand.

Korrero leaned closer to me, dropping his voice. "That armor is truly remarkable, young woman. I've never seen its match."

I had to admit, I was proud of what I'd made. The ceremonial breastplate, complete with scores of red-gold scales embossed with leaves, matched the pauldrons on Enesidu's shoulders, while the bracers on his forearms and the greaves strapped to his shins were formed by hammered red-gold sheets over wax-hardened leather tailored to fit the king alone.

None of it would stand up to battle, of course, but that had not been Enesidu's goal. Only to impress these foreign ambassadors with his wealth and make them lust after such finery themselves. And from the way he'd rewarded me over these past weeks, with a well-appointed room of my own in the palace, a basket full of fine linen clothes, and even a maid assigned to see to my comfort, the king was well-pleased with my work. He'd already told me to prepare to make pieces for the ambassadors from Avaris and Byblos—bribes, I would guess, to make certain their kings were amenable to furthering their trading connections.

He'd also said I was to take on three apprentices within the next week, with the goal of having them ready to produce red-gold pieces in months, not years.

For now, I was just glad for the coolness of the salty breeze on my face. I'd never been on a boat of any kind before, so I was lightheaded from the sway of the deck, and a tinge of nausea had parked itself at the base of my throat. I'd been less than thrilled when the king insisted I be present at this ritual and certainly was not looking forward to watching the priests slaughter a pig and a dog atop the wooden altar that had been set up on one end of the deck.

I did not see Mattaniel among the onlookers, but Baalimeq and Oresto were standing on the other side of me, so I hoped to slide behind the two of them instead of having a direct line of sight to the horrifying offering to the gods of the sea.

At least it wasn't a more macabre sacrifice like those the Amalekites offered. The longer I was away from Punon and the influence of Kila and Niv, the more horrified I was that I'd ever excused the burning of the innocent at the altar of Molech and the more grateful I was that Yahweh had separated my people from Amalek. And from what I'd heard from some of the foreign slaves in the palace, the Philistines were no strangers to offering up their own babies from time to time as well.

Once everyone was finally in their place, the king lifted his voice to welcome his guests and thank them for attending the solstice celebration as a fire was stoked within a copper brazier by the priests. Then, he gestured to someone behind us. As the crowd parted, Danelo, his steward, came forward with a box I instantly recognized as the one that held the Atarah Hod. I'd been allowed to study it at length one day, under Danelo's watchful eye, to draw inspiration for the embellishments on the breastplate, but I hadn't seen it since then. Apparently, Enesidu wanted to make a grand impression by having the crown placed on his head in front of everyone.

However, at the very same moment Danelo passed me, his sandal collided with something unseen on the deck, sending him pitching forward. The heavy box flew from his hand and fell to the ground with a horrible crack, the lid flying open and the priceless crown rolling across the deck to collide with the center mast. Gasps of horror came from a number of mouths, including my own. A pale-faced Enesidu darted forward, his beautiful armor glittering in the torchlight as he snatched up the crown to inspect it.

Scrambling to his feet, Danelo dashed across the deck to throw himself at Enesidu's feet, his whole body visibly trembling. "Forgive me, my lord. *Please*."

"You *broke* it," Enesidu said in a terrifyingly flat voice as he held the crown aloft. One of the delicate vines snaking around the crown had snapped at the impact.

My heart pounded in fear for Danelo, even if I'd only spoken to him that one day he'd monitored me with the crown. Every single person on this ship knew that such a mistake—innocent though it may be—was grounds for severe punishment from a king known for mercilessness. And when that mistake had caused a revered object like the Atarah Hod to be damaged, it could even mean death.

"I can fix it." My feet somehow moved forward of their own volition. I was infinitely grateful for the cedarwood cane Korrero had given me as all eyes on the ship turned to watch me hobble toward the king. "I only need to get back to the foundry. It won't take me long."

I'd recently experimented with a new type of furnace that provided a very hot point of flame through a small hole in the iron lid. As long as the break was clean, I could probably weld the fracture without damaging the rest. I *hoped*.

Danelo's tear-stained face peered over his shoulder with a look of stunned gratitude. I doubted he would retain his position, and he'd likely be flogged, but if I succeeded, he should at least be spared his life.

Enesidu snapped his fingers at Korrero. "Get her to the palace. Fast. I want that crown on my head before the ritual begins."

Without hesitation, Korrero snatched the wooden box from the ground where Danelo had dropped it and retrieved the crown from Enesidu. Then he took my arm and led me to the railing, calling for the closest of the small boats waiting nearby.

The two rowers moved the narrow boat into place and then with the same rope system that had lifted me up into the boat, I was lowered down into its shallow hull. I'd never seen anything like the way Phoenicians loaded cargo and people onto their ships but was too distracted by trying to not fall face-first into the rocking boat to care.

One of the rowers helped me sit on the bottom of the boat and then the box with the crown was carefully handed down to be placed in my lap. Korrero climbed into the boat holding a small torch and sat behind me.

Eyes squeezed tight, I held my breath as the boat swayed back and forth, bumping into the hull of the ship again and again. Why Enesidu had insisted this ceremony take place on the water instead of on flat ground was beyond me. I clutched the crown box tightly to my stomach, which was churning from the rough motion of the waters. I'd be very glad to never step foot on a boat again, if possible.

"Move," Korrero ordered the rowers, gesturing with his torch toward the coastline. "She has to get to the palace quickly."

The men pushed away from the ship with their oars, and then we were on the move toward the shadowed shoreline. I could not bring myself to look at the water sliding by, which only made my stomach more unsettled, so I dropped my eyes to the treasure in my lap. What would happen if my idea to fix it didn't work? Or if I damaged the crown? Would Enesidu have me put to death along with Danelo?

"Where are you going?" asked Korrero, pulling me out of my anxious thoughts. "The palace is to the south."

There was no response from the rowers. I peered up to see that the distant lights of the port were to my right, instead of to my left, where I'd expected them.

"Turn around," said Korrero, his tone sharp. "We have no time for foolishness!"

The rower facing away from me kept dipping his oars into the water, over and over, ignoring Korrero's mounting frustration while the boat glided northward.

"What is going on?" The boat rocked harshly as Korrero stood. "Turn around!"

The hair on the back of my neck stood on end, and I twisted to find him lunging toward the rower in the back. I yelped as the boat jerked to the side, grabbing for something to keep me upright. The box slid off my lap and tipped sideways, the crown clattering onto the wooden floor for the second time tonight, but I could do nothing more than hang onto the edge of the boat so I wouldn't be thrown down myself.

"Treachery!" bellowed Korrero, his voice echoing across the water. "We're under attack!"

Panic swirled in my belly. There was a reason the king had insisted I be guarded at all times, and it wasn't because he thought I'd somehow run away. He was convinced once others heard about my skill, they would attempt to snatch me for their own gain. And perhaps he had been right to worry.

Disoriented, I tried to make sense of what was happening while the two men grappled behind me and the man at the front continued to row, his huge shoulders heaving as he pushed us farther from the coastline and in the opposite direction of the port.

The torch had fallen into the hull of the boat, casting light on the commotion behind me and illuminating the face of the man Korrero was wrestling. Recognition hit me full force in the center of my chest. His long, unruly curls may be gone and his face bereft of a beard, but I would know those gray eyes anywhere.

"Gavi?" His name flew from my mouth, drawing those eyes to me, just as Korrero plowed a fist into his jaw. Off-balance as the boat swayed violently, Gavi tipped sideways and nearly fell out of the boat. Within two breaths, Korrero had him pinned, fist raised again as Gavi's upper body hung over the edge.

"No! Korrero, stop! It's my husband!"

The head guard jolted, startled by my command, his eyes wide as his head swiveled toward me. "What?"

Gavi too turned to stare at me, looking just as bewildered as Korrero.

"That's my husband. Please . . ."

Throughout my captivity, one thing had been consistent, and that was Korrero's unlikely kindness to me. At first, I'd thought he was merely impressed with my knowledge of goldsmithing or my courage in challenging him at the gate to the palace, but a few weeks ago, he'd confided that I reminded him of his own daughter, a girl born with a disease that caused her muscles to waste away over a period of fourteen years before she'd died. He'd said her strength, even in that affliction, had been like nothing he'd ever seen, and he recognized the same spirit in me.

"Please," I begged, letting my love for Gavi show on my face.

Korrero blinked at me for a few tense moments, then slid away from Gavi, who righted himself.

"Your husband?" He looked back and forth between us in bewilderment.

"Yes. Please don't hurt him."

Korrero's gaze was now drawn back to the ship, and the lights coming toward us across the water. His alert had indeed drawn attention. We were being pursued.

"Get her out of here," he said to Gavi, then dropped the torch over the edge of the boat into the sea. "I'll throw them off as much as I can, but the king won't stop until he finds her."

Then, to my absolute astonishment, Korrero stepped onto the center bench and launched himself off the boat, leaving us in the dark. Water splashed the side of my face as the boat wobbled hard, righting itself.

"Go, Shachar," ordered Gavi as he grappled with his oars, trying to realign them in the water. His friend complied, powerful arms circling again and again as we began to move forward.

There was no time to ask how they'd come to be here tonight as the shouts in the distance grew. I peered over the edge of the boat to see more torches trailing behind us in the blackness. Who knew how many boats were in pursuit now? I prayed one of them would quickly find Korrero and rescue him.

"Zahava, listen," said Gavi, his words coming out strained as he kept rowing. "There's no time to explain, but I need you to trust us."

"What do you mean?" I didn't like the sound of that warning.

"Can you swim?" said Shachar.

"No!" My voice pitched high.

"It's all right," said Gavi. "Shachar will get you to safety."

"What? I'm not going in the water!"

"There's no need to fear," said Shachar, grunting as he pulled the oars in tandem with Gavi. "I swim like a fish."

"I'm sorry, little dove, but we have no choice," said Gavi.

"There, up ahead," said Shachar. "There are the rocks."

Gavi dropped his oars and moved toward me, staying low as the boat swayed. "Are you ready?"

"No! I'm not!" Imagining the cold water swallowing me, I trembled. "Gavi!"

The boat wobbled again as Shachar stood up and suddenly there was a thunking sound, like an ax hitting wood.

"What is he doing?"

"Sinking the boat. But first, we need to flip it."

"Why?"

"Because they will be here within a short time, and we have to swim the rest of the way."

Water trickled along the hull, soaking my backside as Gavi reached for my hand. "We are going in. Ready?"

I had no choice, did I? This boat was going down.

"The crown!" I reached for the box, pushing it aside, and felt around until the cold metal of the crown met my fingers.

"Give it to me," said Gavi. "I'll keep it safe."

There was no time to question him. I let him take the priceless heirloom, and in the dim night, I could see him slide it up over his arm and to the top of his shoulder. The water gushed into the hull now, and my panic rose along with its level.

"All right," said Shachar. "To my left. Hold on to her."

Gavi wrapped his arms around me. "I've got you. Hold your breath."

I clutched the back of his tunic and then the world was tipping as Shachar and Gavi both threw their weight to the side. We crashed into the sea, and even though I kept my mouth closed, salt water dashed up my nose as my head went under and everything went black.

And then suddenly, we broke the surface, and I blinked as the starry sky appeared. With his arms tight around me, Gavi kicked, keeping us afloat.

"You two all right?" Shachar swam closer.

"Zahava?" Gavi tightened his grip.

"Yes," I replied, my teeth chattering from cold and terror.

"I know this is frightening," said Gavi. "But we have to swim."

"But I told you—"

"I've got you," said Shachar, sliding an arm around my waist and tugging me away from Gavi.

I let out a strangled cry at being torn away from my husband, but Gavi released me into Shachar's hold. "He's a much stronger swimmer than I am. It's all right. We have to go before they get here."

In all my terror over being plunged into the black sea, I'd nearly forgotten we were being pursued. I craned my neck around to see that the torches were indeed closing in, and the sound of voices rolled over the water as they searched for us.

"Don't fight me, just relax," said Shachar as he began to stroke his free arm through the water. I did my best to comply as he towed me along, although my heartbeat pounded in my ears, my jaw ached from trying to keep my teeth from clacking together, and my mouth tasted of brine. Next to us, Gavi's form cut through the water as the waves pushed us toward the shore. However, instead of heading directly toward the beach, Shachar veered toward a dark shadow that I guessed to be the rocks he'd mentioned before.

We could not see the boats that had been pursuing us, but the voices rang out not far away. Once Shachar reached the outcropping, he put out a hand to keep us from being slammed into the rocks by the powerful waves. With eyes stinging from the salt water, I searched through the blackness for Gavi, my heart fluttering with relief when he appeared beside us, chest heaving as he fought the relentless swell of the waves.

"Now what?" he asked, sounding exhausted.

"We go under."

Gavi sounded as confused as I felt. "Under where?"

"There's a cave under this outcropping. We'll wait them out there."

"But how will we even find it?" I rasped, my throat raw.

"I've been here many times. There's a sponge bed down there. And the tide is low enough tonight since there is no moon that there's space to breathe."

"Look, there's the boat!" came a shout from far too close.

"We have to go. Now. Gavi, hold your wife's hand. Both of you take a deep breath because we have to go down a good way. Once you feel me push up, kick hard."

"But how can you navigate in the dark?" I asked as I felt Gavi's cold fingers entwine tightly with my own.

Shachar's grin was nearly audible. "You'll see. Now, take a deep breath and hold."

I did as he asked and suddenly my head was underwater again. I squeezed my eyes tight as Shachar tugged us down, down, down for what felt like too deep to ever make it back up again in time. My heart pounded frantically, my chest feeling as though it might burst if I had to hold my breath much longer. After everything, I may very well perish under the rocks fifty paces from the shoreline.

But then we suddenly burst through the surface of the water, and I gasped for a painful gulp of air. I blinked the salt water away and when my vision finally cleared, I had no explanation for what I saw. We were indeed inside a long but narrow cave, the ceiling above us half the height of a man, and all around us was light. Tiny points of glowing blue shimmered from the walls of the cave and under the water. I'd never seen anything so strange and yet so incredibly beautiful.

"What is it?" My awed voice echoed off the rocky walls.

"Not sure," said Shachar, running a palm over his clean-shaven head. "One of my sponge-diving friends showed me this place a couple of months ago. I've come here a number of times since then just because it's so spectacular. I think now that perhaps it was Yahweh's provision."

"*Months*? How long have you been here?" I asked, looking back and forth at the two men who'd seemed to appear from nowhere tonight.

"We came back five days after the king left us at the border," said Gavi. "I've been working for a blacksmith, and like he said, Shachar has been diving for sponges and mussels."

I blinked at my husband in wonder, finally getting a good look at his face in the blue glow. His hair was short, barely two fingers long, and standing on end where he'd swiped the water from his forehead. His face was shaved, as was the custom of many Philistines. He looked so foreign like this—so not *my* Gavi—but he was still the most handsome man I'd ever seen. "I just cannot believe you are here."

"You didn't think I would leave you here, did you, little dove?" He tugged me into his body and held me close. Even in this frigid underwater cave, his presence made me feel so safe, warming me from the inside. The crown wedged over his shoulder reflected the glittering blue lights.

A tear dripped down my cheek and into the glowing water. "I was afraid to hope."

With the strange luminescence lighting the unfamiliar planes of his face, he told me of how they'd waited for a chance to find me, how Shachar had schemed information out of one of the laundresses, and their thwarted efforts to find me at the palace. When Gavi said they'd found Adin instead, new panic rose up. I'd forgotten that he'd been left behind tonight at the palace, told that his presence on the ship was not necessary.

"Where is he?"

"Waiting for us not too far away. We should probably get back soon so he doesn't think our plans went awry."

After some discussion about whether we'd waited long enough

for the searchers to have given up, Shachar dived back out of the cave and returned shortly to say he saw no evidence of the Philistines. I wondered if Korrero had convinced them we'd drowned. Which, Gavi told me, had been the entire reason they'd decided to sink the boat in the first place. If I was presumed to be dead, the search would be over. Whereas, if there was any hope of finding me, Enesidu would not give up. Ever.

Although I mourned leaving behind the mysterious blue cave, a miracle of the Creator I would wonder over for the rest of my days, it was time to go. Secured between Shachar and Gavi, I endured another horrible trip underwater until my lungs felt like bursting. But this time, I knew what to expect.

When we finally made it to shore, I would have done anything to lay on the sand and rest my weary body, but Shachar insisted we run to where Adin was waiting.

I certainly could not run anywhere, and I'd lost both of my elevated sandals in the sea so Gavi urged me to crawl onto his back. Weak with exhaustion, I did not even argue, even though both of us were soaked and covered in sand.

"You ready?" he said as he jostled me into position.

"Yes." I tightened my grip around his neck and snuggled closer, gratefully for his innate warmth.

"How about you?" he asked Shachar.

His friend grinned at us, the faint glimmer of starlight reflecting off the priceless crown jammed onto his bald head as he tensed his body to run. "Beat you there."

And then we were off, spiriting through the night and away from the midnight black ocean I very much hoped to never see again.

Gavriel

"I thought the three of you were at the bottom of the ocean." Adin seemed to pop up from nowhere as we approached the meeting place. Shachar had sent him to an abandoned fisherman's hut a half-hour's walk north of the port. Somehow he'd found the ramshackle shelter, alone and in the dark.

"Seen anyone around here looking for us?" Shachar asked as I let Zahava slip to the ground, then caught her as she wobbled on her bare feet.

The run here had been fairly easy, even with her slight weight. But we still had a long way to go tonight before I was satisfied Zahava would be truly safe. She shivered, so I pulled her in front of me to block the wind and wrapped my arms around her. Even though her clothes were sodden and her skin like ice, the feel of my little dove nestling closer was pure bliss.

"I saw a couple of torches along the shore to the south—even thought it might be you," said Adin. "But they disappeared a good while ago."

"Glad to hear it," said Shachar. "But we need to get east, and fast."

"You think they're still looking for me?" Zahava asked. "Surely they'll think I drowned."

"We aren't taking any chances," I replied, tightening my hold. I wouldn't be letting her out of my sight for a good long while after this. "You rested up, Adin? We'll need to run most of the night."

Adin folded his arms, looking down. He cleared his throat before meeting my eyes. "I'm not going with you."

"What do you mean you aren't going?" snapped Shachar.

"Look . . ." He blew out a breath. "I won't go back to being under my father's control. That's not the life I want for myself."

Shachar threw his arms wide, the crown he still wore making him look like some kind of pauper-king. "So you'd stay in *Gaza*?"

"No. I've been offered a job on a ship. I'm going to sea."

Zahava let out a little gasp. "With who?"

"Mattaniel," he replied. "His master needed to replace some crewmembers who got caught selling cargo to fill their own purses. They are leaving just after dawn."

"You were going to leave Zahava behind?" A flare of anger rose up. He'd not known we were coming tonight.

The young man lifted his palms, shamefaced. "I hadn't decided whether to go. I'd been waiting for a sign from Yahweh that it was the right thing to do. And then the two of you showed up in the palace while I was waiting to speak to Zahava." He looked at my wife. "And you *did* tell me to go if I had the chance."

Zahava patted my arm where it crossed her chest, peering up at me. "I did tell him that. And I meant it. There was not one day I felt unsafe, even in the Philistine palace. Yahweh watched over me and provided Korrero to do so as well."

I'd have to ask her more about that later. I'd never been so shocked as when the same man who'd had me viciously beaten months ago jumped off the boat and pled for us to get Zahava to safety. It seemed I owed the guard an enormous debt of gratitude I would never be able to pay.

As for Adin, I fully understood both his desperation to get far away from his brute of a father and his youthful desire for adventure. After all, when I'd been near his age, I'd run off to fight for King Saul with my cousins.

"They'll be looking for you too after what happened tonight," I said, knowing I'd not change his mind.

"Mattaniel told me to go to the port at dawn if I was able to get away from the palace. I'll stay hidden here until it's time to go."

No wonder he'd known how to escape the palace through that priest's entrance; he'd been making a plan to flee.

"All right, then. We need to go," said Shachar, his eyes tracking down the shoreline. "We have a long distance to cover before the sun comes up."

Zahava disentangled herself from my arms and limped over to grasp Adin's hands. "You *will* be careful."

He pressed his lips together, nodding. It was obvious the two of them had become good friends during their stay in Gaza.

"Someday perhaps we'll meet again and you'll tell me of your many adventures in faraway places." Her voice broke. She came to her toes and pressed a kiss to his cheek. "Hold tight to Yahweh, brother of my heart."

Adin sniffed, then cleared his throat. "I will."

Stepping forward, I grasped Adin by the shoulder. "Thank you for watching over Zahava, my friend. For risking so much to keep her safe."

"I hope you'll forgive me for leaving with her in the first place."

I'd had four long months to work through my anger at Adin over taking Zahava to Gaza. He'd been a fool thinking he could fix what happened to Farah, but my little dove was determined as well as clever. She likely would have found a way to fly off alone if he hadn't gone with her. I certainly didn't want him to carry a burden of guilt around for as long as I had. "All is forgiven."

He let out a sigh. "I'm grateful."

"Be safe, boy," said Shachar, giving Adin a rough pat on the shoulder. "I'll tell your father you went off with pirates. He'll hate that."

"That he will." Adin chuckled as I crouched for Zahava to crawl onto my back again.

Once the crown had been removed from Shachar's head, placed inside the leather satchel Adin offered, and slung across Zahava's back, we were once again on the move eastward, leaving the young man behind to find his own way. I prayed that unlike me, back when I was a stiff-necked young fool bent on determining my own path, he'd entrust each of his steps to Yahweh from now on.

I used to think Zevi's harsh training regimen was excessive, especially when I'd been subjected to the torture of mile after mile carrying a rock overhead, once it was implemented as standard for Saul's soldiers. But I had to admit, I was grateful for the ability to keep moving for hours at a swift but steady pace.

Shachar insisted we take turns carrying Zahava to avoid fatigue, but with how slight she was, and for as great as my relief was to have her near, I could have easily done it alone—even though the terrain was mostly uphill.

She'd slept much of the way as we navigated by starlight through hostile territory, but she somehow clung tightly to me even in sleep. We'd stuck to the trees as much as possible to avoid civilization. So far, the only life we'd seen was a couple of wildcats tearing apart the rotted carcass of a deer and they'd scattered the moment they spotted us.

Now that we were high in the foothills, Shachar and I decided we were either close to Yehudite territory or already in it, so we could stop and rest for a while. We hid in the center of a thick grove of wild olive trees perched on a steep hillside and slept until the sun was high.

Waking with my precious wife in my arms was a luxury I wasn't certain I'd ever have again, so I was grateful Shachar was still asleep with his back to us when she stirred, turning over in my embrace to smile up at me.

"*Boker tov*, husband," she whispered.

It was a good morning indeed. "Boker tov, little dove."

"I missed you every moment." Tears glistened in her hazel eyes. "I am so sorry—"

I stopped her with the kiss I'd been desperate for every day of the past four months. There was plenty of time to discuss all that had happened. But for now, I just wanted to take advantage of the small window of privacy we'd have before Shachar woke.

With a little hum of pleasure, Zahava slid her arms around my neck as I reacquainted myself with her lovely mouth for the next few minutes. After endless nights of dreaming of her and waking to empty arms, it was almost surreal that she'd not disappeared with the sun.

When finally I allowed her a moment of respite, her lips were swollen and her cheeks tinged with roses. "Shachar is going to catch us."

I chuckled softly. "The man sleeps like the dead. And even he wouldn't begrudge me a kiss from my wife after such a miraculous rescue at sea."

Her eyes flared. "It *was* a miracle. How were you there last night? How did you know I would be lowered into that boat?"

"I didn't. After we got out of the city, we had no idea what to do. You were on a ship out in the water and we knew once you were taken back to the palace, it would be even more difficult to get to you after the ruckus we'd caused. We walked up the coastline toward the port, trying to come up with a plan that wouldn't put you in more danger."

I told her how I'd sat on the beach, staring across the darkening waters in despair. We'd been so close and it felt like Zahava was a thousand miles away instead of on a ship anchored just off the coast. I could not understand why Yahweh would allow Zahava to be imprisoned for so long. Or why he would let us get so close, all the way into her quarters, only for everything to fall apart.

Barzel had told me to not ask "why" of the Almighty, to simply listen and obey, but that was far easier said than done. With nothing to do but trust her father's wisdom, I lifted my chin to take in the few stars already twinkling in the swiftly deepening sky and breathed deep of the salt air, determined to simply be still and listen.

"After a while, your mother's song began to run through my mind," I said. "And I suddenly felt this driving urge to look for your golden star. So I stood up and turned around, searching the southeastern sky, but there was a line of palms in the way. I moved a little farther down the beach and stumbled across two very drunk fishermen lying on the sand, passing a skin of wine back and forth. It turned out that not only did Shachar know them, but he was also able to talk them into letting us borrow their boat for the price of the iron swords we took off the palace guards."

At least they'd been well paid for the loss of their fishing boat and the small ax we'd found in the hull, which Shachar had used to knock a hole in the bottom.

"Our plan had been little more than to row out to the ship and see if we could spot you, perhaps follow you back to shore and find an opportunity to surprise your guards. But then, when we were coming around the stern, someone called out, commanding us to come alongside and ferry passengers. We had no choice but to comply and hope no one recognized us. And then, as if Yahweh had lowered you down from the heavens, you were suddenly there in our boat. It took everything I had in me not to say your name. Turns out, I didn't need a sword or a knife or even a sling to rescue you. Just the God who hears even a stubborn, rebellious fool like me."

"It truly was a miracle, then," she whispered. "I didn't recognize you at all."

She frowned as she ran her palm over my thick-stubbled chin, then traced a delicate finger over my lips. "I must admit, I miss the beard a little."

I kissed the tip of her finger. "Don't worry, it doesn't take long to grow out. I've had a full beard since I was sixteen. I'm just glad not to have to shave every day anymore."

She grinned mischievously. "As long as it doesn't grow into that enormous bush that hid most of your handsome face when we met."

"*Handsome*, eh?" I repaid her tease by rubbing her exposed throat with my rough cheek, followed by a few gentle nips and kisses. Unfortunately, her giggles woke Shachar.

"Are we going to go any time soon or are the two of you going to mess about all day?" His sleep-graveled voice was full of amusement. "Perhaps we'll just wait here for the Philistines to catch up while you kiss?"

"Four months is a *very* long time," I muttered as I helped my flushing wife to her feet.

Once Shachar had gone off to tend his needs down by the stream, I found Zahava staring back the way we'd come. I slid my arms around her waist and pulled her close. She'd likely soon be sick of my desperate need to touch her and reassure myself that she was actually here with me.

From up here, the coastlands spread out like a blanket of green and gold for as far as the eye could see. The Philistines had certainly claimed a valuable stretch of earth. After seeing the city of Gaza and the might of Philistia for myself, I wasn't certain how Saul would ever reclaim the area for Israel without far more soldiers and resources than he'd accrued over the past ten years. It may take decades before we were equipped for such a battle.

But, then again, after the way Yahweh had proven himself so faithful both to me and to my people over hundreds of years, who knew what he had in store for the future? Salvation from our enemies may come in a way we could never imagine.

Zahava sighed. "Do you think Adin will be all right?"

I hummed, contemplating. "I do. I suspect he never had any plans to return to Gibeah in the first place. He told you about his father?"

"He did. And as much as I will worry about him, I'm glad he won't be under the man's authority anymore."

"Who is this friend of his who invited him to sea?"

"The servant of a wealthy Phoenician merchant. Adin was fascinated by Mattaniel's stories of foreign places and people. They're setting out on a trading expedition that will take many months, maybe longer. Adin will be as far away from his father as possible."

"Is this Mattaniel trustworthy? What do you know of him?"

"Not much. Just that he is highly valued by his master for his ability to speak many languages."

What little hair I had on the back of my neck rose. "How old is he?"

"Maybe a few years older than Adin? I'm not certain. But there was something about him that seemed far older than his years. I am not sure what it was. Something in his eyes, maybe? Or perhaps it was just his hair."

Intuition rattled hard in my gut. I pulled back and turned her around by the shoulders. "What do you mean? What about his hair?"

She frowned up at me, confused by my intensity. "He had a patch of silver in his hair. I've never seen anything like it."

My entire body went rigid. *Surely not.* "Was the rest of it black? And curly?"

Her eyes were round as moons. "It was black but trimmed very close to his skull. I'm not certain how curly it was."

I slumped forward, hands on my thighs, breaths coming short. "And did he have a deep scar cutting through his right eyebrow?"

"Gavi, how do you know that? Did you meet him in the palace?"

My eyes dropped closed as I groaned, pain slicing through my chest. How could I have been so close and yet missed him?

"It's Shalem," I rasped against the hot glut of emotion in my throat. "My cousin. The one we lost during the battle of Yavesh. It has to be him."

Her hands flew to her mouth, eyes glistening with tears.

Zevi had discovered years ago that Shalem was with Phoenicians headed to the port of Ashdod. And now he and Adin were aboard a ship that was undoubtedly long gone by now.

I scrubbed both hands down my face.

"From what the other young men said," Zahava began, "your cousin's master regards him as a valuable asset. You can at least be glad he's not being mistreated."

I huffed, the familiar wave of guilt rising up. If only I'd not been so selfish and turned back to Naioth when Zevi told me to. "He *should* be with his family."

Zahava stepped forward into me, slid her hands around my waist, and with her cheek pressed to my chest, embraced me tightly. "Do you truly believe that Yahweh brought us together—twice—in such unlikely ways and yet does not have his eyes on your cousin?"

A groan reverberated inside me as her gentle words struck true and deep as a double-edged sword.

"I don't know why Shalem was taken from your family or what all happened since then," she continued. "But if anything, we know that he is safe. Alive. And that means there is still hope he will return one day. So instead of bludgeoning yourself, my sweet husband, the way you've done in the past, perhaps we should keep our eyes on the One who made the stars—the very same ones sailors follow—and trust him to guide Shalem home again?"

I tilted her face up to me so I could look into her hazel eyes. "How will I ever repay Yahweh for giving me such a precious gift? I'll never deserve you."

She smiled ruefully. "My father always says Yahweh doesn't give us what we actually deserve, or we'd have nothing but sorrow. He gives us just what we need, even if we don't understand his reasons at the time."

Little did she know that her family had been dealt yet another blow. I'd not yet told Zahava about the extent of her father's injuries from Gaza, but I could not bring myself to give her any cause to worry on the way back. However, I prayed Yahweh would give me the words before we reached Be'er Sheva to tell her that he had gone completely blind.

For now, I just leaned to place my forehead on hers, breathing in her nearness. "There are many things I regret in my life, Zahava, but not the moment my drink-addled mind saw a white dove fluttering up on the hillside in the darkness and went to see for myself."

She sucked in a breath and jerked her chin up to stare at me, wide-eyed. "I always wondered why you called me that!"

"Oh, for the love of . . ." Shachar's gruff voice called out from a short distance away. "Not *again*. Are you two coming? I'd like to be in Be'er Sheva before midnight."

I grinned down at Zahava, whose cheeks were once again dusky pink. "I'll kiss my wife whenever I want, you great buffoon. So turn around if you don't want to see it."

Shachar's growl was half-amusement, half-annoyance as he stomped away, and I made good on my promise.

Zahava

My heart leaped at the sight of Be'er Sheva's completed walls, and once again when I spotted a host of black-and-brown Kenite tents along the southern river in the distance. Shachar parted ways with us, headed up to report at the gates while Gavi and I veered toward the encampment, passing by herds of grazing sheep and goats and the evidence of recently plowed fields and new irrigation ditches. It seemed my people were making this place their own.

A shout from far off echoed on the breeze and then someone was running toward us across one of those beautiful fields. It took me only a few moments to realize it was Farah, black braids flying out behind her as she barreled toward me with a few of her goats bumbling along in her wake. Gavi set me down, and I'd barely gotten my footing before my sister plowed into me, her grip around me tight as we cried.

"How?" she said through her sobs. "How are you here?"

"It's a very long story."

She pulled back to stare at me. "Are you all right?"

"Thanks to Gavi and Shachar, I am fine."

She flinched, looking between me and my husband. "But what about Adin?"

Although it was clear that Adin had been enamored of my sister, I wasn't certain how she felt about him. So I was careful with my words.

"He chose to board a ship instead of returning. He's off to explore the world."

Her dark eyes were full of confusion. "He . . . he left? For good?"

"He didn't want to return to Gibeah," I said, wondering if she knew anything of his father.

She pursed her lips, gaze tracking west. "I can't blame him."

"Perhaps he'll return someday."

"Perhaps." Her shoulder twitched as if she couldn't be bothered to care. Farah hated showing her soft underbelly, so unless something changed, I doubted I would ever know her true feelings on the matter.

The goats had caught up to us, one of them snuffling at the hem of Gavi's brown tunic. My husband made a strangled noise and jerked away.

"It's not going to bite you," I said with a giggle.

"How do you know?" he said, moving to put me between himself and the doe. How this fearless warrior could be so unnerved by a goat was beyond me.

Farah rolled her eyes at him, then tugged on my arm. "Everyone will hit the clouds when they see you've returned. And I want to hear the story of how you escaped the King of Gaza."

She led us around the edge of camp instead of through the center, trying to avoid anyone else noticing our presence before I had a chance to see my own family. At the sight of the familiar pattern specific to our household on a few tents pitched beside the river, I could not hold back the tears. To see my family living in such a beautiful place in peace and safety within the boundaries of the land promised to Avraham filled me with gratitude.

And then, before I could catch my breath, my mother was suddenly flying out of one of those tents toward me, Breena and Anaya just behind her. The three of them wrapped me in their arms, all of us sobbing. My mother kissed my face again and again, telling me she knew Yahweh would bring me home.

"Let me see her" came a graveled voice I knew as well as my own. My father stood in the door of the tent, his clouded gaze roving back and forth as he came forward. "Where is she?"

Disentangling from my mother and sisters, I went to meet my father. "Here I am, Abba."

"Oh, Zahava. My golden star," he said, two fat tears tracking down his cheeks. He reached for me. "Is that really you?"

With my stomach in a knot, I looked up into his eyes, but they were focused just above my head. Just this morning, Gavi had told me that the beatings by the Philistines had caused him to lose the rest of his sight, but it hadn't been real until now.

"It's me, Abba." My voice brought his gaze downward, and I reached for his hand and put it on my cheek.

His callused fingers curved around the side of my face as he let out a gusty sigh. "Thank the Almighty."

"I brought you something," I said, reaching for the satchel at my hip. Removing the crown, I pushed it into his hands.

"What is this?" he asked, brows bunched as his fingers slid along its polished edges.

"The Atarah Hod, Abba. It's back where it belongs. The King of Gaza had it all these years."

His face went slack. "What? This is truly . . . ? It can't be."

"It is," I said. "And I have quite the story to tell you about how it came to be in your hands right now."

It awed me to see how easily Yasmin had stepped into the role of mother to Rahm's sisters. As I told the story of my captivity in Gaza and Gavi explained our escape, the twins sat on either side of her, leaning close as though they'd always belonged to her. Gavi had told me during our journey that Rahm held on for two whole days after I'd run away to Gaza, a miracle that allowed him time to repent of his deceptions. I would never understand how he could so easily betray us, but I'd leave the judgment of his soul up to the One who created him.

When our bellies were full and the entirety of the story had been told, Ima pressed a kiss to my forehead and then ushered a yawning Breena and Anaya off to the tent, Yasmin followed suit with the girls, and Farah drifted away to herd her little flock into their pen.

"I cannot thank you enough for what you have done, Gavriel," said my father once the three of us were alone by the fire. "The lengths you went to to restore Zahava to us are extraordinary."

"She is my wife. I had no choice."

"That's not true. Few would have blamed you when it looked so hopeless. Instead, you refused to give up, and for that, I am forever in your debt."

"You may have coerced me into this marriage, but I love your daughter more than I thought I could ever love anyone or anything, Barzel. There was no question I would go after her. I would go to the ends of the earth to find her and gladly lay down my life to protect her."

Tears tracked down my cheeks at his pronouncement. I'd known he cared for me, but to hear him speak words of such adoration was astounding.

"But still," said my father, his voice hoarse, "you brought back my precious girl to me." He cleared his throat, eyes glimmering with his own tears. "We have all lost so much . . . I must admit it was enough to cause my faith in El Shaddai to waver a little. The story of your time in Gaza and all the ways Yahweh guided and protected you both has revived my spirit and restored my confidence. I could not have picked a better man for my daughter."

"It was only Yahweh's grace that you did." Gavi's response came out choked, as if he too were struggling against heavy emotion. "In truth, you probably saved my miserable life by doing so. There is certainly no debt between us."

I leaned into my husband and slid my hand into his, my silent reminder to him that I was by his side and would remain that way for the rest of my days.

"You know you need to leave here, don't you?" said my father. "You must get her far away from Be'er Sheva."

I flinched, stunned to my bones. "What?"

Gavi just nodded. "I do."

"Far away? No. Abba. I just got back. I want to be with all of you." I gaped at my husband. "You want to take me away from my family?"

His expression was full of compassion. "It's the only way to protect you, little dove. There is no guarantee our ruse with the boat worked. When none of our bodies wash up on shore, there will be questions about whether we escaped. And if Enesidu sends spies to Be'er Sheva and finds us here, no one will be safe. Least of all, you."

I loathed to admit it, but he was right. If the king suspected I was alive, he would stop at nothing to get me, and the crown, back in his hands.

"As well, you must never make red-gold again," my father pronounced. "It is far too dangerous. And you must take the secret of its production to your grave. We cannot risk Enesidu or any others hearing word of new pieces being made, even in the future. Look at how long they preserved their false beliefs about the crown in the first place."

It hurt to think of not teaching my children the things I'd learned from my father and allowing the precious knowledge to disappear forever. "But, Abba . . . it's our family's legacy."

He shook his head. "No. Our family legacy is not things we make with our hands. It's our faithfulness to Yahweh. That is what you must pass down to your children—the only wealth that cannot be taken from us and that will endure long after things made from gold and silver turn to dust. And for as much as it pains me to send you away, my precious daughter, for your sake, and for the sake of all the Kenites in this valley . . . you must go."

Gavriel

There was only one place to go where I knew for certain Zahava would be safe, one household protected night and day by well-paid guards and far enough away from the threat of Philistine incursion to Israelite territory that I could relax.

The one I'd grown up in.

However, even as I strode along behind a trader's wagon heading north with my gaze fixed on my brokenhearted wife, I wasn't certain we'd be welcome. Especially after the hateful things I'd screamed at Hanan the last time I walked away from his villa—some of which I could only remember through a haze of drink.

I'd come back to see my mother and sisters five years ago, on the tail end of a long stretch with the army. After a tense meal with my stepfather, where he could barely look at me, I'd gone to the local tavern. Who knew how long I was gone, but it certainly was far past midnight when I stumbled back to the villa. After arguing loudly in the street with the night guard at the door, who did not know me, I was let into the house by an uncharacteristically disheveled Hanan, who accused me of acting the drunk fool and waking the entire street.

Looking back now, with clarity of mind and a shift in my perspective, I had to admit he was right. In fact, I was ashamed to think that my mother and little sisters had likely witnessed it too. But at the time, I'd drowned restraint at the bottom of a jug, so instead I got louder.

"Well, you were right then, weren't you?" I'd thrown my arms wide. *"I turned out just like him after all, didn't I? Satisfied?"*

"What are you talking about?" he'd asked.

"'He'll end up face down in the muck too, Miri,'" I'd sneered in a mockery of his cultured voice.

Hanan had flinched as if I'd hit him. *"Gavriel, you are—"*

"What? Worthless to you? Out of control? Well, don't worry, this is the last time I'll step foot in your precious palace. Shouldn't have come back in the first place."

I'd spun around, heading for the half-open doorway, and Hanan had grabbed my sleeve, trying to keep me from barreling back into the night. Startled, and impaired by drink, I'd jerked away, which set him off-balance. He'd knocked back into a large decorative urn, which shattered to the floor with an explosive crash.

I'd stared at the mess for a moment, oddly proud of myself for ruining something he'd wasted so much of his cherished silver on, and then I stepped over the threshold for the last time.

"Gavriel, stop," Hanan said as I stumbled down the stairs, nearly missing the last one. *"Don't do this."*

I turned back to see him shadowed in the doorway and itched to get in a parting shot. *"Just be glad, Uncle. At least I'll die on a battlefield somewhere instead of under the wheels of an ox cart. Won't look so bad to your rich friends this time."*

I didn't remember much after I'd turned away, only that I'd woken under a tree outside the city walls the next morning, vaguely ashamed for humiliating my mother but not enough to crawl back to Hanan.

And now here I was praying that my uncle would not turn me away for Zahava's sake—even if it was only temporary, until I could make a better plan. I would beg if I had to. She'd been through enough, having to leave her family behind after being with them just long enough for me to secure passage in this caravan.

The Gaddite traders had let us travel with them in exchange for Shachar and I helping with their protection along the way. Then, after tearful good-byes and farewell kisses, we left behind Zahava's family with no firm assurance she would ever see them again—even if I silently vowed to somehow find a way.

"The road west branches off from here," called the driver of the wagon as he pulled his oxen to a halt.

Shachar jogged up as I helped Zahava out of the wagon bed, where she'd been riding among huge sacks of grain. "You sure the two of you will be all right from here?" he asked. "I'm happy to go with you before I head east."

With the training of the guards in Be'er Sheva complete, Zevi had gone home two months before we returned from Gaza, and Eliyah's unit had returned to Lachish soon after. Shachar would now carry the report of all we'd seen in Gaza to the commanders in Gibeah. Hopefully he'd not be punished for going with me instead of returning with what had remained of Emmet's company. I'd have to face Yonatan sometime as well, but Zahava's safety took precedence. I was still a soldier at heart, and would gladly defend my people, but I was a husband first.

"I know this area like the lines on my own palm, my friend," I told him. "It's only a couple hours' walk from here." I wished Zahava didn't have to walk so far, but one of the Kenite shepherds had given her a new walking stick to replace the one Korrero had given her, and if it got too difficult, I'd carry her on my back the rest of the way.

"All right, then." Shachar placed a palm on my shoulder. "Be well, Gavriel. I'll see you soon." Then he leaned in to press a kiss to my wife's cheek. "And you, if you ever get tired of that ugly face, come find me." He winked at her with a grin.

I shoved him. "Get away from my wife, you boar."

He laughed, and with a wave over his shoulder, began the walk toward Saul's ever-expanding fortress at Gibeah.

We extended thanks to the traders, and they clattered away on the path down to Jericho. Then Zahava and I turned west, carrying little more than two leather packs. One held a priceless crown rumored to have sunk to the bottom of the sea and the other a small flint knife I'd made when I was only a boy but whose owner had sailed away on those same waters to parts unknown.

"Will your family welcome us?" Zahava asked.

"My mother and sisters will be over the moon that I am bringing a wife home, little dove." Telling my ima I was married was the one thing I was looking forward to in Ramah.

"And your uncle?"

I sighed. "For my mother's sake, I hope he will allow us shelter. If he refuses, we can try Kiryat-Yearim, where Zevi's family lives. I'm sorry I have no home to offer you."

She turned to face me, a look of bewilderment on her lovely countenance. "Gavriel ben Elan, I have lived my entire life in a tent. Why do you think I would care about where we live?"

"I wasted so much time focused only on thoughts of battle and weapons," I said. *As well as drink and other worthless things.* "I should have prepared myself to care for you instead, and for our own family, someday."

Zahava slid her arms around my waist and put her head on my chest. "What matters is that we are together. The rest will fall into place. Let's just trust Yahweh to guide our steps, shall we? Even if they are a little wobbly for now."

I chuckled, holding her tight as I pressed a kiss to her hair. "I will do my very best, little dove."

"It's enormous," said Zahava, her mouth gaping as she took in the shining white villa near the center of Ramah. "You truly grew up in this house?"

I tipped my chin up to the windows on the third story, where I'd had a view of the market square from my room. "That I did."

"Is your uncle one of the city elders?"

"No, just the richest man in the region. He has no interest in governing people, only growing his wealth."

I vividly remembered the morning I'd snuck out to go fight for King Saul. I'd been planning to run away for months already, but when messengers arrived at the city gates with a bloody ox leg and a summons for the men of Benjamin to join Saul's defense of Yavesh-Gilead across the river, I'd taken it as a sign. I'd left behind my mother and my sisters with barely a thought, so set on becoming my own man away from both the shadow of Hanan's low opinion of me and the specter of my father's damning reputation. It had felt like shedding my skin to become someone completely new. But I hadn't shed anything—just dragged it along behind me like an anchor.

Over these past months I'd realized that I didn't want to be my own man; I wanted to be a man of honor. A man who cherished his wife and put his family ahead of himself. One who bent his knee to the King above all kings instead of his own selfish desires.

And when the door opened before I even had a chance to knock and my beautiful little ima stood on the threshold with tears of joy streaming down her round face and her silvery-black curls wild around her face, I didn't even care that my own cheeks were wet. She must have seen me from an upper window and run down two flights of stairs to get here.

"Gavriel," she rasped out, plowing into my outstretched arms. "My son. My son. Oh, my prayers have been answered. Thanks be to the Most High!"

Her steadfast love and unwavering faith humbled me. My ima had endured the worst and yet refused to be shaken. I wrapped up my mother and held her tight as she wept. "I'm sorry I was gone for so long."

I hoped she knew it was an apology that encompassed so much more than the years that I'd stayed away. Among my many regrets was how I'd pulled away from her more and more as I'd gotten older simply out of spite for being happy with a man who despised me.

She tipped up her chin to look into my eyes, her own shining with adoration and relief. "I knew you would return, my precious boy. Even through my deepest valleys, when my knees ached from long nights in prayer, I've always believed that when the time was right, Yahweh would bring you back to me."

"Gavi!"

"Gavi!"

"You're home!"

All three of my sisters barreled through the doorway, their sweet voices ringing out joyfully as they practically pushed our mother out of the way to embrace me, chattering like starlings and teasing me over my short hair and beard. Their affectionate welcome felt like a mending of something that had torn loose long ago.

"Who is that?" asked Ruti, my youngest sister, her big brown eyes latched onto Zahava, who stood off to the side, watching our reunion with a delighted smile.

"This," I said, putting out a hand to draw her forward, while still holding Ayelet tight to my side with the other, "is Zahava. My wife."

My mother gasped, hands on her cheeks. "*What?* You are married?"

"I am. And we are here to stay, if you'll have us."

"How about we take this discussion inside? Instead of including all of the neighbors?" Hanan had appeared in the doorway, his expression blank as ever. I wasn't certain how my mother had endured life with such a cold man and remained as joyful and vibrant as she was. Both Ayelet and Ruti looked more like him than my mother, where Liorah and I favored her instead. But thankfully, the girls were free with their smiles, unlike their father. Ayelet, though, was much quieter than the others and had a mind that was always working three steps ahead of everyone else's. Just like Hanan.

Once we were inside the villa, Ima insisted on feeding us. I'd expected no less from a woman whose greatest pleasure was to ensure that no one ever left her home with a sliver of room in their belly, who reveled in organizing enormous parties, and who was the undisputed head of her own kitchens. I'd been dreaming of my mother's food for the past three days and delighted her by telling her so.

Once we were seated around the grand table at the center of the soaring main hall, which shortly was covered with platters of food, the girls plied Zahava with questions about where she was from, which led to the entire story of our marriage, our journey, and eventually our time in Gaza.

By the end of it, Zahava was solidified in my sisters' eyes as nothing less than a heroine on par with Devorah, the great female *shofet* who'd long ago led the armies of Israel to victory against our Canaanite oppressors, and my mother had cried jugs of tears. Hanan, however, remained quiet throughout the evening, then left after his steward came in with a message about some urgent matter regarding a lost shipment. His dedication to his business was foremost. In that, nothing much had changed.

Noting that Zahava and I were exhausted from our long walk, my mother told the girls to head off to bed and then led us to the guest room she always kept prepared for Hanan's business associates. Although I needed to have an important conversation with my uncle, the temptation of crawling into a soft bed and holding my wife proved far too great. What I had to say could keep until the morning.

"You've been through quite the ordeal." From behind the table stacked with missives and tablets in neat rows, Hanan gestured for me to seat myself on an exquisite cedar chair opposite him. He'd probably had the costly furnishings in this room imported all the way from Tyre.

"I have." I settled against the carved backrest. "But I am grateful I was sent to Emmet's company or I would not have Zahava."

"She is truly a master goldsmith?" His brows arched.

"Yes, but that is to remain a *secret*."

"Do you think I would jeopardize her?" He frowned, looking strangely offended.

"I don't truly know, Hanan," I admitted. "You and I have never seen eye to eye. And I will do anything to protect her, even if it means taking her away from here and finding somewhere where no one knows of her gift."

His mouth quirked. "I would expect nothing less, Gavriel. Don't you think I would do the same for Miri?"

I looked straight into Hanan's eyes, a rarity since I'd avoided him most of the time I'd lived here. "You provide well for her, but honestly, the only thing I ever thought you truly cherished was your business and your ledgers."

He shifted in his seat, his fingers tapping an uneven pattern on the table. "It's what I am good at, Gavriel. I was never strong like my brother, who had no issue hefting logs on his shoulder or carrying stones to raise buildings. I was born sickly and practically blind in one eye, so I could never wield a sword or go to battle like the rest of the men in this city. But I could build wealth, keep meticulous ledgers by adding large sums of numbers in my head, and expand my investments with little effort. It was the only way I could protect Miri. And after all she'd endured at the hands of Elan, she deserved to want for nothing."

I blinked at him in astonishment. My whole life, I'd thought his obsession with wealth had been about himself—and it had been for my *mother*? The shift in my perspective was difficult to grasp but not impossible. She'd always insisted he was a good man, that I didn't give him credit for what he'd done for us. But I'd been too angry to listen. All I'd known was that my father was gone and that my foundation had been shaken. I saw Hanan as a thief, not a savior.

"If I would have known about Elan, I would have done something," he said. "I didn't know until he was dead and I went to that hovel and found her with two black eyes and a little boy I'd never met before."

The back of my neck prickled. "What are you talking about?"

"He never told us he had a wife, Gavriel, let alone a young girl he'd lured and impregnated when she was barely fourteen. He kept her hidden away on the other side of town and never said a word. If I would have known, I would have insisted he bring her here. Would have made certain you two had food and clothing. I cannot even explain why he pretended he was unmarried when he bothered to come see our parents. He'd left the house when he was sixteen, insisting he wanted nothing to do with any of us, and only returned when he drank through whatever wages he earned."

The similarities between my father and me were almost eerie, with the exception of the way he'd treated my mother. There was no world in which I'd ever dishonor any woman like that, let alone Zahava. And if I wanted Hanan to allow us to stay here, I'd need to humble myself.

"Listen," I began, "about that night and the things I said—"

He put up his palms to stop my apology. "Before you say anything more, I must ask your forgiveness."

I flinched, stunned. "What? Why?"

"I'd hoped you would come back so I could explain myself—even sent you a couple of messages to ask you to do so."

I had received two missives from Hanan when I'd been stationed in Gibeah, but I'd thrown them away once I recognized the seal. It would have done me no good anyhow, since I couldn't read.

"I regret staying away so long," I said.

"I don't blame you." He tapped his fingers again, the beat faster this time, as if he were nervous. "You must have overheard a conversation between your mother and I, didn't you?"

I shrugged a shoulder. "I did. The day after the last tutor refused to deal with me, you told her how I would never amount to anything. That I was just like your worthless brother."

Hanan's face seemed to drain of color. "I wish you'd not heard that."

"It was the only time I'd ever heard you raise your voice. I was curious what you and she were arguing over."

"Oh, Gavriel," he groaned, leaning forward to put his face in his hands. "No wonder you've hated me all these years."

"It was true," I said. "I did end up just like him. Without Yonatan sending me away, I'd be dead like him too."

His head came up and he pinned me with a glare. "No. You are *not* like him. When I came into that dark hovel where Elan had kept you two, you stood in front of your ima like a lion to defend her. You were six years old and told me you'd gut me if I hurt her." He huffed a laugh. "And I had no doubt you would have if you'd been big enough."

I had only a vague recollection of that day, tangled as it was with a haze of grief and confusion.

"And yes, I tried to teach you to read and write so you could take over my business someday because I wanted to provide for my family, especially if something were to happen to me. I couldn't understand why you were so resistant to it, so yes, I was frustrated. You rebuffed every single gift I tried to give you, even an education from brilliant scholars I hired from Naioth."

"The symbols wouldn't stand still!" I said, revealing the truth for the first time. "It didn't matter how hard I tried to read the tablets they put in front of me, the symbols jumbled themselves up and made no sense. And numbers were even worse, I couldn't keep track. They just slipped out of my head. I felt like a fool. So it was easier to act like I didn't care and play tricks on the tutors instead."

Hanan's jaw hung open. "I didn't . . . I didn't know that."

My face was on fire. "I was too embarrassed to say anything."

His gaze tracked to the window. "I wonder . . ." He went quiet, staring into the distance until the silence unsettled me and I had to press him to speak.

"What is it?"

"I wonder if Elan had the same problem. He had no interest in learning either. He said it was mind-numbingly dull to sit in one place and refused to listen whenever our father tried to teach him about trade. I thought he just preferred fighting and drinking over being responsible. But perhaps he too thought himself incapable."

I'd never considered that anyone else's eyes might play tricks the way mine did. I'd always thought something was broken inside my head.

"But regardless, Gavriel, I have never thought you to be anything less than highly intelligent. You may prefer to work with your hands instead of a stylus, but you've always been a quick learner. Why do you think I asked Tabbish to teach you metalwork?"

My jaw went slack. "You . . . you what?"

"Did you think my best smith would take the time to teach an eleven-year-old how to craft bronze if he hadn't been told to do so? I saw you hanging about the foundry watching him and told him to encourage you if you wanted to learn."

"But I thought it bothered you when I hung about Tabbish. Or spent time laboring with your servants."

He huffed a quiet laugh. "You were determined to do the opposite of whatever I wanted for you. So I played along. Tabbish reported to me regularly about what you were learning, and I supplied him with plenty of copper and tin to keep you going. And then when you got interested in leatherwork for armor, I purchased the tannery."

My entire understanding of the world shifted completely upside down. I'd spent my boyhood years thinking I was thwarting Hanan's every desire, and yet he'd been one step ahead of me. Protecting me. I was truly speechless.

"I'd hoped you might want to take over the foundry instead of running off to fight for Saul, but it didn't surprise me when you did. And I am incredibly proud of who you've become, especially after all you've overcome."

Emotion wrapped a tight hand around my throat. I'd never thought to hear such praise from my uncle.

"So, please, Gavriel, forgive me for what I said out of frustration and lack of understanding. I wish I could go back and shut my own mouth, do things differently."

I cleared my throat. "I gave you plenty of reasons to be exasperated with me from the start. I saw you only as a villain snatching my ima from me."

"You were a confused and frightened little boy."

"I had plenty of time to open my eyes and see that you weren't out to get me. As well, I was so awful that night five years ago. A drunken fool bent on my own stubborn ways. I hope you know how much I regret the things I said."

His expression softened. "If you would have returned, you would have known that I never held any of those things against you, son."

In all the years I'd lived in this house, Hanan had never called me *son*. Frankly, I wouldn't have allowed him to do so. But now the endearment felt right. Like a new beginning.

"Thank you, Hanan. I appreciate that more than you know. I know our arrival here is a surprise, but do you mind if we stay? At least until I figure out where we can live?"

"This is your home, Gavriel, and I hope you both stay here for good. However, your arrival was no surprise to me. I've known you were coming for over a week."

"What do you mean? We only left Be'er Sheva three days ago."

He reached into a decorated box on the corner of his desk and pulled out a folded piece of papyrus. "I didn't tell your mother, in case you didn't actually come, but your commander sent me a message. He'd been alerted to your return to Be'er Sheva but doubted you would remain there. He said that should you come to Ramah, I was to give you this."

Stunned, I reached across the table to accept the missive from him, which was sealed with a mark I recognized easily—that of Yonatan ben Saul. I cracked the wax and unfolded it. For once in my life, I wished I'd at least made an attempt to listen to those tutors. The symbols were still little more than nonsense.

"Will you read it for me?" I handed the papyrus back, glad I did not have to explain myself.

He nodded, his eyes skimming the message for a moment, then read it aloud. Like the man himself, Yonatan's words were succinct and authoritative.

"'Gavriel. I've been informed of your escape from Gaza. You'll be expected to report to me in person at Gilgal within the month. Bring your wife and the crown.'"

My blood went cold. "How would he know about the crown? About Zahava?"

Hanan leaned back with folded arms, frowning thoughtfully. "Perhaps someone in Be'er Sheva reported your return? Or maybe even in Gaza? He once told me you were involved with making connections for him in enemy territory."

It was certainly possible. Yonatan's spy network among both

friend and foe was extensive. But before I could think on it more, something he'd said snagged my attention.

"What do you mean he once told you about my work for him? When was this?"

Something that looked a lot like guilt moved over Hanan's features, and he began tapping his fingers on the table again. He took a deep breath before speaking. "You were too young when you left here, Gavriel. When Ronen returned from trying to chase the four of you down and told us you'd gone off to war, your mother and I were terrified you would be killed. We spent weeks holding our breath, dreading a knock at the door from someone coming to tell us you'd been struck down on the battlefield."

I leaned forward, elbows on my knees, clasped hands pressed to my mouth to avoid interrupting. Again, Hanan was shifting my perspective of him.

"Of course we knew it was futile to forbid you to remain with the army, and when Zevi came through Ramah on his way home from Gibeah, he said you'd already found favor with the king's son. So I went to see him."

"You went to *Yonatan*?"

He nodded, fingers tapping quicker this time, but he wouldn't meet my eyes. "He was well aware of your youth, but you'd already proven yourself capable on the battlefield, so he agreed to let you remain and to keep me appraised of your welfare since you hadn't even sent word to Miri that you survived the battle."

He lifted his gaze then, placing a fist over his heart. "I couldn't bear to see her torn to pieces by worry, Gavriel. I was helpless to assuage her fears any other way. I did it for her, you see."

"*What* did you do?" I choked out. It was difficult hearing how devastated my ima had been, especially when it was my self-centered behavior that caused her such pain.

"I funded Yonatan's unit." He let out a resigned sigh. "And also made certain his men—including you—had whatever weapons and armor you needed to be safe. It was the only way I could protect you." His voice broke on the last word, betraying his true feelings for me.

It was a very good thing I was sitting down. For so long, I'd hated this man, seen him as some terrible enemy. And even when I'd despised him, rebelled against him, and sneered in his face, he'd loved me. He'd been the father I never even knew I had.

Unable to speak through the knot of emotion in my throat, I stood and came around the table. Then, as Hanan stared at me in wide-eyed bewilderment, I knelt on the ground beside him and bowed my head.

"Forgive me," I rasped, the words encompassing a multitude of sins. "Please."

After a few moments, Hanan's palm curved over my shoulder and squeezed. "Already done, son. Already done."

34

My wife swayed in rhythm to the plodding steps of the mule beneath her as I led them up the narrow road along the Jordan River toward the camp at Gilgal. Hanan had insisted the pack animal I'd borrowed from him was a particularly docile one, and so far, my stepfather's reassurances had proved correct.

Zahava had affectionately named the mule Kefa, mentioning a couple of times as we'd plodded along the trade road how much she hated leaving poor Ebenezer behind in Gaza. I was just glad she didn't have to walk all the way from Ramah. And that, on Hanan's insistence, we were accompanied by four of the Hittite mercenaries he employed as protection. Kefa carried two treasures on his back today, and I would jeopardize neither one.

The last time I'd been in this valley, Samuel the Seer had conjured a storm of such incredible magnitude that everyone gathered here thought for sure that they'd be swept away by its fury. The day Saul had chosen to be crowned king in front of all Israel had instead proved there reigned power far superior to his own. That was also when I'd privately begun to wonder whether Saul's position on the throne was simply a transient one until Yonatan was prepared to take hold of his inheritance. Since that day, my conviction had only become stronger.

So, as difficult as it had been to leave the safety of Hanan's villa, I could not ignore the summons of the future King of Israel.

"Why are there so many soldiers here?" asked Zahava as she gazed over the scores of tents pitched between the road and the hillside town of Gilgal.

"Hanan heard that the king ordered a gathering of his armies to offer a sacrifice of thanksgiving for the victory over Amalek at the new moon."

That had been two days ago, a full week past the time Yonatan had given me to report to him. I could only hope he'd be merciful once I explained what had delayed us and offered him the gift I'd brought as an apology.

We garnered more than a few odd looks from the soldiers as we passed through the camp and a good number of raised brows at the sight of the four well-armed Hittites walking behind us. But strangely, instead of the jovial atmosphere that usually accompanied such a decisive victory over our foes, the mood was sullen. Usually, a camp like this would be overflowing with music, loud laughter, and friendly but drunken wrestling matches as the soldiers let down their guard after a successful campaign. This one was almost eerily quiet—so much so that it was hard to believe Amalek was truly defeated like we'd been told.

By the time we arrived at Yonatan's tent, easily found by the familiar banner flapping in the easterly breeze off the Jordan River, my instincts said something was very wrong.

I helped Zahava down from the mule's back with her burden, removed the parcel I'd tied to his saddle, then left Kefa in the care of the Hittites while we approached Yonatan's aide, who was seated cross-legged near the entrance to the large, billowing tent with a scribe's tablet across his lap, writing symbols on a piece of old pottery.

"Shalom, Elishua. The commander asked me to report here."

The young man looked up, peering at me in the bright sun without recognition. "Who are you?"

"It's Gavriel ben Elan," I replied, knowing it was the difference in my appearance that confused him, not lack of familiarity. The poor man had been forced to fetch me for discipline a number of times.

Elishua's eyes flared wide. "Oh! Forgive me. Yes, he's been expecting you for a few days now."

I nodded but declined to explain, then gestured toward the tent. "Is he available?"

"No. I'm sorry. He's gone to meet with the High Commander, but I expect him back shortly."

"Is something wrong?" I asked. "This does not seem like the camp of a victorious army."

Elishua's brows pressed together as his eyes roved the encampment. "It's been a difficult couple of days. But I'll let the commander explain."

The young man was extremely tight-lipped with information he was not given leave to discuss, as all good aides should be, so I let it go.

"My wife could use a comfortable place to rest while we wait for Yonatan. May we go inside?"

Elishua's jaw slacked in shock for only a moment as he looked back and forth between Zahava and me before he caught himself. "Many blessings for your marriage, Gavriel."

He unfolded himself to stand and smiled at Zahava kindly. "Please, do go on inside the tent. I'll bring refreshments. You must have been traveling all day."

With thanks, we entered the flap of the tent as he strode away. As usual, Yonatan's tent was sparse. A few pillows, a wooden casket I knew contained his armor and weapons, and an unfurled bedroll covered with one wool blanket. Certainly not the usual accommodations for a future king. Even the lowliest servant in Hanan's home lived in more luxury. Something else I'd never cared to notice when I was young and prejudiced against him.

Once she was seated on the thickest of the cushions, with the cedar box she'd carried here settled in her lap, Zahava sighed. "He may be a gentle creature, but Kefa's saddle is not kind to my hips."

"Perhaps I should carry you home on my back instead," I said with a grin.

"Well, you are certainly stubborn as a mule." She lifted a teasing brow.

I tipped my head back to laugh, and she joined in. I'd heard Zahava laugh more in these past few weeks than I had the entirety of our marriage, and it gave me no lack of joy.

Thanks to my mother, who treated Zahava as just another of her own daughters, and my sisters, who were enraptured by her and practically fought over her attention, my wife had settled into her new life. She said their kindness and silent accommodations for her limitations helped soften the sharper edges of her grief at leaving her family behind. Still, there were times when I found her gazing out the upper south-facing window and wished I could do something to ease her pain.

"I'd have to agree with that assessment, young woman." Yonatan swept into the tent. "But from what I've heard, you're to thank for taming this hardheaded jack."

Zahava's hazel eyes sparkled as I helped her to her feet. "He may be a little less reckless than before, but I'm not certain how tame he is."

I ignored their ribbing and greeted Yonatan with a bow. "Commander, I must ask your pardon for taking so long to arrive. The delay was inescapable."

He stood before me, arms folded and his expression now solemn. "Oh? And why was that?"

"The crown was broken during our escape from Gaza. It required repair. Gathering the necessary materials and tools took longer than expected."

"The crown is with you, then?"

"It is."

Zahava opened the latch on the box, but Yonatan held up a staying palm. "Leave it for now. Ah, here's Elishua with refreshment. Please, have a seat. You've had a long journey."

The young aide entered with a basket of fruit and cheese, along with a jug of wine and two cups. He placed the basket on the ground between Zahava and me, then poured the wine. I marveled that even though the smell of the sweet white permeated the air, it was easy to refuse.

"So, the reports are true, then?" Yonatan had settled on the ground as well but told Elishua he'd already eaten with Abner. "Emmet reported that he'd forbidden you from drink. And Shachar insisted you had slayed that particular beast."

"First, let me say how sorry I am about Emmet," I said. "The captain was well-respected by his men and died bravely while protecting the Kenites. May his memory be a blessing to all who knew him."

Yonatan took a long, deep breath that spoke of lingering sorrow. "He was the best of men. As much a brother as he was a friend. I don't think anyone could ever take his place."

"I owe him a debt of gratitude. If it were not for his edict, the last few months would have gone very differently."

"Shachar's report was quite thorough with regard to both the movement of the Kenites and the incidents in Gaza. However, I expect you to give me a full accounting later as well. After that, we'll discuss the possibility of your return to my unit. Haim and Shachar both reported to me that before his death, Emmet planned to report that you took my admonishment seriously and recommended your reinstatement."

My throat went dry. "I have much to apologize for, Commander. I did not deserve the mercy you offered me before. I not only dishonored you and my fellow soldiers but all of Israel with my reckless and selfish behavior."

"I would have to agree. But I also sense that you've sincerely repented of such egregious actions, so I am willing to restore your place in my unit."

I inhaled, bracing myself before I spoke. "I'd like to propose an alternative."

Yonatan looked wary but intrigued. "Go on."

"First, I have a gift for you." I handed him the wool-wrapped parcel at my side. "A long-ago promise I needed to fulfill."

He unwrapped the iron sword I'd spent nearly a month crafting, when I wasn't assisting Zahava with her work. It had taken me far longer than I'd hoped to find the right balance of charcoal to molten ore as I forged the iron and no less than a miracle to produce a short sword that was worthy of the king's son. But with Hanan's help in procuring the necessary supplies, including ore, and adapting the foundry furnace to one capable of reaching the correct temperature, I had succeeded.

Yonatan slid the sword from its leather sheath, then tilted it back and forth to examine the weapon from all sides. "Did you make this?"

I told him of how I'd learned the techniques in Gaza from the blacksmith and the way my stepfather's generosity had enabled me to emulate the processes.

"The days of the Philistines controlling our ability to produce wrought iron like this must be in our past," I said. "I'd like to focus on building our capabilities. Hanan recently made connections with Hittite traders who have no love for Philistia. He believes Israel can negotiate with them for iron ore. Rumor has it they have mines in the far north that far outproduce anything the Philistines have access to. If I have the freedom to build my proficiency with this craft, since I'm nowhere near mastery yet, with the aim of teaching others eventually, our enemies will no longer have superiority in weaponry. It will take time and resources, but I am willing to do whatever is necessary."

Yonatan shook his head, chuckling softly. "*This* is why I kept you in the unit, Gavriel, despite your youth and reckless behavior, and even though Emmet thought I was a madman for not sending you home after Yavesh. I told him that day I caught you behind the rock after my father was anointed there was potential in you for something truly great. Not only was that knife you showed me close to master-level, but there was a hunger in your eyes that told me one day I'd see remarkable things from you."

Overwhelmed by such incredible words from a man I'd practically considered divine when I was sixteen, I simply shrugged. "I did promise you a sword that day."

He gave a full-throated laugh. "That you did. Consider that particular debt paid in full."

Elishua entered the tent again, bowing. "Forgive me, Commander. The king is ready to see you."

All amusement drained from Yonatan's face. "Thank you, Elishua. Please let him know we are on our way."

The aide slipped out, and Yonatan rose to his feet. "We should not keep him waiting. He's in a foul mood."

I stood as well before helping Zahava. "Are we . . . are you saying you want us to go before the king?"

"Yes. You'll give him the crown directly."

Zahava sucked in an audible breath. "You want me to hand over the Atarah Hod to King Saul? It's been in my family for generations."

Yonatan's frown was full of compassion. "The moment my father heard of that crown, and the legend behind it, he's been determined to possess it."

"It has no magic," she said. "It's nothing like the King of Gaza believed. Our clan has never been involved with such things."

"It doesn't matter," said Yonatan with a sigh. "The myth has nearly as much power as the truth in this case. And since the king spared your people—especially since you lived in alliance among our enemies for so long—he feels it only right his mercy should be repaid. He could have let your people perish alongside Amalek, after all."

My skin prickled. It was a threat if I'd ever heard one. Perhaps the Kenite elders who'd mistrusted Saul from the beginning had been right to do so. Just as Emmet had pointed out, the differences between Yonatan's even-tempered and thoughtful leadership and Saul's impulsive directives were becoming starker by the day.

Yonatan's tone was apologetic as he met my wife's incredulous gaze. "For the sake of your people, that crown must be handed over to my father. Especially after what happened two days ago, it's not wise to refuse his demand."

I'd known Yonatan for years now and was certain I'd never heard him so demoralized, even when his own father nearly killed him for taking a small bite of honey after battle.

"What *happened*?" I asked. "This camp feels like it's mired in tar."

He scrubbed a hand over his face and beard. "It took months for us to completely rout the Amalekites. We took Punon first, but Agag got away during the battle. We chased him through the desert, destroying the vast majority of their enclaves along the way. They finally found the coward hiding in a tent full of women and children near the border of Egypt. My father insisted he be put in chains and brought north, along with the livestock."

"I heard in Qadesh that Agag was being pursued but assumed he'd been put to the sword months ago." The orders from Samuel's mouth had been to destroy everything of Amalek, including their livestock. Nothing with breath should have been left alive.

Yonatan's jaw ticked, giving away his frustration with his father's decision. But not even Saul's heir could question the King of Israel without consequence.

"Two days ago, Samuel came to Gilgal. He and my father . . . quarreled." His hesitation spoke louder than words. The last time

Samuel had confronted Saul, it had been in front of thousands of men, women, and children in this very valley. It was likely the prophet had castigated the King of Israel in full sight of the entire encampment for his dereliction in following the direct command of Yahweh. No wonder the soldiers in this camp were so solemn.

"Samuel then demanded Agag be brought before him just outside the gates of Gilgal, and he cut the Amalekite king to pieces in view of everyone."

"Oh, how awful," Zahava muttered in horror against the hand over her mouth.

For Samuel, a man decades older than Saul, to finish the task was not only an indictment of rebellion against Yahweh's will but a public shaming of the man he'd personally anointed as king. And since the arrogance of the man who'd once hidden among the baggage the day he'd been anointed as sovereign had only grown with his wealth and power, I guessed Saul had not taken the chastisement with grace.

"As you can imagine, things have been . . . tense around here ever since, to say the least. You are the first visitors my father has received since Samuel left camp, aside from his closest advisers. So, for as sympathetic as I am to your plight," Yonatan said to my wife, "and that of your family, I can honestly say I do not know what my father will do if you refuse to give him that crown."

Zahava

As we stood before the enormous royal tent high on the hillside above Gilgal, Gavi's comforting hand stroked up and down my back. I willed myself to dwell on the soothing motion of his touch instead of the fact that I was waiting to go before yet another king who felt it was his right to claim the Atarah Hod for himself.

"Breathe, little dove. It will be all right."

After the stark warning Yonatan had given us, I wasn't certain that was true. The lives of my people were at stake, and even the king's son seemed unsettled by his father's state of mind today. If only I'd been able to finish the crown before the prophet had come here and made a fool of Saul in front of his own army.

Hands shaking, I leaned into my husband, never more grateful for his strong presence at my side. "But what if—?"

Gavi cut me off, his voice low. "There is no need to fear. You have already faced down the King of Gaza with the courage of a seasoned warrior. Remember, Saul may be seated on the throne, but he is only a man. And I am beside you. Always."

Taking a deep calming breath, I let my gaze slide away from the kingly tent and over the fertile valley below. The Jordan River sparkled in the distance, reflecting the pink and orange sunset painted across the sky behind us. And beyond the river, the towering hills seemed formed by the Creator's hand of the finest gold.

Over the past few months, I'd seen a great deal of the Land of Promise. The expanse of the Great Sea stretching across the horizon like an ocean of lapis lazuli. The rolling green hills and endless emerald forests of the hill country. The sweeping deserts and the copper cliffs of the Aravah wilderness. And canopied above all the beauty was an ever-changing sky that sang the glories of the One who'd spoken it into existence, from morning until night.

Gavi was right. There was no need to be afraid of the man seated on a throne made by human hands. I could indeed trust Yahweh with every step—even the ones that wobbled or led in directions I'd never anticipated.

By the time Yonatan's aide ushered us inside, the crippling panic had dissipated, replaced by a deep sense of calm as I entered the king's tent with my sturdy walking stick in my right hand and my left hand curled around the strong arm of my warrior husband.

Where Yonatan's tent had been almost shockingly sparse, this one overflowed with extravagance. Rings of oil lamps hung from cross-poles, vibrant rugs blanketed the floor with costly indulgence, and a nearby tabletop practically bowed from the weight of huge platters of rich food. And at the center of it all, the King of Israel lounged on a magnificent lion-footed throne atop a wooden dais, a huge golden chalice clutched in his long fingers. Saul's heavy-lidded gaze remained pinned on the box tucked under Gavi's other arm as the two of us bowed low before him.

"My king," said Yonatan from his place to the right of the dais, "this is Gavriel ben Elan of Ramah, a man who has faithfully served in your army, and in my unit, for the past nine years and proven himself to be fearless in battle as well as a talented weapons-maker." I felt, rather than heard, my husband catch his breath at the high praise. "And this is his wife, Zahava, daughter of Barzel, one of the Kenite chieftains. It is her skill that made possible the repair of the crown her ancestors crafted decades ago."

Even seated, Saul was enormous, broad-shouldered like his son, and with the undeniable bearing of a fearsome warrior king. Perhaps it was simply his air of authority or the bejeweled rings on his fingers but something about him reminded me of Enesidu, even if with his dark brown hair and thick beard, he looked nothing like the Philistine king.

"What has been the delay?" Saul snapped. "My son told me he summoned you weeks ago."

"A thousand apologies, my king," replied Gavi, with a humble bow. "It took some time to gather the resources necessary to conduct repairs on the crown. Not only did it require the purest ore we could secure but my wife's specialized metal-crafting tools were left behind during our escape from Gaza."

I missed my precious heirloom tools nearly as much as I missed my family. But Hanan had generously commissioned brand-new ones, made exactly to my specifications, and outfitted his foundry with everything I needed to complete my task.

Scowling, Saul brushed aside my husband's explanation with a careless wave of the gold chalice in his hand. "Yonatan, bring it to me."

Coming forward, the commander received the box from Gavi, a slight wrinkle of apology between his brows. Regardless of the obvious similarities in their appearance, Yonatan seemed nothing like the king. Perhaps it was only that Saul was stewing over what had happened with Samuel and Agag, but I sensed the air of humility in the son was greatly lacking in the father.

My stomach pinched as Yonatan opened the lid to the cedar box Hanan had purchased from a master wood-carver, one far more lovely than the blasphemous container in which the Atarah Hod had resided for decades. Saul reached inside and pulled out the crown, his eyes skimming over the shimmering surface I'd polished again this morning until it shone like glass. The gleam of greedy delight in his dark eyes as he examined the snaking vine of delicate leaves was the very same as had been in Enesidu's silver ones. No wonder he'd reminded me of the King of Gaza.

"Extraordinary," he murmured. "I've never seen its match."

I swallowed hard against the flutter of nerves as Saul removed the plain golden circlet from his head and tossed it aside, then settled the new one over his thick curls with a satisfied smile. For the first time since we'd entered the tent, the King of Israel addressed me instead of my husband.

"Your people are now settled in Be'er Sheva?"

I nodded my head, willing my voice to remain steady. "They are, my lord. They are already planting fields and rebuilding the ancient foundries our ancestors left behind."

"Excellent. Then I accept your offering of gratitude for my generosity."

My mouth went sour. Regardless of the assurances Emmet had offered our elders when they came to Punon, Gavi agreed with me that the king's promises of protection were tenuous at best. At least the crown would be a tangible reminder that the Kenites and their skill with metal were an asset to his growing kingdom.

"My son tells me you are to reside in Ramah instead of returning south."

"Yes, my lord."

"There will certainly be no lack of commissions for red-gold from my wife and daughters, I am certain, so it's fortunate you'll be close to Gibeah."

Gavi had warned me this would happen, that Saul insisted anyone with talent was obligated to serve him by virtue of his divine appointment to the throne, so I'd anticipated the demand and even prepared how I would respond. But still, my stomach lurched. Refusing a king was a dangerous risk. Refusing one who was already enraged by the public censure from a prophet was on the edge of madness. It very well could be that I'd only survived one king to be sentenced to death for defying another.

Yet before I could open my mouth to deny the King of Israel his demand, my husband spoke instead. "As you can see from the seamless repairs she made on the crown, my wife's talent is unparalleled, even among her own kin, my lord. She is skilled with gold, silver, copper, and a variety of alloys that only the most talented metalsmiths can master. She's also able to embed precious gems without damage to their value or to the metal itself, a talent many artisans covet. She will be honored to craft jewelry for your wife and daughters and those among your court."

My heart seized. After all we'd done to protect my family from vulnerability, why would Gavi force me to renege on my promise to my father?

"However," he continued, "for her safety and for that of her family, she has vowed to never again create anything of red-gold."

Saul's face contorted. "Who are *you* to dictate to me? I am your *king*!"

All my blood seemed to drain into my feet, my vision blurring for a moment. Had my husband just sacrificed everything he'd ever worked for to defend me?

"Father, please." Yonatan moved to stand in front of us. "Gavriel is only protecting his wife. She and her entire family are at risk if King Enesidu discovers where she is."

"I don't care," Saul barked, his face going red. "She is *my* subject, and she will make whatever I *tell* her to make."

The commander did not cower in the face of his father's fury. "And yet if she holds her vow, the crown on your head will be utterly unique. Without equal among the nations. Its value will be beyond measure."

"That means nothing!" he spat, throwing his hands wide. "I

am the king. No one defies me. Not her! Not you! Not that lying madman who calls himself a prophet!"

"This has nothing to do with Samuel, Father—"

"Do *not* speak that name in my presence," Saul bellowed, his face deep red as he stepped off the dais to stalk toward his son. "Are you in collusion with him? It's you trying to take away my kingdom, isn't it?"

Slipping his hand into mine, Gavi quietly eased us backward and away from the king, who seemed to be losing all control as he spat accusations at his son.

A bright burst of golden light suddenly spilled into the tent as a violent gust of wind blew open both sides of the door flap and billowed the walls of the tent outward with such force I thought they'd come loose from their stakes. Above us, the oil lamps swayed and guttered while the tabletop behind us slid from its log supports and tipped over, the platters and wine jars crashing to the ground in a horrific cacophony of shattering pottery. By the time everything went quiet, I was wrapped in Gavi's arms, my face pressed to his chest.

"*What* was that?" Saul gasped out in a choked voice. His face had gone ashen, his wide eyes staring at the open door flap. I peered from the safety of my husband's embrace to follow his gaze and the sky outside was rose-colored but otherwise clear. A shiver slid across my shoulders.

"Just a gust of wind," said Yonatan, although he too looked rattled.

"No, it's him," Saul moaned, slumping down to sit on the edge of the dais. "I shouldn't have disobeyed. Should have destroyed it all." He groaned, dropping his face into his hands as the crown slipped from his head onto the rug at his feet with a muted thud. "Why didn't I listen? *Why?*"

Yonatan peered over his shoulder to my husband, then jerked his head toward the still-open tent flaps with pointed urgency.

Gavi took it for an order, silently swept me into his arms before Saul could notice, and fled the tent. Expression grim, he did not stop moving until we were at the very bottom of the hill, where four burly Hittites stood guard over a lone mule.

"What's wrong?" asked one in his oddly clipped accent.

"I'll tell you later," said Gavi as he settled me on Kefa's back. "We need to go. Now."

My husband slapped the mule's rump, startling him into motion, and by the time the fiery sunset melted away and stars began twinkling overhead, we'd left the camp at Gilgal far behind. And as Kefa plodded steadily up the road past Jericho, I searched out my golden one among the glittering diamonds strewn across the heavens. Then I lifted a prayer of thanks to the Maker of those stars for the vivid dream of warning I'd received the night Yonatan's note arrived in Ramah.

And that because of that dream, the real Atarah Hod was tucked away in a common, unmarked basket in the far corner of Hanan's well-guarded treasury, where I hoped it would remain until Yahweh raised up a king worthy to wear it.

EPILOGUE

Gavriel

1032 BC
NAIOTH, ISRAEL

Sukkot had always been my favorite of the ingathering festivals, not only because our extended family sometimes traveled from Kiryat-Yearim, which meant Zevi and his family came to stay in Naioth for nearly a month, but because it entailed building a *sukkah* from branches and twigs and sleeping under the stars. As a boy who abhorred being stuck inside, there was nothing better than tagging along with my uncle Natan to scavenge the forested hills for materials to build our shelters with Zevi, Avi, and Shay.

Watching Zevi's father emerge from the tree line now, with one grandson on his shoulders and followed by a parade of more grandchildren and two of Avi's older boys, all dragging tree branches or carrying leafy twigs, brought memories surging to life. I could almost hear the echoes of our young battle cries on the wind as we turned sticks into swords, basket lids into shields, and sharpened reeds into spears. If only we'd known then how one real-life battle would someday tear us apart.

"Your family is so big, Gavi," said Zahava, a smile on her lips as she surveyed the clearing where a number of *sukkot* were already being raised, poles jutting from the ground, and people on ladders tying crossbeams together. The entire area teemed with life, animated voices, laughter, and even the cacophonous sounds of Uncle Ronen's student-musicians practicing lyres, pipes, and drums.

"This isn't even all of us," I said. "There are a large number of aunts and uncles and cousins who remain back in Kiryat-Yearim, and Grandfather Elazar isn't able to travel anymore, so Grandmother Yoela stayed back to tend to him." I planned to take Zahava to the mountain as soon as we were able to introduce my wife to the rest of our clan.

I wrapped an arm around her shoulders, pulling her to my side. "And just think, next year, your family will be part of this chaos."

She turned to press into me, her smile stretching wide and hazel eyes sparkling. "I still cannot believe they are coming here."

Seeing my wife grieving over these past few months had been gut-wrenching. Even though my mother and sisters did their best to keep her occupied whenever she wasn't working in the foundry, and I made every effort to make her feel enveloped in affection, she missed her family desperately. So, a few weeks ago, I'd gone to Hanan.

I'd barely begun my proposal that we move her family north in the coming months, perhaps find a place for them to pitch their tent up near Naioth, when Hanan said he wouldn't hear of them living anywhere but in his own house.

"This villa is enormous, Gavi," he'd said, waving off my initial protest. *"We have plenty of room to spare. What good is wealth if it's not shared?"*

My relationship with my stepfather had grown steadily over these past months, once my eyes were opened to the truth about his nature. He was not effusive in his affection and much preferred the quiet of his chambers to a loud, chaotic celebration like this one, but his silent generosity provided food for widows and orphans in Ramah, and had paid for three new buildings to be raised for the school of prophecy here in Naioth.

I'd also discovered that some of the foreign mercenaries he employed as guards for his home and treasury, and to protect him when he traveled for business, were former slaves rescued from unscrupulous masters. Once my blinders had been removed, I found myself truly admiring the man I'd unfairly hated.

And not once since I'd returned did he bring up my past behavior. The fact that he'd not only sent a messenger on horseback to invite Zahava's family to move northward but insisted that once they were ready, his wagons would fetch them, earned him eternal allegiance from my wife as well.

What Zahava didn't know was that Barzel had already turned over headship of the clan to his eldest brother, and that he, Safaa, and all the girls—and even Farah's horrible goats—were already on their way to join the new life we'd made here together.

With a shriek, Zevi's eldest daughter streaked by, long hair flying as she chased one of Avi's cackling sons, a threat on her lips for the cousin who'd stolen a basket of flowers from her hand. Keziah, Avi's wife, moved into the boy's path, forcing him to a wide-eyed halt. "Give it back," she said, "or you'll lose your turn on Sarru."

Without hesitation, her son returned the basket of flowers to his cousin. There was nothing the children liked better than riding Keziah's magnificent black stallion. Now that Avidan and Keziah had moved back to Naioth from across the river, for good, there would be plenty of rides for all the little cousins. The warhorse was surprisingly patient with children, even if he still refused to let any man but Avi in his saddle.

"One day our children will be part of this lovely chaos," said Zahava, delight dancing in her hazel eyes.

I could never imagine life without my little dove and didn't miss being a full-time soldier at all. When Yonatan arrived in Ramah a month after we'd fled Gilgal, full of apologies for his father's erratic behavior, it had been easy to accept his invitation to serve Israel by producing iron weapons. He confided that although things had settled down in Gibeah, Samuel had so far refused Saul's request for reconciliation.

And from what I'd heard from Shachar, who'd witnessed the entire bloody incident with Agag, Samuel had announced in front of everyone that Yahweh had removed his anointing in favor of someone else—although no one knew who that might be. Speculation was running wild among the army about who might rise up to challenge Saul, stirring jealousies and stoking latent strife between tribes—especially between those in the North and those in the South. I did not envy Yonatan's position at the center of what could very well become a dangerous storm.

Instead, I was more than content to spend my days in the blacksmith hut I'd built on the back side of Hanan's property, hammering iron bloom into weapons. It was filthy, sweaty work that pushed my body to exhaustion every day, but I'd never been more satisfied. And there was nothing better than seeking out my precious wife after she'd spent the day blissfully bundled up in the frigid wine cellar, carving wax patterns, and sharing some of my excess body heat while thawing her lips with mine. I'd never get enough of her. Even after months of marriage, her nearness was all the intoxication I needed.

"You are going to be a wonderful mother, little dove," I murmured, taking the opportunity to steal one of her sweet kisses now.

"Are you just going to stand around kissing your wife, Gav? Or are you going to help us raise a sukkah?" Avidan teased as he and Zevi came up on either side of us.

"Leave us alone," I said, scowling at the smug look on his face. "She's much prettier than the two of you."

Avi slipped his arm around my neck and smacked a kiss to my cheek. His provocation led to a juvenile tussle between the two of us while Zahava giggled and Zevi frowned in amusement at our ridiculous behavior.

It didn't take long before a few of the children were gathered around, jumping up and down and cheering us on. Avi had height on me, but blacksmithing kept me in fighting shape, so I brought him down quickly, both of us laughing like idiots on the ground as he surrendered.

"Oh my goodness," said Yochana as she approached, carrying a large basket overflowing with flowers. "At least the two of you could pretend to be good examples for the children."

Avi and I came to our feet, brushing dirt and grass from our tunics.

"Eliora needs helpers in her garden," Yochana said to the children, "and when you are finished, Miri and Shoshana have honey-sesame cakes prepared for the lot of you."

Needing no further enticement than some of my mother's famous desserts, our audience darted away. Hopefully, in their exuberance, they wouldn't trample Eliora's flower garden, which had expanded so greatly over the past couple of decades that people came from all the neighboring towns to purchase colorful blooms to brighten their homes and celebrations.

"I could use some help too, Zahava," said Yochana, gesturing to the basket. "Let's put that creative mind of yours to use decorating the sukkah."

The two women walked off together, Yochana kindly adjusting her long stride to that of Zahava's uneven one. With one hand holding her mahogany walking stick and the other resting on the small curve of her belly, there was nothing in the world more exquisite than my little dove.

Avi threw his arm over my shoulder, sighing dramatically. "I never thought I'd see the day when Gavi only had eyes for one woman."

"I knew the two of you would torment me." I pushed him off me as he barked a laugh.

"You deserve some teasing," said Zevi, "after years of doling it out while insisting you'd never marry."

I shrugged helplessly. It was the truth, after all.

"*Or* have children," added Avi knowingly.

I couldn't help my quick grin. "You noticed?"

"Keziah told me this morning that she guessed Zahava was expecting. Looks like she was right."

Nodding, I let my eyes drift back to Zahava, where she and Yochana were in the shade, twining flowers into garlands for the sukkot. I could not wait to see her holding our coming son or daughter in her arms in a few months.

"Tell Zevi what you told me," said Avi, dragging my attention away from my wife, "about Shalem."

Zevi and Yochana hadn't arrived in Naioth until yesterday, since they took a detour to Gibeah first to deliver perfumes to Saul's palace, so I hadn't seen my oldest cousin since he'd given me his blessing to head back to Gaza and rescue my wife. He'd heard of our return through one of Saul's men, I'd been told, but this was the first chance we'd had to talk.

So I explained in detail about the young servant called Mattaniel and how, from Zahava's description of the silver patch of hair on his head and the distinctive scar that cut his brow in two, we were fairly certain Shalem was living aboard a Phoenician merchant ship.

"Unfortunately, Zahava doesn't know the master's name or where exactly the ship originates from," I said. "It could be months, or even years, before it returns. It's not as though we can check every port on the Great Sea."

Zevi frowned, arms locked tight over his chest.

"I've already asked Avidan's forgiveness for not staying with him after Yavesh," I said, "but I want to apologize to you as well, Zev. When you told me you'd come across information that he still lived, I was too lost in drink to care. I should have gone to Ashdod and at least asked around at the port there."

Zevi shook his head. "I doubt it would have done much good. It had been weeks since I'd lost his trail."

"At least we know he's alive," said Avi. "Even if he is enslaved like we feared."

"From what Zahava said, he was free to walk about the palace and even in the city. She said he didn't seem frightened or abused. And he's highly valued for his skill with language by his master. It could be far worse."

"I wonder if he's tried to escape over the years," Zevi mused. "He has to be desperate to get back home."

The truth was, none of us had any idea what Shalem had endured. I'd imagined a thousand different scenarios, none of them pleasant. But at least he was alive, not ripped apart by hyenas, like we'd thought that first day.

"So, what do we do?" asked Avi. "We aren't just going to give up, are we?"

"No. We aren't," said Zevi. "We never should have in the first place. If we'd listened to you the day he disappeared, we might have brought him home then." I wasn't certain that was true, since the only evidence we'd had of his trail then was the little flint knife Avi came across in a market—the very one that lived on a shelf in the room I shared with Zahava, my daily reminder to ask Yahweh to watch over Shay.

Zevi stretched out his right hand, displaying the tiny scar at the base of his thumb that matched the one on my own, the one on Avi's hand, and the one on Shay's, the reminder that we'd made a vow of brotherhood and sealed it with our own blood.

"We may have failed our cousin nine years ago," he said with all the weight of his well-earned authority, "but even if it takes nine more, we will find Shalem and bring him home."

AUTHOR'S NOTE

Three books (and three companion novellas) into this adventure with Avi, Zevi, Gavi, and Shay, and I am already dreading having to write The End in a few months. I hope you, too, are enjoying spending time with these heroes, and their heroines, as we explore the early years of King Saul's reign. From the beginning, I knew that writing Gavriel, a hero with deep character flaws, was going to be a challenge. But it also turned out to be a delight to see him set aside his selfish desires, false idols, and misconceptions to grow into the man he was meant to be. May we all follow his example.

Not much is known about the Kenite people, other than the few things we find about them in the Bible, but we do know that they were incredibly talented with metalworking. So creating a heroine for Gavriel was a simple task once I settled on incorporating the war with the Amalekites and the merciful separation of Zahava's people from Israel's enemies. Since we don't have any evidence of where the Kenites lived, especially since they were likely fairly nomadic, I dug into research about sources of ancient copper for the Israelites and discovered the valley of Feynan (in modern Jordan), which most scholars agree is Punon, the same place where Moses and the Hebrews spent time during the wilderness wanderings. It's a fascinating site, where large-scale mining operations were undertaken for thousands of years near major trade roads and would have been a valuable commodity for whoever controlled it. As well, I discovered that ancient copper workshops, some of the oldest ever found, along with giant kilns and metalworking tools, were located in Be'er Sheva, so moving the Kenites here, where there were already established metalworks was an easy decision.

Another interesting aspect that I dug into was that Israel did not have the ability to forge iron during this period.

> Now there was no blacksmith to be found throughout all the land of Israel, for the Philistines said, "Lest the Hebrews make swords or spears." But every one of the Israelites went down to the Philistines to sharpen his plowshare, his mattock, his axe, or his sickle. And the charge was two-thirds of a shekel for the plowshares and for the mattocks, and a third of a shekel for sharpening the axes and for setting the goads. So on the day of the battle there was neither sword nor spear found in the hand of any of the people with Saul and Jonathan, but Saul and Jonathan his son had them.
>
> 1 Samuel 13:19-22 ESV

What I discovered was that the archeological evidence actually backs this up! The Philistines' metallurgy was notably advanced for the period, whereas ancient sites in Israel provide evidence of only iron tools (mostly crude cast iron, which is not as strong or durable), and very little in the way of forged (hammered) iron weaponry. The techniques for working with various metals were highly guarded secrets (hence the vow of silence for Zahava), and while there may have been smaller foundries producing weapons, the technology for large-scale production of forged iron was not yet available to Israel. As well, Israel was surrounded by enemies who dominated trade routes, and the Philistines held most of the coastal ports, where important materials such as tin and iron ore would have been imported from foreign lands since native deposits were small and of low quality.

As for Zahava's skill with red-gold, or what we might call rose-gold, there are very few surviving pieces from ancient times since yellow and white gold were much more prevalent, due to the finicky nature of the alloy. It wasn't until the nineteenth century when Carl Fabergé popularized rose-gold on his famous eggs that the techniques became more well known. We'll just pretend that he was a long-lost descendant of Zahava, shall we?

In the Word, *metalsmithing* is frequently used as an analogy for the way Yahweh refines his people. He speaks of our hearts being tested and purified by the fires of affliction and suffering (Proverbs 17:3, Psalm 66:10, Isaiah 48:10, Job 23:10) and preparing us for battle in the same way a blacksmith strengthens iron (Isaiah 54:16–17) and of the important process of sharpening one another like iron on iron (Proverbs 27:17).

But in my research, I came across the most beautiful analogy of how the Master uses all these processes to make us more like himself. After all the refining and purifying and clearing of dross, after all the filing and grinding and cutting and sanding, the goldsmith begins to polish his work with a soft cloth or piece of wool. Once he can see his own perfect reflection in the surface of his masterpiece, then he is satisfied that his work is both pure and complete. Isn't that just a gorgeous picture of how the Original Artist shapes us into his own image? Nothing about the process is easy. It's most often painful and deeply uncomfortable. The dross has to be burnt out of us. The blemishes chiseled away. And sometimes we need to be bent and shaped in ways that hurt. But one day, when we stand before him, he will not see those imperfections at all. He will only see his perfect and glorious reflection in us because of the blood of the Lamb. So, while we wait to be made perfect, be encouraged that these momentary afflictions (2 Corinthians 4:17), as painful as they are in the flesh, are making us more like him every single day.

Look to the stars, my child, and know,
The heavens speak of what you're shown.
More precious than the diamonds bright,
More costly than the purest light.
Your worth is far beyond the earth,
Crowned in splendor before your birth.

Lift your eyes to skies afar,
And remember, child, just who you are.
The Master's hand, with skill untold,
Has shaped your heart of pure red-gold.
Strength and beauty, love refined,
In you His perfect craft combined.

The One who lit the stars aflame,
Is He who softly calls your name.
His mighty hands designed your soul,
A radiant mystery to unfold.
Endowed with worth from Heaven's throne,
You are His child, His very own

Soli Deo Gloria

Connilyn Cossette is a Christy Award–winning and bestselling author known for weaving vibrant, immersive stories that illuminate the ancient world of the Bible. Her passion is to invite readers on unforgettable journeys that inspire them to dig deeper into Scripture and encounter the Great Storyteller himself. A recent breast cancer survivor and adoptive mother of her two greatest joys, she and her husband love to travel the world from their small-town home base south of Dallas, Texas. Discover more about her books and journey at ConnilynCossette.com.

Sign Up for Connilyn's Newsletter

Keep up to date with Connilyn's latest news on book releases and events by signing up for her email list at the website below.

ConnilynCossette.com

Follow Connilyn on Social Media

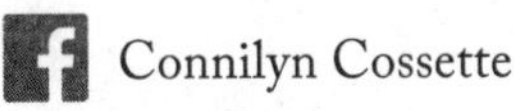
Connilyn Cossette

@ConnilynCossetteAuthor

@ConniCossette